NEVEREND

Blake Rudman

A HellBound Books Publishing LLC Book

**A HellBound Books LLC
Publication**

Copyright © 2025 by HellBound Books Publishing LLC
All Rights Reserved

Cover and art design by Tee N Art
For HellBound Books Publishing LLC

www.hellboundbooks.com

Dedication

For my daughter, Selah,

Your mortal station is temporary. Use your precious blessing of life wisely to gain as much wisdom and understanding through selfless, warm and kind acts with the abundance of all giving and encompassing Love, Long-suffering, Charity and Mercy

"But the more they afflicted them, the more they multiplied and grew. And they were grieved because of the children of Israel."

Exodus 1:12

Love Dad

Prologue

It was the grind that got to her, yet there was something strangely hypnotic about the relentless repetition that had the young woman addicted to the screen and playing the game even though her thumbs ached like the devil.

The rhythmic churn and click of stone-on-stone awoke something deep inside her, as if her pulse were an echo of that gravelly beat—and not only because she was wearing the G-Flex 30S Haptic Feedback Vest. Its vibrating motors and automated air bladders thrummed as they conveyed the timbre of the grind, but even without the vest, the woman would have felt that churning motion, the sonic whirlpool that drew her ever deeper into the immersive world of *NeverEnd*.

She never referred to it as a *game*. To her, *NeverEnd* was an experience, an alternate life, a *passion*.

She'd been stuck in the endless loop of one of *NeverEnd*'s myriad side missions in an attempt to regain the prizes she'd lost along the way of her journey through the game and, hopefully, to attain the holy grail—immortality. *NeverEnd* was clever that way: It gave out virtual prizes—gems, cash, energy, extra lives, and the like—in return for achieving kill levels, completing tasks and quizzes, or finishing a level, which invested the player ever deeper. Of course, there was always the opportunity to buy those prizes using real-world money converted into *NeverEnd* coins, but it was far more gratifying to earn or win your way through the game's seemingly endless labyrinth of imaginative worlds, deadly tasks, and vicious monsters.

In concept, the mountain task was simple, and that's what made it so damned addictive: She had to gun down the harpies, zombies, and other hellish abominations that struck at Sisyphus, the immense, bronze giant of Greek legend who struggled endlessly to roll his stone up the mountain. The sound of that mighty stone was the source of the grind she felt throughout her entire body.

She dreaded the moments it stopped.

One came the moment after the woman took aim at a diving ur-harpy, a ferocious, leather-winged, snaggle-toothed abomination that swooped down from the heavens amid a thick swarm of flying, biting insects to chomp off the heads of unwitting players with Fairplay's sniper rifle, her player avatar. His buxom female sidekick, Fury, shouted a warning, but it was already too late.

Before Fairplay could pull the trigger and blast the creature out of the sky, the entire screen turned red and Fairplay's hit points plummeted. As they dialed back to zero, the hero's body tipped over the edge of the precipice and vanished into the blackness of the abyss.

More troubling than Fairplay's death scream was the eerie silence once the screaming was done; it was broken briefly by a hideous crunch. Sisyphus had lost his endless war with gravity and been crushed by his own stone.

NeverEnd didn't flash "Game Over" on the screen. Instead, it presented the same prompt it had shown so many times before:

YOU HAVE DIED. IS THIS THE END?
NO!
NEVER!

The third option didn't appear.

Still, the woman knew by rote that by pressing a particular combination of buttons, a player could save and/or quit. It was the game's version of a necessary evil. Some people who devoted their days to helping Sisyphus would have to return, albeit briefly, to their everyday, humdrum lives. The woman had used the button combination in the past, but had no use for it today. With hardly a conscious thought, she thumbed the selection arrow from NO! to NEVER! Fairplay had died at the end of a good run.

The woman promised herself the next would be even better, and her ultimate prize of everlasting life was well within reach.

She *always* played standing up and clutching the controller tightly in her sweating, throbbing hands, which helped her focus better, made sure her head stayed in the game. So, when her haste to answer the prompt and continue the game made her lose grip on the controller, it had several feet to fall before it reached the floor. Reacting quickly, she bent over to attempt to catch it, missed, and stumbled backward.

Her heel struck something soft.

The woman looked down at the corpse that lay on its

side at her feet, its jaw open and slack, eyes open and staring blankly at the blood-soaked carpet.

The player frowned in annoyance; she could have *really* hurt herself had she fallen over the woman she'd killed long enough ago for her corpse to begin to stink. She figured that if she dragged the dead woman *under* the coffee table, it would prevent any further mishaps. But moving the body would take energy—energy she needed to put into *NeverEnd*.

Before she could decide, the vest rumbled and jolted her back from her reverie. The controller had fallen on its face. The selection button had been pressed, and a new journey up the mountain with Fairplay, Fury, and Sisyphus was getting underway.

Quickly, the player snatched up the controller, wiped her moist palms on dirty jeans, and blasted the afterburners of Fairplay's flying sledge. Maybe, she hoped, in the game's eagerly awaited sequel, players would be given a choice between controlling Fairplay *or* Fury. That would certainly make a welcome change.

But playing a man—even a scruffy steroid junkie like Fairplay, was perfectly fine in the meantime.

Anything was fine, so long as *NeverEnd* got her away from the reality of what she'd done to that poor, innocent woman and back to the endless grind.

PART ONE

1

"Gauze." Doctor Jon Edom's voice was calm, monotone.

At his direction, the pretty young nurse removed the fat, blood-soaked wad from the patient's chest cavity; it had been in the way of Jon's next planned suture.

"Gently," he told himself as he inserted a curved needle into the small, delicate arterial wall. He applied a tad more pressure behind the patch of synthetic material that would help seal the artery, but eased off again as the sharp needle made a second puncture in the blood vessel. Pausing to breathe, he heard the nurse let out her own breath.

Jon glanced across; he couldn't see much of the nurse's face through the mask, although he knew she was pleasantly attractive beneath it. Her name had been wiped from his memory by the intense concentration of surgery. Even if he had remembered, he couldn't spare the time to thank her or break the tension they both felt with small talk. Jon had to be careful with how he dealt with the young nurses at the hospital; many of them had developed a crush on him at one time or another, taken in by his tall, muscular frame and chiseled, all-American good looks. Not even flashing his wedding band seemed to fend them off.

Branches of the patient's aorta had been clamped for a long time now, her tiny heart slowed to a fraction of its regular beat. Now that the aneurysm was repaired, Jon had to work fast to finish his stitching, reverse the bypass, and remove the clamp. The neatness of his sutures would have definitely earned the praise of the Violet Crown Charity Medical Center's chief surgeon, but that would mean little to Jon if the patient died.

A quick glance up at the utilitarian analog clock on the theater wall: Three hours, twenty-four minutes had passed since the clamps were applied. In an adult patient, he might not have worried, but the undernourished six-year-old was frail as a nursing kitten. Jon had balked at the thought of sending her home again only to bring her back tomorrow— he knew she would only have grown weaker.

He got back to work.

At three hours, forty minutes the nurse sponged his forehead again, as she'd done two or three times in the past quarter hour. Jon hoped, when surgery was over, he'd remember the pretty nurse's name.

The clock was at three hours, fifty-four minutes when Jon finished the last suture in the patch and began removing the bypass. They were in the home stretch now, and all was looking good.

Sighing with relief, he recalled the nurse's name: Aegypt, spelled with an *Ae*. Jon had suppressed a chuckle when she'd first told him about that little flourish; it made her stand out among all the other pretty young nurses at the hospital.

One successful closing later, Jon smiled beneath his mask as Nurse Aegypt and his surgical assistant, Rohan Majumdar, congratulated him with sincere applause. Then, Jon and Rohan went for a much-needed post-op shower while the nurse tidied up and orderlies wheeled the young patient to recovery.

Dried off, dressed, and making his way along the staff-only hallway with Rohan, Jon's phone vibrated. He raised a finger to silence Rohan's banal chitchat. Taking the hint, Rohan turned aside to check his own phone while Jon took the call.

The screen showed a smiling picture of his wife, Chelle, he'd snapped on their Bali vacation the summer before.

Thumbing the screen, Jon held the phone to his ear. "Hey, babe."

"You missed dinner." Chelle's voice was level. She wasn't surprised. Jon's job meant he missed plenty of dinners, but he knew she was disappointed and trying hard not to let it show; tonight was supposed to have been a special one.

"I am *so* sorry, sweetheart. We had some emergency plumbing to do. Client sprung a leak. It's fixed now, but I really should have called you. I know we had plans."

"It's fine," Chelle insisted. She spoke too quickly to mean it. Jon pictured his wife biting her pouting lip, putting on that brave smile of hers. "I *do* understand. Don't worry about dinner. I'm proud of you, honey. You're *so* good with your hands. If you can get home in an hour, I'll let you demonstrate on me just how good you are with them."

"Perfect timing." Jon couldn't suppress the knowing smile that curled his lips. "I'm nearly done here."

"I know. Laura said you were out of surgery ten minutes ago." Laura was that night's scheduler. "I have the after-party timed."

"Am I really that predictable?"

"Not at all, my darling," Chelle teased. "But you *could* surprise me by getting here on time."

"I'll run every yellow light if I have to. Oh, hey. We never finished our conversation about Luke. The blood test at Longevity Therapeutics. I meant to ask—"

"It was nothing." There was relief in his wife's tone. "Everything looks good. No nutritional deficits or weird allergies. Nothing unexpected in the DNA."

"I'll be happy to look over the report."

"There's nothing for you to worry about."

Jon was a little taken aback by his wife's insistence. But, since he was already in the doghouse for breaking their date, he figured there was no point aggravating her further.

"If you're sure, babe."

"I am." Chelle made her tone playful. "Hey, do you know what day it is? We're officially a week past my depo. That means once you wrap up there, you won't have to do any more wrapping over here."

"I'm counting the seconds here. Kiss the kids for me."

"They're down for the count. Love you."

"Love you so much." Jon hung up.

Rohan raised his eyebrows from across the hall. "You getting lucky tonight?"

"Maybe." A wry smile.

"Don't tell me you're in trouble."

Jon let the smile turn into pursed lips. "Chelle worries, is all. She's not crazy about the neighborhood. The *Crown*'s neighborhood, I mean." Nobody ever used the charity hospital's full name; the primary donor's name sufficed. Jon was sure the late Violet Crown would have agreed with Chelle about their corner of Chestnut: the Austin neighborhood had definitely gone downhill in recent years, in much the same way as many other Texas downtown suburbs. The hospital itself had retained much of its dignity, although splashes of colorful graffiti were beginning to appear around the rear entrance to the basement parking lot. The hospital's dated façade, columns of beige brick interspersed with tinted windows, had so far escaped the tagging, but it really was only a matter of time.

"Gotta get myself home too, my friend." Rohan smiled. "Treat the wife's fears with these healing hands. It's what I do best."

"Listen to the husband of the year. How are your energy levels doing?"

"Fine until you asked." Rohan bent his knees like he was on the verge of collapse. Jon knew they were both close to exhaustion, but they had a few minutes left in the tank before the adrenaline washed out.

"You think you could keep it together for a quick visit?" Jon asked his colleague. "I want to check on the kid—the one who came in wearing that gray puffer vest. I thought that style went out with Marty McFly."

"Everything comes back eventually," Rohan said wryly. "Okay, let's check on the kid. Keep it quick, though; you're not the only one with a hot wife at home."

Normally, Jon left checking on patients to the nursing staff. There was no medical reason for him to see the kid— he was in the very best hands as it was. Curiosity motivated Jon that night: In his decade plus as a surgeon, he'd seen plenty of strange wounds, and plenty of wounds with strange causes.

But the puffer vest kid's case was special.

The patient's vest, along with his upper trapezius, had been run through with a hunting knife. The injury itself was straightforward, the weapon itself only slightly unusual. What was strange, though, was what the kid was doing when he got stabbed.

After Jon had finished stitching the kid up, he'd asked the admitting police officer for details. The officer didn't know everything, but he'd pointed Jon to another care station where a preteen girl was being treated for a head wound.

It seemed the kid had been stabbed during a fight with the young girl. One look at her showed the kid had given nearly as well as he took. The girl's face was all bruised to hell, one eye was blackened and swollen shut, and the gash on her forehead had clearly exposed the skull before aid was administered. It was the girl's clothes Jon found the most interesting. The kid's vest had given him an idea about why the two youths might have been fighting, and the girl's outfit confirmed his guess.

So, knowing what he did, he couldn't help but check on the kid before he drove home to make things up with Chelle.

Jon, with out-of-shape Rohan panting beside him, arrived at a nurse station. He asked the location of the kid patient, and the nurse, a plump, middle-aged lady with a kind face, escorted the two along C-corridor to a double room. Jon checked the nameplate and was shocked to see two names: One was the name of the puffer-vest kid, the other that of the preteen girl.

"Why have these patients been put in a room together?" Jon inquired of the nurse.

"They're cousins," she explained. "It was the family's request."

"And the police didn't object?" asked Rohan.

The nurse shrugged and opened the door. "Ask him." She pointed to the police officer inside; he sat quiet and still against the large window that looked out onto the dark, cloud-filled sky beyond. Beyond where he sat sentry on the hospital-standard white plastic chair, Jon saw both young patients sleeping peacefully in their beds. The officer nodded a polite greeting; he was the same cop Jon had spoken to earlier.

"Long night for you too?" whispered Jon.

"I've had longer." The cop had a mellifluous cowboy drawl that Jon was sure made him a hit with the ladies. His badge read: G. KELMAN.

The nurse shut the door as she left.

"Are the patients giving you trouble, Officer?" Jon asked with a smile and a nod to the slumbering kids; even in the darkened room, he made out the family resemblance now that they were in close proximity: same round, freckled faces; same strawberry-blonde hair; same upturned button nose.

"Nawp," Kelman grunted. "They've been out for hours—nurse doped 'em up real good."

"Mind if we take a closer look?"

"Be my guest."

With Rohan at his heels, Jon stood between the kid's bed and that of his preteen cousin. Their distinctive clothing had been changed for pale green hospital gowns, of course, but Jon's eye was drawn to the kid's unique injury. Crouching down, he pointed out the boy's cheek to his colleague. There, a dark, crusted scab ran down the smooth skin, from beneath the eye socket all the way down to the lower jawline. And, concealed by the boy's scraggly hair, was a second scab that ran parallel to the first. It parted the right eyebrow and stopped shy of the hairline.

Jon said to Kelman, "I guess you know *NeverEnd*, the game my wife created?"

Rohan nodded and rolled his eyes. "My nephews are obsessed."

Jon glanced back at the sleepers. "I'd say these kids are too. Those scratches, the puffer vest . . ."

Rohan curled his lip. "Fairplay—the tough-nut hero."

"Yeah," Jon replied. "And the girl was wearing a camo-print halter top when she came in."

Kelman grunted. "Why they make stuff like that in a kid's size is beyond me."

"That's Krysis, one of the female characters." Rohan scratched at his chin, as if contemplating something.

Jon nodded. "We've seen cases like this before. Cosplayers pulling dumb stunts they copy from the games.

LARPers with live steel stabbing at each other like they're gonna regenerate when they die," he said, using the slang term for live-action role-players. "Now we have kids acting out a game where the whole hook is coming back from the dead. I've got a bad feeling these two are gonna be the first in a long, long line, and it won't be long before we have the first one down on Sandy Fry's mortuary table."

"First?" Kelman looked shocked. "I hate to tell you, Doc, but I've already seen a dozen kids dressed like those two get hurt—and I mean *really* hurt."

Jon was deeply troubled by the cop's revelation. It was bad enough Chelle had followed her mother into the video game industry, bad enough she'd helped create an addictive online game that had managed to hook more kids and adults worldwide than even the worst-abused opiates. Now the game was bleeding into the real world, inspiring children to get into violent fights and scar themselves so they resembled their virtual heroes.

"But Fairplay and Krysis are on the same side," Rohan chipped in. "So why did these two get into it?"

Before Jon or Kelman could answer, they heard a small, hard *thump* at the window.

With a start, all three men turned around in time to see something small, brown, and moving fast ricochet off the outside of the window.

"What the—?" The cop choked on his words and stood up from his chair.

Another *thump*, a smear of green-brown goo on the glass.

Then another.

Another.

Like some gruesome rainfall, the hospital room's window was assaulted by countless insects, each one three, four inches long and sacrificing itself to the imperviousness of the glass. Mesmerized by the spectacle, Jon winced as the insects pounded hard against the window, bursting like the overfilled water balloons he loved to throw at his siblings on those hot summer afternoons of his childhood.

Soon, the window was a sickening mosaic of insect guts, disembodied legs, antennae, fragments of chitin, and delicate wings, so much that the sky was obliterated from view.

And then, as quickly as it had begun, the onslaught was over; the cloud of insects disappeared back into the night.

"Locust swarm," Kelman stated the obvious.

"Third one this week," Rohan grunted. He wrinkled his nose at the smeared mess on the window.

"A big one, too," Jon said as he glanced at the two fair-haired kids who had slept soundly through the whole attack. "Make sure you get some rest, Officer."

"Relief's on the way. My shift's over in ten," Kelman assured him.

Rohan followed Jon back out into the hallway. "What's with all that?" he asked as the two made their way toward the exit sign.

"The locusts?" Jon said.

"Yeah. And the kids. Maybe Chelle's right about the neighborhood going to hell in a handbasket. It's getting really bad out there—actually, it's bad *everywhere*. Now there's damned locusts—it's all a bit too biblical for my liking. I'm beginning to wonder if I ought to join your church. The end is nigh and all that, right?"

"I left the Church of the Resurrected," Jon reminded him. "I'm freelance these days."

Rohan gently thumped his own temple. "Sorry. Forgot." He waved good night to the plump nurse before adding, "What do you think?"

"About what?" Jon's tired brain wasn't keeping up too well.

"The end. Could it *actually* be nigh?"

They reached the elevator. Jon stabbed at the well-worn silver button. The doors hissed open.

"Rohan, my friend," he said, "I think that, in some ways, it always has been."

2

*T*hud! Thud! Thud!
Murphy Gore couldn't make out if it was his head pounding or someone knocking on the garage door. He punched the illuminated button on the wall that swooshed the automatic door up and out of the way.

No one was outside.

It was his head, then. He left the door up, despite his wife's constant fear of letting locusts inside; there had been a bunch of swarms in Driftwood over the past few weeks—just like those Austin was experiencing—and Sharon had become quite paranoid about them getting into the house. Going around the hood of his Civic and through the door at the rear of the garage, Murphy entered his laundry room and peered past the washer and dryer into the kitchen, then beyond that to the off-white carpet of the living room. He knew, because he'd checked, that no one was at home. Still, he called out. "Sharon?"

The only answer was silence.

Sharon was at her sister's house. He knew that. For the twenty-two days Sharon had been there, Murphy had been all alone.

The laundry room smelled damp, of old detergent and rust. Murphy hadn't run the machines since before Sharon left. His clothes reeked, he was sure, but he'd gotten used to the smell, just like the itch in his unkempt beard and the creep-crawly feeling of his unwashed skin and hair, especially his scalp.

At the kitchen door, he paused.

Did he *really* want to go in the house again?

He had a purpose tonight, a plan, and nothing about that plan called for him to enter the house. Still, it beckoned him.

Upon entering the kitchen, Murphy was hit by a flood of memories: family dinners, raucous games of Chutes & Ladders and Monopoly with the kids, precious time spent helping with homework. Of course, Sharon was in nearly every flashback, and always with a worried expression. In his memories, Murphy was happy, easy, as though nothing bad could happen to the people he loved.

Thud! Thud! Thud! His head was seriously pounding.

Above him in the empty house was the second-floor hallway. At the end of that was the junk room, stuffed with ski boots, hula hoops, and roller skates with missing wheels. To the left of that, a bedroom.

The bedroom door hung open because, three weeks ago, he'd slammed his head so hard against it, he had bent the hinges. Murphy knew by heart the furniture on the other side of the crooked door, the bedspread that changed color from mauve to magenta depending on how the light hit it, how many frilly cushions lay on top of the bed, and how the giant stuffed panda on those cushions hid all but the ears of the green, stuffed rabbit behind it—like the panda had green bunny ears.

The kid-sized table and chairs still had a tea party all laid out. The bookcase was half-filled with oversized books, the other half, home to art supplies. A Hello Kitty wall clock stood on the dresser, its six o'clock hidden by a pair of clean socks, matched in a bundle but never put away. Dust covered every surface of the room. Sharon would dust, when she finally came home. Murphy wouldn't be here when she did.

His left knee felt weak, as if tired of supporting him. Murphy rested a hand on the kitchen counter to keep himself from falling, even though he didn't really think his knee could buckle—not with the shin guards and heavy kneepads he was wearing.

Pushing himself away from the counter, Murphy made his way back to the garage where the Civic waited, its dull silver paint job throwing off gleams from the pole lights outside. It wasn't easy to sit in the little car with his full body armor on, but after a minute or so of awkward shimmying, Murphy stuffed himself behind the wheel. He cranked on the engine, jerked the shifter to reverse, and drove away from home for the last time.

Nothing on the radio could drown out the pounding in Murphy's head. He gritted his teeth against it, half blind with pain. His knuckles ached from gripping the steering wheel, but at least that gave him some focus. He gripped harder as he put the old neighborhood behind him, harder still as he drove onto the street that just happened to be his way to work, and even more so as he pressed his foot down on the pedal to accelerate steadily for nearly a mile. The Civic was going eighty, its engine complaining, when he finally relaxed, first his hands then his foot, and turned onto a narrow side street that housed the service entrance to Driftwood's old, run-down baseball park.

The baseball field itself, and the spectator stands, were inaccessible from this side. A chain-link fence bordered the ball field; a wooden perimeter fence blocked off the stands. Murphy would have had to trek through the trees or hike along a long, gravel path if he wanted to park on this side and still see a ball game. But that wasn't why he had come tonight. He was done with games. Forever.

As he pulled off the service road onto the dead grass, he lifted a hand to shield his eyes from the lights shining on the chalk diamond and its empty bases. A tall man stood on the pitcher's mound. After an overly elaborate wind-up, the man pitched an imaginary fastball. Murphy was sure it was imaginary but could have sworn the back fence clanked as if it had been struck by a ninety-mile-per-hour pitch.

The tall man descended from the pitcher's mound with his arms spread wide. He was dressed just as Murphy had always seen him dressed: cowboy boots, blue jeans, and a sand-colored shirt, which was set off by the large turquoise stone of his bolo and the even larger matching stone of his belt buckle. The ensemble was covered by a long, suede duster. The man would have looked exactly like he'd walked out of a cowboy flick were it not for the absence—unforgivable in Texas—of a Stetson.

Murphy opened the Civic's door and got out. "Evening."

"My excellent friend." The tall man's accent wasn't local; it sounded old-fashioned to Murphy's ears and was impossible to place.

"Okay, I'm here." Murphy shook his cramped, armored limbs as if to bully them into life. "I'm ready."

"So you are," said the tall man. "So you are."

As the tall man approached the fence, he grinned, which made Murphy's skin crawl more tonight than usual. The man's teeth were perfect, stainless, with a flawless bite; they captivated Murphy's focus.

Murphy watched the tall man approach, arms wide for an embrace. His head pounding, Murphy closed his eyes and pressed trembling fingertips against his forehead, trying to squeeze out the pain. When he opened his eyes again, the tall man stood directly in front of him. He held a pistol in one hand, an automatic rifle in the other. Nodding to Murphy, he offered the firearms.

"This is somebody's blood," he said.

"Huh?" Murphy squinted at the man through his aching eyes.

"Merely trying to lighten the mood. Now, take, Murphy Gore. Isn't that why you came here tonight?"

Murphy selected the pistol; it perfectly fit the holster he had strapped on his thigh. The rifle was lighter than he expected—it felt good nestled there in the crook of his arm. He'd trained with similar weapons under the tall man's direction, but these felt different. They thrummed with an energy, straining like hounds on a leash, sporting for a hunt.

The tall man took a step back and grinned once more. "You've done well, Murphy. You've earned your reward."

"And *her*?" said Murphy. "What about her reward?"

The tall man lowered his eyes. "That's not my decision to make. You know it's not up to me or the interests I serve. Those who go alone to the end . . ." He made a gesture of dismissal, like brushing away a troublesome insect. "We can but try. You still want to try, Murphy?"

Murphy's throat was too dry to answer yes. It was one of the few moments since he met the tall man that he seemed, even by accident, less than committed to his course. Ever since the doctor had given him the news, Murphy's life had run on automatic. Only the sudden dryness of his throat threatened to divert its straight course.

The tall man gazed into the distance. "You *can* change your mind."

Murphy swallowed. "Never." His pulse was elevated, his breath rapid. "I want to try. I *have* to!"

The tall man seized Murphy's shoulders. Even through the thick layers of padding, the man's touch was ice cold.

"That's what I like to hear. The world needs men like

you, Murphy. Men of action. Men who can face harsh truths and say, 'Bring it on.'"

Pausing, the man studied Murphy. Murphy felt the trickle of perspiration beneath his armor and clothing; he reckoned he had to reek worse than ever. If so, the tall man gave no sign.

In a heartbeat, the tall man struck Murphy between the eyes with the smallest two fingers of his left hand. The movement was so quick that Murphy didn't have time to dodge. It wasn't until the second strike that Murphy realized the impact was timed with the thudding in his head.

The third and fourth strikes were equally well timed. And after the fourth strike, the thudding headache ceased. Murphy was stunned.

He'd lived with the pounding for months. When it did go away, it was never for long, and always in the brief moments between waking and sleep. Now, it was gone completely. The tall man had banished it, along with the last of Murphy's doubts.

"Thank you." Murphy's knees felt weak again. He stumbled forward, holding the rifle to one side, and fell down onto his kneepads. Lifting his chin, he thanked the tall man again.

The tall man didn't answer.

When Murphy wiped the tears from his eyes, the tall man was staring into the distance. Murphy rose with some effort, cradled the stock of the rifle in the crook of his arm, and took one last mental picture of the tall man. Then, he climbed back in the Civic and placed the rifle on the floor in the back. His helmet with the plastic face mask sat in the passenger seat. Without so much as a second glance at the tall man again, Murphy drove away.

Somewhere between the ball field and the service road, excitement set in. Murphy tried the radio again; it played his favorite song.

Murphy sang along with the line about letting the sun shine in!

When the song was over, Murphy switched off the radio and sang it to himself a capella. He was on his fourth time through when he braked in front of the Violet Crown Charity Medical Center. He pulled on his helmet, still singing, and adjusted the mask.

Then, gunning the Civic's engine, he drove straight through the glass entrance of the ER waiting room.

3

As the elevator doors slid open to allow Jon and Rohan out, the men heard the crash and accompanying screams. Both paused, startled, questioning what they'd heard, momentarily paralyzed. The doors started to close. Jon reached a hand out to stop them, and the men stepped out.

Then the shooting began.

No single first shot; the crackling staccato of a rapid-fire barrage filled the hospital's hallway. Jon sprang into motion, a burst of adrenaline overpowering his fatigue in a dash that left Rohan behind. A backward glance saw his friend and colleague retreating back into the elevator, terrified, embarrassed. Ignoring his every instinct, Jon ran in the direction of the shots; he'd dodged a half-dozen people before it dawned on him everyone else was running the other way.

Jon stopped when he came across a man leaning against a wall clutching his side, trying in vain to stop thick, crimson blood oozing through his fingers. Jon took the man's hand and pressed it firmly against the wound as the gunfire fell momentarily silent.

"Calm down. You're gonna be okay." Jon helped the wounded man to sit down against the wall. Just then, a blond emergency medical technician with an impossibly handsome, bearded face pushed a gurney at speed toward them. "Here!" Jon hailed the EMT as he might a taxi.

Leaving the wounded man in capable hands, Jon hesitated. Exactly what *was* his plan? The shots were clearly coming from the direction of the emergency department; most likely the shooter—*shooters?*—was in the waiting room. Jon shuddered to think what might happen if they were to reach the patients beyond, helpless in their beds.

The rapid bursts of gunfire picked up again, jarring Jon into action. Doctors, patients, and nurses flooded the corridors, all running past Jon in their panic, crying, screaming, praying. Among them ran hospital security guards, some badly injured. Jon paused briefly to check on a man with a gaping chest wound that bubbled bright, frothing blood. He was critical but breathing—for now. Jon left him with a nurse in a blood-soaked uniform and ran on. On his way around an abandoned, overturned gurney, he tripped and went sprawling.

Picking himself up off the well-polished beige floor, ignoring the pain that shot from his elbow to his shoulder, Jon saw a face he knew: a volunteer he knew only as Jessica. Her eyes were half open, still. A solitary fly—fat, bloated, lazy—settled on her left eyeball. Of course, she made no move to swat it away. A thick puddle of dark blood and bile congealed on the floor near the volunteer's gaping mouth; she obviously had a stomach wound and punctured lung. Jessica had choked to death on her own fluids.

A burst of gunfire came from close by.

"*Stop!*" Jon shouted.

Another burst.

He bunched his hands into fists and screamed, *"Stop!"*

Then Jon was running, seeing only the dead, not the injured. He ran to the end of the corridor, turned onto a perpendicular hallway, and stopped at a double door. Terrified screams, sobbing, and a voice came from the other side, pleading in words he couldn't make out.

Gunfire spat; the pleading stopped.

Jon pressed the ID on his lanyard to a wall pad. The door swung open, and he stepped into the emergency waiting area. There, furniture was kicked over, and the acrid stink of gunpowder hung thick in the air. Jon saw the bloodied bodies of a man and a woman, hugging each other in death, just a few feet in front of him. Eight or nine bodies were draped over and around the nurse's station; the sight reminded Jon of how his eldest daughter, Cass, strewed dolls all around her bedroom.

At the far end of carnage, the crushed wedge of a decades-old silver Honda Civic was perched at an impossible angle atop the shattered metal column that had been part of the now-smashed sliding doors. A security guard's body, crushed from waist to neck, lay under the vehicle's back end.

There, standing center stage, was a bulky man wearing SWAT-style body armor and holding an automatic rifle.

Jon straightened his spine, furious, and walked straight toward the armed man.

The shooter didn't register Jon's approach at first. The clear face mask attached to his helmet had a thick black border that likely limited his peripheral vision, giving Jon a slight advantage, some element of surprise.

Jon was ten feet away when the shooter snapped his head around. He was a large man, out of shape and breathing heavy, caught in the middle of loading his pistol with a fresh magazine. A rifle was cinched in his armpit. Caught unaware by the approaching doctor, he dropped it, along with the magazine. He dropped the rifle, too, but caught it by the shoulder strap and swung the barrel at Jon with a grace that told of training.

Jon flinched as the pistol and magazine clanked to the floor. Instinct told him to duck. Fighting that, forcing his head up, keeping his back straight, he showed open, empty palms to the man he knew could kill him without a second thought. Anger at the senseless slaughter still drove Jon, but he didn't let it make him stupid.

He wasn't there to fight.

He was there to save lives.

He stared the shooter straight in the face. "What do you want here?"

With some relief, Jon saw the gunman relax the finger that had been about to squeeze the rifle's trigger. The face on the other side of the mask appeared puzzled—and also familiar.

"Mister Gore." Jon took a chance. "I'm sorry. It's Doctor Decker's night off." Actually, the chief surgeon *never* worked the night shift. Jon recalled that he had assisted on Gore's daughter's surgery the day before, but it had not ended well.

Gore flinched at Jon's news. He stared at Jon, his expression most unsettling. Jon tried to maintain eye contact but couldn't help his eyes flicking away from Gore. He was surprised to catch a glimpse of an elderly woman who'd managed to stuff herself, along with two small children, under one of the waiting room's sofas. Jon was amazed that one person could fit under there, let alone three. More distracting than the hiding place was the blood seeping from a hole in the side of one of the children.

As if he had read Jon's thoughts, Gore grunted, "Blood."

"What?"

Gore pointed with the rifle. "On your cuff."

Jon saw blood on his right cuff and recalled the man he'd helped moments before.

"Mister Gore . . . *Murphy*. You may not remember, but I assisted with your daughter's surgery. I can answer any questions you have."

"*Why?*" Trembling, Murphy's voice was barely above a whisper.

It was the one question Jon could not answer. Not in the sense Gore meant. What Gore *truly* wanted—*needed*—was a meaning behind his senseless loss.

"It was a heart attack, Murphy. Meg's heart tissue was simply too thick. Doctor Decker did his best to thin it out, but her heart couldn't take the strain. She went into shock. We did everything we could. I'm so very sorry."

Usually, when Jon made this speech, he would place a hand on the parent's arm and press gently when he mentioned the efforts he or a colleague had made to save a patient's life. When he got to the apology, he would ease the pressure, letting the parent know he, too, was powerless. Doctor Decker had taught Jon the technique. At first, Jon had been worried he might come off as insincere. Thankfully, he never did.

A distracted air settled over Murphy Gore, as if he was listening to a sound only he could hear. Plainly, judging by the bereaved father's face, Jon's speech had done little to ease his pain.

Jon took a moment to imagine what his own spiritual counselor, Rabbi Max Sophar, might have said. Something wise, no doubt. Clearly, Gore wasn't in a patient mood. His eyes snapped back to Jon. They were furious. Jon said a silent prayer.

"You're hurting." The words were out of Jon's mouth before he knew what he was saying. "Nobody should have to hurt like this."

Gore's face went through another change. The fury

eased, replaced by brutish determination. He struck Jon with the rifle's barrel. Instinctively, Jon raised an arm to shield his face, and the gun struck his forearm. Using a trick learned from Rabbi Max, Jon moved with the blow, letting its momentum turn him. He then dropped to the ground, facing away from Gore, and let him think he'd done serious damage.

"I made my choice." It sounded like Gore was having a conversation with someone else.

Jon tensed, ready to leap back to his feet and try for the rifle. But before he could, gunshots rang out.

It wasn't another barrage from Gore, but a trio of shots from somewhere behind Jon. The first shot clipped Gore's helmet, the second blew a divot in a column behind the armored man, and the last bullet hit Gore square in the chest. He wobbled but remained on his feet. His armor might have been only imitation SWAT, but the vest, at least, appeared to be bulletproof.

Jon turned his head to see Officer Kelman framed in the double doorway. As Gore leveled his rifle at the cop, Jon made his move. He sprang up on his knees, seized Gore around the waist, and wrenched him to one side.

Gore fired.

Kelman was hit in the lower ribs and hip, but the best Jon could tell from a distance, the spray of bullets missed his heart. As for Gore, he tipped over sideways, still firing the rifle. A body lying belly-down on the nurse's station did a gristly dance. Gore's shoulder struck tile. He grunted and lost his grip on the rifle. In the split second this bought him, Jon grabbed for the weapon.

Jon's fingers closed on the handle, just above the magazine. Even caught in the split-second moment, he knew enough not to grab a hot barrel. Gore was strong, but Jon had knocked his breath out in the fall. The doctor pulled at the gun, loosening Gore's hold, but fell short of tearing it free.

"Murphy," he said, still grappling for the weapon, "this can't be worth it. You don't want to make other people hurt like you do."

Gore clenched his eyes shut. "Why?" This time there was no pleading tone, and he didn't speak to Jon but into the air. "Why did you take her?"

With a surge of inhuman strength, he tossed Jon aside, but Jon, to his own surprise, kept a grip on the rifle. He was lying on his back, some distance from Gore, squeezing the rifle close to his belly. Gore was on a knee, blinking at Jon, clearly stunned and staring at his empty hands. Jon considered pointing the rifle at Gore and putting an end to his madness but quickly dismissed the thought. He sat up, still holding the gun but threatening no one.

"Lie down, Murphy," Jon told the shooter. "More police will be coming."

Gore didn't answer, but he did look at Jon. His gaze was pitiful. His eyes seemed to beg Jon to point the rifle his way and end the pain.

"Lie down," Jon repeated. "Save yourself."

"Save myself?" said Gore. "I didn't do any of this for me."

Gore got to his feet. Jon expected him to rush, to go for the rifle. Of course, he'd forgotten about the pistol and its ejected magazine.

Gore remembered, though. Slowly, he bent down to pick them up from the blood-splattered floor.

"Don't do it, Murphy!"

Gore stooped forward, the pistol inches from his hand.

"She ended alone. There's no *NeverEnd*!"

Jon squeezed the trigger. Gore's arm, the one reaching for the pistol, jerked as the bullet tore through its flesh, shattering the bone beneath. He seemed not to notice. Instead, he grabbed the pistol in one hand, the magazine in the other. He slammed the magazine home.

Jon's heart gave a queasy thump. He glanced at the old woman and the two children hiding under the furniture, and in that moment, he was sure Gore had seen them too.

Gore raised the pistol.

Jon switched his aim to Gore's clear mask and pulled the trigger.

The rifle bucked like a living thing desperate to escape his clutch. Most of Jon's shots flew over Gore's head, but one struck the target. The plastic mask offered no protection; it splintered as, beneath it, Gore's face blew apart. He swayed a moment before crumpling to the ground and blood began spreading in crimson pool around his head.

Jon bent over slowly and set the rifle on the ground. He allowed himself a moment to get his nerves under control before unbuttoning his already-bloodied cuffs and got to work on the closest of the living wounded.

"Nurse! *Nurse!* I need someone to start triage over here!"

4

A wave of exhaustion washed over Pamela. It was so heavy, so insistent, she actually hunched forward, folding her body until her breasts sagged to the patio railing. It was a shame, a real shame: they had been so perky in her ankle-length gold silk evening gown. Now they had come to this. Sad.

After a while, Pamela straightened her back. She took a moment to shake out her long, rather dull brown hair, then tried on a smile. It didn't fit. She didn't feel much like smiling. She *did* feel like drinking, however, so she drained the champagne flute in her hand. She also felt like smoking, which kinda made sense, since the two first fingers of her free hand were pinching a lit cigarette.

Pamela took a long drag, enjoying the way the hot smoke tickled the back of her throat. She didn't even mind when it set her to coughing, since it reminded her of sneaking smokes in the little patch of woods behind the fellowship hall of the Church of the Resurrected's satellite compound. The satellite was defunct now, but the Faith Center—the church's longtime home in Texas Hill

Country—was thriving.

Having recovered from her coughing fit, Pamela took a moment to take in the bright white pole lights that swept down the hill from the house she shared with her mother and brother. The lights lit up the long, sweeping road that led to the grand, nine-story tower that served as the Center's administration building. Her father, Doctor Ezra Erasmus Berger, had commissioned the tower and paid for most of it himself.

It was called God's Footstool. Dad had proposed the name, and since the money was his, the executive committee had little choice but to readily accept it. Pamela pictured a giant pair of sandaled feet spiking their heels on top of building. The image gave her a chuckle, and the chuckle brought on a second bout of coughing.

A voice came from behind: "About time you gave up those death sticks, don't you think?"

Pamela didn't have to turn around to know her brother, Phillip, had slid open the patio door. Soft notes of a classical music track and snippets of polite conversation drifted out on an air-conditioned breeze. It was late September but hot enough in Texas to raise sweat from the skin of their guests. Pamela's skin was bone dry; her blood ran colder than most.

She lifted a finger to Phillip to signal him to wait until she got the coughing under control.

He stepped out on the patio and slid the door shut behind him.

Pamela said, "You know what tonight is?"

Phillip didn't answer straightaway. He had been quiet as a boy and had grown into a man who liked to weigh his words. "The night of my oh-so-important dinner party?"

"Important." Pamela sniffed. "Right."

She set the empty champagne flute on the railing and dropped in her smoldering cigarette butt. The railing was narrow with a slightly rounded top, and as Pamela took her hand away from the glass, it slipped off and tumbled to smash on the concrete two stories below. She glanced back at Phillip. He'd flinched at the sound of shattering glass, she was sure. He looked so dashingly handsome in his light-blue striped suit, but she didn't tell him so; her brother's ego was big enough as it was, and the boyish way he dangled his black dinner jacket from his hand detracted from the picture.

"It *is* kind of important, sis. All our friends are here, all the important people, not to mention most of the town council and that weird county commissioner. I was hoping you could turn on your charm."

Pamela turned once more to face Phillip, arms crossed over her chest. "You hoped I'd give him a little, isn't that what you mean? Clear the way for your land grab with some bedroom diplomacy?"

Phillip's own hands shot up. "Whoa. You must be thinking of somebody else, trustee. There's nothing I value more than my sister's sacred chastity."

Pamela sneered at her brother's sarcasm but fought the urge to snap back; it was better to give up a fight with him early on than try to win his way.

She gazed out at the lights and the administration tower. "Are you being dumb about the date, or did you really forget?"

Phillip joined her at the railing. After a moment's deliberation, he spread his palms in defeat.

"It's Dad's birthday," Pamela said. "He would have been sixty-five today, if the Big C hadn't gotten to him."

Phillip drummed the railing with his fingertips, a dull, rhythmic sound. "Another argument against those death sticks, don't you think?"

Pamela glared. "Is that all you have to say?"

"What do you want, P. J.? Dad made some bad choices.

He made good ones, too." With a wave of the hand, Phillip indicated God's Footstool and everything it loomed over. "But he's gone. I'm not happy about it. Doesn't change much."

Pamela wanted nothing more than to pull another cigarette out of her clutch purse on the patio chair, but the one she had dunked in the now-defunct champagne flute had been her last. She felt a little bad about how she was treating Phillip. He was older than her by only a year but always acted like her little brother. The act was made easier by his height, which was at least three inches shorter than her own five foot nine—more so given the vertiginous heels she wore that night.

"I'm sorry," she said. "I'm not being nice. I'm feeling off tonight . . . thinking about Dad."

Phillip bumped her shoulder with his own. "It's no sweat, Peej. Honestly. This is my thing. I don't need you to host . . . or do anything else."

"*'Peej*? Ugh. Way to spoil a moment, bro. Stick to P. J. if you can't say Pamela. But ditch the Peej, okay."

"Sure Peej . . .ay." Phillip grinned as a wave of laughter wafted from the house, as if beckoning them both back in. As Pamela pushed away from the railing and picked up her clutch, Phillip held up a hand. "*Sixty-five*, really? That's retirement age."

The siblings laughed together. As if Dad would ever have retired—from work, from his involvement with the church, or from anything else for that matter.

"Seriously," Phillip added, "what do you think he'd be like now? Would he have lost his figure? Let his hair go white?"

Pamela shook her head. "The immortal Ezra Berger? Never."

A chill ran up Pamela's spine, despite the heat. She hugged herself against it as her ever-attentive brother stepped forward and raised his jacket as though to twirl it around her shoulders. She stepped back, forgetting the railing until she knocked against it with her thigh. It was too high to tip over, but Phillip caught her by the wrist, a look of alarm on his handsome face. She let him pull her away.

"Careful," he said. "Geez."

"*Geez*? That's the Jesus version of 'Peej.' Maybe ditch that too?"

"You think He's sensitive?"

"Do you want to find out?"

"It's funny," Phillip said, staring at God's Footstool, "I've been thinking about Dad a lot lately, but his birthday completely slipped my mind."

"It's not like you had to buy a present."

"I could have, though. For Mom, I mean. Or you, or Rochelle. Dad is somebody we should celebrate, don't you think?"

"I don't . . ." Pamela couldn't complete her thought. She snagged Phillip's jacket and draped it around her bare shoulders to ward off a second chill.

Phillip touched her arm lightly. "We'll talk about it some other time, okay?"

He then returned to the patio door and slid it open. Another wave of laughter beckoned. Phillip gestured with a shrug to invite Pamela inside, but only if she felt up to it.

"Give me a minute," she said.

Phillip nodded and stepped back into the house.

She watched her brother cross the staircase where Jake Korvus, the church's senior pastor, stood waiting. Phillip greeted him heartily with a hug and a vigorous handshake. His exuberance reminded her of their father. So much did, these days. She hugged the jacket tighter. She usually felt warm, thinking about Dad. It seemed, after all these years, the fact of his absence had finally sunk in.

Pamela was broken from her reverie by the appearance of headlights below. One of Phillip's guests had missed the meal, it seemed, but didn't want to miss the champagne and networking possibilities of the rest of the evening. Pamela always found the artifice of these events distasteful. She didn't actually think Phillip wanted her to seduce the commissioner, but having to kiss up to the man and all their VIP guests was almost as bad. The sparks of family sentiment her talk with Phillip had kindled were now extinguished. She felt exhausted again and wondered how long she could stretch out her minute before he got annoyed.

The cell phone in Pamela's clutch buzzed. The hour was too late for a spam call, and the only person who might be calling out of the blue was Rochelle, her older sister. Fishing the phone out, she saw Rochelle's name on the screen and thumbed the green reply icon.

"Hey!"

"Hey, yourself." Rochelle sounded happy. In the background, a little boy gave a *whoop*. "You two. Bed. *Now*. Sorry, P. J. One sec."

It was more than a sec, but Pamela was happy to wait. Hearing Rochelle's voice gave her an immediate boost. Hearing the boys at play was pure joy.

"Sorry about that, P. J." Rochelle returned to the call; all was quiet in the background now.

"Don't apologize. Live your life."

"I try. Listen, I won't keep you. I know you're at Phillip's fancy do. I just wanted to make sure I'm on the calendar for next week."

"Next week?" Pamela struggled to recall what was meant to be happening.

"Yeah. Friday or Saturday. Either's fine. Jon'll be at the conference, remember?"

"Oh." Pamela *had* forgotten, of course. If she'd

remembered, she might have been in a better mood for her brother's shindig. The only thing that made Pamela happier than spending time with Rochelle was spending time with Rochelle and her two boys. A whole day of visiting was a rare treat indeed.

Time flew by as the sisters made plans for a girls' morning out, followed by an afternoon with the kids at the Thinkery and/or the aquarium. It would all happen next Friday. By the end of the conversation, Pamela was sure the anticipation would keep her smiling for the next eight days. The only thing that dampened her mood slightly was when she asked how Jon would feel about missing the fun.

"Couldn't tell you," said Rochelle, "and I can't ask. The doctor is supposed to be home by now, but he's late—as usual." Jon was a medical doctor, not a renowned scientist like their dad, and Rochelle had a way of saying his title that made her sound almost embarrassed.

"I'm sorry, love," Pamela soothed.

"Don't be. Not for me. God's in his heaven. All's right with the world. My husband will have to learn is all, or he'll have to leave. I'm fine either way."

This leaving talk was new to Pamela. "You two? You don't mean . . ."

"Don't listen to me, sis. I'm rambling. Ragged out from a long day with the kids. Jon and I are fine. We're *very* fine."

Pamela heard the lie in her sister's voice. She had no idea how she could help or what to say, so she spent the last minute of the call sending love to the boys and saying goodbye.

5

"Bye, love," Rochelle Edom said and hung up the phone. Rochelle, who went by Chelle, sat on the front steps of her house. It was dark outside, but she couldn't see anyway: Her elbows were on her knees and the hand not holding the phone covered her eyes.

How late *was* Jon? She checked the time on her cell. The time he'd promised her he'd be home was long gone. Was he still at the hospital? Dead in a ditch?

No way of knowing

She tried calling once more, only to get her husband's automated voicemail.

Chelle went back in the house and tried to get some sleep, but an anxious stomach wouldn't let her drift off. Getting up, she checked on the boys. Paul, her five-year-old, was sound asleep. Luke, the seven-year-old, peeked her way when she opened the bedroom door of the room the boys shared, but shut his eyes as soon as he saw her. She went downstairs.

Her tablet was on the dining room table. Chelle brought up her email and breezed past the messages about church business, the school open house, and the inevitable avalanche of spam. She read through the results of the tests she'd run on Luke. *Some* of them, anyway. An earlier email, the one that went into more depth, was in her trash folder. The shorter email, the one currently on her screen, held all the information Jon needed to see. Chelle had planned to show her husband tonight, before his first delayed homecoming. There wouldn't be time now; Jon would be too tired. She'd be tired too, if she weren't so anxious. Or was it anger she was feeling?

She'd told Jon a thousand times they had to get out of the city, away from the hustle and bustle in the heart of Austin. He'd assumed his wife would have wanted to be close to her family, which had been true once, but not anymore. Now, Chelle was worried. The neighborhood that was home to the Violet Crown Charity Medical Center had gone to the dogs in recent years: It had fallen to the worst scum of humanity—the drug pushers and pimps who cared less about other people's lives than cockroaches cared about sanitation ratings.

If only Jon had listened to her years ago. Then they would never have come to the city, and Chelle would never have gotten caught up in her mother's obsession. Of course, Chelle was proud of her work on *NeverEnd*, but the years of intensive, time-consuming work had come at a bitter cost. If not for the game, Chelle could have been a stay-at-home mom to the twins, Cassidy and Simon, instead of having to wait until the birth of her second batch of kids, Luke and Paul, to make mothering a priority. Instead of skinned knees and lunch boxes, her life had been design meetings, market analysis, and endless streams of code.

Working for Mother at Endless Loop Games had been like living through an alternate childhood, one in which Mother paid rather than scolded her into compliance. Of course, the high-concept action and online reward components that made *NeverEnd* so addictive to players was a collaborative effort, but it had been Chelle who'd put in overtime to make that effort pay. As a result, she'd missed out on most of the twins' lives. Falling unexpectedly pregnant with Luke woke her up to the need for change.

And now Jon was making the same mistake she had: spending all his time in that pit of a hospital! It made Chelle so angry, so resentful that she'd felt compelled to go outside so her disapproving face would be the first thing Jon saw when he *finally* arrived home.

A low humming sound filled the still night sky, the twinkling stars and crescent moon flickering out of sight as an expansive cloud of locusts passed overhead. Chelle considered going back inside; the insects still disgusted her, even though they seemed to be an all-too-regular occurrence these days. Instead, she watched the black cloud buzz over the treetops, blanking out the streetlights as they flew east to seek the dawn.

Somehow, the notion of chasing daylight made Chelle think of Vivek. She was sure he wouldn't leave her lonely on a night like this. If she called, he'd come over at once. Only, the phone wasn't how they kept touch these days. Vivek would get angry if she called.

Reawakening her phone, Chelle went through the sequence of steps her lover had detailed to send him a message. It was overly complicated and involved multiple servers and a VPN that rerouted to Canada. Chelle's own technical knowledge told her there were easier ways for two people to message without anyone else knowing, but Vivek's approach felt more like a ritual, part of some elaborate foreplay on his part. And her life already had more than enough of that. Nonetheless, Chelle did things his way because it made him feel respected and confident. If only Jon would make such a sacrifice for her!

Chelle typed a medium-length message to Vivek but

didn't hit send. Her emotions were too raw. She was afraid of scaring him away, though she wasn't sure that was possible; he seemed besotted with her almost to the point of obsession. When Vivek had offered to leave Mother's company, abandoning his meteoric rise to the top so they could run away together, telling him no had nearly broken Chelle, but it seemed barely to take a puff out of Vivek's sails. When Mother retired to a part-time consulting position within the company and Vivek succeeded her as Endless Loop's CEO, Chelle had spent a week in bed, mourning the lost opportunity. The next time she contacted Vivek, he responded like nothing had changed, despite their years apart.

If only Jon was so devoted, so unshakeable. Jon, the man she'd chosen over Vivek and lost in the end to his obsession, his fool's crusade.

She'd always known Jon to be a crusader. In fact, his passion was what had attracted her in the first place, long before it became an acid eroding their marriage. Jon had refused all his wife's begging to move the family out of the city, and ignored her pleas to accept a position at Longevity Therapeutics, the company her father founded. Every denial of Chelle Edom's wishes had driven her deeper into despair. The last insult was when Jon left the church.

She knew from the start his road to Damascus conversion was false, made only to get close to her back in their early days together; at the time, Chelle had found it most romantic. That his Christianity was all a front hadn't made Jon's defection any easier. In a way, it was harder, since she knew his staying was tied only to his husbandly devotion. What did it say about them as husband and wife that he'd left?

A breeze stirred the fringe of Chelle's red kimono, which sat mid-thigh on her freshly shaven legs. The flimsy swirl of printed silk was all she wore; Chelle had meant what she'd told Jon on the phone earlier. Tonight *should* have been special, but it had turned out like so many others she'd spent waiting, watching, barely daring to breathe until her husband turned up at last with some hero's excuse for leaving her alone. Her mind drifted to what Vivek would say if he saw her dressed this way, and goose bumps dappled her barely dressed flesh. Probably nothing. Her lover's actions always spoke louder than words.

The sound of a car engine caught Chelle's attention. A police cruiser, an Austin black-and-white, rumbled along Cedar Park Drive. Standing up, heart thumping hard and heavy in her chest, Chelle started down her front path as the vehicle turned into her driveway. The concrete was rough beneath her bare feet, but Chelle picked up the pace, running to meet the car.

Stopping the car in front of her, the cop killed the engine. The cruiser's windows were tinted, the sparse moonlight too dim for Chelle to see anything but her own reflection. As the uniformed driver opened the door to climb out, she peered past him at the passenger seat.

It was empty.

Chelle was stunned. She was convinced she'd see Jon's tired eyes peering at her from beside the police officer. This wouldn't have been the first time he had been dropped off, too tired to drive, and not even the first time he had been dropped off by Austin PD.

Everyone, aside from Jon, knew the Crown's neighborhood was dangerous. Friends, workmates, and the police did their best to get her husband safely away from the hospital and home. But would he take the hint?

No. Not Crusader Jon, whose passion for saving the world made him eager to give up his life to anyone who wanted it—except his wife and kids.

Chelle's cheeks felt hot. She was embarrassed, woefully underdressed for greeting a uniformed police officer on her driveway. What would the officer think? Well, maybe he wouldn't mind at all; she was, after all, still a beautiful, desirable woman.

The cop was youthful, athletic, and tall. He had dark skin, light eyes, and a smooth-shaved head. Broad shoulders contrasted nicely with his narrow waist. On pure aesthetics, in Chelle's opinion, he was more attractive even than Vivek. Evidently, he didn't mind the difference in their ages; his lingering glance up and down the brief length of the kimono told Chelle as much.

"Evening, ma'am," the cop said.

Chelle almost laughed. The cop's tone said so much more than his words. Her body had changed in the twenty years since she started having children, but she had been careful to preserve the ratio between her breasts, waist, and hips. Men didn't care about measurements, in her experience. It was the proportions that counted, and hers were the same as they had been at her wedding, no matter the uptick in numbers.

"Evening, Officer," she purred.

"You're Mrs. Edom?"

"It's Berger-Edom, actually." The response was automatic, conditioned into Chelle after years of using the hyphenated name at work. "What's your name?"

"Officer Barnes, ma'am."

"Good to meet you, Officer Barnes." Chelle tugged the kimono tighter around her body to allow Officer Barnes a better look at what little it covered. "If you want my husband, he's not home."

She turned toward the house, daring the officer to invite himself in. The twins and Paul were sound sleepers. Luke had a tendency to wander. It was one of the traits that made him unique, but she was sure, if she went ahead of her guest and shut the boys' door, they'd get no disturbance. She had told Vivek as much, more than once, though he never took her up on the offer.

"I know he's not in the house, Mrs. Berger-Edom," Officer Barnes said. "He's a hero, ma'am. A *real* hero."

Chelle widened her eyes. What *was* he talking about? Had he missed the signals? He'd have to be blind, or perhaps gay?

Then, the thought hit her. Hard.

"You don't mean . . . ? Is he . . . ?"

Officer Barnes stepped to the rear passenger door of the cruiser. "Nothing to worry about. He's fine, ma'am." He opened the door. "Doctor Edom? Wake up, sir. You're home."

Chelle felt another blush redden her cheeks as Jon stepped out from the cruiser's back seat. Absently, Chelle straightened her hair with one hand. The moment Jon turned to her, eyes bloodshot and a little melancholy, she lunged for him, flung her arms about his neck, and kissed him full on the lips.

He kissed her back with eagerness, despite his obvious fatigue.

"Where were you, Jon?" Chelle broke the kiss. "An hour, you said. That was—I don't know how long ago."

"I'm sorry." Jon spoke softly. "There was a little trouble at work."

Officer Barnes cleared his throat. Chelle saw him shake his head. "You'll come in to the station to make that statement in the morning, Doc?"

"Bright and early." Jon yawned. "Well, bright, anyway."

Chelle frowned, troubled. She adjusted her kimono, feeling something of the chill as she noted Jon's smell was . . . *off.*

The usual tang of hospital antiseptic was there, as always, but buried beneath other scents. The most obvious was laundry starch. The service she used for Jon's shirts never used enough. She squinted, trying to make out the details of her husband's shirt. It was black, with short sleeves, and two pockets on the breast.

Not one of his own.

"That's my shirt, ma'am." Officer Barnes read her mind. "A spare."

"Mine got a little wrinkled."

Chelle saw Jon eyeball the officer. Barnes did that headshake again, as though he couldn't believe Jon's modesty.

He approached Jon, holding out a gloved hand. "Get your rest, hero. The paperwork can wait."

Jon shook hands. "Thanks."

Then, Chelle watched the black-and-white reverse back down the driveway with Jon at her side. She felt foolish, embarrassed, and angry at Jon for keeping whatever it was to himself. Once the car was out of the drive, she rounded on Jon.

"What happened, Jon?"

"I'll tell you everything, I promise. Just let me get some sleep first."

Chelle crossed her arms, covering her breasts; she didn't want Jon to see her the way she had wanted Officer Barnes to see her, or Vivek, or any other man who paid her any attention in that way.

"Tell me *now*," she said.

"Babe, I'm so sorry. You know how it is at the hospital. Always some crisis. Just let me shower, okay? Then I'll tell you."

Chelle felt her anger surge. Jon could be so casual, so infuriatingly *dismissive*.

"It's that woman, isn't it? Doctor Susan *something*."

"Doctor Grunberg?" Disbelief registered in Jon's eyes. "She doesn't have anything to do . . . Chelle, nothing is going on between Susan and me. Nothing has ever gone on.

We've been over this before, babe. It's old ground."

"Is it?" Chelle considered the evidence. The call, earlier, to say he was coming home, then hours without as much as a text. The mysterious ride home in a police car. Why? Maybe he'd had a glass of wine too many with the delectable Dr. Grunberg to drive and the cop was a friend who knew about his affair? "Feels like *new* ground to me. What's this about a crisis? What sort of a crisis keeps you from texting your wife?"

Jon grew distant. "I'll tell you. I will. Not out here." He turned to the door.

Chelle held the door closed, reaching a hand past him.

"Need time to put your story together, huh?" She jabbed a finger at her husband's chest. "Why can't you admit . . ."

Hands closed around her elbows. Chelle gave a gasp as Jon spun her around.

"Stop that. Shush," Jon hissed.

"Am I too loud for you, Jon? Afraid the neighbors will hear?"

"The kids." His weary expression was replaced by a look of deep suspicion. "Did you take your lithium today, Chelle?"

"It's two in the morning."

"*Yesterday*, then."

"I forget. Don't change the subject."

"Babe, you can't go cold. How many days have you been off your meds?"

She lashed out, snarling, trying to shove Jon or scratch him—or both. Dodging her attack, Jon caught his wife in a bear hug and lifted her off her feet. As he set her back down, he gave a slight push so the backs of her knees struck the front of an Adirondack chair. She lost her balance. Jon caught her arms and lowered her into the seat.

"Get off me. I'm not a child! *Let go!*"

Jon did as he was told. Out of her reach, he stood and

watched her for a moment with what looked disgustingly like pity. More than anything, Chelle hated to be pitied, especially from *him*.

"I'm truly sorry I'm late. There was a crisis, a *real* one. I will tell you all about it later, *after* you've had your pills."

Then he left her, making his way into the house. Chelle wanted to follow, wanted to scream more in his face about the other woman, but strength suddenly left her. In a shallow, raspy whisper she said, "I'm so sorry. Oh God, Jon."

And she promised herself she would say it again when he was close enough to hear.

6

The morning was half gone when Tasmin Beale pulled her dirty brown F-150 into the reserved parking space in front of the administration tower of Church of the Resurrected Faith Center. The impressive, gray stone building sat on the outskirts of the small ranching town of Wimberley, Texas, which was home to fewer than three thousand people—perfectly quiet for the church. Usually, she was an early riser, but last night's conference with Senior Pastor Korvus had run late, and Tasmin had slept in. Half an hour out of bed, she had treated herself to pancakes at the Center's diner, then driven out to Blue Hole Park to walk off their extra calories.

But it was her fascination with nature that made Tasmin late to her meeting with the two most important trustees of the church.

Tasmin didn't blame herself. It wasn't her fault that she'd happened across the carcass of a yearling deer on her trek through the woods. She figured the deep gash in its belly was probably the work of a coyote; the poor little creature was just the perfect size to be a tempting target for a solo predator. Tasmin had squatted beside the body and poked at the raw, gaping wound with a stick as she listened for signs of anyone, or *anything*, approaching. Nothing. So, she had stroked the fawn's fur and drawn in long breaths of its scent as she backed away to watch the scavengers at work.

Carrion spotting was Tasmin's favorite pastime—had been for as long as she could remember. She recalled losing hours watching a swarm of red ants carve up a still-wriggling beetle when she was barely old enough to walk. From there, she'd progressed to hiding out to look on as rats, badgers, and raccoons picked over carcasses, most of which Tasmin found already dead. Really, the source didn't matter to her. It was the ability to blend in with nature so perfectly that carrion eaters, who were a cautious lot by nature, failed to notice her, which gave Tasmin such a thrill.

The corvids were her biggest frustration. She'd spent so many hours buried under piles of brush or crouching in a hastily made dugout while solitary ravens or whole murders of crows refused to gorge on a nearby corpse. They were too smart for their own good, these feathered eaters of the dead; they knew she was there, likely *smelled* her. Tasmin would never harm a scavenger—she admired them too much. And still, the overly cautious corvids *refused* to make friends. Tasmin knew people who trained ravens and others of the genus, some who spoke to their birds, and even some who got the birds to speak back. But for some reason she couldn't fathom, the corvids avoided Tasmin like the plague. They would circle, caw, even nip warily at a carcass she was watching every now and then, but never, in all her years of carrion spotting, had a raven or a crow gorged itself freely when she was closer to their target than a stone's throw.

Was it any wonder, then, that when a raven landed right in front of the dead deer that morning, she'd lost track of time? Tasmin hadn't even been hiding, not properly; she was sitting on the ground, shoulder against a tree, when the bird arrived. Paying her no mind, it plunged its beak straight into the deer's opened belly.

Tasmin's breath caught. She felt the thrill of discovery. Here was something new! When the raven's beak came out capped with a bloody mass of rotting innards, a feeling of warmth had spread from between Tasmin's breasts, across her belly, down to that special place between her thighs.

"My God," she'd whispered in reverence. "Who told you that you could do that?"

The raven had seen her. More than seen, it had *looked* at Tasmin with its narrow, pitch-black eye. The bird was ancient, almost a corpse itself. Patches of pink, goose bump skin showed where feathers had fallen off its back; its face looked ancient and *tired*. But as the raven tipped back its head to swallow down the gobbet of intestine, Tasmin was struck by a premonition: This bird would live long enough to tear chunks from her own flesh, from her moldering carcass, the body she left behind.

She'd sat in silent contemplation with that unnerving sensation for quite some time after the raven took flight and left her alone once more with the deer's corpse.

So now she was late.

"Who cares?" Tasmin said to the empty pickup.

Like so much else in her life, the convenience—and *in*convenience—of others was none of Tasmin's concern. She would have skipped the meeting completely if she hadn't been eager to see how other attendees would respond to Korvus's revelation. And eager she was. The information he had was priceless; it would change the lives of everyone it touched, including Tasmin herself.

After today, she would forever divide her life into *before* and *after*. Nothing would be the same after today.

Using a leather shoelace to tie her long, auburn hair in

a ponytail, Tasmin leapt from the pickup's cab. Her chief of security waited at the door of the admin building, nodding as she approached. Tasmin nodded back with a smirk at the M4 carbine cradled in the security chief's muscular arms. That rifle was genuine army issue; he'd bought it off a crooked quartermaster a few years back at one of the five Texas army bases. He never did say which one.

"Boss lady," he greeted her with a flat tone and nary a smile.

Tasmin made a sour face. "Why'd you call me that, Billy Weaver?"

The tilt of Billy's head drew attention to his missing right ear, along with the mottled skin that had grown back after an IED had blown away the original flesh. Tasmin checked her six. Nobody was around, so she took the chance to lay the flat of her hand on Billy's damaged skin.

"Bless you, my child," said Billy. It was an old, dark, and quite sick joke known to only two people in the world: Tasmin and Billy Weaver.

She smiled. "Get on inside," she ordered. "I need you."

Hesitant, Billy scratched at his salt-and-pepper goatee.

Losing her patience, Tasmin barged past Billy and opened the door for herself. He followed behind her in silence.

The reception desk was manned by a church member named Darrin. The pale, clean-shaven young man with bony features reminded Tasmin of a stray dog, but he had enough beef to him that she'd advised Billy to consider him for the Ezekiel Nine special force. The other trait that made Darrin a prime candidate was his unquestioning loyalty. Tasmin treated Darrin to a smile that didn't drop when he let her know the others were waiting for her in the boardroom; his tone let her know they were less than impressed at her tardiness.

Let them wait.

The walk from reception took under a minute, and Billy shadowed Tasmin the whole way. He maintained his usual trick of shifting right or left every time she tried to look at him over the opposite shoulder; it was kind of a little game the two liked to play. The man could be a ghost if he wanted, and in his profession, it was a talent worth cultivating.

Tasmin paused at the door to the boardroom. She turned to Billy. "Before we go in, I want you to remember something," she said.

Billy raised a quizzical eyebrow.

"Youngsport."

Billy's frown was almost a grimace. "I'm not likely to forget."

"See that you don't."

"Sure." Billy cursed under his breath—just loud enough for Tasmin to hear. "*Youngsport.*"

Tasmin opened the door.

The boardroom she and Billy entered was longer than it was wide. Windows occupied the entirety of one wall, monitor screens the others. The space between Tasmin and the far wall was taken up by the long table that filled most of the room.

Jake Korvus, her nominal superior, sat at the head of the table. At his right hand sat Phillip Berger. Phillip's sister Pamela Jean Berger sat across the table at Korvus's left hand. The siblings had a sort of similarity about them that played tricks with the mind: the same slight bump at the bridge of the nose, high cheekbones, hazel eyes, and flawless skin—they even shared the same cheek dimples that emerged when they smiled. Tasmin could never see one without thinking of the other, but they weren't twins. Phillip, P. J., and the other Berger sibling, Rochelle, possessed an uncanny likeness that seemed to surpass simple genetics. It was as if Ezra Berger, the late patriarch, had stamped his features on his offspring by sheer force of will. Tasmin suppressed a shudder. Actually, she wouldn't have put that past Ezra, the sly old dog. After all, he'd willed practically everything else around the Center into existence, so why not his wily old face on his kids?

From the end of the mahogany table, Korvus broke the silence. "It's about time, Pastor Beale. Thank you so much for joining us."

Tasmin slid her hands deep into the pockets of her jeans and gave the black-suited man a level stare. The title of senior pastor said little about what Korvus did in the church; most of his role involved dealing with the public. If scandal threatened to raise its ugly head, or the church achieved some noteworthy milestone, Phillip Berger was face number one in front of the news cameras as the church's appointed spokesman. Korvus was always face number two, and appeared on command to give smiles and nods and stirring prayers.

Tasmin's own position as executive pastor was much more practical, and gave her a different perspective on the work of the church. Public outreach meant little to her, and public opinion even less. All she cared about was keeping the authorities happy so they would leave the church alone to get on with its business. Tasmin mostly achieved that without interference from Phillip and Korvus. Youngsport had been the exception, and it was Tasmin herself who'd swept that particular fiasco under the rug.

Still, she was forced to admit, Korvus could be useful at times.

Thoughts still with the fawn's mutilated corpse, Tasmin smiled at the utilitarian beige folder on the desk in front of Korvus and said, "Oh, is it after nine? *So* sorry."

Moving down the table, Tasmin took the chair next to P. J. At her signal, Billy moved to stand opposite; the security chief loomed over Phillip.

The eldest Berger cleared his throat. "Pastor Korvus, you said you have something to share with us, something vitally important."

Tasmin widened her eyes at Phillip in mock surprise. He was a good-looking man, despite that disturbing resemblance to his sister, but he was nothing like Tasmin's type at all. She loved to flirt with powerful men, enjoyed the buzz it gave her to spurn the advances they thought she was inviting. To date, Phillip was one of her failed anti-conquests. He'd not shown even the slightest interest in her faux advances, but she wasn't one to give up that easily.

"*Important*, trustee?" she said. "That's an understatement."

P. J. glared hard at her. "Don't try to be funny, Tas."

Tasmin countered the glare with an innocent blink. "Funny, *me*? You've got me all wrong. In the Lord's own name, I'm serious as the grave. Fact is, trustee, what you're about to listen to is about the most serious thing you ever heard."

P. J. scrunched up her face in derision, her distaste of Tasmin Beale painfully clear. She obviously wasn't buying the woman's self-aggrandizing. "Short of the last trumpet, you mean?"

Tasmin looked her straight in the eye and slowly shook her head. "What the pastor's got to tell you is *very* short of nothing at all."

Korvus cleared his throat to break the palpable tension. "How 'bout we begin?"

And begin they did; the experience was even more delightful than Tasmin could ever have hoped for.

Just a few minutes in, P. J. sprang from her seat with tears in her eyes. She dashed from that conference room like Satan himself was on her tail, the door vibrating as she slammed it behind herself. Phillip attempted to follow his sister, but when he pushed back his chair to stand up, Billy caught it and held on.

Tasmin slid into the chair P. J. had vacated; it was still nicely warm. All the better to gaze deep into Phillip's eyes. "Settle down, trustee. Looks like your sister's scared of skeletons in the family closet. But she's only just seen a few scattered bones. The *really* good stuff is still to come."

She held Phillip's gaze until she was sure he wouldn't try to bolt. If she had wanted, she could have told Billy to grab Phillip by the collar and make him stay. Now, that *would* have been fun, but Tasmin held back from the command. She was sure Phillip's reaction to the rest of what Korvus had to say would be even more pleasant to watch.

7

Jon scuffed his Oxfords on the curb. He set down the crate of raw carrots he'd been hefting and told his friend and spiritual advisor, Rabbi Max, "I wore the wrong shoes for this."

The two men were a block away from Austin's Food for All Food Bank. Putting "Food" in the name twice had felt like a syntax mistake to Jon, but he reckoned the charity may have done it for emphasis.

The rabbi didn't stop to comment on Jon's shoes. Instead, he gave his attention to the crate of canned pears he carried. It was a jumbo-sized crate, easily twice as heavy as Jon's carrots, but the rabbi didn't complain. He didn't ask to swap with Jon, either, despite the thirty years of joint pain that separated the pair.

"A beautiful day," Rabbi Max said. "We've done this how many times now? It's nice you got the day off."

The rabbi had a habit of switching topics anytime Jon started grousing about something trivial, and he had his own ideas about what was and what was not trivial. Jon's "day off" was certainly not. Far from being a vacation, it was a mandatory weeklong leave, ordered by the Crown's chief of behavioral therapy after the previous night's ER massacre. Jon didn't often take time off. In fact, the last time he'd more than two days off in succession was more than a year ago, the last time a violent episode had interrupted his life.

Rabbi Max's other annoying habit was accurately reading Jon's mood. "That friend of Rochelle's, what was her name? The accountant."

"Hannah," Jon replied.

"Hannah, right. Like Samuel's mother. A good name. Did the police ever say anything about what happened?"

Jon took a deep breath. "They think she had a boyfriend we don't know about. Most murders are domestic, apparently."

Rabbi Max harrumphed. "Unless there's a war. Listen. You've had a tough year, Jon. It's good you're giving back."

"I'm not sure I follow."

"You're *alive*, yes? You breathe the clean air, you see your kids most days, now and then you eat out with your wife. How do you think you've made it so far?"

"I'll take a wild guess. God?"

"Good boy. There's hope for you yet. God sustains the righteous. Since that poor girl died, maybe earlier—what do I know—he's been working overtime for you. It's good you're giving back."

Jon couldn't help but smile; the rabbi's attitude was infectious.

"Rabbi Max?" Jon said. The Rabbi paused and half turned, no doubt hearing the change in Jon's tone. "I truly appreciate you looking out for me."

The Rabbi shrugged. "It's a living." He walked toward the food pantry's entrance again, but Jon's next sentence brought him up short.

"I think my marriage is over." Jon sounded so matter-of-fact. "Her mom hates me. The church, the Church of the Resurrected, I mean, has gone way out on the lunatic fringe since Chelle's dad passed. The new pastors are raking in millions in tithes, and they're using the money to buy weapons. Chelle knows this, but somehow she seems not to care. I don't know if it's her illness or something else at play. I've begged her to get out before something happens, before it's too late. She won't listen to me, Rabbi. We fight all the time. And I'm pretty sure she's cheating on me."

Rabbi Max set down his crate. He walked back to Jon and laid a comforting hand on his shoulder. Jon felt the age-old callouses through his shirt.

"My son," the rabbi said, "*Tzedakah tatzil mimavet.* You know what that means?"

"*Tzedakah,*" Jon repeated. He paused, trying to work it out. "Sorry, Rabbi. Bar Mitzvah was a long time ago."

"*Tzedakah tatzil mimavet.* Charity saves from death. Did you think it only meant the receiver?"

Jon answered with a smile.

"What the—?"

Jon followed the rabbi's gaze into the distance, from where the all-too-familiar sound spilled across the quiet streets. There, he saw the all-too-familiar sight of a locust swarm flying high over the rooftops. The unmistakable hum of so many thousands of tiny wings drifting across the still air triggered memories of the previous night in Jon's mind: the dozens of crumpled bodies, blood puddling on the hospital's polished floors and spattered high up the white walls, the crazed look in the gunman's eyes at the moment the bullets brought him down. It was almost as if the locusts had been a wicked portent.

The locusts that had plagued Austin and several outlying small towns since late July had thinned considerably with the start of September, but there were still enough of the insects for their clouds to cast shadows. The swarm swerved in the food bank's direction.

"We need to get the food undercover. Quickly." Jon tried to keep the panic from his voice; they were delivering a lot of fresh produce to the food bank, and he knew how destructive the insects could be. "I'll go back to the truck and let the driver know."

The Rabbi squeezed Jon's shoulder tightly. "Stay, Jon. Have faith." He closed his eyes and began murmuring softly in Hebrew.

Jon fidgeted, wishing he knew what the rabbi was saying. He'd have loved to have been able to pray along with Rabbi Max, in his own words of course, but simply couldn't take his eyes off the swarm; he braced himself for the locusts to descend upon the vegetables, pummeling him and the rabbi with their stiff, brown bodies in the process. The locusts had already stripped Austin's parks bare; they seemed to have no fear of people and had thus far proven immune to all the insecticides the authorities had thrown at them.

The rabbi finished his prayer. He looked warmly at Jon as the buzz of the locusts grew louder, louder still, and Jon imagined he could feel the breeze of their wings lapping at his face . . .

Then, the buzzing faded away, and Jon watched in disbelief as the locusts passed by overhead.

"How did you know?" he asked the rabbi.

"I had faith." Rabbi Max tightened his cheeks and tipped back his head, as though smelling the air. "And I had a good feel for how the wind was blowing. It's mostly blind faith, though."

"I guess the prayers helped too?" said Jon with a wry smile. Stooping forward, he picked up the crate of pears.

The rabbi took it from of his hands. "Never underestimate the power of prayer, Jon," he said.

Jon went to retrieve his abandoned carrots and jogged back to catch up. Somehow, the day seemed brighter, his burdens less, but that only gave him the space to search deeper into what was troubling his soul, and he wasn't quite sure he was ready to do that.

Caught in his reverie, another memory of the night before played out in Jon's mind: Standing there in the hospital, holding the power of life and death in his hands in the form of the rifle, should have felt like just another day. Hardly a day went by when he didn't hold someone's life in his hands, but aiming that gun at Murphy Gore had been different. The moment he menaced Gore with the rifle, he'd felt all-powerful, invulnerable, free from all fear. He tried to fool himself that the shots fired over Gore's head had been intentional and those that killed him an accident—but that was a lie. The instant Jon fired the rifle, sparing Gore had been the furthest thing from his mind.

"Jon?" called Rabbi Max. After his short jog, Jon had lagged behind; the rabbi had reached the entrance of the food bank.

Jon quickened his pace. Before him stretched a long line of men and women, the homeless, the addicted, the destitute. The line ran out of the building, turned the corner, and went on up the block, so the sight of one man— scrawny, filthy, middle-aged, with a full bush of a black beard—leaving a spot near its front was unusual.

As the man stepped away, Jon saw him stumble like someone had shoved him. As Jon hurried to the rabbi's side, the scrawny man recovered, turned, and threw a punch. His target, presumably the man who had done the shoving, took a hard fist to the chin. He answered with a quick fist of his own.

"Hey! Quit that!" The security guard stationed outside the entrance ran toward the brawl. He tried to get between the two men and got a bloody lip for his trouble. As he stumbled back, reaching for his cell phone, Jon advanced, determined to help.

Rabbi Max restrained him with a firm hand upon his arm. "Fools rush in, Jon. Look."

One of the brawlers—the one who'd started the fracas with a shove—had leapt away just far enough to pull out a pocket knife. It snapped open, and Jon saw the keen blade glint in the sparse sunlight. Shaking the knife at his opponent, the man shouted in a dialect Jon couldn't quite place.

Slowly, it occurred to Jon that, while he didn't understand the words, he knew where they were from. Strictly speaking, they weren't words at all but a verbal emote, one of the dozen prepackaged expressions Endless Loop Games had programmed into their two hits, *Infinite Quest* and *NeverEnd*, as a replacement for the curses players yelled into their microphones. While the company downplayed its ties to its founder's church, they made sure to censor their voice chat. Some die-hard gamers complained, but the international fans who embraced the games quickly adopted the emotes as a lingua franca.

"*Ichaka!*" shouted the knife wielder.

"*Po ki yi!*" his opponent countered.

Translated, the phrases meant: "Your mother!" and "Come here and say that!" so far as Jon could remember. The unarmed man took a step forward, daring the other to make a move.

"Stop this at once!" Rabbi Max stepped forward. Unlike the guard, he didn't attempt to insert himself between the men. He didn't have to. The power of his voice alone caught the brawlers' attention, and they rounded on him as one. The rabbi shifted his crate to his hip, as if to block Jon from getting involved. "Gentlemen. No good will come of violence."

The man wielding the knife grinned at the rabbi. His

eyes widened and he lifted the thin blade to his own forehead. In a heartbeat, he slashed downward, carving a long, red cut into his forehead and cheek that resembled Fairplay's. What happened next was almost too quick for Jon to follow.

The man swung his bloodied blade at Rabbi Max. In the blink of an eye, the rabbi pivoted, caught his would-be assailant's wrist, and used their combined momentum to twist the man's knife hand backward; Jon heard bone crackle. As the attacker screamed loudly in pain and dropped the weapon, Rabbi Max spun him to the ground. He finished the skilled maneuver by rolling the man on his belly and wrenching his arm behind his back, so much so, his fingertips touched the back of his head. The man screamed again. The unarmed man glanced from the rabbi to the other man and ran.

Rabbi Max sighed. "*Tanto tori*. Thank you. That's the first chance I've had to use that outside of class."

The security guard holstered his phone and rushed to lock the captive in a set of handcuffs. Rabbi Max helped, and when that was done, he paused a moment to accept back slaps from his astonished audience.

"The cops are on the way," the guard told Jon and Rabbi Max, and the two made another couple trips to and from the truck as they waited.

Twenty minutes later, the ordeal was over. The handcuffed man was being held by police. No one seemed to know the other brawler's name, but Jon was able to give a description. The knife wielder wore blue jeans and a duffel coat, but the runner's outfit had been a variation of that worn by Jon's juvenile patient: instead of a puffer jacket, he had worn a gray vest that had once been a regular shirt before it lost its sleeves. A pair of green camo trousers and army boots completed the outfit. The boots, in fact, were a closer match to Fairplay's than Jon's patient had worn. Why the adolescent and the middle-aged brawler had both chosen the grizzled veteran of the games for a role model was a mystery; *NeverEnd* offered plenty of character choices. Jon made a mental note to ask Chelle about the appeal—if they ever made up, that was.

Jon and Rabbi Max watched the police cruiser drive away with the cuffed brawler looking spaced out in the back seat.

"What do you think set all that off?" Jon asked the rabbi.

Rabbi max shrugged, but a man in the line heard the question and approached them. Despite his disheveled appearance and unholy stink, the phone the homeless guy produced from his jacket was the latest iPhone. He unlocked it with a face scan, tapped the screen, and held it out for Jon to see. A news feed played. Kate Boldwin, local star reporter with Channel 6, held a microphone in one hand and pointed the other at a bend of the Colorado River, where the rippling water had turned a deep red.

"I know that spot," said Jon. "It's close to here."

"You're right," said the phone's owner. He breathed in, whistled. "Whew! Try that. Take a whiff."

Jon did as he was told. Chelle always said his taste for spicy foods would kill his sense of smell, but he'd hardly begun filling his lungs before he detected the odor.

"Smells like diesel, and maybe dead fish. And is that *blood*?"

The scruffy man tucked the phone back in his jacket. "News broke about a minute before the trouble started between those two. I was around the corner." He tapped his nose. "The wind was blowing my way, so I *knew* something was coming."

Rabbi Max had his own phone out, scrolling. "It's a chemical spill. Or so says the AP."

"What else could it be?" asked Jon.

The rabbi didn't answer. He hefted a crate he had set aside and carried it into the food bank. Jon trailed after him with another crate. As the door swung closed behind him, he heard a shrill voice in the distance.

"Repent! Repent before The End!"

8

Blood was in the air at the Cross Guard Ranch. The 120-acre patch of undeveloped land sat a little under nine miles south of Austin, in Bluff Springs, Texas, itself a town of fewer than a hundred souls and home to scattered, white-boarded ranch homes, fancy retirement homes, and cheap apartment complexes. Its owner, Silas Bram Bundy, liked to say it was far enough from the city to have its own bouquet. He usually said it while showing off his prize cattle, the source of the particular bouquet he had in mind. But on this day, the twenty-four-hour news channel Silas favored reported that a blood-like odor could be detected in a twenty-mile radius around the Lake Austin Marina, where a chemical spill had occurred. They also said the authorities believed the spill had been intentional.

Silas breathed in the sickly funk with satisfaction. For once, the authorities were right. The skiff he'd purchased had sunk beautifully, according to the boys he paid to sink it. The open-top barrels on the small rowing boat had deposited their contents, and in mere minutes, the river had turned red as cherry wine. Panic set in; the news vans arrived.

It gratified Silas to see a plan come together so seamlessly. He would have to ask his cousin Graham for the recipe of what was in those barrels. Sending that boy off for a bachelor's in chemistry had been worth every penny.

The blood stink boosted Silas's spirits so high, he barely felt the chill running down his spine when the man he knew as Coppersmith said, "Good morrow, Abraham."

Silas turned on his heels to see the tall, lanky figure standing five feet behind him. He had heard nothing, sensed nothing, until Coppersmith spoke; the man had a knack for appearing seemingly out of nowhere.

"Lord above," said Silas, his heart pounding. "You some kinda Injun? I never knew a white man who could sneak up on a fellow like that."

"You must be behind on your Fenimore Cooper." Coppersmith fixed Silas with a grin. It was a peculiar habit of his—to finish some nonsense statement by showing his teeth. Silas had a fancy to count those pearly whites. It always seemed to him, whenever Coppersmith grinned at him, there were a sight too many for any regular man.

He said, "What do you want?" He knew better than to draw out Coppersmith's opinion of his plans, even those that worked flawlessly, like the bloodied Colorado.

"What I always want, Abraham."

Silas clenched his jaw. Only Coppersmith called him by that name. It wasn't even the right name. The "Bram" in Silas Bram Bundy stood for nothing but itself.

"Oh, I know. The COTR is evil." Silas preferred to use the initials of the Church of the Resurrected, as if saying the words out loud would somehow soil his mouth. "The Bergers are devils incarnate and Jake Korvus is the gen-u-wine antichrist. I get it, okay? What I don't get is what you want me to do about it. We're on our own out here, Coppersmith. There ain't a soul in Christendom who'd spit on a brother or sister of the Texas Cross Guard if they was on fire. And here you are, wanting me to start a war. Well, get somebody else is all I can say. Or show some patience. We'll be ready to take on the church in three, maybe four years. Move any faster and they'll be sure to wipe us out, unless the gov'ment gets wise and wipes us out first."

The tall man grinned all the way through the end of Silas's speech. Only when he was finished did Coppersmith allow that toothy grin to fade. Turning, he stared silently into the distance before returning his gaze to Silas's face. When he finally spoke, it was like he'd forgotten the earlier conversation.

"Have you visited the upper forty today, Abraham?"

Silas groaned with frustration. That was the trouble with Coppersmith. Sure, he was useful: If Silas was honest, Coppersmith had been downright indispensable in forming the Cross Guard. But lately, every time Silas tried talking to him, it was like nothing he said mattered. None of his questions got answered, at least not in a useful way, and barely anything he stated got a comment from the tall man. He'd been more flexible in the old days, or at least more talkative. These days, all Coppersmith seemed to care about was accelerating the timeline on a physical attack against the church that abandoned Silas in his time of need. That is, when he wasn't making random suggestions about how Silas ran the ranch.

"You really *should* visit the upper forty," Coppersmith said.

Silas cursed quietly beneath his breath—he never knew who could be listening—and marched off down the hill. The Guard's fleet of golf carts was parked a stone's throw from the bottom, under a rusty metal canopy that kept at least some of the rain from soaking the seats. Silas picked his favorite of the twelve carts—black, and one of only six that actually ran—and squished his round belly behind the wheel. Coppersmith sat daintily in the back seat, which faced backward; he swung his long, spindly legs over the safety bar and kicked his black boots in the air.

"That Faith Center of theirs is a cesspool," Coppersmith said as Silas started the engine with the press of a button; the electric motor whirred to life. As they drove away from the shelter and onto the dirt path that would take them north, the tall man continued his diatribe. "You've seen the membership roster I sent over, I trust? It's full of social dropouts, phony spiritualists, and the mentally inept. Your fear of the authorities is understandable, Abraham. You've been on their bad side. But honestly, you have nothing to fear from the church. You're stronger than you imagine, *much* stronger than they are, and you have something on your side they can't hope to beat."

"Right?" asked Silas.

"No," said Coppersmith. "*Me*."

Silas drove the cart over a rock to deliberately jostle his passenger. "Stronger? Then how come the COTR's got a compound, thirty black Chryslers, and twelve thousand registered members, while the two hundred sixty of us here hunker down in trailers and drive around in these kiddie carts?"

Coppersmith answered without hesitation. "Priorities, Abraham. The holy gentlemen and sainted ladies around here have taken the wise course. They've divested earthly interests, repudiated wealth. Their focus is on far higher pursuits."

Silas cursed again, this time out loud, not caring who heard his displeasure. "Do you even hear yourself, Coppersmith? You know what I saw out my window last night? One of our sainted ladies falling down drunk off Lloyd Cooper's back step. She fell over because her sainted panties were down 'round her ankles. I guessed at drunk because the fall didn't seem to hurt her any. She hopped right up, laughing, and duckwalked over to Jed Land's trailer next door with them polka dots still about her feet. Jed was happy to see her, of course. He must have owed her money, 'cause he tossed a fistful of bills in the air and watched her pick 'em up one by one before he and his nephew Tommy hauled her inside. Nice boy, Tommy. Always happy to lend a hand."

They drove along in silence for a time. Finally, Coppersmith spoke. "Silas, I'm concerned by your lack of empathy for your fellow man. It's like you expect your brothers and sisters to be without flaw. Who was it who said something about a plank in the eye?"

"That would be Jesus, you fool."

"Right. Him." A chuckle escaped Coppersmith's throat. "It was a nice speech, but not my favorite. I like the one where he told the sinless man to throw a rock at the whore."

"He didn't—"

"Good thinking, that. A sinless man would be disciplined, focused. You'd have to imagine he'd have a lot of stored-up energy. The right rock, thrown by his hand . . . Well, he might not have needed another one."

The golf cart lurched as Silas applied the brakes with a heavy foot. He'd driven to Michmash, the highest hill on the ranch. A patch of earth almost damp enough to call a mire had formed near the base, and Silas steered around it to where a more-or-less dry trail began. The trail wasn't meant for carts. In fact, it wasn't really meant for *anything*. Cattle had worn it into the dirt by zigzagging upslope in search of fresh grass. Only one side of the cart's wheels could occupy the trail at a time, leaving the other to skid in mud, dust, or crusted cowpats.

A third of the way to the top of Michmash, Silas's patience gave out. He parked the cart, hopped out, kicked a tire, and started to hike up the incline. When he checked on Coppersmith, he saw the tall man had left the cart as well and was actually ahead of him. He swung his long legs in great arcs, which had the tail of the black leather duster he wore in all weathers swishing with his rhythm.

Silas grunted. September it might be, but the weather was far too hot for a man his size to hurry. He slapped his belly and started after Coppersmith at a moderate pace. Not that Coppersmith seemed to mind. When Silas came out on top of Michmash, his partner was surveying the scene with indifference. Spread out before him was the forty-acre spread that ran all the way to the ranch's north border. Occupying that spread would be about a fifth of the dairy cattle on the ranch, though only a few hundred head could be seen from Michmash at that moment. All were cows and their calves; the bulls were kept elsewhere. The upper forty cattle sat in small clusters on the hillside or roved aimlessly in mini-herds, grazing the valley below. A couple of ranch boys watched over them on horseback from the smaller hill opposite. One had a rifle on his back in case of coyotes; the scene was quite tranquil.

"All right. We're here," Silas panted, his breath labored, wheezing. "Now what?"

The tall man pursed his lips but didn't speak. This troubled Silas as he paced the crest of Michmash, studying the valley and the scattered lower hills. The Bundys were no greenhorns when it came to raising cattle. Silas's fifth-grandpappy back had been roping steers when Texas was declared a state. Prior to Silas's most recent and quite lengthy stretch behind bars, he'd chalked up twenty-five years as a cow puncher, flank rider, and ranchman of Pa's ranch in the Blacklands. If something was wrong with the Cross Guard cattle, Silas was sure he'd know.

The words "ain't nothing" had just come out of his mouth when he saw it. A heifer standing downslope of Silas took a step and stumbled sideways. Her calf had to scurry to get out of the way and not get itself crushed to death. The cow caught herself and ambled onward, but something about how she walked made Silas's neck itch. He lifted his hat, fanning his face as he pondered. Gritting his teeth, he spun his cell phone out of the holster clipped to his belt. After taking a moment to skim the duty roster, he phoned up Bill Sharp, the rider with a rifle on the opposite hill.

The phone rang only once before Bill answered. As Bill's slow, steady voice said, "Yeah, boss?" Silas held up a hand. In the distance, Bill shifted his phone from right hand to left and waved back. Silas heard Bill cuss as the barrel of his rifle clipped the phone. Swearing was on the list of vices the Cross Guard brethren pledged to give up when they devoted their lives to the Lord. Silas would have to remind the brothers about swearing in his sermon on Sunday, though it would be tough to fit that in, what with all the drinking, gambling, and passing women around he already planned to preach about. The thought made him tired.

"Bill," Silas said, "how they movin' today?"

The rider considered before he gave an answer. "Kinda lazy out of the gate, boss, but we got 'em going."

Silas glanced at Coppersmith, who had stopped staring idly to give him a grin. Once again, Silas was struck by the urge to count the man's teeth. He punched the button to switch to speaker phone—figured Coppersmith ought to be in on the conversation.

"Stir 'em a little, Bill. I want to see how they go."

Bill signaled his partner and both spurred their horses. The beasts came to a trot, then a gallop as the ranch hands circled behind a group of idling cattle with voices raised in a cacophony of hoots and hollers.

It was a sweet show, and it got the job done. In seconds, every cow and calf that had been lounging was up on its hooves, and each one already up was loping ahead of the cowboys with panic in their eyes. Silas nodded to himself as more of the herd was drawn in and, before long, the riders had eighty animals trotting a tight circle in the valley on Michmash's north side.

Silas held the phone near his mouth. "Keep 'em hopping. Keep 'em hopping."

The eighty loping cattle should have been a sight to warm any rancher's heart, but it didn't take long before Silas saw something that chilled his. Out of the eighty-odd, he counted fourteen that showed the similar labored, wobbly gait of the heifer who'd almost flattened her calf. Some wobbled worse than others, and the more afflicted of those tottered around with heads low and legs stiff. It was almost as if they'd forgotten their joints could bend.

"Bill," Silas grunted. "Put 'em in."

"Boss?"

"Put 'em in *now*!" Silas snapped as he hung up on the ranch hand and put in a call to his cow boss. "Hooch, get Doc Harley down. We've got BSE." It was all Silas could do not to throw down the phone after he hung up on Hooch too.

Down in the valley, Bill had the herd on the move. He had clearly noticed the gait of the animals affected with bovine spongiform encephalopathy, or mad cow disease, and was putting in special effort to speed them along to the pen. The other rider was equally competent, which left Silas nobody to yell at but Coppersmith. He made to stomp over to the tall man, but found he had moved. Coppersmith was a quarter of the way down Michmash, already heading back to the golf cart.

"Well," Silas shouted after him, "I saw what you wanted me to see. What's it mean, Coppersmith?"

Coppersmith stopped dead in his tracks. It was so unlike him to acknowledge a prompt from Silas that the simple act brought on a feeling of dread. When Coppersmith turned around, Silas felt his cheeks go numb. He had never in his life been on the end of such a malevolent glare.

"Are you stupid?" Coppersmith asked, his tone flat, dry. "We have been friends, partners, *brothers* for years, Abraham. And yet you claim not to know The Will."

Silas wanted to say something smart in reply, but all he got out was, "Will?"

"*The* Will, Abraham. The definite article. You think to deny it, to go slowly when The Will says you must go fast. Who do you think has done this thing to us, Abraham? Do you think it is God who has stricken the cattle with disease? An *enemy* has done this. An enemy with hands already red with the blood of our lambs."

Silas pondered carefully what he said next. He knew Coppersmith too well to assume he was speaking metaphorically. The tall man clearly had a specific bloodletting in mind.

"What lambs?"

Before Coppersmith could answer, the phone in Silas's hand beeped. Coppersmith folded his arms, clearly intending to wait while Silas checked the phone. The alert took him to a text message. The message contained an internet address, a link to a URL. From the corner of his eye, Silas saw Coppersmith twirl his hand impatiently. He clicked the URL link.

The first photo was of a woman with her head twisted around so far, her chin rested on her back. The barrel end of a gun and a pair of dusty brown boots could be seen at the edge of the photo. Silas scrolled down the page and saw more bodies, of both men and women. Slowly, the memory of their faces came back to him. Every last one was a Cross Guard member.

Specifically, they were Cross Guard members who had been chosen to infiltrate the Church of the Resurrected and report back on what they found. Coppersmith had suggested the program, but it had been Silas who selected the spies. Nearly six years had passed since his chosen had been sent out. After a few months of stealthy communication, all contact had ceased. Silas had guessed the worst, but seeing the photos caused his guts to knot.

"Why am I only seeing this now?"

Coppersmith hummed a tune. It took only a few notes for Silas to recognize *Turn! Turn! Turn!* by the Byrds.

As Silas continued to scroll, he saw photos of soldiers posing with some of the bodies. The red triangle of the Church of the Resurrected showed clearly on the breast of their uniforms. There was also a patch, visible on the right shoulder, that showed three block-capital letters: EIX. One photo showed a soldier shielding his face with his hand. He shouldn't have bothered. Silas knew who he was from the scarred skin around the missing ear. Billy Weaver must have thought hiding his face while planting his boot on a dead man's back was funny.

Silas didn't see the joke.

He lowered the phone, his head along with it. Coppersmith wanted to go to war. So did Silas, now he'd seen the evidence of how brutal their enemy could be. Yet, still, a quiet voice muttered away in the back of his head, telling him they were too weak and they stood to lose everything.

"They've struck at your home," Coppersmith said.

"Huh?" The photos had all but driven out all thought of the diseased cattle. "You think COTR infected the cattle with BSE?"

"Naturally they did. Your numbers are up. Korvus feels threatened."

Silas considered. He was no greenhorn, and neither were his ranch hands. There was no way the disease could have progressed so far without someone raising the alarm. Except if someone—an enemy, as Coppersmith hypothesized—had helped with the spreading. He dialed a number, listened to the ring tone.

"Silas." The voice at the end of the line greeted him after three rings.

"Coachman." Silas took in a deep breath. "We been hit where we live. Get your best boys together. I want plans for a counterstrike."

"Target?"

Silas hesitated, remembering the compound, the twenty black Chryslers, and the twelve thousand registered members. Off to his left, Bill and his partner had brought the herd around Michmash's east end. Silas watched the stumbles, the mother cows blundering into the little ones; his mind showed him the cattle funeral pyre that was now inevitable. There was no point delaying. The enemy had brought the war to his door.

"A cesspool of wickedness," he told Coachman.

He lifted his eyes, but Coppersmith wasn't looking at him. The tall man stared off into the distance. His mouth was straight, lips closed. Yet, as Silas looked at him, a trick of the light made it appear he could see straight through Coppersmith's skin to those myriad teeth he was sure were in the shape of a grin.

9

The Alphon Hotel in downtown Houston was an expensive, modernized boutique establishment with three-hundred-dollar-a-night rooms, ostentatious décor celebrating the city's oil barons, and a bar that stayed open all night. It sat smack bang in the center of Houston, a huge, glass-fronted building dwarfed by the tall office towers that surrounded it. Fancy or not, the Alphon smelled the same as pretty much every hotel Jon had ever stayed in: a bouquet of day-old roses in a vase filled with Lysol.

He tossed his keys on the bed with a scowl. His mood had been bad all day. After his mandatory post-incident time off, he was having a hard time getting back into the groove of his working medical life. The drive down from Dallas had been tedious, and all he'd been able to think about was his failure with Chelle. She was outwardly pleasant toward him, yet inwardly cool; it was as if the incident at the hospital had thrown up a permanent wall between them.

It was hard on the nerves, too. Not for the first time, Jon wondered if his life wouldn't be better if he ended things with Chelle. The twins were grown up and the boys stuck so close to their mother, they hardly seemed to notice him much at all. If Chelle didn't care that much for him, if she didn't want to make up . . .

He picked up the keys and squeezed hard to press one key painfully into his hand; the sharp jab brought him a little clarity. How could he think that way? He didn't want a divorce, or even a separation. The very thought made him shiver. Jon dropped the keys in the faux-walnut bedside table, next to the Gideon Bible. Rabbi Max would have referred him to the Torah, but Jon decided what he needed to lift his mood was to sweat.

He hung his garment bag in the closet and riffled his duffel for gym shorts and a shirt. Twelve minutes later, he stumbled on the Alphon's exercise room almost by accident, after a desk jockey and a bartender gave him conflicting directions, and hopped on the stair climber. He was getting up to speed when a familiar face walked in.

"Jon!" Susan Grunberg, MD, called to him; her enthusiasm was flattering. Jon thanked her with a smile. "Are you just in? Traffic on 610 was ridiculous."

"I took the 290. It was just as bad. Got in maybe half an hour ago."

"Ha," said Susan. "Beat ya. I had time for nice, hot bath."

She was the sort of woman who could never have wet hair without a man noticing; it would appear dark auburn or light chestnut, depending on the light. Damp, it reminded Jon of melted caramel oozing down the inside of a chilled sundae glass. Today, Susan had it in a ponytail, but her hair was so thick, it draped against the back of her neck and clung wetly to her skin. She didn't seem to care.

"You had a bath *before* your run?" Jon feigned disapproval. "Isn't that a waste of water?"

Susan stepped onto the treadmill beside Jon's machine.

"According to my philosophy of life, a good soak is never a waste. And besides, it ain't my water bill!"

Intoxicated by Susan's presence, Jon staring straight ahead, as if transfixed by the climber's digital display. He had to pretend he couldn't see the sensuous body covered by dark blue, skin-tight spandex active wear in his peripheral vision. Susan was younger than him by almost a decade, but she wasn't the sort who got hung up on ages. She looked at him with hungry eyes, but not for sex, exactly. She craved the flattery she loved to give and receive—but Jon knew that didn't mean sex was off the table.

Far from it.

For Susan, sex was flattery's sincerest form.

Jon poked at the speed-up button on the climber. Maybe if he got himself out of breath, Susan wouldn't expect him to talk.

No such luck.

"Did you drive down alone?" Susan made the question sound innocent.

"Just me," Jon puffed; the climber's new speed was really beginning to kick his ass. "Chelle's got the kids." He considered punctuating the statement by clacking his wedding band on the stair climber's handrail, but realized he wasn't wearing it. He had a clear mental picture of placing it next to his wallet on the dresser in his room, just before he slipped his driver's license and hotel room key card in his shorts pocket.

"Poor Chelle," said Susan. "She's going to miss all the fun. You know what the hot topic is this weekend, right?"

The LED display on Jon's machine showed he'd reached a steep hill. Groaning, he paused while gears ground and the pitch adjusted. It would have seemed awkward not to meet Susan's eyes at that moment, to share a smile and pretend not to notice the small split in her sports bra.

Susan moistened her lips.

"Based on the program," Jon said, "I expect it'll be violent video games."

Susan nodded. "This afternoon's keynote is 'The Pathology of Online Gaming Addiction and Its Attendant Psychosis.'"

Jon rolled his eyes. "'Online Gaming Addiction.' Makes it sounds like they're talking about video slots and digital blackjack. Why can't people just say what they mean?"

Susan pressed a control on her treadmill that increased both speed and pitch. Instead of waiting, as Jon had done, she raised her voice over the growl of gears. "They'd get sued if they came out and said *NeverEnd* was the problem. Sued by your mother-in-law, yeah? How cool would that be?"

Jon didn't comment, partially because he was out of breath, partially because nothing he could say would come out right. The climbing was most of the trouble, but exchanges with Susan were always tiring. He'd taken a vow not to look at any woman who wasn't his wife, figuratively speaking. It didn't matter Chelle had broken a similar vow to him.

Susan noticed he was struggling; she matched her breathing to his and said, "Hey . . . how about . . . we get a bite . . . after the session?"

Jon used the first lie that came to mind. "Sorry. I'm . . . meeting someone."

"Anyone . . . I know?"

Jon yawned to buy himself some thinking time. He thought about who he knew in Houston, but all the names that came to him were professional contacts. Susan would likely know most of them better than he did.

"College friend. From before premed. It'll probably be

a late night."

Susan tapped her speed control again and raised her voice another notch. "You know me, Jon. Night owl to the end." She'd dropped the heavy breathing act in favor of accenting her words with a throaty purr. Keeping that up while she moved so fast was a neat trick. "If you want a midnight snack or someone to hit the minibar with, give me a knock. Room 319." With the help of the handrails, she leapt off the whirring treadmill and stood on the strip beside the running deck. Reaching up past Jon to the number pad that was part of his machine's controls, she pressed the key for each number she repeated, "Three . . . one . . . nine."

Jon's stair climber lurched as it switched between programs. At that point, Jon couldn't have answered Susan even if he'd wanted, he was so distracted by the ridiculous surge in speed. He pulled the safety tether to stop his machine and rode a step to the ground. His feet touched the gym floor in time for him to wave to Susan as she walked out the door.

"Bye, Jon. Hope to see you later." She winked and, as she walked out, Rohan made his way in.

"Hey, Doc." Rohan smiled as he turned his head to take in Susan's retreating derriere. "I figured you'd be here. Want to get some lunch before this shindig starts?"

Jon checked his watch. It was a bit early for lunch, but the first half day of the weekend conference was due to kick off promptly at one.

"Probably a good idea."

Rohan said, "Cool. Don't tell me Doctor Grunberg's hands were a disappointment."

Jon sighed and stepped back from the climber. "You saw her."

"Bro, I *smelled* the pheromones. I'd ask what she wanted, but those hips were moving, and they don't lie."

"I fought her off, if you're wondering."

Rohan smiled. "You're a better man than me."

After a cold shower and a change of clothes, Jon met Rohan in the lobby. Lunch at the deli across the street turned into a strategy meeting. Rohan had a cousin in Houston he hadn't seen in years and, at Jon's urging, he got in touch. The three men made plans to meet for supper. Jon would be paying, of course.

"It won't make any difference," Rohan told Jon. "319 will still want her midnight snack."

"She'll have to find me, first."

Rohan's wry smile told Jon he knew that if Susan Grunberg wanted to find him, she would.

As Rohan filled up a tray with sandwich wrappers and napkins, Jon checked his phone. Chelle had texted an hour ago, asking for a call. It probably wasn't serious, so he texted back, promising to call after the session.

The conference's kickoff happened twenty minutes later. Jon and Rohan were seated near the back of the converted ballroom that functioned as the conference room, so Jon was grateful for the two large screens, one on either side of the stage. They showed the keynote speaker's face. Gerhard Wolff, MD, PhD, was a large, gruff man with a strong chin, strikingly full lips, and a fringe of gray hair. Wolff surveyed his audience for several long, pregnant seconds before graciously thanking the conference organizer who had introduced him, and launching into his speech.

"Friends and colleagues, I stand before you in the role of the disappointed prophet. I am not disappointed with my own prophecies, you understand, nor with the prophecies of other experts in my field. What has come to disappoint me is the reception our warnings have been given by the general public. Since before the inclusion of internet gaming disorder in DSM-5," he said, referring to the *Diagnostic and Statistical Manual of Mental Disorders,* "clinical psychiatrists have been sounding the alarm, not only about internet gaming in particular, but about the internet in general *and* gaming in general. The combination, I have warned, is like mixing bleach with ammonia. Each has its uses, but you would serve neither at a dinner party, and would not think of poisoning guests with the mixture."

From this sobering mental image, Wolff's keynote continued on into darker territory. His first graphic, which flashed garishly up onto the twin screens, showed a line chart of teenage suicide rates over the decades. The numbers alone were alarming, but what really caught Jon's attention, and evidently that of the rest of the audience, was the second graphic. It compared the rates of suicide with the rates of homicides committed by teens.

"You will no doubt be familiar with the so-called pandemic crossover, when homicides among teens aged fifteen to nineteen surpassed suicides for the first time in ten years. I would like to draw your attention to the detail only hinted at by statistics. Who were the victims of these homicides? And what were the motives? Where psychosis played a part, what interventions were attempted? Since the beginning of last year, I have led a team that examined these questions. I am now prepared to share our results."

The graphic disappeared, replaced once more by Wolff's imposing visage. "But before I do, I would like to ask you, my friends and colleagues, why bother? I am the disappointed prophet, the psychiatric Jeremiah. My doom has ever fallen on deaf ears. If I speak again of a decline in moral responsibility, of the growing distaste for right and wrong as a concept, will anyone hear?"

This last turn of phrase reminded Jon of Jake Korvus. The Church of the Resurrected's senior pastor was the polar opposite of Doctor Wolff in so many ways: He didn't bemoan his role as prophet, more reveled in it, but both men did weight their words with apocalyptic sentiment. All at once, the peculiar cadence of a Korvus sermon came back to Jon. He couldn't listen to Wolff's tale of woe without hearing the bouncing rhythm that held Korvus's congregation spellbound every Sunday. He heard the emphasis Korvus would have put on the words, if he had been giving the speech and not Wolff.

"*What* if I tell you that *this* nation, the *United States of America*, has *passed a pivot point* in history? That *the world beyond* this pivot point, the world *we live in today*, is in a state of *social*, psychological, and *moral* crisis?"

The Wolff-Korvus hybrid that had taken root in Jon's head told how the threat to human life was more dire than that of all modern diseases put together, that it surpassed even the dangers from climate change, nuclear war, and rogue artificial intelligence. If Korvus himself had been the speaker, he would have held his silver-lettered copy of *The Grand Cycle* above his head and proclaimed The End to be so close, it had actually passed, and the listeners were living through a sort of cosmic spasm in the final seconds before death.

What Wolff actually said was, "What will be your reaction, friends and colleagues, if I tell you our crisis promises a future grimmer than the biblical Armageddon?"

In the silence that followed, Rohan leaned toward Jon to whisper, "Whoops. He shouldn't have said the *B* word."

Jon was about to comment that he didn't blame Doctor Wolff for wanting to shake people up when a new image appeared on the screens. Instead of a still graphic, the screens showed a video clip of *NeverEnd* players in action, in which a pair of five-man squads swarmed over a battleground already crowded with fallen dead. Jon had played his share of first-person shooters in college, and he was always impressed by the way the *NeverEnd* characters moved through their virtual world. Instead of their digital boots flicking past the scattered body parts, they kicked some out of the way and stomped others into the mud. The next clip showed the squads transformed into an army of skeletal warriors, their bones covered with scraps of decayed flesh and ancient, rusted armor.

It was a low-level skirmish, so the enemies were armed with swords and spears, while the players carried oversized rifles. Muzzles flashed and skeletal bodies were exploded into smithereens. One player launched a rocket-propelled grenade, and a thick plume of dust and splintered bone burst high into the air. Though the clip itself was silent, Jon found he could imagine the battleground noises so vividly in his head, it was almost like being there. Blood rushed to his cheeks. His neck muscles tightened. He flexed his fingers, half expecting one of the comic book rifles to appear in his hands.

"Did you see?" Doctor Wolff said from the podium. "The details are not so engaging as the *Sturm und Drang*, but they are educational. Let us go back."

He turned to face one of the screens as his image was replaced, again, by the *NeverEnd* scene: The player squads charged. The skeleton army rose to meet them. The players fired a volley of shots.

The video paused. A second later, a white circle appeared on the screen. It surrounded a figure in the enemy ranks. Like the others, the figure was mostly bone, only covered in a few places by flesh. But it was smaller than all those around it. Jon's experience told him at once the bones belonged to a child. The video clip advanced by one frame, then another, and another. Frame by frame, Jon and the rest of the rapt audience watched the child skeleton take a half-dozen bullets to the skull. As the last bullet exploded out its occipital, the clip advanced a final frame and stopped. All at once, Jon was no longer looking at the skeleton of a child. The video game enemy had become, in the last frame, a girl with blonde hair, red blood, and pale skin.

The audience gasped. Some of the less-hardened medical professionals actually groaned. The freeze-framed toddler was as lovingly rendered as any of the *NeverEnd* graphics; even her powder-blue sundress was freshly pressed. The video clip editor had censored the girl's face, replacing the game's depiction with a pixelated blur, but that left the audience to imagine the mess six bullets had made of the child. Her body was contorted by the impact, her arms spread wide and one bare foot kicked into the air. Even without seeing the face, Jon found himself so close to vomiting, he was actually grateful for the anger that closed off his throat.

The video advanced another frame. The little girl disappeared and was replaced by a skeleton in the same pose. Whoever was operating the video allowed the clip to play, and the small bones crumbled and blew into dust.

Then the screen went black, which allowed the audience to take a much-needed breath before they were confronted once more with the dour face of Doctor Wolff.

"You are shocked to find content of this sort in a popular online game? The Entertainment Software Rating Board was shocked also. So were rating agencies in Europe, South America, Australia, and parts of Asia. And yet the game has been on our shelves, and in our homes, for more than three years.

"Within that time frame, the *modus operandi* of adolescent homicide cases have shown a distinct change. My team found more evidence of intentional homicide—cold-blooded murder, if you will—in that period, as well as an increase in the number of victims with no previous connection to their killers. It may not surprise you to learn the average age of the victims has also declined in the same period—from sixteen to thirteen and a half. Although what I have shown you here today is just one of many, many depictions of brutality suffered by victims of practically every age and description in *NeverEnd*."

Jon and Rohan shared a look. The surgical assistant had been too good a friend to shame Jon for supporting Chelle as she toiled to make the abomination of a game. He didn't have to, as Jon felt ashamed already.

"Please don't misunderstand," Wolff droned on. "This is no evil, subversive mind-control plot; subliminal messaging has been proven to have little power over human behavior. What power the game does carry, however, is in suggesting how people may satisfy their psychological drives. Those drives are preexisting, and the most common among them have the simplest titles: hunger, thirst, lust, rage. An argument might be made that there can be no harm in showing people, even children, where their inborn, natural drives may lead. But I say there *is* harm!"

The screen showed a still of a newscast Jon remembered seeing live: a wave of protesters swarming a police line, battering one shielded SWAT member while one of his colleagues opened fire on the lightly armed crowd. If one or the other group had been an army of animated skeletons . . . Jon decided not to finish the thought.

"We have seen the evidence, my friends and colleagues. As physicians, administrators, and other leaders in the medical field, we have seen the undeniable evidence of this harm. There has been, in recent years, a catastrophic rise in the number of beating, stabbing, and gunshot victims admitted to our hospitals. This is the reality internet gaming has brought to our door. I urge you to play *NeverEnd* yourselves, if you have not already—so you will be prepared for what's coming. Brutal violence, of the sort once confined to the battlefield, now overflows into our streets. We must be ready to stand against it or be swept aside by the abhorrent tide."

With a dry smile and cursory nod, Doctor Wolff left the

platform to muted applause.

Wolff's words had transported Jon back in time, back to the bloody, chaotic mayhem of Murphy Gore's attack on the Crown. Still haunted by those terrible memories, Jon's fingers itched to hold a rifle, to defend himself.

Rohan tugged at Jon's sleeve. "Let's get some air."

Jon followed his colleague to the hotel exit and out into the hot Texas sunshine. They stood on the sidewalk, a stone's throw away from another group of conference attendees who appeared stunned by Wolff's talk. Rohan let Jon keep his peace; the men stood in silence, breathing the warm, asphalt-scented air as the conference rolled on indoors.

After a minute, Jon heard himself say, "How can she be part of that? How could Chelle have ever been a part of kids dying and killing each other like that?"

Rohan held up his hands but kept his distance. "Don't be so hard on her, Doc," he said. "I mean, she quit the company, didn't she? She's not making games now. I'm sure Chelle never knew anything about all that, the kids."

Jon sighed. "I'm not sure about that, Rohan. I'm not sure at all."

The urge to pull out his phone, to call Chelle and ask if she knew about the hidden images in her addictive video game, was palpable. But Jon controlled his temper, leaving the phone in his pocket. Most likely, Rohan was right: Chelle couldn't have known the lengths to which her mother's company was willing to go. She was a peaceable woman, for all her faults, except when she shoved him, or threatened him, or . . .

Jon balled his fists and tried not to think the worst of the woman he'd once loved more than life itself.

10

The wind stirred the freshly cut grass of the Edoms' fenced backyard. Chelle pressed the function button of her phone and closed the last app she'd been browsing. She didn't care much for the way the wind brushed her cheek and ruffled her hair; the caress was gentle, but she couldn't help thinking it was trying to lull her into a false sense of security. And she couldn't be lulled, couldn't let herself be lulled, not when her whole future, and the future of her children, was hanging in the balance. She took a moment to compose herself before she turned her back on the yard and entered the house through the patio door.

"Boys!" Chelle's eyes blinked against the sudden switch from dusk to bright, artificial light. "Luke. Paul. Come here."

"Coming, Mommy!" Luke, the oldest of the pair, shouted. Together, he and Paul formed what she and Jon called the *new set* of Edom children. Simon and Cassidy, the twins who formed the first set, were already weeks into their freshman year at the University of Texas at Arlington.

The day Chelle waved goodbye to the twins had been her last day of peace; she had been feeling their loss ever since, especially Cassidy, who'd helped so much with the boys.

"This is all on me now," Chelle whispered to herself and willed her hands to quit trembling. "*All* on me."

Luke appeared in the doorway connecting the hall to the kitchen. As with most Texas homes, the kitchen was open plan with the dining and living area, as well as the space in which Chelle stood—a former breakfast nook. A year after moving into the house on Cedar Park Drive, Chelle had given up trying to coax her doctor husband, the teenage twins, and an energetic toddler to sit down to breakfast. Instead, Jon had packed away the table and chairs and stuck a wooden toy chest in the nook. Tonight, a firetruck sat in front of the chest, its ladder extended, evidently to help the plastic pterodactyl—clinging on with grim determination with one wing—reach the open lid.

Luke rushed to the chest with a "sorry" and started tidying up. Chelle stopped him with a touch on the shoulder.

"Leave it," she said.

"Mommy?"

"Leave it." Chelle dropped to one knee, set her cell down on the carpet, and brought her face so close to the seven-year-old, she could feel his breath on her cheek. "Luke, baby. We're going away for a little while. Get your pj's. Get your brother's too. And your toothbrushes. And a book. No, not a book. It's dark. Get some toys, something to play with in the car."

Luke's confusion was plain. A less perceptive child might have run off immediately, excited by the change in the nightly routine. Chelle was sure a young Jon would have dashed off. He would have grabbed his book and forgotten his pj's, and probably the toothbrushes, too. But not Luke. Luke had been raised to be obedient but self-sufficient. He thought on his own, like his mom.

"Where are we going?" the kid asked her, a slight tremor in his voice.

"The lake house. You remember the lake?"

"Grammy's lake?" The house belonged to Luke's grandmother, and extending the ownership to the lake itself was natural enough for a kid his age.

"Yes. Grammy's lake. Grammy won't be there, but that's where we're going. The house on the lake."

"Will Daddy be there?"

"Daddy's busy working, baby. You know that."

"But how—"

"Go." Chelle was firm; she'd had her fill of Luke's questions. "Get pj's, toothbrushes, toys. Be at the door in five minutes?"

Luke looked around for a clock. He was learning about seconds, minutes, and hours in school, though Chelle had taught him the basics long ago.

"Minute hand on twenty-six. I can do it!"

"Good. Go."

"Okay. But Mommy? I can't get Paul's pj's."

"What? Why not?"

"Because he's wearing them."

Luke gave her a smile Chelle didn't like. It was far too snide for a little boy. If any of her other children had given her that smile, she would have snapped at them. However, Chelle reminded herself that Luke was special.

"Of course he is. That's fine. You get the other things, baby. I'll get Paul . . . and his pj's."

As Luke ran off with a whoop of excitement, Chelle crossed to the kitchen cabinet that held her medicines and the boys' vitamins. She stopped short of opening the door; Jon would have finished his day at the conference and she'd heard nothing from him. She had nothing to say to him, of course, but it annoyed her he hadn't called. Momentarily forgetting the cabinet, she scrolled through her phone, searching for his texts.

That morning he'd sent, *Arrived safe. Checking in.*

She'd replied with a thumbs-up emoji and, *Call soon?*

Chelle had waited an hour before he answered that one: *Sorry. Love you. Call tonight.*

Had Jon forgotten to call, or was there a good reason for the delay? After the shooting at the hospital, Chelle reckoned she had every right to be paranoid. She considered calling someone else at the conference but talked herself quickly out of that. She knew Jon could be absent-minded at times, especially with distractions, and she guessed he was simply spending his free time with that buddy of his who assisted on the surgeries.

Unless, of course, he was making it with that god-awful Grunberg woman.

Chelle knew damn well Susan Grunberg would have shown up at the hotel in some inappropriately tight skirt, push-up bra, and low-scooped top. If she hadn't tackled Jon at the door, she would have lurked by the elevator waiting for him. They'd have stood hip to hip as she covered Jon's hand with her own and steered his finger to the call button. Then Jon would have forgotten all about calling his wife and the door swooshed open and they entered together, Grunberg pressing the button for her floor.

Chelle's phone screen shattered with a resounding *crack*. She jumped at the sudden sound, scared from her troubling daydream. Without knowing what she was doing, she'd slammed the cell phone down on the kitchen counter—hard. Chelle recoiled, staring at the hand that had done the deed. Her heart pounded, her head felt full, painfully so, as if it was filled with too much blood.

Without thinking, Chelle reached for the knife block, for the stainless steel paring knife that sat there. The pressure was unbearable. She ought to cut herself, let the blood out—

"Mommy?" Luke interrupted. "I can't find my shirt."

Chelle blinked. The light in the room was too bright. She had to shield her eyes as she slid the knife back into the block and turned her attention to her son.

"What shirt, baby?"

From his place in the doorway, Luke held up the bottoms to his pj's. "My pj shirt. I've got the pants part, but I can't find the shirt part."

"Don't worry about the shirt. You can sleep without it."

Luke's eyes went wide at the prospect of sleeping shirtless.

Chelle glanced at the clock. "Three minutes," she informed him.

As Luke scurried off, Chelle touched fingertips to her temples. The fullness was still there, but the idea of cutting herself to relieve the pressure had lost all appeal. She opened the cabinet and dry-swallowed two Tylenol Extra Strength. Then she pocketed the boys' vitamins but left the bottle with her lithium prescription untouched. Jon had watched her take the pills on the morning after his ordeal at the hospital. He had watched her again the next morning, and the morning after that. The next day, he'd forgotten, and Chelle had gone back to dropping them down the garbage disposal.

Luke was a minute late getting back. At least he'd been thorough and packed an extra shirt in case Mommy changed her mind as well as plenty of action figures to play with in the car.

Chelle had driven for ten minutes before she realized she'd neglected to pack any of her own night things. She considered turning around, but the boys were strapped in, and her urge to get to where they were going had become too compelling. No problem; she could sleep in the clothes she had on, and one night of neglecting her teeth wouldn't make much of a difference.

She passed the next hour half-listening to a talk station on the radio while the boys alternated between dozing and staring out the window. Her thoughts were hundreds of miles south. What was Jon doing right now? Probably being wined and dined by whatever pharmaceutical company was sponsoring his conference. He'd chew his steak and smile as Susan Grunberg flirted with him across the table with plenty of cleavage on display and maybe even playing footsie beneath the table. Chelle had seen the way Grunberg looked at her husband on the few occasions they had all been together in person. It was much like the way she looked at Vivek, the longing that was a hunger for a change in her life, and she knew her jealousy toward Grunberg made her one hell of a hypocrite.

Thinking about Jon and Vivek made Chelle remember her cell phone.

"Luke?" She kept her voice low so as not to wake Paul. "Luke, look in Mommy's purse and see if her phone is there."

The boy had to shake himself from weariness. His search was slow and reverent. He wasn't used to handling Mommy's things; he knew better than to ever rummage through the purse. In the end, he came up with nothing.

The phone was clearly not there.

Chelle thought back. Had she left it on the countertop? Very likely. Again she considered turning back, but why bother? She wasn't sure if the damage stopped at a cracked screen or the phone was totally dead, as she'd smashed it down pretty damned hard.

A check of the SUV's rearview mirror brought on a fresh worry. How long had that black sedan with the blunted chevron hood been behind her? The electric lights of the highway showed only a few details, but she knew the shape of the Chrysler 300 well. The sinister black paint reminded her of an argument at a meeting of church trustees last year. Chelle had been on the side of her sister, P. J., who agreed the fleet of sedans the church planned to purchase should all have the same paint job in the name of *branding*, but argued against funereal black. P. J. wanted a fleet of white 300s, but her motion had been voted down. Black had won, and a short time later, the order was fulfilled. Obviously, not every black 300 belonged to the Church of the Resurrected, but seeing one behind her conjured in Chelle a storm of jumbled memories.

She flashed back to her feelings at the meeting, and at every meeting of trustees since Father died. Father's funeral, his bedside, and the horrible family supper when he announced his cancer was in its very last, terminal stage. Every one of Chelle's moments between then and now had been haunted by death . . .

First, there was Dad's, then poor Hannah had been killed. The shooting at the hospital that nearly took Jon had returned Chelle to a nightmare she'd been foolish enough to think was nearly over. Some nights she awoke fighting for breath, drenched in sour sweat, convinced there were bony fingers at her throat. She spent entire days smelling rotten flesh, and every cold breeze that brushed her cheek made the hair at the back of her neck stand on end.

She thanked Luke for his help as she put the pedal down. The SUV sped past 75 to 80, 80 to 85, 85 to 90. Chelle glanced in the rearview. She could still see the Chrysler, but as a black smudge behind starburst headlights. She eased off the gas, and the other car held its distance. She drove on for another ten minutes, and it was gone. Other vehicles had taken its place—sedans and SUVS, and what she guessed by its single headlight was a motorcycle—but no more black Chrysler 300s appeared in the rearview.

Chelle breathed a long sigh of relief and continued

along the highway, wracking her brains for the names of Mom's neighbors at the lake house as a welcome distraction. If something went wrong tonight, she would have to borrow a laptop, so remembering names would be useful. Of course, she knew her email app login by heart, so she'd be able to access it from anywhere; she'd just have to remember not to allow the laptop to cache or passkey it.

Unfortunately, she hadn't remembered a single neighbor's name by the time she stopped for gas about a mile before from her turn off.

Paul slept through the refueling, while Luke ran inside for the bathroom. He was snoring soundly by the time she turned off the TX-105 at Montgomery. Then, as Chelle crossed a bridge that spanned a branch of Lake Conroe, the name of a woman Mom had once run into at the grocery store popped into her head. Marge—like Homer's wife with the big, blue updo. Had she been a neighbor, though, Chelle wondered, in the down-the-road sense? It was impossible to know.

She passed the store where they'd met Marge what seemed a lifetime ago, and took a right turn at the church on the hill. The white clapboard building looked very *Little House on the Prairie*, and had been Chelle's landmark since the first time she'd made this trip alone. It meant she was close to the lake house, though she still had some twists and turns to make through the various scattered neighborhoods that led to Lake Conroe.

It was a touch after ten o'clock, and the neighborhood was quiet; it seemed eerie to Chelle. She sped up and was going well over the speed limit when a car on a side street flashed its headlights at her. Chelle guessed the driver was warning her of police ahead and slowed down. The car revved its engine as she passed. When it roared into the street behind her, Chelle's heart skipped a beat. She looked back, past the sleeping faces of Paul and Luke, but the car had killed its lights and she couldn't make it out.

Chelle faced the road ahead just in time to see a transit van backing out of a driveway. In a split second, she stomped on the brakes and the SUV fishtailed.

The houses on Chelle's side of the street had sturdy, brick-built mailboxes, so Chelle's first worry was hitting one. She made a quick, jerky motion of the steering wheel, and the SUV zigzagged, missing the nearest mailbox by inches. Chelle's relief of avoiding the mailbox evaporated when the car behind rammed her rear bumper. Chelle's SUV skidded, clipped the next mailbox, and went into an uncontrollable spin.

Time slowed to a crawl as Chelle tried desperately to remember if she was supposed to steer *into* a spin, or *out* of it.

In the end, it didn't matter. Her back wheel slid into a drainage ditch. The SUV tilted, came close to rolling over, and clunked to the ground in a dead halt.

Chelle was dazed, sure she'd momentarily blacked out. Her left cheek was sore and there was the stink of gunpowder in the car; her airbag had gone off. She coughed to get the smell out of her lungs.

Paul was whining, terrified.

Luke spoke up. "Mommy, what happened?"

She turned to comfort the boys, but the driver's side window suddenly shattered inward, spraying glittering crystals of safety glass in Chelle's face.

She screamed.

A man, face obscured by a black mask, reached inside and unlocked her door. In his other hand, he held a claw hammer. It was the last thing Chelle saw before someone slipped a cloth bag over her head.

No! No!

The inner voice that had urged Chelle to make the trip to Conroe now told her to fight. So Chelle lashed out at the man who had a strong grip on her, to jab her manicured fingernails into his mask's eye holes. Nothing worked, and the men got Chelle out of her seat belt and from the SUV. As they carried her, flailing uselessly, Chelle heard her children crying and shouting to be let go. Their voices were muffled, and Chelle guessed their heads were covered by bags as well.

Back in college, the freshman Rochelle Berger had taken self-defense classes. It had mostly been a lark, something to do with friends on a Thursday night, a neat way to meet older boys. She'd not paid too much attention at the time, but one piece of sage advice had stuck with her: *Don't panic.*

Remembering that, Chelle calmed herself and managed a controlled landing on the transit van's floor. When Paul and Luke fell in beside a moment later, she located them by sound and drew them into a protective hug. Paul was bawling, and Luke, her brave little stoic, was sobbing and sniffling and tugging at the string that secured his head covering.

"Leave the hood on," said a voice, cold and stern.

Footfalls of at least three men reverberated around the van's metal shell. The door slammed shut. Before the sound had quit echoing, the van was already in motion.

Luke pressed his head into Chelle's shoulder. Showing maturity beyond his years, he whispered, rather than sobbed, "What do we do now, Mommy?"

Chelle considered being honest with him: there was *nothing* they could do. They were trapped, helpless, and no one but their kidnappers knew what was going to happen next. However, none of those facts were of use to a terrified seven-year-old.

"We're fine, baby," she soothed. "We don't have to do anything. Just hold on to me, and we'll be fine."

In her mind's eye, Chelle summoned the last image she

had seen before the transit van forced her into fight-or-flight mode. The car had flashed its headlights only briefly, but the glimpse had made an impression. Now that she had time to process, she was sure the broad grill and sloped angles belonged to a black Chrysler 300 sedan.

PART TWO

11

"Hey. This is Rochelle. I can't answer the phone right now. Leave a message and I'll get back to you after the crisis."

Jon punched *End Call*.

He'd already left a message. Several, actually. The first had been last night. He'd called late, both in terms of the actual hour and how long he'd put off checking in for the day. He understood why Chelle would be angry, why she might have let the call go to voicemail on purpose. He could even understand her ignoring his second call, and maybe his third. But ignoring the fourth, the fifth, and all the calls he had tried throughout the morning seemed an extreme reaction—even if Chelle had been off her meds. He was pretty sure that wasn't the case, as he'd watched her taking the lithium in the days leading up to his trip . . .

Jon thought for a moment.

When *was* the last morning he'd watched his wife take her meds? He chastised himself for letting the habit slide.

Jon's call vibrated in his hand. He answered without looking. "Chelle?"

After a brief pause, his sister-in-law's voice said, "No, Jon. It's P. J."

Jon took a breath. "Thanks for getting back to me. Did you—"

"Yeah," P. J. interrupted. "I went by the house like you asked. There's nobody there. Everything looks fine. Normal, I mean. Only, nobody's there."

"Okay." Jon's stomach knotted a tad. "Thanks for checking." In their earlier conversation, he'd asked P. J. if Chelle had said anything to her about plans after their girls' day out. P. J.'s answer had been a definite *no*. Jon didn't bother asking the question again, particularly as what he had to ask next would be painful. "You asked Lisa, right?"

P. J.'s pause said more than any words could. "She remembers *someone* was with her yesterday, but she doesn't know if it was her grandkids. If Chelle said anything to Mom . . . I'm sorry, Jon. If Mom knew anything before, it's gone now."

He'd expected as much. "I'm coming home early. And before I do, I'm calling the cops."

"Are you . . . Are you sure?" There was concern in P. J.'s tone. "I get how you feel, but this is Chelle we're talking about. She probably got an itch to see . . . I don't know, Vegas? You know how she can be."

Jon *did* know. All too well. And *that* was why he was worried. But he didn't say as much to P. J. Instead: "Even if she got an itch to run off on one of her excursions, she'd still take my call."

"Well, maybe her phone's out of juice." Again, P. J. paused. The moment stretched out so long, Jon thought she might have set down the phone without hanging up. He had nothing more to say and was about to hang up himself, when P. J. sighed. "You're right, Jon. I'm sorry. You do what's best. I'll call around to some more of Chelle's friends."

"Thanks," said Jon. It was a weight off his shoulders to have P. J. make calls to the friends she shared with Chelle. They would mostly be Church of the Resurrected faithful, and Jon hadn't exactly been their favorite person since he broke off ties.

As Jon hung up the phone, the stress of the past couple days swept over him like a flood. He felt suddenly dizzy and had to sit down; he took one of the few open seats in the hotel lobby. Rohan was nearby, and when he saw Jon slump, he came straight over. The session they were supposed to be attending had started twenty minutes earlier, but Rohan refused to go in without Jon. He'd paced the lobby while Jon made his worried calls.

"What happened? Is Chelle okay? The kids?"

Jon gave Rohan a weak shrug. "Nothing. P. J. went by the house. There's no sign of Chelle or the boys. Listen, I'm going to call it here. I need to phone the police, then I'm heading home."

Rohan nodded. "Makes sense. Hold on two seconds while I call Farosh. He can take my car back, and I can drive yours."

Even under the circumstances, the generous offer brought a smile to Jon's face. "No. No thanks. You stay. Somebody has to take"—he swept his hand in a gesture that summed up the conference—"all this in."

Rohan frowned; his eyes urged Jon to change his mind.

Undeterred, Jon showed he was firm in his decision, and Rohan knew it was best to give up. "Well, at least let me grab your bags while you call the APD, okay?"

"Thanks." Jon dug out his key card from his pants pocket and handed it to Rohan.

"Gimme two," said Rohan, and left.

It took Jon a few seconds to work up the nerve for his call, and to google the right number on his cell. He was sure 911 would have redirected him to the precinct station closest to home, but he wasn't sure he wanted to label the loss of contact with Chelle an emergency. Not yet, at least.

After a courteous female voice assured Jon he'd successfully reached the Austin Police Department, Jon explained his situation. The woman listened intently.

When Jon was finished, she said, "Doctor Edom, I'd like to dispatch a couple officers to your house for a wellness check. How does that sound to you?"

"It sounds fine, but I don't think it's necessary. I just got off the phone with my sister-in-law. She went by the house. There's nobody home."

"That's fine, sir. I'd like to send someone anyway."

The woman's thick Texan accent wasn't quite as thick as Officer Kelman's, but it was pretty close. "Tell you what," she added. "The wellness check will take twenty minutes, tops. Can you stay where you are until I get back to you?"

"Stay where I am? Look, I'm not distraught, if that's what you're worried about. I'll drive the speed limit all the way home."

"Honestly, Doctor, there's no rush. You've done the right thing by calling us. Right now, there's nothing more you can do. I expect there's a simple explanation for why you can't get in touch with your wife. I dispatched the officers while we were talking—a car is on the way to your house right now. All I'm asking is for you to relax for the next nineteen minutes or so. Can you do that?"

Jon sighed. He knew the dispatch lady was right. The likely situation was that Chelle had been mad at him for calling late. She had ignored his first call, and her phone had gone dead before his second. Her battery was over three years old. It didn't hold a charge like it used to, and she was awful at remembering to plug the damn thing in. The likely situation was that Chelle had ignored one call, missed the others due to a power drain, and been out shopping, or visiting, or doing any of the thousand-and-one things that could have taken her out of the house when P. J. visited. Yep, that was the more likely situation.

The problem was, Jon didn't believe any of that. Chelle might have been mad at him, but one of the Christian ideals they lived by was *don't let the sun go down while you're angry*. Dead phone or no dead phone, she would have gotten in touch before now—even if it had been to admonish him for being an inconsiderate husband or ask him if he'd bumped into Dr. Grunberg.

It seemed too much to express to a stranger, so Jon replied with a simple, "I guess."

"Doctor Edom, is there something you're not telling me? Have you been getting along with your wife okay?"

Jon was taken aback by the personal question. "I . . . There's been some tension lately. But nothing that would make Chelle run off and not get in touch like this."

"Are you sure?"

The Kelman-like accent conjured the memory of the shooting and with it the memory of Jon's homecoming that night. Despite how tired he'd been, Jon remembered the argument with Chelle clearly and how pissed she'd been that he'd not wanted to talk about it when she wanted to. The reluctance to expose his family's pain clashed with Jon's guilt about not watching Chelle more closely; what the hell was he thinking going to this stupid conference anyway?

Guilt won. "She might have had an impulse, if she's off her medication."

The woman let a second go by before saying, "What sort of medication, please?"

Jon's jaw tightened. His lips went cold. "She's on lithium—Eskalith—1,600 milligrams a day."

"Doctor Edom, is your wife bipolar?"

"She . . . She suffers from bipolar mood swings, yes."

"Okay. I've noted that for the officers. We've got sixteen minutes before they check in. I have to free the line for other callers. Will you wait at your current location for me?"

"I will."

"That's a yes?"

"Yes."

"Thank you, Doctor Edom. You did the right thing by calling. I'll be in touch."

As the dispatcher hung up, Jon felt like he'd just bet his entire life savings on a spin of the roulette wheel. In his mind, he could hear the ball clicking ominously from number to number, the dull sinking feeling in the pit of his stomach letting him know it was never going to land on *his* number.

He'd calmed down by the time Rohan arrived, just a few minutes later. He wheeled Jon's small suitcase to him and handed over his duffel and garment bag. Jon offered a fake smile. Rohan evidently bought it, and the smile he returned was all teeth.

"You're looking better," Rohan said.

"I'm *feeling* better," lied Jon. He said nothing about the call to Austin PD, so Rohan wouldn't know he was less than truthful when he returned his key card to the front desk and left the hotel in a hurry.

Of course, Jon knew what the officers from the wellness check would report before the dispatcher called back; the next time he heard that cowgirl accent, it told him what he already knew: Chelle and the boys were nowhere to be found.

Jon pulled his ancient-but-reliable Volvo XC90 SUV to the side of the road so he could use the app on his phone to disable his home security system. He gave the Austin cops permission to enter the house. The dispatcher assured him they'd have a good look around and be waiting when Jon got back from his trip. No doubt they'd leave and come back, seeing as he was a two-hour-forty-five-minute drive away.

As Jon pulled back into the steady stream of traffic, a jarring sense of unreality made the highway seem to blur. It was likely the stress of worry, and Jon made sure to keep within five miles per hour of the speed limit; the last thing he needed was to get pulled over and delayed even more.

Houston was an hour behind Jon when a chime told him he was almost out of gas. The Edoms cared about the environment, but not enough to move up from their trusty, old hybrid to a full electric vehicle just yet. On the drive down from Austin, Jon had watched his fuel gauge dip in the knowledge there was plenty in the tank to get him there. At the time, it had seemed more important to get the trip over and done with than to top off his tank. Now, Jon reproached himself for not stopping and asked Siri on his phone for the nearest gas station.

A mile and a half later, Jon steered the hybrid into the almost-empty parking lot of a Sunoco; only one other car was getting gas, so Jon had his choice of pumps. He chose one at random and pulled the Volvo alongside.

Jon held his debit card over the tap-to-pay symbol to prepay for the gas. But, after he'd put in his zip code to confirm his identity, the display told him he had to go see the cashier. Jon tried once more; he had no desire to waste time talking to the damn cashier. The message repeated.

Growling foul expletives beneath his breath, Jon locked the Volvo and made his way into the store.

There, a skunky odor greeted him as he stepped through the door. The attendant was a red-eyed, pale-skinned teenager with dreadlocks that looked like rat's tails.

Jon said, "My card was declined—said I have to come see you."

"Oh. Got another? I can put it through here." He pointed

at the register.

Of course Jon did, but curiosity had him wanting to find out why his debit card had been declined; his gut told him it might have something to do with Chelle.

"You know? I'd like to find out what's wrong with this one," he told the cashier. "Is there a message for me on your register?"

"Let me check." The teen stabbed away at the register's keys. "It says you have to call your bank."

Jon told him thank you and walked a few feet down the chip aisle. There, he flipped over the problem debit card and dialed the customer service number on the back.

A computerized voice answered, steered him through an automated menu, and finally prompted him to enter his card information.

"A hold has been placed on that card," the robot voice declared. "Would you like to speak to a representative? Press one for yes, two to return to the main menu."

Jon pressed one. A couple rings came down the line, followed by wait music, which was soon interrupted by a second artificial voice that advised Jon that, "Your estimated wait time is . . . forty-five minutes."

Jon pulled the phone away from his ear, fighting the urge to hurl it across the gas station store. However curious he was about the card, he wasn't about to delay his trip home. Jon was about to end the call when his phone clicked and a human voice said something he didn't quite catch.

He put the phone back to his ear. "Hello. Sorry, what was that?"

"Hello. Thank you for calling Minders Bank and Trust. This call may be monitored for training purposes. My name is Devon. With whom do I have the pleasure of speaking?"

"This is Jon Edom."

"Would that be *Doctor* Jon Edom?"

"Yes."

"How can I help you today, Doctor Edom?"

"I'm having trouble with my card. Your system said something about a hold."

"Let me check." Devon spoke English like a US native and had no discernible accent. "I see, Doctor Edom. It looks like the hold was put in place because someone attempted to use your card at a service station outside your usual area."

"That was me," said Jon. "I'm heading back from a conference in Houston."

"Sorry, Doctor. I should have been more clear. The hold was placed because of multiple charges at *unusual* locations. Someone recently used the card in another place you don't usually visit."

"I've been in Houston," said Jon. "I'm about an hour northwest of there now."

"Yes, sir," said Devon. "This was somewhere else."

Jon's heart rate shot up. "Can you tell me where?"

"Certainly. A service station called The Wagon Hut. It's a Shell with an address on Texas Highway 105, close to Montgomery, Texas."

Montgomery. Jon had passed through there plenty of times. It was on the way to Lake Conroe, where Chelle's family kept a vacation home.

"It had to be my wife," he told Devon. "She must have been traveling down there."

"So, the charge was authorized?"

"Yes."

"Shall I release the hold?"

"Please do."

"All right. I'll just make that change, sir . . . there. Your card should be active, Doctor Edom. Is there anything else I can do for you today?"

No sooner had Jon said no than he thought better of it. "Actually, can you tell me if there were any other charges in the area after the one you mentioned?"

"The Montgomery area?"

"Or any unusual location, aside from Houston."

"I'll check. No, sir. There don't seem to be other charges."

"What time was the Montgomery charge?"

"Let me see. Ten seventeen last night."

"And there's been nothing since."

"Right."

"Thanks. You've been a big help."

Jon hung up while Devon was in the middle of returning his thanks. The clue to Chelle's actions was as unexpected as it was concerning; Jon almost ran out of the Sunoco without filling up. When he did prepay at the pump, it wasn't with the debit card: he felt better leaving the charges as they were until the story played out.

On his way back to the car, he told his phone, "Siri, take me to Lake Conroe." According to the GPS directions, the trip would take him under an hour.

Jon clicked the phone into the bracket projecting from the Volvo's dashboard and started the engine. It was only later that he'd regret not making a second call to the police.

12

The long, bony finger pointing out Dani's passenger window belonged to her partner, Saul Troyer, as did the creaking voice. "Chryslers. Think they call them 'Chryslers for Christ?'"

Dani looked away from the pair of identical sedans entering the main gate of the Church of the Resurrected Faith Center just long enough to roll her eyes at Saul. The girls at the station had a nickname for the senior detective. They called him Saul the ____ Whisperer. What filled in the blank depended on how Saul had been treating the speaker. The girls he sweet-talked said something crude and complimentary. The ones he ignored stopped at crude.

"Listen, Saul," Dani said. "They'll all be *ladies* in here. Religious types. I need you to be on your very best behavior."

Saul flipped down his sun visor to check his mustache in the mirror. "Quit worrying. I'm always at my best when ladies are round."

Another eye roll.

A few minutes later, Dani pulled her silver GT Mustang

into a parking space in front of the Faith Center's central tower. Her escorts, the twin Chrysler 300s that had led her through the gate, followed the road around the building and out of sight. The woman who'd waved Dani into the parking spot watched them go. Only when Dani opened her door did the petite redhead return her attention to the visitors.

Actually, "petite" wasn't quite the right word for the redhead. The church woman's features were nice enough on their own, and they combined in a face Dani might have called cute, except for the way the lips and eyes crowded to the center. In a similar way, the young woman's body was more *compact* than petite. The way the woman's forearms bulged beneath the rolled-up sleeves, Dani expected she had more muscle than Dani herself, despite being shorter by a head and a half.

"Hey there." The redhead had a confident drawl. "You're the detectives."

"Detective Cavallo." Dani held out a hand to shake. "This is my partner, Detective Troyer. Austin PD."

The redhead said, "Look around, Cavallo. You see Austin anywhere?"

"Point taken. We're here to ask a few questions, but if you want to talk to the county sheriff, I can get him on the line, Miss . . . ?"

"Beale. Tasmin Beale. Executive pastor. And that's fine, just so long as we understand each other."

"I think we do, Executive Pastor Beale."

"Great. Come on in."

Beale turned her back on the detectives and, as she marched off to the door of the tower, Saul stepped up beside Dani.

"Listen, I need *you* on your best behavior too," he whispered.

Dani glared at her partner and picked up her step to keep

after Beale. The trio passed into the tower and strolled past the front desk. The attendant was the only part of the building's security system the operators had made visible. Dani finally caught up with Beale when she stopped at the elevator.

"You've got a lot of trust in your people," she said.

Beale shot a glance sideways. "What makes you say that?"

"No metal detector. No obvious cameras. You're shut in tight behind your walls and gates, but once you're actually in here, the security's light."

The elevator arrived and Beale stepped inside. "We know who our friends are, Detective." She pressed 7 and waited as the elevator dinged. "We know our enemies, too. And they're mostly on the other side of the gate."

As the floors continued to ding by, Dani said, "*Mostly*?"

"We get visitors now and then." Beale shot the detectives a barbed glance.

The elevator arrived at the seventh floor. Beale led the detectives to a large, open lounge with an amazing view of the entire complex. Several office buildings and the Faith Center's impressive worship hall lay at the feet of the people Dani and Saul had come here to interview; each one stood on a square of the checkered carpet.

Dani mouthed "behave" at Saul as she spotted Lisa Berger, widow of the late Ezra Berger, whose donations had built much of the Faith Center. According to rumor, the sixty-eight-year-old woman's mind was failing, but up until a few years back it had been keen as a razor and every bit as dangerous. She had built her own gaming company, Endless Loop Games, Limited, from the ground up and had conquered the gaming world with two runaway hits. After her retirement, the company continued to thrive, and the church she fed with the profits just kept on going from strength to strength.

Lisa Berger stood at a small bar ahead and to the left of Dani. One hand rested on the bar, gripping the wood lightly as she lifted a glass of orange juice to her thin lips. The young woman on the opposite side of the bar kept her hand an inch under Lisa's glass, prepared to grab it if Lisa's trembling hand dropped it. Dani had seen all the Berger family in photos, and knew them by heart: The woman with Lisa was her daughter, Pamela, and the man standing across the room from the pair, next to a potted plant, was Phillip. Weirdly, he bore a striking resemblance to his sister, but hardly any to his mother.

Apparently, Phillip, official spokesman for the Church of the Resurrected, appeared often on local TV—he was kind of a local celebrity. She hadn't actually seen him on TV because she only owned one to play *Call of Duty*. She'd never hooked up the cable, and only checked the news on her phone when she was working a case. Phillip was attractive in a boyish sort of way, and the close resemblance to Pamela didn't do him any harm. Both brother and sister had deep-set eyes and strong, masculine jawlines, and Dani found looking from one to the other was a little disorienting—kinda like seeing side-by-side reflections in angled glass. After letting her eyes flicker between the Bergers for a moment, Dani had to turn away.

The detective's gaze had nowhere else to settle than on the man standing at the far end of the room; she knew him from the file as Jake Korvus. Stationed in front of the floor-to-ceiling windows, he appeared to be enjoying the view. In contrast to Beale's jeans and work shirt, and the business-casual outfits of everyone else, Senior Pastor Jake Korvus wore a long, white robe with gold trim at the cuffs and collar. Dani had expected to see an oversized cross on a chain, but as he turned to face her, the pastor's neck was bare. He must have figured the robe was enough to mark his vocation. Or, if not the robe, the large black Bible he hugged tight to his chest.

Wait. *Was* it a Bible?

Dani looked again and picked out the book's title in large silver letters, which was partially covered by Korvus's arm. Filling in the gaps, Dani read the title as *The Grand Cycle*. Before Korvus or the Bergers rose to power in the church, its founder had written that particular study of Bible prophecy, Greek philosophy, and Jewish mysticism. According to his teachings, they all shone light on each other, and explained how the human race would eventually break out of the cycle of history that kept tearing down civilization after civilization every few thousand years or so.

Dani was skeptical, but success required keeping her hosts on side, so she approached Korvus and opened the conversation with, "I see you're keeping the Good Book close, Pastor Korvus."

The pastor did not meet her eyes, even as every other eye in the room snapped to Dani. She suddenly felt nervous and would have stopped in her tracks if the badge in her pocket and the gun on her hip didn't urge her on.

As he spoke, the pastor's voice rose and fell as if he were delivering a sermon. "This is a fine book, indeed, Detective. Yes, a *fine* book. But there is only one Good Book, one perfect, divine book that holds the mystery of ages. This book is fine, but it is not the Good Book. Its author and its believers are very clear on that."

Dani stood on a checker square that put her in line with the Bergers. "Sorry. I didn't mean to offend."

"You didn't." Phillip Berger strode purposefully across to Dani. "Please, Pastor Korvus, be nice to the detectives."

Korvus gave a chuckle. "I took no offense, and meant none."

"It's all good," Dani said as she turned to accept Phillip's handshake. But instead of shaking, he bowed over her hand and pretended to touch it with a kiss.

"*Ciao bella!*" he said with a theatrical flourish.

Both the gesture and the greeting were *way* over the top, but Phillip evidently thought he was charming enough to get away with it. Dani agreed—he was one of only a few who could pull such a show off—but didn't want her opinion to show. Dropping her hand, she maintained her poker face.

Phillip had the grace to be embarrassed. "Sorry. When I heard your name . . . I used to spend my summers in Italy."

Dani released some of her tension. The missing woman's brother seemed harmless enough.

"I'm a quarter Italian," she told him. "Papi married a Lakota, up north. Dad met a Tigua girl. After he split, we moved down here. Well, west of here, but not far."

Phillip smiled. "We're four quarters German, so I'm told. It's *Danielle* Cavallo, correct?"

"Call me Dani." She pointed to her partner. "That's Detective Troyer."

A set of bony fingers reached out. "Saul."

Phillip addressed both detectives, "My sister, Rochelle, and my nephews, Luke and Paul, are missing. If I've done my math right, we've already passed the crucial forty-eight-hour mark."

Dani straightened her shoulders; it was time to get down to business. "Officers made a wellness check at the Edom house after Doctor Edom called from his conference in Houston. They found no one home, so obtained permission from Doctor Edom to enter. Inside, they found evidence of a hasty departure. The closet was open. Clothes were strewn across the bed. But they found nothing to suggest where Rochelle or the children had gone. Other officers have since interviewed Doctor Edom. He had reason to believe the family's trip was to a house on Lake Conroe, about three hours east."

"Our lake house," said Lisa Berger. Dani was surprised to hear her speak. "Ezra is at the lake house. We should go to him?"

"Careful, Ma," Pamela said as Lisa let the glass of orange juice slip. Pamela easily made the catch.

Phillip sighed. "I'm sorry, Detectives. Mom gets confused." He turned to Pamela. "P. J., would you take Mom somewhere else, please? The detectives and I should speak in private."

Dani pulled out her notebook from a back pocket. The simple flipbook was a little old-fashioned, but she never worked a case without it. She began to scribble a note that Pamela was known as P. J. to her family, but the look in the siblings' eyes distracted her. There was something unspoken in the expression. Resentment, Dani thought. Phillip was the boss, P. J. the beast of burden.

Dani was about to say that Lisa and P. J. should stay, that she needed to speak to them both. But the eldest Berger's face suddenly changed: her lips stiffened and the creases in her crinkled old brow straightened. She stared at Phillip with such anger, Dani expected the old lady to bare her teeth like some cornered animal.

"Shut up, Phillip," Lisa admonished sternly. "My money built this place. Don't you ever forget that."

In a heartbeat, Lisa Berger had switched from frail dependent to powerful aggressor. Dani rocked on her heels, showing wide eyes to Saul. Her partner appeared less shocked but more interested in the sudden change. The others in the room had clearly seen behavior like this from the matriarch before. Korvus and Beale turned away, and Pamela crossed her arms protectively across her chest.

Phillip had just confirmed Dani's assessment of where the family power rested. With his mother practically foaming at the mouth, he tucked his chin low and slipped his hands deep in his pockets. The sentimental spokesman was gone. Phillip was another man now.

"And you know I appreciate every cent, sweetheart."

Lisa's rage vanished as quickly as it had appeared. She gave Phillip a warm smile that Dani thought most flirtatious and inappropriate from a mother to her son. The old woman left her drink with Pamela and walked from the bar to Phillip. Taking his hands in her own, she stared deep into his eyes.

"Ezra. I thought you were at the lake house."

"I'm here, my love," Phillip spoke softly. "I'm right here." Then he held his mother, squeezing her tightly.

Dani spoke over the beaming old woman's shoulder. "Maybe a private talk would be best."

13

R abbi Max squeezed Jon's hand. "*Gam zeh ya'avor.*"
"Huh?" said Jon.
"This too shall pass."
They sat together in a room of the finished basement of Temple Beth Shalom in West Lake Hills. Jon had walked there from home. After spending all of Sunday in a Montgomery jail and half of Monday morning speaking to Austin police, his need to move had overridden exhaustion as a motivator.

"Have faith. Even impossible situations are temporary," the rabbi said sagely.

Jon couldn't help but blurt out, "What if they're dead, Rabbi? Chelle and the boys."

"Then you'll say kaddish and wait for the world to end," said the soft-spoken man. "Even death is temporary, my friend. You did well, by the way, coming here on foot. Move a muscle, change a thought. Motion plus faith is the formula to beat depression. The *prescription*, I'd call it, if not for my respect for your profession."

Jon would have resented the obvious attempt to cheer

him up if it had come from anyone else. But the rabbi genuinely cared. As Jon passed a hand over his dark hair, he said a brief, grateful prayer. Only a few minutes in the rabbi's presence had left him feeling steadier than he had for three days. Almost steady enough to call the twins.

A policewoman had offered to make the call for him, but Jon had insisted on delivering the news himself. That had been an hour ago. Jon had spent the time since then signing paperwork, getting dropped off at home, and staring at his phone—all while he tried to work up the nerve to make that damned call.

"Are you ready to talk about what happened at the lake house?" asked the rabbi.

Jon sighed. So far, he'd told Rabbi Max about his concern for Chelle and the boys, about calling the police, and about the block on his debit card. He had mentioned the lake house but stopped the story there; thinking back on that part of his story was too painful to face just now.

"I don't mean to rush you, Jon," the rabbi added.

"It's okay. *I'm* okay. I need to tell someone. Someone without a badge."

Bracing himself with a deep breath, Jon took up the story again.

"It was around eleven o'clock when I got to the lake house. Old Ezra Berger used to love that place. On our very first visit there, he took me fishing. Can you imagine *me* fishing, Rabbi? That was a month before Chelle and I got married. I was just settling into my residency, and the family had high hopes for my future. Little did they know."

"It's modesty that becomes a man, Jon," Rabbi Max said. "Not outright lies."

"Who's lying? What I am and what they wanted me to be are two very different things, I promise you. Anyway, the family used to throw out more invitations to the lake house than we could accept, but after the wedding, Chelle and I made memories there. Simon took his first steps in the living room. Years later, Cass almost drowned when she hit her head on the dock. We found out Chelle was pregnant with Luke three weeks before a lake house barbeque. She kept quiet and switched up the wardrobe—all so we could spring the good news on her folks up there. Life got real busy after that. The next time Chelle and I were at the lake house was a week after Ezra died, about three months after he was diagnosed terminal."

Jon paused there, thinking back on that somber family gathering. Ezra Berger had loomed large in life, and his death struck Jon like nothing since 9-11.

"Jon?"

"Huh? Sorry, Rabbi. Got lost there a second."

"That's fine. I asked what the place is like."

"It's cute. Gray exterior. An oversized cottage. Modest by Berger standards, huge for anybody else. Two and a half stories and ten rooms, if you don't count the walk-in closets. I searched every one of those rooms on Saturday, but to be honest, I can't remember much of what I saw. I was worried, distracted. I said it was eleven when I pulled in—that's what I told the cops too—but the truth is, I didn't look at the clock. I didn't look at much of anything when I arrived. There wasn't much to see. It was misty outside. I could barely see the roof of the house until I was halfway up the drive. There were no other cars, I'm sure of that much. The house was quiet, but I had this feeling, you know, like somebody had been there. Plus, the drive is gravel, and the tracks I followed in looked kinda fresh to me."

"What were you thinking when you got there?"

"That Chelle had left me. That maybe she was so upset, so out of her mind and off her meds that she did something horrible to herself and the boys. To be honest, I don't know what scared me more: that I wouldn't find her, or that I would.”

“But you went into the house alone. You’re a brave man, Jon. Braver than most.”

“I went around the house, first. There’s an alarm system. Very high tech. I don’t know the code. I went around the back and— Wait, I forgot something. On my way around, I heard a noise, or thought I did. I went back to the car and got The Club from the running board. You know The Club?”

The Rabbi laughed. “Before I quit driving, I had a 1956 DeSoto. Yes, I know The Club.”

Jon could almost feel the cool, metal body of the safety device in his hand. Chelle had bought it off the internet a week after he started working at the Crown. He had only locked the hooks to his steering wheel a few times since, and only because Chelle had been in the car.

“If there was a burglar, or something, I’d probably have been shot, but it made me feel better to hold *something*. Anyway, I went around back. There’s a lawn back there, some bushes, a fence. The family pays a gardener to keep everything tidy, even though they haven’t been out since Ezra passed. I used The Club to poke the bushes. Aside from an old burn barrel, I didn’t find anything, but the grass looked trampled, like somebody had walked there before I arrived. I wasn’t sure how to feel about that. I told myself the boys had done it. I pictured them running around, having fun. But the house was so quiet, I knew things must have . . . *changed*.”

That was when he’d decided to call P. J. She’d let the phone ring several times before answering. When she did come on the line, the first thing she did was apologize.

“I’m so sorry, Jon. Phillip was talking. I didn’t hear the phone. Did you hear anything?”

“No. I’m at the lake house now.”

“The lake house? Why?”

He kept the explanation brief. Too brief, it seemed, to convey his urgency. When he told P. J. his plan to smash a window with The Club and asked her for the alarm code, she hesitated.

"I understand why you went there, Jon. But what I don't get is how a broken window will help. Did you try knocking?"

Jon looked sheepishly at Rabbi Max when he got to this part of the story. "I hadn't, actually. The lawn gives access to a deck. I climbed the steps and peeked in the glass doors. The blinds were open. They're usually closed when no one is at home. Anyway, I saw the TV, the fireplace, the hardwood floors, and the usual furniture. Nothing strange, no people, and so far as I could see, no signs anyone had been there recently. I said as much to P. J., told her I wanted to check upstairs."

"Let me guess," said the rabbi. "She didn't give you the code."

"She really, really didn't want me to break the glass."

"Sensible girl."

"Always has been. Not like her sister."

"I take it you smashed it anyway?"

"Of course. And before you ask, P. J. was right. It was pointless. I searched all I could in the eight minutes it took for police to arrive. There was nothing. Nothing obvious, at least. I had a sense that somebody had been there, but they'd covered their tracks. I couldn't tell who they were, why they'd come, or what they had to do with Chelle and the boys. I got myself arrested for nothing."

"Were the police sympathetic?"

"They didn't beat me with night sticks, if that's what you mean."

"But they did hold you overnight."

"And most of the next day."

The rabbi rose from his chair. He paced slowly up and

down the small, square room. It wasn't his office. That was upstairs. The rabbi had told Jon long ago that he came to this room to think about new problems. To him, "new" meant anything less than three thousand years old.

He stopped pacing. "I have someone I'd like you to meet, Jon. He's a lawyer. A good one. What do you say to breakfast tomorrow?"

"Rabbi," said Jon, "I don't need a lawyer."

"Maybe you don't. But you need friends, Jon. And friends with connections are the best friends to have."

"Wait. What connections are you talking about?"

The rabbi touched a finger to the side of his nose. "How's eight o'clock for you?"

"I . . . eight's fine," said Jon. There seemed little point in arguing; the rabbi never took no for an answer. Besides, his listening ear and positive attitude had given Jon the courage he was after. He thanked Rabbi Max, climbed the stairs from the basement beside him, and said his farewells at the door.

All the way home, Jon thought over what he was going to say to Simon and Cass. Upon reaching his block, he made the call. He tried Simon first. The call went to voicemail. Jon hung up and tried Cass.

She answered on the second ring. "Dad? I'm between classes. Can I call you back?" The sounds of laughter, footfalls, and distant traffic made it obvious she was walking outside.

"Sorry, honey," said Jon. "Can you take a minute? I've got something to tell you."

In the pause between his question and Cass's answer, the phone gave a buzz. Jon listened to Cass say, "Yeah. Sure," on speaker as he checked his texts.

A new text had come from Bev DePalma. She did schedules at the Crown. *Doug sick*, the text said. *Can you scrub in for 2?*

Jon thought through the offer. Going into surgery at two meant he would have to work an eleven-hour shift. At the moment, that sounded like bliss. Rabbi Max had said to keep moving.

"Dad," said Cass, "did I lose you?"

"No. I'm here." He listened to the background noise a moment longer and added, "Hey, are you somewhere safe? A sidewalk, I mean. Not crossing a street."

The sounds of life two hundred miles away faded as Cass drew an audible breath. Into the silence between them, she said, "What's wrong?"

There was nothing he could do but swallow hard and break the news that Chelle and the boys were missing.

14

The space Tasmin and Billy slid into would have made a decent closet; it wasn't anywhere near wide enough to call a room. It was crammed with electronic gizmos, most of which were spare parts for the security system Tasmin had designed herself and spent more time than she cared to admit keeping up. Tucked away in a corner was a sleek, metal rectangle with lights that flashed when it was in use. The rectangle sat on a low shelf and had two coiled wires connected to two sets of headphones on top of it. The headphones had large, cushioned ear pads that did a good job blocking out the world when Tasmin wanted to be alone with her thoughts.

Of course, today, alone time was off the menu. Tasmin lifted both sets of headphones and passed one back to Billy. He'd turned sideways to fit through the door and now stood with his back pressed flat to the wall, frowning at the mountains of junk on the shelves like he expected it to fall on him at any moment.

As the big man took the headphones from her, Tasmin licked her lips suggestively. "What's wrong, stud? Don't you like a tight fit?"

Billy grunted. Tasmin frowned. She had hoped for a bit of banter to go along with the espionage, but the guy seemed dead from the neck up.

The volume knobs on the receiver were turned down to zero, so Tasmin put on her headphone and plugged in. She turned up the volume and voices came through. First, they were a low murmur, but once they were loud enough to be distinct, the first thing Tasmin heard was the woman detective, Cavallo.

"—ference was for three days. Did Rochelle say anything to you about what she wanted to do with the time?"

"I think I should clear something up," said a voice Tasmin recognized immediately as Phillip Berger's. "Your question makes it sound like Jon being away from home was unusual. Do you know any doctors, personally?"

The question must have been directed at both detectives; after a brief pause Cavallo's partner said, "I've known a few."

Phillip said, "I've known Jon Edom twenty years. And, of course, I knew my father my whole life. In my experience, *doctor* is another word for *workaholic*. So, no. Rochelle didn't say anything to me about her plans. I have no reason to think she made plans. Why would she? There was nothing special about Jon being out of the house."

There was a sound like flipping pages in a notepad. Cavallo said, "What about her plans with your sister?"

"P. J.?" Phillip sounded confused, if not downright annoyed. He recovered in the next breath. "Oh, you mean that shopping thing. P. J. said something about that. But it was girls only, nothing to do with me. I think . . . Well, you can ask P. J. for those details, but as far as I know, they were together a few hours, that's all."

In the confines of the small, stuffy closet, Tasmin shot

a look across at Billy. He seemed not to notice.

"Okay," said Cavallo. "We'll ask her about that. What about Doctor Edom's associates? You say you've known him twenty years. How well do you know the people he works with?"

Phillip hummed softly, as if deep in thought. The sound came clearly through Tasmin's headphones like some annoyed insect. "Honestly, I'm not sure I could name a single one. I'm sorry, Detectives. When Jon left the church, he burnt a lot of bridges. It's not like he was ever a social butterfly to begin with, and since the split, whole months have gone by when we barely saw him. If I ever knew the names of his workmates, I'm afraid I've forgotten."

The notepad pages fluttered again. Cavallo said, "So you wouldn't recall a Mister Rohan Majumdar?"

"Sounds Indian. *East* Indian, I mean." Phillip seemed to be floundering.

Cavallo chipped in. "Mister Majumdar is of Indian heritage, yes. He's a surgical assistant. He works with your brother-in-law. He was at the Houston conference. I thought you might have heard the name."

"No. Sorry."

"That's fine, Mister Berger."

"Please, Dani. Call me Phillip."

Tasmin imagined Cavallo exchanging a glance with her partner. Phillip wasn't being subtle in the least. They *must* have heard how he deepened his tone, changing the offer of his first name into a come-on. Tasmin stifled a laugh. What was Phillip thinking? He wasn't nearly man enough for the detective and, from what she could tell, Detective Cavallo was the last woman to have her head turned by a stuck-up worm like Phillip.

Cavallo said, "What about a Doctor Susan Grunberg? Does her name sound familiar?"

"No. Wait. Did you say *Grunberg*? I don't believe

we've met, but yes, I have heard the name."

"And where did you hear it, Phillip?" said the male detective.

"I'm not sure. Probably here, at the Center. Rochelle mentioned a Doctor Grunberg a few times. I know she works with Jon. I got the impression they were close and that irked Rochelle."

"Close?" The male detective jumped straight onto that word like a dog with a bone.

Cavallo added, "What do you mean by *close*, exactly?"

There was horror in Phillip's voice as he replied, "I didn't mean to imply—" He sounded genuine, though of course Tasmin knew it was an act. Rochelle had been clear about what she thought was happening between "that Grunberg woman" and her husband. She even detailed her suspicions to Tasmin, which had come as a surprise since the two women had never been close.

"Look," Phillip continued, "it's like I told you. I've known Jon forever. He's a good man. He's no saint, but I'll say this for certain. There's nothing on earth that would make Jon hurt his wife or kids."

"I'm sure that's true," said Cavallo. The rustling of pages in Tasmin's headphones ceased as the notepad clapped shut. "Well, that's all the questions I have for you, Phillip. Anything else, Saul?"

"I'm good," wheezed the old man.

"Then we won't take more of your time," Cavallo wrapped up. "But I would like to interview your sister. Is there someone who can take care of your mother while I do that?"

"Um, no," said Phillip. "I don't think there is."

"That's fine." Cavallo's voice said the opposite. "We'll leave you to figure that out, okay? P. J. can come by the station when she's ready. So long as you understand *ready* means business hours, today."

Tasmin heard Phillip say, "Of course" as she removed the headphones.

Done, Tasmin shoved past Billy and made her way out of the storeroom door. They were on the sixth floor of God's Footstool. Tasmin's office was down the hall, and Phillip's office, the office they had been spying on, was at the end of the hall around the corner. Tasmin slipped into her office just in time to poke her head out and watch the detectives coming her way. They had to pass her office to reach the nearest elevator.

"Hey," she said. "Y'all done with Phillip? I bet he's plum chargrilled."

Cavallo raised her eyebrows. "Yes, we're done, Miss Beale."

"Got a minute? I'd like to bend your ear." Tasmin eyeballed the male detective, who gave her a smile she didn't return. "And let's make it just us gals, if that's okay."

Cavallo nodded yes and Tasmin stepped back and ushered her into the office. It was impressively spacious, actually the largest non–corner office in the tower. Tasmin had picked out all the furnishings herself, a mix of classic and modern pieces. Her guest assessed the room appreciatively as Tasmin shut the door. She led Cavallo to the office's crown jewel, a taxidermied lynx crouched on a rock behind a half-inch pane of clear glass. The lynx was a masterpiece; it looked almost alive, except for the lifeless glass eyeballs.

"I did that," said Tasmin. She meant the taxidermy, not killing the creature; the animal had been the victim of one of the church's Chryslers.

"You're a talented woman," Cavallo said.

"Funny you should mention *talent*," said Tasmin with a wry smile. "Dr. Jon Edom's got a few himself. I guess you met him?"

Cavallo turned to face her. "Not yet."

"Well, I'm sure he'll be nice. Jon's as sweet as a lamb to near about everyone. A talent for acting, I'd call that. There's only a few folks ever get to see the real Jon, or even hear about him. And you'd have to be one of them to know where his talents lie."

Cavallo lifted an eyebrow. "What are you trying to tell me, Miss Beale?"

Tasmin held up her left arm to show the underside of her bare wrist. "You know, I never saw Rochelle wear short sleeves. Can you guess why, Detective? To hide the bruises Jon gives her. He likes to pin her down, dominate her. It isn't even a sex thing. He just likes the power. Rochelle told me more than once that her husband is the sort of man who likes hurting women."

Cavallo reached for the notepad in the back pocket of her suit pants, but stopped. She said, "You're telling me Doctor Edom is an abuser. Do you have any evidence to back that up?"

Tasmin tipped back her chin and set her hands on her hips. "I reckon evidence is your department, Detective. The only evidence I need is what I see and hear."

Cavallo folded her arms. "That's a strange sentiment, coming from a woman of faith."

"I see my path clear enough. Listen, Detective. Rochelle and I were like sisters. I know what Jon does to her. The 'hero doctor' is all a show, a blind to hide the monster he really is."

Cavallo's eyes widened. To Tasmin, it seemed an exaggerated reaction. The cop had taken Tasmin's words to heart much easier than expected. For all her coolness, the pretty, straight-haired detective had taken Tasmin's word about Dr. Edom on board. Better than that, she seemed ready to act on what she'd heard. Those red lips and blushed cheekbones surely hid some past damage from men. What woman didn't have some to hide? If Cavallo wasn't a card-carrying man hater already, she was close enough to want to see a bad one burn. And thanks to Tasmin, Jon was now directly in her sights.

Some of Tasmin's smugness must have inadvertently shown through, because Cavallo blanked her face and made a last-ditch attempt at objectivity. "Hold on. If the abuse was as bad as you're making it out to be, why didn't you report it?"

Fake tears sparkled in Tasmin's eyes. "Because Rochelle loved him, that's why. I begged her to say something, or to let me say it for her. She shut me down. Bruises or no bruises, Rochelle loved Jon Edom. She never complained; she might say something about his schedule, make jokes about feeling neglected now and then, but the deeper stuff, the *serious* stuff? She kept it quiet. I don't even know if there was anyone else she told but me."

For a moment, Cavallo peered at her, as though trying to read her thoughts. Tasmin wondered if she'd overplayed her hand. Then the detective's eyes widened once more, and Cavallo's look of conviction came back. The dog had returned to its vomit.

"All right. Thank you," said the detective. "I'll . . . keep what you said in mind."

"Do that," said Tasmin. The detective made a move to go, but Tasmin wasn't quite through with her. She added, "While you're at it, how 'bout I give you something else to chew on?"

That brought Cavallo's attention back to Tasmin, but with a hint of reluctance. She seemed to be on the verge of distrusting Tasmin for being *too* helpful. Tasmin would have waved her off, let her go, if she hadn't thought so highly of what she had to say next.

"It's about the lake house, up at Lake Conroe. You said something about Jon thinking Rochelle was there. You know Jon went up Saturday, right? P. J. will tell you, if you ain't heard it yet. He called and asked P. J. for the alarm code. He said he was thinking about breaking in."

Cavallo pulled out the notepad and jotted a few notes.

Tasmin was thrilled her information had sparked some interest, but the silence that stretched out after Cavallo's scribbling made her nervous.

"Anyway," Tasmin went on, "I was thinking. Don't you think it's funny Jon would go all that way without telling anybody? I checked Google. Houston to Lake Conroe is more than an hour by car. P. J. says Jon called the cops before he left Houston, but this thing with the lake came up later. Why didn't he call again? He could have left checking the lake house to somebody local, instead of driving all that way."

The notepad pages made a rustling sound, but Cavallo failed to write anything else. "That's interesting about the call. I'll be sure to ask P. J."

"Don't you think it's funny?" Tasmin sensed Cavallo's reluctance, the typical cop skepticism that said she might dismiss everything Tasmin had said if she pushed her too far. But Tasmin couldn't help one more push. "Jon gets this brainstorm that could solve the whole mystery, and he doesn't even call y'all back; he doesn't even call the cops at Conroe. That'd be the smart thing to do, if he was *really* worried about Rochelle and the boys. And Jon is smart, I can tell you. Smart like the devil."

"What are trying to tell me, Miss Beale?"

"Jon's call to the cops, and his story about the lake house, is a smokescreen."

Cavallo's reaction wasn't as strong as Tasmin would have liked. She folded her hands over the notepad, cocked her head slightly, and said, "How so?"

Despite the lukewarm response to such a dynamite revelation, Tasmin was eager to answer this question. It was what she had been building up to, after all.

She said, "Well, I've been thinking. Jon says he went to the lake house because of the bank hold on his card. Of course, you can find out if that hold really happened, but what if it was an excuse, a cover for the real reason he went looking for Rochelle there?"

"And what would be the real reason?"

"Because he asked Rochelle to go there, of course. Probably called her, said, 'Come on down to the lake house, babe. We'll put our problems behind us,' or something like that. Maybe he told her to make sure it was just her, that she shouldn't tell anyone. I swear, Detective, I loved that girl, but she could be a sucker for Jon's smooth talk."

Finally, Cavallo made a note.

Tasmin tried to see what she wrote, but Cavallo's hand blocked her line of sight. When she was done writing, Cavallo held the notepad to her breast and turned a doubtful eye on Tasmin.

"You're saying Doctor Edom lured his wife to the lake house."

Tasmin nodded.

"What do you think happened then?"

Tasmin was ready for this question too, but she tried to look surprised. "He killed her, of course."

Cavallo echoed the look. "Dr. Edom killed his wife?"

"Why not?" Tasmin thought she may have stretched her credibility a tad too far. "He's been working up to it for years. I don't reckon he wanted to kill those boys. Maybe he thought Rochelle would leave them behind. When she brought 'em down with her, they had to go. Or maybe he hated the boys too, because they were part of Rochelle. I don't know. Point is, Jon did the deed and cleaned up his mess. I reckon he could have done it that morning, after calling y'all. Or he could have gone up the night before, and the call was after. Only, when he made it, he got worried he missed something in the clean-up. So he went back to the scene. That's the cliché, right? The murderer goes back to the scene of the crime. I did some research on that and it's for real. Some murderers, the careful kind, do go back. I don't guess I have to tell you that *careful* is a must-have quality for a doctor."

Absently, Cavallo tapped the notepad with her pen. "What about the calls to Rochelle's cell phone, Miss Beale? Jon said her not answering was what made him worry in the first place. He called multiple times in the evening, and again the next morning. We've verified the calls were placed and we know they weren't answered."

The detective was holding something back. Tasmin could tell. The police had evidence they weren't sharing. Tasmin hated to be left out.

She said, "What does that prove?"

"Two things," said Cavallo. "First, if the couple had plans to meet, why make the calls? Second, if they were on good enough terms for Rochelle to accept the invitation, why didn't she pick up?"

Tasmin stalked away, hands on her hips, thinking. The answer came in a flash. She spun back to the detective and met her dark eyes.

"Something's wrong with Rochelle's phone." It was a statement, not a question. She said it with confidence. "Jon broke it ahead of time, or stole it, or—"

Cavallo broke off eye contact. "No, that's . . . I'm sorry, Miss Beale. That doesn't fit the evidence."

Tasmin suppressed a grin. Cavallo was *still* keeping secrets, but something in her phone hypothesis had the detective rattled.

She said, "I ain't all wrong, am I? I can read it on your face, Detective."

There was a long silence. Tasmin once again wondered if she really had pushed the detective too far.

At last, Cavallo said, "Your theory is interesting, Miss

Beale. I won't say it's correct, but there are points I will look into." She continued, "You're convinced Rochelle is dead?"

Tasmin lifted her arms to remind Cavallo about Rochelle's bruised wrists. "I *know* she is, detective. And I know Jon killed her."

Cavallo stood and thought a moment. She flipped to a new page in the notepad and jotted something down. "Like I said. I'll look into that."

"You do that."

Tasmin's heart thudded, and her muscles were so pumped with adrenaline, they felt fit to burst. Somehow, she managed to hide her euphoria.

"Is that all, Miss Beale?"

"Ain't it enough, Detective?"

Cavallo studied her closely, and for an uncomfortable amount of time. Finally, she closed her notebook and shook Tasmin's hand. As Tasmin showed her out of the office, she kept her face neutral, but she was beaming on the inside.

15

Jon stood at the edge of a cliff, one foot firmly planted on soil, the other stretched out to probe the void. It was a cloudy afternoon, the cliff high, so much of his view was obscured. He could make out trees, a little farmland, and a distant hill—no, a *mountain*—that dwarfed the cliff as its peak stood far above the horizon. It was his awareness of the unusually tall mountain that moved Jon to question where he was and how he'd gotten there. He could think of no answers, and the effort of thinking made him feel shaky. He tried to withdraw the extended foot and found he couldn't. It was paralyzed.

He couldn't move the foot at all, or feel it. All he could do was stare at the thing, willing it to move in the same way he used to will bullies at school to turn their backs so he could sneak past them to class. The method worked as well as it always did.

Frustrated, Jon quit staring at the paralyzed foot and concentrated on pivoting away from the cliff. As soon as he tried, the scene before him shifted. He hadn't turned. He remained standing at the edge, but the mountain, one distant, had moved closer. Now it filled the center of Jon's vision and stretched far above his head, blocking out the sun. Part of Jon was terrified of the mountain. Another part was curious.

"Why am I here?"

A low rumble of thunder sounded from the far sound of the mountain. Jon thought a moment.

"Why can't I move my foot?"

This time, the thunder was nearer but no closer to human speech. Jon asked himself what Rabbi Max would have done in his place.

"What do you want from me?"

There was thunder, an earthquake. The sky around the mountain burned, and great rifts tore in the very stone of the cliff. Through it all, Jon stood quiet, awaiting the end of the disaster.

It ended. The world fell silent. Jon felt the warmth of the sun. A soft voice said, "Doctor Edom? I'm sorry. I didn't want to wake you, but the woman on the phone says it's urgent."

Jon blinked. He lay on a cot in a linen closet the doctors used to catch naps and sometimes hook up with the nurses.

Nurse Aegypt had a hand on his shoulder; she'd shaken him awake. In his groggy state, mind still filled with the dream of the mountain and the cliff, the nurse resembled Jon's wife. "Chelle?" Jon mumbled.

"Chelle?" said Nurse Aegypt. "Oh. No, Doctor. It isn't your wife on the phone. It's the police."

Quickly, Jon came to his senses. "Police? Where's the phone?"

They moved across to the nurse's station, where the nurse on duty passed Jon a handset and punched keys on a keypad. "Connecting you now."

The phone switched from dial tone to heavy silence. Jon said, "Hello?"

"Hello." It was a voice Jon didn't know, but he pictured a woman in her late twenties or early thirties. Based on the woman's impatient tone, he knew she'd been waiting longer than she liked. "Is this Dr. Jon Edom?"

"It is." Jon nodded his thanks to Nurse Aegypt and the duty nurse. They left him alone.

"Sorry to disturb you, Doctor," said the woman, although Jon didn't think that was true. "Your scheduler said you're used to working nights."

Jon squeezed his temples between thumb and forefinger, feeling the pressure there. "I don't know if anyone really gets used to it. But I'm fine."

"Good. Doctor Edom, my name is Dani Cavallo. I'm the detective in charge of the missing persons case."

"I expected your call hours ago." It was Jon's turn to sound disgruntled.

"I *did* call, Doctor. It went straight to voicemail."

"I switched it off during surgery. Normally my assistant reminds me to check my voicemails, but he was called away—"

"Doctor, it's late," said the Detective Cavallo. "If you don't mind, I'd like answers to a few questions, then we can both get some sleep."

"Fine," said Jon.

The impatience in Cavallo's voice had grown more pronounced, so Jon wasn't about to argue. He waited as she did something to prepare—it sounded to him like she was flipping through a notepad—and cleared her throat.

"Would you say your wife is happy, Doctor Edom?"

"In general? We all have our ups and downs."

"Is she happy in your marriage?"

"Our marriage?" Jon paused in thought. "I'm sorry. This is going to sound unhelpful, but the answer's the same. We've had ups and down, just like everyone does. If you're talking about lately, I'd say we're on an upswing."

"An upswing?"

"Yeah."

"Upswings start on a down, Doctor. What would you say was your most recent low?"

Jon dropped his voice so no one passing could hear. "That would be the shooting, here at the Crown. Chelle has been stressed about my job, about the neighborhood, for years. Having her worst fears confirmed that night didn't help much."

"I'm sure it didn't." Up until now, Cavallo had seemed sympathetic, if only slightly. But the cursory pretense dropped as she asked, "Did you fight?"

"Did we—"

"Fight, Doctor. Did you and your wife fight about your job, about the neighborhood, about *anything* else?"

Jon's instinct was to say, "No," and hang up the phone, but that wouldn't help Chelle—or himself; Jon was forming the distinct impression he was rapidly becoming a suspect in the disappearance of his wife and sons. He'd caught a lift in Cavallo's tone when she said *anything else* and decided to make a point of it.

"What else do you mean?"

She didn't answer, but said quietly, "Doctor, did you hurt your wife?"

Jon sighed. "Never. I have *never* hurt her. I can guess where you got that idea, though. You should know, Detective, there's bad blood between me and my old friends at the Church of the Resurrected. When I left, they cut me off completely. Even Chelle's family kept their distance. I didn't hurt my wife, Detective, and I didn't drive her to suicide, if that's what you're implying here."

"Suicide?" said Cavallo. "No. I wasn't thinking that at all."

"Listen, if you want to know what the church is like— what it's *really* like—I can tell you who to talk to. Not a personal friend or anything like that, but someone who can tell you what's in the Kool-Aid, if you catch my meaning."

Several hours later, when Jon related the conversation with Cavallo to Rabbi Max, he left off this offer, and its result. Instead, he concentrated on his confusion at Cavallo's denial she was considering suicide as an option.

"I was tired. Not thinking straight. I couldn't imagine what she might mean, but afterward . . ." He lowered his voice. "I think the cops suspect me of killing Chelle and the boys."

The two men sat across a table from one another, a heaped pile of scrambled eggs in front of Rabbi Max. He'd been about to take a bite but stopped his fork in midair to stare at Jon over the yellow mound.

"Jon, the fact this is only just coming to you now shows you need help."

"Yeah. I guess it does."

The stiff wooden booth they were crammed in was near the front of a greasy spoon called the Last Stop Diner. Rabbi Max had chosen the location; it had been a favorite spot of his for years. There were faded spots on the walls where railroad signs might once have hung—either that, or pictures of half-dressed lot lizards draped over eighteen-wheelers. All the tacky, mood-setting bric-a-brac had been removed, and the only theme at the Last Stop was "Good grub, cheap." A sign over the host station said exactly that. Jon had declined to take the owners at their word; the only thing in front of him was a coffee cup.

"Sure you won't have some of this?" asked the rabbi. He glanced at the extra plate he'd requested when Jon refused to order food.

Jon winced at a stabbing pain in his side. "I'm really not sure I could handle it."

Rabbi Max grunted. "Nerves, or are you growing an ulcer?"

"I don't know."

"Do we need to reschedule?"

"No. It's passing. Give me a second . . . Okay . . . I'm okay now."

"Good timing." The rabbi pointed to the diner's glass front door. The tiny brass bell above it rang as a man walked in. "There's Fitz now."

A storm had blown in outside, so the lawyer entered folding his umbrella. He was a tall, silver-haired man with a perfectly straight back and square shoulders. He strolled over to the hostess station like he owned the place. Rabbi Max rose to wave him over.

"Shalom," said the rabbi. "You're late."

"Business is good, my friend," said the lawyer. He shook hands with the rabbi. "Shalom." He held a hand out to Jon. "Jim Fitzgerald. Call me Fitz."

"Jon Edom."

"It's good to meet you, Doctor."

"Likewise."

It wasn't until the greetings were over that a second stranger joined the party. Jon figured he must have entered the diner with Fitz, as the bell had only rung once, but Jon hadn't noticed him until Fitz shifted position.

Jon couldn't have imagined two more completely different men if he tried. Where the lawyer was tall and stood straight, his companion was short and slouched. Fitz wore a three-piece suit, probably bespoke and expensive, in autumn leaf brown with copper pin-striping. The quiet stranger was casually dressed in black cowboy boots, blue jeans, and a rusty red–colored hoodie. He was the sort of man Jon would have easily missed in a crowd, but now he did see him, two details catching the eye: The first was the way the man surveyed the room. Instead of turning his head at the neck as he assessed the place, the man kept his chin tucked and moved only his eyes. Jon once knew an ex-boxer who did that, but he didn't have anything like the second notable detail that distinguished Fitz's shadow. The man's lower lip appeared to be permanently swollen; it jutted below his upper lip like that of a bulldog.

"Max, Jon," said Fitz, pointing at each, "this is Charlie Castro, my senior investigator. Charlie used to be with Austin PD."

"Good to meet you." Charlie Castro shook hands all around before all four men took their places at the booth. Rabbi Max sat next to Jon so Fitz and Castro could sit across from one another. After they shifted plates, the waitress came to take orders from the newcomers.

When the four were alone again, Castro jutted his lip at Jon and said, "Edom, right? I heard your name from a friend on the force. He was on the Bernstein case."

Jon nodded politely. "That seems so long ago."

"Not long to the law," said Castro.

"May I ask," broke in Fitz, "what you know about the investigation into your wife's disappearance?"

Rabbi Max said, "We were just speaking of that. It seems a Detective Cavallo has it in for Jon."

"Hold on," said Jon, "I didn't say she had it in for me."

"She as good as accused you of murder, my friend."

Jon nodded. "I guess she did."

Fitz steepled his fingers. "This is important. Let's hear the details."

And so, Jon related his conversation with the detective once again. He'd just finished when the waitress returned, carrying eggs Benedict for Fitz and a double stack of blueberry pancakes for Castro. Again, Rabbi Max urged Jon to eat. Again he declined. He'd hardly even made a start on the coffee.

"Okay." Fitz took up his fork and knife. "This is how I see it: Whatever the police may think, we've yet to see evidence that Rochelle and the children have been harmed.

Our chief goal, then, is to get them home safely. Do we all agree on that?" Jon and the rabbi nodded. Castro paused his diligent work on the pancakes to hold up a thumb. "The police may or may not be helpful, and this thing with the investigating detective is troubling. Even if she's not fixated on Jon, the fact she made us wonder shows her eye is off the ball. For this and other reasons, it's critical to move forward with our own investigation. Jon, this is my usual fee." He held out a slip of paper but gave Jon barely a second to read the figure scribbled upon it before turning it over; the back side was blank. "And *this* is what I charge friends of the rabbi. No objections. I've never added up all I owe Max, but just the matchsticks I've lost to him in Mahjong would be enough to build a house. Accept the offer and move on, is my advice. Will you take it?"

Years of working in a charity hospital had cured Jon of the notion that a man needed to pay his way, no matter what. He bobbed his head graciously.

"Great!" said Fitz. "That seals the deal. My secretary will send over the necessary papers later. What I need from you now, Jon, is a promise to do everything you can to help Charlie out. He's the best investigator I've worked with in a long, weary career. Charlie will find your family, of that I have no doubt."

"That's good to hear."

Castro gave no indication he heard the lawyer's praise. He'd finished half of the first stack of pancakes and carried on eating as Fitz continued, "Okay. I know the basic story—the medical conference, Rochelle's disappearance, the lake house. After breakfast, Jon, I'd like you to come by my office so we can get everything you remember on file. I know you've been through it all with the police, so maybe this is a good time to ask: Is there anything you want to share with me or Charlie that you didn't feel the police needed to know?"

Jon took a moment to recall what he had said in the police interviews. He'd gone over everything the last time he had seen Chelle, even speculated about her state of mind, and mentioned how she might act if she was off her lithium. He'd also given them the names of her family and friends. Finally, he had taken the police interviewer through the lake house trip step-by-step. Even his phone call with Cavallo had been perfectly frank, despite her hostile attitude.

But there was one detail Jon hadn't divulged.

"Chelle had an affair," Jon said quietly, as if the revelation embarrassed him. "Actually, I think she had more than one, but so far as I know, only one was serious. It was years back, and I never asked her the details, but if the police want to find a motive for me to hurt Chelle, there's a chance they'll dig up the old boyfriend."

The rabbi patted Jon's hand.

Castro, who had just finished the whole first stack of pancakes, set down his fork. "Who else knew?"

"About the affair? No idea. Her sister, maybe. Actually, now I think of it, P. J.'s the only person Chelle *would* tell."

"P. J.," mused Castro. "Okay. And the boyfriend, you know his name?"

"No. I never asked."

Fitz set his fork aside. "Is that *all* you held back from the police, Dr. Edom?"

"That's all I held back."

Fitz nodded. He'd made inroads on the eggs Benedict, though nowhere near as much as Castro had on the pancakes. He took up his fork and scooped a shallot off the top. "Well, it's a start."

Jon raised an eyebrow.

"Don't get me wrong," Fitz explained. "I want you to help the police, but from now on, anything you say to them needs to come to me, first. Understand? Everything you and

I talk about is privileged. Some of what we say will go to the police. Some of it won't. All I'm asking is that you let me decide which is which."

That sounded wonderful to Jon. The police had been on his mind every waking minute since the lake house. When he wasn't answering their questions, he was worrying about what to say next. And to think that now, he could just hand over the responsibility!

"Thank you," Jon said. "That's actually a huge relief. Is there anything else you need from me?"

Castro said, "Pictures would be nice."

"Pictures of what?"

"Of your wife, Doctor Edom. Her and the missing boys."

"Of course." Jon brought up a folder on his phone. "I've got plenty."

Castro said, "Do you mind?" and reached out a hand for the phone. Jon handed it over across the table and watched as Castro swiped from photo to photo until one caught his attention. He turned the phone around so Jon could see. "Was this at your lake house?"

The picture was not of the house itself, but of the family—Jon, Chelle, and the twins—standing out back in their swim clothes. They all appeared happy, carefree. Jon had to blink back tears before answering.

"It's my wife's family's lake house. But yes. I think I have better pictures than that."

"This is all good stuff." Castro pulled the phone back before Jon could reclaim it. "I see your wife has tattoos. You ever get ink yourself?"

"No. It was kind of Chelle's thing. She went through a phase, right after we got married. That's when she got the sleeve, the tats on top of her right leg, and a couple only I'm supposed to know about."

If Castro heard Jon's resentment in *supposed to*, he let

it pass. Spearing his last bite of blueberry pancake, he said, "A *phase*, huh? So she didn't keep it up."

"Oh, she goes in a couple times a year. Mostly she gets her old ink retouched. Sometimes she gets new work done."

For the first time since the small man had appeared behind Fitz, his round face broke into a smile. "One thing I learned as a cop: There's stuff people will tell their tattoo artist they don't tell anyone else. Do you know where your wife gets her work done, Doctor Edom?"

"I can find out."

"As soon as you can, please."

"Anything else?"

Castro swiped through a few more photos. "I'd like copies of these."

"I'll text you them."

Fitz produced his phone from his jacket, and with them, a set of reading glasses. He peered at the screen. "How's your schedule for the rest of the week, Jon?"

"I'm trying to work as much as I can. Maybe that seems callous, but aside from meeting with you gentlemen, it's the only peace I get."

Rabbi Max placed a hand on Jon's shoulder. *Lo alecha hamlacha ligmor, v'lo atah ben chorin l'hibatel mimena.*

Jon was about to ask for the translation, but Castro beat him with a, "Huh?"

"'It is not your responsibility to finish the work, but you are not free to desist from it either,'" Fitz recited. "I think the rabbi is saying you should do what you can, Jon."

Rabbi Max shrugged. "Close enough." As he spoke, a stiff wind from outside blew open the door. The bell dinged, and everyone in the Last Stop, about fifteen people total, turned to look.

Suddenly, alerts rang out on every cell phone in the diner.

Someone said, "Twister."

Jon thought it was Castro, but the rush of wind made it impossible to be sure.

The hand gripped Jon's shoulder as Rabbi Max pulled Jon to his feet. "Come on. Let's go. Let's go!"

"Where?" Jon was confused.

A thready, white cloud billowed in the street. As Jon watched, it lifted several feet off the ground, turning as if moved by a giant hand, then suddenly plunged like a dagger into the clothing store next door. The glass front shattered, broken bricks flew out into the street, and Jon saw broken mannequins spinning wildly in the whirlwind; he was certain at least one was not a dummy, but a human being.

Rabbi Max quit pulling his shoulder; there was nowhere to run. The four men huddled under the booth table as the tornado raged outside. Something slapped the diner's window. Everyone jumped; there was a huge spiderweb crack in the glass. As the wind roared up and down the street, Jon's eyes fixed on the crack, positive it would grow and spread. A waitress stood frozen before the window, as if mesmerized by the sights outside. If the glass exploded inward, it would slice her to ribbons of flesh.

"Get down!" Jon shouted, already running toward the waitress. He tackled her from the side at the same instant the glass shattered inward. Shards of window sprayed over the empty tables. At that moment, as he lay protectively over the trembling waitress, all Jon could think of was the deep, resounding thunder from his dream. At any moment, he was sure, the roaring would quiet, its tone would pitch upward, and it would speak to him in a quiet voice.

Jon kept listening for the voice for the minutes it took the storm to level the clothing store and the apartment building across the street. He was still listening when he stumbled out of the diner and began searching through the debris for people to help.

16

"Well, ain't you a sweet little thing?" said the hillbilly manning the gate. His beard alone was old enough to be Dani's father, to say nothing of the man himself.

"I'm a sweet *cop* thing, actually." Dani Cavallo flashed her badge. "*Detectives* Cavallo and Troyer. We're here to see Pastor Bundy."

The creep barely peeked at the badge. He eyed Dani with disdain. "Pastor? Ain't no pastor here. The Brotherhood of the Cross Guard are all free and equal."

"Good to know," said Dani. She looked past the man to the rifle resting against the wall of his shack. "If you're not in a hurry, maybe we can talk about your firearm. I'm sure you can show me a license."

"I'm sure I could. But I don't want to keep you."

The hillbilly stepped away from Dani's Mustang and made a quiet call on his walkie-talkie. An answer came quickly and, two minutes later, Dani was parking the car in the dirt on the outskirts of the ranch.

In place of the matching black Chryslers that had

escorted them at the Church of the Resurrected, the detectives were met by a golf cart. Its driver was a woman, her body odor so pungent, Dani kept her mouth closed. Foul as she was, the driver did her job well: as the golf cart bounced hurriedly along a rutted woodland tract, Dani counted a dozen places she would have flipped the vehicle had she been behind the wheel. Eventually, the sour-smelling woman got them out of the woods and onto a large, dusty plain strewn with faded old trailers.

Saul nudged Dani in the ribs and pointed to a paddock. There, a large palomino frolicked with two pointed bays. "How you feel about horses?"

Dani pursed her lips and shook out a few strands of glistening black hair. Saul had never ragged her about the indigenous thing. After several seconds of waiting for him to cringe and apologize, she decided he probably wasn't trying to start now.

"All girls love horses," she told him.

"Sure."

The cart left the paddock behind and began to weave through the gaps between the trailers that passed for roads. Here and there, members of the Brotherhood peered at the visitors from doorways or makeshift porches. There were no women, aside from the driver, that Dani could see, and she saw absolutely no kiddie pools, kid-sized bikes, or any other signs of children.

Thanks to the police files she'd pored over, Dani knew why: Excluding the prisons, there were more registered sex offenders per acre at the Cross Guard Ranch than anywhere else in the state. The locals put up with the place because the residents kept to themselves; of course, they absolutely kept all children out. Dani couldn't help but wonder how the Brotherhood dealt with pregnancies. She made a mental note to ask Pastor Bundy.

As the cart emerged from the shadow of a trailer, a man

on horseback came into view. He gripped the reins and patted his horse's neck. The creature stood with one foreleg straight and the other bent, its head tossing nervously in a way that made Dani think it wanted to bolt, although she saw nothing that might have spooked the animal. The only other living thing around was a tall man in an ankle-length duster. He had his back to Dani, but so far as she could see, he wasn't doing anything to the horse, except, perhaps, smiling at the skittish thing. The thought of that imagined smile caused the back of her neck to prickle and a chill to sweep through her, despite the ninety-degree heat.

As the cart swung away, the tall man, the horse, and its rider were lost behind another trailer. Dani shut her eyes and tried to squeeze out the feeling of unease that had settled across her mind.

Then, a strong, somewhat nasally voice broke her thoughts. "This the cops?"

The cart's driver didn't answer. Instead, she turned the cart to give the speaker a view of his guests and hit the brakes.

When they'd come to a stop, Dani stepped out and looked down into a ditch at a powerfully built man with bowed legs, a beer gut, and a naked barrel chest. Silas Bram Bundy hadn't changed much from the mugshot in his police file. His hair was just a touch grayer, and he had shaved off his mustache, but otherwise, he appeared much the same as the last time he was arrested by police, fifteen years earlier.

"Mister Bundy?" said Dani. "I hope this is a good time for you."

"No you don't," Bundy growled. He closed a fist around the handle of a shovel, its head stuck deep in the earth. "You hope it's a lousy time for me, and you're right. Any time I spend with cops is lousy."

Saul stepped up behind Dani as Bundy heaved himself out of the ditch, using the shovel for leverage. He dismissed the golf cart with a wave of his hand and set off for a trailer.

Dani and Saul followed. "My name is Detective Dani Cavallo. My partner is Detective Saul Troyer. We're Austin PD."

"I reckoned." Bundy didn't bother to look back.

A cheap, plastic-topped card table had been set up in the shade cast by the trailer. On it were a pitcher of iced lemonade and a stack of red Dixie cups. After brushing dirt from his hands, Bundy poured himself a cup of lemonade. He took one sip, then another, watching the visitors as if daring them to ask for a drink.

True to his usual habit, Saul tried to break the ice. "That's thirsty work you were doing back there."

Bundy glared. "What do you know about running a cattle ranch, cop?"

"Not much," Saul admitted.

Bundy set the cup down on the table. "It's *all* thirsty work. Now, you got questions for me, or what?"

"*I* have questions." Dani made sure to stress the *I*, so Bundy would know she was the one in charge.

"Great." Bundy slurped at his lemonade.

Dani pulled out her notepad. She wasn't sure Bundy would say anything worthwhile, but since the ex-con-cum-ranch-owner clearly hated the police, she figured the best way to get the most from him was to get straight to the point, which was to talk about Bundy's sworn enemy.

"We are investigating a disappearance and have been told some details we need to verify." She paused. "What do you know about the Church of the Resurrected?"

The change in Bundy was amazing. In the blink of an eye, his hostile demeanor disintegrated, replaced by surprise.

"So that's what this is about." He smiled and flipped over two cups. "Y'all want lemonade?"

With Dani and Saul carrying a cup each, Bundy led

them to the back of the trailer. A concrete patio had been poured there, though the work wasn't what Dani would have called professional. Bundy directed his guests to a pair of deck chairs. A heavy, wooden bench sat next to the stainless-steel propane grill. Bundy lifted the end and dragged it over for himself.

"Now, what do ya wanna know about the good ol' COTR?"

Dani made a note in the notepad: *COTR = Church of the Resurrected.* The dismissive way Bundy spoke about the church showed he would be happy to tear it down with his bare hands, given the chance.

She said, "We recently paid a visit to the Texas Hill Faith Center. Some serious allegations were made, and we're trying to decide if we can trust the source. A knowledgeable party said you may have some perspective."

Bundy laughed. "Oh, I do. I surely do." Rubbing his hands together, he looked rather excited. Pausing to take a sip of the lemonade, he used the brief pause to study Dani and Saul with fresh eyes. "'Fore we get to that, I'd like to know who disappeared."

Expecting the question, Dani nodded to Saul.

He said, "You've seen the news about the game developer who went missing with her two boys? Rochelle Berger-Edom."

"Ezra's oldest girl." Bundy wiped his mouth with the back of a hand. "Yeah. I saw that. Well, I don't know if it'll help any, but I can tell you about her old man. He near about *was* the COTR back when he was alive. The folks in charge now still things do mostly like he did."

Dani asked, "How did you know Ezra Berger?"

A bloated horsefly settled on Bundy's shoulder. Swatting the insect before it could bite, he smeared it with a fat hand and scrubbed the guts on the bench. "We got right friendly back when I was a member. That was before my last term at George Beto U."

Dani wrote *Beto U* in the notepad. The biggest favor the state of Texas had done its inmates was adding the word "Unit" to the names of its prisons. It allowed former residents to pretend they'd wasted years in a C-list university instead of within the penal system. George Beto Unit was a maximum security men's prison about 150 miles south of Bundy's ranch.

"Ez and his clan started coming to sermons years after me," said Bundy. "He had brains, friends, and money. Between us, though, I'd say it was money that got him appointed trustee inside of three months."

Saul smoothed his mustache, his tell in the department poker games. In interviews, it meant something had caught his interest. He asked, "How long does it usually take to become a trustee of the church?"

Bundy leaned forward, closing distance with the detectives. "Let me put it this way, Detective. A house of many abodes, the COTR ain't."

Dani waited for him to explain. When he didn't, she prompted him, "Its top positions are exclusive, and Ezra Berger bought one for himself. Is that what you mean?"

Bundy showed her a mouthful of crooked teeth. "That's about the size of it. From the day Ol' Ez joined up, he had eyes on the prize. He snatched what he'd come for and set up his lady. Then his kids—Rochelle, Phillip, and that youngest girl—they all got their share. I was away when the big moves happened, understand, but even from a distance, it was easy to see."

"Big moves?" Saul chipped in.

"Changes," Bundy answered. "Changes to how the church was run. Denning was still alive back then. You heard of him?"

Dani flipped back in her pad to a note from her research. "That would be *Pastor* Denning?"

"Right. They called him pastor out of respect. Pastor Sharp had taken over preaching before I came around. But Denning was the founder. He called the shots, when he wanted. He had a right to. You know he wrote *The Grand Cycle*? There were other books just as good, real stirring material. I thought so then and think so now, despite all the sinning of his disciples."

Dani pictured the silver-lettered tome she'd seen Pastor Korvus clutching. She knew little about the author apart from his name, and nothing about any other books. Bundy had said Denning "was still alive back then," which meant the man was dead now. She asked Bundy if that was the case, and saw sorrow cross the man's round, grimy face.

"Last I saw Denning was a week before I went away. Two weeks later, he was in the ground. His final letter reached me after the funeral."

"You were close enough for him to write personally?" Saul asked him.

Bundy shook his head. "I was a nobody. Nobody at all. But Denning was special. He kept his finger on the pulse of the church. No lamb was beneath his notice. He wrote to me before and after my conviction, and never once a word of judgment."

The conviction had been for brawling and manslaughter, plus several petty drug charges. Dani wrote *judgment* in the notepad and withheld comment.

"He was too weak to visit," said Bundy, "but he got others to come down to Beto U on the church's dime. After he died, the visits dried up. I'd been treated like Paul on the road to Rome while Denning was there. Soon as he passed, I was an outcast. I found out later it came down to a vote. The board of trustees voted to end the prison outreach. And guess who cast the deciding vote?"

Dani guessed. "Ezra Berger."

"Got it in one. I got the scoop from Sharp himself, after

he got booted out as pastor. The Bergers—Ez and Lisa, I mean; the kids were still on the rise—they pushed to end the prison program, plus every other program that connected the church to the outside world. Inside a year, all the money that had been going out was staying in. Only it wasn't. Not really. Word got around the cash was turning into guns."

Saul chimed in. "I remember that. It was on the news. *Local Church Spotlighted by FBI—Fears of Another Waco.* Something along those lines."

"I remember too," said Dani. "A professor of mine suggested the changes were so Pastor Korvus could take the church in an apocalyptic direction."

Bundy laughed so hard that the rest of his lemonade splashed out of his cup and onto his white-haired belly. "That professor of yours never read Denning! Or his Bible, I reckon. The apocalypse is all in there. Don't get me wrong—I've heard Korvus preach. He calls more fire from heaven than the Sons of Thunder. But the changes had nothing to do with him. Not the important ones. Ending the outreach cut costs, for example. Everything else that changed was about increasing donations. *Money*, in other words. And the money man at COTR was Ezra Berger."

"So," Saul ventured, "you blame Ezra for getting kicked out."

Angry, Bundy crushed his empty cup. "I didn't get kicked out of *nothing*."

Dani tensed, hoping the next word out of Bundy's mouth wouldn't be *boy*. That would start a whole other discussion. Saul would let the slur pass; he prided himself on his luck with the ladies, that ridiculous mustache, and being unflappable where words were concerned. Dani, on the other hand, was ready to accept slights to herself—her sex, or heritage—as part of the job, but she drew a line when it came to her friends.

It was part of *her* pride.

The expected slight didn't come. Instead, the next sound Bundy made was a sigh as he calmed himself. When he finally spoke, he seemed like a different man.

"I *left* the Church of the Resurrected." Bundy's words were slow, deliberate. "It was God's will. If you want to know, I met someone at U who helped me break free. The Cross Guard was my calling. We got started before I got out, and I got in touch with all the other inmates Ezra abandoned. We wrote our families, got them to write to others of our jailed brethren. The work just snowballed from there. We ain't rich like COTR. We don't have a big tower or a fleet of cars. But we're real. We're authentic. We're *Christian*."

Absently, Dani watched a teardrop of lemonade drip down Bundy's belly to pool on his crotch. He'd proven more talkative than she expected, and she wanted to move the conversation from the past into the present. She decided to try the direct approach once more.

"Mister Bundy, some of the comments I heard at the Faith Center focused my interest on Rochelle Berger-Edom's husband, Doctor Jon Edom. Can you comment on their relationship?"

The broad, hairy shoulders shrugged. "I don't know the Berger kids much. Ezra was the star. Lisa had a shine to her too. The younger set sort of faded into the background, though it was easy to see Phillip would break out. Doctor Edom wasn't around when I was there, but I know who he is. The *hero* doc, right? I met him once—a sister of the Guard needed surgery, and Edom was up for the job. I'm no Denning, but I do what I can. I met the doc at Crown Hospital. He was COTR then, one of the faithful, but not quite dyed-in-the-blood. Issues with Korvus and concerns about what went down at Youngsport. I guess you've heard of Youngsport, Detective?"

Dani nodded.

Bundy's forehead wrinkled, deepening the shadows under his eyes. He seemed about to say something else but paused first, noticing the crushed cup in his hand. He tossed it against the side of the trailer and watched it fall to the dry grass. "Pretty much all I know about it is what was on the news. Anyway, I know enough about how COTR does business to be sure the full story is . . . *darker* than the reporters could ever dare say. Anyway, when I talked to Edom, I got the idea he was ready to jump ship. I offered him a tour of the ranch—we could always use a good sawbones around here. He turned me down, and I got the impression his 'faith' was about keeping a happy home. One thing we don't need in the Guard is pretenders, so I let Edom off the hook, but I gave him plenty to think about."

"Like what?" Dani pressed.

"A few doctrinal points, a bullet list of how COTR changed under Korvus versus Denning and Sharp. It's all on our website, if you want the fine detail."

Dani said, "We can look that up. If you don't mind my asking, what happened with the surgery?"

"Surgery? Oh. Never happened. Our dear sister got her upward call the same day."

"Condolences," said Saul.

Dani added, "You can't tell us any more about Doctor Edom or Rochelle Edom? You have no personal knowledge, or even any rumors you might have heard about their relationship?"

Bundy responded with a sincere shake of the head. "But I'll tell you this, though. Take anything you hear at the Faith Center with a big grain of salt. Make that a mouthful, actually. In the name of the Father, Son, and Holy Ghost, I wouldn't trust a word from any soul on the COTR membership roll."

"What about the trustees, the inner circle?" said Saul.

"I wouldn't stand close enough to talk to one."

"You're afraid of what they'd say?" Dani asked him.

"No, ma'am. I'm scared they'd spit poison."

Dani closed the notepad. It was clear Bundy knew nothing about the Edoms, or had nothing he wanted to share. His warning was interesting, but too broad to be of use to Dani. Her gut had told her not to trust Beale, who had made the claims about Edom and how he allegedly treated his wife. Her gut was saying much the same about Bundy. As for Edom himself, Dani had her own reasons for not trusting the "hero doctor." All things considered, it seemed her and Saul's trip to the Cross Guard Ranch had been a waste of time. And it was time she couldn't afford to waste, not with a missing family to find.

She got to her feet. As Saul stood up, a little more slowly, a statement of Bundy's flashed back into Dani's mind. "Mister Bundy, why do you think Ezra Berger moved to cut costs?"

Bundy looked puzzled. "He was the money man."

"You said. But the Bergers had money before they joined the church. They could have easily increased their donations without asking for changes in the outreach program. How much were they spending on letters and visits to prisoners, anyway? Whatever it was would have been peanuts next to the construction of that tower they had built. And then there's Youngsport. It was a satellite church complex, from what I understand. We're talking eight figures, at least. Based on the files I've read, the church has never lacked funds. And the biggest impact to their bottom line has always been membership. So why did Ezra risk upsetting parishioners just to pinch a few pennies? It just doesn't make sense."

Something sparked behind Bundy's eyes. He crossed his ankles, scratched his chin, and resembled an awkward, sweaty English professor more than Dani would have thought possible.

"That's an interesting question." Bundy furrowed his brow. "Ezra was greedy. That was enough for me. But there were rumors, way back when, about money getting funneled into *special* projects."

Saul said, "Special as in—?"

"Secret. Illegal, or near enough. Nothing the trustees would ever mention in public. The wildest rumors, and the ones I trust, knowing who was involved, were end-of-the-world stuff. COTR wants to help the end happen, you know?"

"They're proactively apocalyptic, you mean?" said Dani. She got a nod. "Do you have firsthand knowledge of these special projects?"

Again, Bundy answered with a head shake. He stretched his back; it gave an audible crack. "Don't forget, it was all after my time. I bet if you look hard enough, you can find out more, though."

Dani stared at the bare-chested ranch owner. She tried to picture him in the same room as Pastor Korvus, Phillip Berger, and others of the Church of the Resurrected elite.

Saul touched his mustache. "I don't guess you can tell us where you heard these rumors."

Bundy shook his head sternly. "I'll say this, though. The Berger girl who's gone missing? I'll lay odds you find her dead and in pieces."

That caught Dani's attention. "Why do you say that?"

"Call it intuition," said Bundy. "Maybe even prophecy. Or just say I knew ol' Ez. Men like him leave secrets behind. And secrets like his get folks killed."

Bundy rose and pulled out his cell phone. He called Brenda to come fetch the guests. In the minutes it took the golf cart to arrive, Bundy made small talk about expanding the ranch's sewage system; it was, apparently, the purpose of the ditch he was digging.

"Are you expecting more members?" asked Dani.

Bundy smiled but said nothing. As the cops climbed aboard the golf cart, piloted by the effervescent Brenda, he raised a hand in farewell.

"Be seeing you."

Dani opened her mouth to thank Bundy for his help, but he'd turned away before she uttered a word.

17

The sign in the window of Devil May Care Tatts spelled out "OPEN" in multicolored neon light. Charlie Castro enjoyed watching it pulse; the vibration reminded him of how the engine of the white-and-black 1972 El Camino he called Betty rattled when he turned the key in cold weather—not that they got too many cold days in Austin.

The ding of the bell got zero reaction, which suited Castro fine. He liked to take his bearings in a new place. Devil May Care's lobby was the size of a postage stamp. A counter whose only purpose seemed to be holding business cards took up a third of the cramped space. Another third was taken up by a short bench. It looked suspiciously like it belonged in a bus station. There were deep knife cuts in the wood of the counter, on the side that faced the bench. Castro traced one with his finger when the curtain at the back twitched. He saw a face. Female. Not young, but lively—her smile reminded him of the killer clown from *It*. Then the curtain parted, and Pennywise was forgotten. No clown ever looked like that.

"Been here before, hon?" said the plump red lips that were but a whisper of the rest of the woman's curves.

"I'm ashamed to say no," said Castro.

"Well then," the lips said, "you'll want to check out the merchandise." She planted her elbows on the counter and gave him an eyeful of an overflowing cleavage. At first, Castro was too distracted by God's handiwork to notice much else besides those magnificent twin orbs, but then he remembered where he was and focused on the woman's copious amount of ink.

Most of the scenes were from nature: the slope of one fleshy globe showed a rock that had been split open and was spilling a cataract, and above the rock was the fine lacework tattoo of a swirling starscape. The stars within that were flesh-colored, naturally, but so perfectly outlined, Castro could have very easily traced the constellations with a finger. He suppressed the urge, instead using his eyes to follow Ursa Major across his host's sternum and start up the opposite slope. That fine stretch of land showed a river and craggy mountain ringed by fierce thunderclouds. At the fringe of the woman's straining white blouse was the hint of an army driving chariots. They appeared to be chasing somebody, but Castro knew he would have to be a lover or a doctor to see exactly who their quarry was.

"I got the idea from *Ten Commandments*," the lips told him. "You want to see Charlton Heston?"

"I'm here on business."

"You are?" She sounded quite disappointed. "What business would that be?"

"Questions." Castro flipped open his wallet. Flashing the badge was a cop habit. These days, he wasn't a cop. But he did have his PI license.

"Private Investigator," read the lips.

"You don't sound surprised."

"Take a whiff, honey."

Castro inhaled a lungful of equal parts incense, pot smoke, and spicy perfume.

"You know that smell? Secrets. You can choke on 'em in this biz."

Castro tucked in his underbite to give a crooked smile. "Mine, too."

Lips said with a suggestive drawl, "Come on back, hun. You'll want to talk to Sketch."

Castro would have followed those curvaceous, swiveling hips anywhere. Where they happened to lead was through the curtain to the rear of the salon. On the far side was a waiting area with several benches and mismatched, battered chairs. Sample artwork and polaroids of work done was pinned to every available inch of the walls. His hostess fluffed her curly, bottle-red hair and motioned for him to take a seat. As he sat, Castro heard the buzz of a tattoo gun. The woman crossed to another curtain and stuck her head into the next room.

"Sketch!" she said.

The buzzing stopped.

If words were exchanged, Castro didn't hear them. He was too busy watching a black cat appear from under one of the benches. The ex-cop went rigid. Had it been under the bench all along, or had he missed seeing it cross his path? He knew plenty of saints he could pray to for luck, but he didn't want to bug any one of them too often. He tried to spread them all out. There was a saint he'd read about last week that he'd never prayed to before. Saint Fortuna came to mind, but he was pretty sure that was a character from one of the lamentable *Star Wars* sequels. He made the symbol of the fig with his fist and shook it at the cat. Undeterred, the animal cocked its head and walked over.

Castro put both feet in the chair. As he stood shakily on the seat, the curves and lips that had made him feel so welcome came back in the room. She was followed by a guy who looked like a snakeskin on feet. He was thin as a rod, and every inch of him not covered by jeans and a leather vest was thickly inked. His head was topped by a two-inch Mohawk, and upon his sloping nose balanced a pair of old-timey reading glasses, of all things.

Lips scooped up the cat. "Leave our guest alone, Nicky." Then, to Castro, "Don't you like cats?"

"It's nothing personal." Castro offered an embarrassed smile. "I broke a lot of mirrors growing up. Been making up for it ever since." He climbed down from the chair and extended a hand to the tattooist. "You're Sketch, I guess. I didn't mean to pull you away from a client."

"Huh?" said Sketch. "Nah, man. The sound you heard was the doctor treating himself." He thunked a sneakered heel on top of a bench and rolled up his jeans. Fresh ink and traces of blood circled his ankle. "Got to practice somewhere."

"You're quite an artist," said Castro as he eyeballed the cat, who snuggled into the biblical epic of its owner's chest as she carried it out. He guessed it was lucky after all.

Sketch said, "Nette says you're a PI."

Castro nodded. "I'm here about a missing person."

Sketch sat down on the bench. "What can I do?"

"Do you know this woman?" Castro held up his phone for the artist's scrutiny. The image on its screen was a close-up of Rochelle in her swimsuit. Castro had it zoomed to show her face, her neck, and some of the tattoo sleeve.

Sketch didn't hesitate. "Shay-Shay? One of my best customers. A favorite, anyway. She don't come in much, but she was here, like, last week."

"When, exactly?"

Sketch took a second to think before he called out, "Nette! When was Shay-Shay last in?"

Nette peeked through the side curtain, those lips freshly

red and glistening. "Friday. I got that package, remember?"

"Oh yeah." Sketch smiled. "The package." He looked pleased at the memory. Castro guessed whatever had been in that package had gone up in smoke. "She was here with her sister."

That was good news to Castro. He'd gone from vague ideas to definite knowledge of how Rochelle had spent the day before she vanished. The sister would no doubt be Pamela Jean, called P. J. by the family. Austin PD would have interviewed her by now; Castro made plans to do the same.

"Did they get ink done?" he said.

Sketch nodded. "Sure. Shay-Shay did. The sister no. Shay-Shay tried to talk her into it, but she wasn't down."

"How did she pay?"

"She didn't have to, man. It was maintenance. Part of the service."

"You don't charge for touch-ups?"

Sketch pointed to a Chinese dragon on his own arm. The rich jade and crimson highlights practically shone. "Advertising, man. Got to get the word out."

Castro smirked. The information filled in a gap in Rochelle's timeline. Granted, it wasn't the most important gap he needed to fill. He pushed on.

"What sort of mood was . . . Shay-Shay in when she visited?"

Instead of answering, Sketch's bony shoulders slumped. "Hold on. You said *missing person*. Is Shay-Shay the one missing?"

"I'm afraid so."

Sketch shuddered, visibly stunned. "Whoa. She, uh, she was her normal self on Friday. Except maybe a little worked up."

"Any idea about what?"

Sketch hung his head in thought. The old and dainty

reading glasses slid off his nose; deftly, he caught them in his left hand before they could hit the floor.

"Family, I think. Or a job. Not her job, her husband's. Yeah, that was it."

"Did she tell you what her husband's job is?"

After scrutinizing the ground a few seconds more, Sketch looked up. He set the glasses back in place.

"A doctor. Yeah. He's a doctor."

Castro raised an eyebrow. "Most wives are happy to have a doctor in the family."

Sketch shrugged. He probably didn't see a lot of doctors. "Not every doctor works at a hospital that gets shot up."

Castro said, "You lost me," to keep Sketch talking.

"Sorry, man. This husband of Shay-Shay's? He works as a doctor in a charity hospital downtown. Some nut job rammed his car through the doors and shot up, like, a hundred people a couple weeks ago. I must have done twenty portraits of the guy since his pic hit the news—like he was some kind of hero sticking it to corporate America, ya know."

There were nowhere close to a hundred victims of the Crown Hospital, but Castro wasn't at Devil May Care to argue. Instead he asked if mass killer portraits were big business.

"You've got no idea, man. I'm not into that scene personally, but your boy's got to eat."

Sketch slapped his lean belly. The artist actually looked sad that so much of his work came from violence. Castro wondered if the delectable Nette ever posed as a fine-art nude.

He shook off the mental image. "She was upset her husband got shot at?"

"Yeah . . ." Sketch sounded uncertain. "I mean, maybe. I think what really upset her is he won't change jobs. She wants him to quit the charity hospital. It's in a hell of a rough neighborhood. She wants him to get a job someplace safer. And get paid more, too. Girl knows the value of a dollar."

Castro declined to tell Sketch how much the client he was touching up for free was worth: she still got fat residual checks from the video game she programmed years ago. Her home cost upward of two million bucks, paid for, and the family had another three or four million in savings and trust funds. When Fitz had tried explaining the Edom family's stock options to Castro, his mind had wandered to baseball, chicas, an itch on his chin, and cars.

"She says the doc won't make the change?" he asked Sketch.

"Right. Shay-Shay got extra mad when her sister tried to defend the guy. But that only lasted a second or two. The sister said it wasn't worth fighting out, and they talked shopping after that."

"Only shopping. Nothing else?"

"Just shopping, man. You know, chicks and their shopping."

Castro brought up a new picture on his phone. It was an alternative shot of the lake house with no people present.

"Has Mrs. . . . . Shay-Shay ever shown you pictures of this place, or talked about a house on Lake Conroe?"

Sketch peered through his glasses. "Lake what?"

"Conroe. It's about three hours east, highway driving. The family has a place there."

"Hold on. A lake house? Just a sec."

Sketch left the room, mumbling. He was gone for a minute. Castro filled the time scrolling through pictures on his cell, all the while keeping an eye on the curtains. He was wary of the black cat, but wanted another glimpse of its owner. Neither came through the curtain before Sketch returned. He carried a drawing pad. Opening it, he showed

Castro a picture.

"This the place?"

Castro studied the design. A tree that also features in the family photo was there, and there was no mistaking the railed porch that approached the front door. He nodded.

"I knew it. This is an old pic, one I did for Matt, the dude who used to own this place. He was an ace with a brush, you know? Not so much with a pencil. He hired me, gave me my name. This was an early pic I was proud of."

"And Shay-Shay liked it?"

"She was stoked, man. Big time. I could have taken her back to the office for a— Hey. Who'd you say you're working for, man?"

The last thing Castro wanted was for Sketch to clam up at the mention of Shay-Shay's husband.

"A concerned citizen. So, Shay-Shay liked the lake house? That's cool."

Sketch turned his head, as if to call out to Nette again. Maybe she was his bouncer, as well as his receptionist. After a moment, he let the suspicion that closed his lips go. "Yeah," he said. "You can see it on her sleeve, actually, on the side. That pic you showed me was the wrong angle, but if you've got another, you ought to check. It's good work."

"I don't doubt it," said Castro. He leaned closer to Sketch, who stood with the drawing pad. "Between us guys, does Shay-Shay like to party?"

The Chinese dragon around the artist's arm showed its fangs to Castro as Sketch turned to check the side curtain. It was clear he knew the answer but didn't know if he ought to share. Castro put on the smile he had invented for moments like these, the smile that said, *I get you, buddy. I'm on the level.*

Sketch took the bait. "She talks like a party girl, man, but I never had the pleasure. But Matt? She was *so* into him. I wouldn't be surprised if he let the gun buzz while they explored the canvas together, if you know what I mean." Sketch lowered his voice even more to add, "Matt and Nette were an item back then."

Castro touched a finger to his lips and allowed himself a private smile. So, Rochelle had at least *one* boyfriend outside her social circle. On the other hand, she cared about her husband's safety, and felt an attachment to the family getaways. It didn't sound like the profile of a woman about to split her family apart by running off to Mexico or wherever in the dead of night.

He said, "I'd like to talk to Matt. Got a number?"

"Sorry, man. He died of lung cancer a couple years back."

"That's too bad."

Sketched crossed himself and nodded sadly.

Castro decided it was time for a new tack. "Let's talk about the sister, again—P. J. What was she like with Mrs. Edom—Shay-Shay—apart from the fight about the husband?"

"She was happy. Enjoying the day. Enjoying life."

"There was nothing about Shay-Shay or her sister that made you think something was up?"

"Nothing but the spat over the husband, and they got over that fast."

"Right," Castro said. "Right." He felt just about finished with Sketch. "One more thing and I'll let you get back to your practicing. This past Friday, what exactly did Shay-Shay get touched up?"

Sketch beamed. "It was just one tatt, and the parts I touched up are in UV ink."

"UV?"

"Ultraviolet, man. The kind you need a black light to see. When I first put it on Shay-Shay, about six years ago, I asked her what clubs she was hitting. She laughed and said it wasn't about that. She showed me a pic, asked me to do some of it full color, the rest in UV. I don't mind telling you, man, it's some of my best work."

"Work you touched up on Friday."

"Right."

"Did it need it? I mean, were the lines fading, or what?"

"You know, I asked Shay-Shay about that. It's not like it's on public display, if you get me, and it's sunlight that wears out ink fast. When I checked with a black light, the lines were all good. But Shay-Shay wanted the touch-up anyway. Some folks like the needle, you know? And then there's the sister angle."

"What angle is that?"

Sketch put on a grin that convinced Castro he hadn't been named for his talent alone.

"She watched me work, man. I could tell the gun freaked her out. She kept fidgeting, hugging herself. Shay-Shay was into it. She kept talking to the sister, asking her questions, so she couldn't turn away. It was some kind of game, the kind only a sister would think of."

The cruel twist of Sketch's grin told Castro everything he needed to know about the artist's darker side. It told him plenty about the missing Shay-Shay as well.

"Do you have a pic of the special tatt?"

"The UV tatt? You can find it online, man."

Sketch walked over to the side room and returned with a laptop. The image he showed Castro was strange, but somehow familiar. It showed a bird—a flaming phoenix—spreading its wings. A pair of hooked horns sprouted from the head, and above the horns floated a fiery halo. A serpent was clutched in the phoenix's talons, which made Castro think of the Mexican flag, only this serpent wasn't being eaten by the bird. Its head had coiled around to swallow its own tail. It was eating itself.

"Picture that on a smooth, creamy thigh."

"I don't have to."

Castro scrolled to the original picture Jon had sent. The bird was high on Rochelle's right thigh. The thin bikini strap passed through its head.

"Nah, man. That's the plain ink. Even if your girl was here and feeling frisky, you'd still need a black light to see the rest. The flames and the snake, the horns and the halo. They're invisible in normal light."

Castro zoomed in on the image as close as he could. It was no use. He couldn't see enough detail to verify Sketch's statement.

"Why'd she want those parts in UV?"

"Don't know, man. I don't know what the piece means to Shay-Shay. She never explained."

Castro stared at the image a few seconds more. He was sure he'd seen it before, but where? He pointed at the laptop.

"You said I can find that online. Where?"

"Check it out."

Sketch showed him the image again, and this time scrolled so Castro could see the web page address. Once Castro read it he knew exactly where he had seen the image before.

"You've been a big help," he told Sketch.

"Any time, man. Any time. Say hi to Shay-Shay when ya find her." There was sadness in his tone.

By the time he left the tattoo shop and started the two-block hike to where he'd parked Betty, Castro had the boss on the phone.

18

Lieutenant Randall shoved his knuckles against the edge of his desk. They gave out a good crack.

Standing before him, Dani's own knuckles were stiff, but she couldn't have cracked them if she tried.

The lieutenant was a giant. Even seated, he barely had to look up to meet Dani's eyes. But it wasn't physical intimidation that made Dani tense. It was frustration at the fact that nothing she had said in her report to the boss, and nothing she was about to say, was likely to get her what she wanted.

Randall asked the question Dani had been dreading. "So . . . what's your play, Detective?"

Dani kept her voice steady. "I want to work all the angles, sir. Doctor Edom, the church, Bundy. Saul and I can handle Edom. I need FCU to run numbers on the Bergers and FRU to check firearms at the ranch. And I'm not satisfied with the lake house forensics. I want our team up there—with sonar and shovels, if that's what it takes."

The lieutenant managed not to roll his eyes. Dani saw the effort. "It's nice of you to think of the other divisions, seeing as we're so understaffed and underfunded," Randall said. "Too bad they are, too. Listen to me, Detective—why make this complicated? You've got a triple mis-per, a mom and two kids. Mom has a mental health history. Bank records put her close to the Lake Conroe house, and we know she was with her sister part of Friday. Smart money says she got partway to the house, decided she wanted a nice swim with the kids, and drove her SUV into the trees somewhere. It's alligator country out there. There's snakes, too, all sorts of nasties. Why don't you give the sheriffs time to find the vehicle before you rope in other divisions?"

He meant the Montgomery County Sheriff Department, who weren't Dani's favorite people. Not only had they been slow about handing over forensics, but some sort of technical issue had rendered the DNA they'd collected practically useless—especially in a court of law. Still, based on conversations she'd had, Dani was sure the canvass for the vehicle had been thorough.

She replied, "The SUV's not by the water, sir. I think we can trust the county cops that much." Pausing, Dani gave Randall a chance to add something helpful. When he didn't, she decided to probe. "Sir, is this *really* about the department's money?"

The lieutenant's outraged expression came on a little too quickly. "What the hell else would it be about, Detective Carvallo?"

That was precisely what Dani wanted to know, but she dare not say as much.

"I know the budget is tight. I know you're under pressure to get this case right. But I also know you want the truth. There's more going on here than some bored, depressed housewife woman stopping her meds and going off in the woods. There's something suspect going on at that church, sir. Embezzlement, misuse of funds, God only knows what else. It's possible Rochelle Edom found something out and was silenced. Or she may have run across someone from the Cross Guard. They're religious rivals with her family's church, and both have a history of stockpiling guns. Even if they have nothing to do with our mis-per, somebody really ought to check them out."

Randall stared at the detective gravely. For a moment, his silence gave Dani hope she had gotten through. At last, Randall opened a folder on top of his inbox.

"You're looking at Doctor Edom?"

"I have, sir. I'm not sure—"

"This came in today. It's the transcript of a call from a Mister Vivek Singh. He worked with Rochelle Berger-Edom, and claims they had an affair. On the day of the disappearance, she got in touch with him by private email. Singh says she confessed the affair to her husband, and he was furious, made threats. According to the email, Rochelle and the boys spent Thursday night locked in the bedroom, listening to Jon Edom rant. Rochelle got out in the morning, when Jon left for his conference in Houston."

Tasmin Beale's theory of the purported crime popped into Dani's mind. The weakest point was the notion Rochelle would agree to meet her husband, who was supposedly abusing her, in such a remote place. If Singh's story was true, that was clearly ridiculous. But it might explain why Rochelle left her home. She had her planned day with her sister finished, and got to thinking about what life would be like when her husband returned. Dani pictured Rochelle fretting, maybe watching the boys play. Were the stories of abuse true, Dani could actually imagine Rochelle making the decision to run.

"Did Singh speak to her on the day she disappeared?" asked Dani.

"No," the lieutenant grunted.

"So why is he only saying all this now, three days into the investigation?"

"Apparently, he doesn't check his email account every day. It's for sensitive emails. He saw the email on Saturday and was thinking what to do when the news broke about the disappearance. He says he's very sorry and he should have said something sooner. He gave us the usual excuses we hear from people all the time who don't want a scandal."

Dani chewed her lip. "Do we have a printout of the email from Mrs. Edom?"

"Just his word, for now. Do I need to order you to get on this? I want you to make Jon Edom your focus, and let me worry about the church and that ranch of yours."

Dani felt a sharp twinge that started at the top of her head and ran down, through to her solar plexus. It was the closest thing she could imagine to being torn in two. Singh's story was compelling . . . but so were the signs Pastor Korvus, Silas Bundy, and the rest of their feuding circles were up to no good. The difference, in the end, came down to priorities.

Chasing down the church's financials might lead to a new suspect in the disappearance. But Dani had a suspect already, and time was ticking. If Edom had stashed his family somewhere, instead of killing them outright, she had only days, at best, to find them.

The Cross Guard's illegal firearms were worrying, but the detective couldn't see a connection between them and Rochelle Berger-Edom. Bundy's sworn enemy was Ezra Berger, not the family. If Ezra was still alive, maybe Bundy would have done something to hurt his family—but not this. Dani honestly didn't think Bundy the type, though. He talked tough, but after their cozy chat and the shared lemonade, she couldn't believe he was dangerous.

She nodded firmly at Randall. "I'm on it already, sir. One hundred percent."

The lieutenant shut the file with a theatrical flourish and held it out to the detective. "Good. One hundred percent is a good number. It's *exactly* the amount of your energy I want devoted to the husband. You understand?"

"Yes, sir."

No sooner were the words out of her mouth than Dani felt another twinge. She wasn't being torn apart, this time. It felt more like the sting of cold air. Her interviews in the tower, the visit to the ranch—it had been a little dreamlike, even surreal. Now she was awake and the path ahead concrete.

"Doctor Jon Edom," she said. It gave her a warm feeling, especially the "doctor" part.

"Go get him," said Lieutenant Randall.

Dani took the folder from him and left the office.

19

The crowd's whoop made Silas think of an old Western movie, and the sound was more like thunder as the trailer crashed down from vertical to horizontal. He saw Hooch keeping his grip on the controls of the crane. The last two crane operators, a couple of young guns from Dominguez, had both lost the job because they got too excited. Each one had pumped a fist when he should have kept a firm hand on the controls. The cow boss was far more reliable.

Silas understood the excitement, though. It *was* exhilarating to watch the crane hoist a trailer, snap the underpinnings, and allow the plumbing to flex and crack, until the tin-plated rectangle stood poised on its end. It was a thrill to watch the trailer balance momentarily, before momentum or a nudge from the crane arm tilted it sideways and had it crash down in a crumpled heap. His work crew had started demolishing trailers this way because it added some excitement to what was otherwise a humdrum job. But it was also wasteful, even though the waste had its uses. Smashing a trailer to bits told his crew and all the brothers and sisters who turned out as observers they were doing just fine. They could afford the waste.

Silas was all for excitement and for the strategic wastefulness, but he always insisted his workers play it safe. All workers wore safety glasses and, along with the gathered observers, they stuffed in the sponge ear plugs. Silas insisted on the protective gear, just as he insisted on his crane operator keeping his hands on the controls. He would have liked to work the crane himself but found the seat belt uncomfortable, on account of his fat gut. Hooch wasn't his second choice for the job, as operating a crane kept him from the cattle, but better to use Hooch than to let someone get killed.

As the echoes of the trailer's fall and the crowd's whoop faded, Silas stepped forward and watched for the signal from his spotter that it was safe to approach. He caught the signal and returned the spotter's wave.

"All right, boys," he hollered. "Get to capping them pipes. I want this site leveled for pouring in two hours. The rest of y'all, get back to your lives—show's over."

The observers gave a brief round of applause before they moseyed away, stuffing the used earplugs in their pockets. Silas was happy they'd enjoyed the show, but was less so to see some of the unmarried brothers and sisters pairing off, and downright annoyed when he saw Dwight Moon, an electrician from Clarence N. Stevenson U, slap the shapely, denim-clad backside of a woman whose name escaped Silas but who was definitely *not* his wife.

He growled softly to himself as he watched Dwight and the woman flirt outrageously and in open view of everybody out there. Dwight was boasting about some imaginary exploit, as he was prone to do, and the woman laughed, tossed her head, and swished her hips.

Her firm hips.

Her firm, round hips.

Her firm, round, *available* hips.

Coppersmith said, "Is this a bad time?"

Silas spun around, startled. His partner was standing six feet away, his body turned like he'd been watching the worksite, with his head turned back to speak over his shoulder. Coppersmith gave the impression he'd been there a long time, only Silas hadn't seen him all day.

"I see that I am." The tall man sounded disgusted.

"What are you talking about?" Silas asked.

"A botherance, Abraham. Evidence of a wandering mind."

Silas glanced to his left and right, trying to figure out what Coppersmith meant.

"Look down. That's where it lives. And don't turn sideways, whatever you do. It makes things inescapably noticeable."

Silas felt himself blush. He stuffed his hands into his pockets and strode away from Coppersmith, in the direction of the cement truck that was going to pour a pad on the ex-trailer site once it was clear. Coppersmith walked along with him.

After a few pointless steps, Silas halted. "You need something from me? I'm busy."

"Are you? It's hard to tell. Everyone else is moving and sweating. You're doing that too, but less so."

"I work plenty hard, as you well know. I'm serious. What do you need from me, Coppersmith?"

"Not much. Not much at all. I only wondered . . . Sorry, could you look just there?"

Silas had to shift position to follow the tall man's finger. He still had no idea what Coppersmith wanted him to see. He faced a patch of perfectly blue sky over a green, distant hill. There were no clouds, aircraft, or even birds to be seen.

"There's nothing there."

"I never said there was. I simply wanted to get the . . .

unpleasantness out of sight."

Silas had his back to Coppersmith, who pointed vaguely at his own crotch. He cussed to himself and walked on, but Coppersmith continued to follow. Silas halted again.

"You can be a trial, you know," he said.

"How very clever of you," Coppersmith said dryly.

"Huh?"

"A trial is what I wanted to talk to you about. *Two* trials in fact: one active, one pending. What did you make of our visitors yesterday?"

Silas replied with equal dryness, "The Native cop and the Black cop? Not much."

Coppersmith clucked his tongue. "Don't be distracted by appearances, Abraham. The two detectives offered us a unique opportunity."

One of the workers hit a pipe with a sledgehammer. The loud, resonant *clang* forced a pause in the conversation. Silas waved for Coppersmith to follow him to a clearing some forty feet away. He sat at one of the picnic tables set up for the workers; its top was strewn with Tupperware containers and sandwich bags. Silas lifted the lid on a green bean casserole but saw Coppersmith grinning with those extra teeth of his and shoved it away, his appetite suddenly gone.

"What opportunity?" Silas asked.

Coppersmith knocked a bag of chips to the ground and perched on the table. "Isn't it obvious, Abraham? We have a chance to strike while our foe is distracted."

Silas didn't have to ask if "foe" meant the Church of the Resurrected. It always did with Coppersmith. Which he found ironic, since it was Silas, not the tall man, who had reason to bear a grudge.

"And by distracted, you mean—?"

"Ah! Now that really is obvious, friend," Coppersmith

interrupted. "Those archfiends, the Bergers, have suffered a loss. One of their own is missing. *Three* of their own, if the little people count."

"Seeing as those *little people* are Lisa Berger's grandkids, I reckon they do."

Coppersmith twirled a hand to dismiss the comment. "Whatever the case, the signs clearly favor action, Abraham. We must strike like Jehoash!" He slapped the table hard and locked eyes with Silas. "Don't you ever read that book you're always talking about? Second Kings 13. Elisha and the arrows. *He was told to strike. Strike!*"

Silas folded his arms. Some of the crew looked over; Silas glared back until they got back to work.

He said, "The point of that story is he didn't strike enough."

Coppersmith showed Silas his palm. "Exactly! We must be like Jehoash, but bolder. Vigor, Abraham. It's not just for blowing your nose."

Silas scowled. The insults were wearing thin, but he knew pointing that fact out to Coppersmith wouldn't do any good.

"How did you know those detectives were here about Rochelle Berger and her kids?"

Coppersmith waggled a finger like a chastising schoolmarm. "You're asking the wrong question. Don't you want to hear my idea?"

Silas didn't, of course, for so many reasons. Top of the list was the work it always took to execute any idea of Coppersmith's. He gestured at the job site. "This is all for you, Coppersmith. All part of your big plan. A plan you ain't explained yet, I might add. The Cross Guard has been digging, building, renovating for months. And you haven't told me why."

"Patience," came the tall man's answer as he gazed off into the distance.

Silas waited. And waited. Finally, it was his turn to thump the table. "All right, you win! What is your big idea?"

Coppersmith took a moment before speaking. "Did I say it's *big*? I don't think so. It's not a big idea, Abraham. I'd call it right-sized. The time has come, I say, for the Brotherhood of the Cross Guard to advocate for change by means of its media presence. We need to get out there, on all the social networks, and make people question the Berger clan's motivation. Are they seeking their missing members in earnest? Or might they, just might they, know more than they are letting on in public?"

Silas was intrigued. "You think the church has something to do with the disappearance of Rochelle Edom and her kids?"

"Given their general wickedness, I wouldn't rule it out for a moment. And wouldn't it look bad for them if they did?"

It certainly would.

Silas wasn't much of a social media user himself, but the ranch employed a team of members and freelancers who were more than happy to post their message to every corner of web—and beyond. So what if some of the posts Coppersmith was suggestion would be half-truths, at best? The Cross Guard was fighting a war and couldn't realistically expect to keep their hands clean.

"Interesting." Silas scratched his chin. "I reckon I can get our boys started on an information campaign. Or should that be *dis*information?"

Coppersmith rubbed his hands together like some comic book villain. "Excellent. That will leave me free to attend to the other matter."

"A different part of your plan?"

"No, actually. An addendum to the present idea. Still, it's all much of a muchness, Abraham."

"I'm sure it is." Silas was growing weary of his visitor. "And when will you fill me in on the details?"

"Patience," Coppersmith repeated himself, but this time with a wide, toothy grin. "In fact, I do mean to tell you very soon about the part of the plan that involves you directly. You'll need to sign invoices as usual—"

"Of course."

"—but there will be an opportunity for you to act more directly than before. We both know you're a man of action, really, though your stomach obscures it."

Silas let the crude slur pass. "I like the sound of that, Coppersmith. Why not explain it now?"

"Oh, irons in the fire, Abraham. I like to keep my promises, so I must be cautious about making them. Suffice it to say, I have been working with Coachman and the militia. If all goes well, I'll be able to show you the fruits of our labor in roughly a week."

The thought of Coppersmith working directly with the militia brought a sour taste to Silas's mouth. They had worked together to create every facet of the Texas Cross Guard, but one of the roles Silas had always played was carrying the direction from Coppersmith to the men. That he might be excluded completely from the chain of command was a new and troubling thought; especially so to think he might be cut out of directing the Guard's paramilitary wing.

Silas had to know more about what Coppersmith was doing. But he knew his partner would clam up if he was asked directly. Subtlety was the order of the day.

Cautiously, he said, "Coachman. He's one of the best."

"Absolutely. He's so *marvelous* at violence."

Silas hid his alarm behind a smile. "You, uh, you said you'll show me something next week?"

"If all goes well I will, certainly."

"And what if all doesn't go well?"

Coppersmith shrugged. "Trust me, Abraham. You're in a wonderful position. The best there is to find out everything of importance in the end."

"Everything of importance," Silas imitated. "Right. That's fine, so long as this end you're talking about ain't too far in the future."

The sinister grin returned to Coppersmith's lips. In Silas's racing mind, it seemed to stretch beyond the confines of the man's face, practically splitting it into two.

"Oh, my dear Abraham. You can bet your bottom dollar on that."

20

The rabbi's ringtone was as perfect a copy of those old rotary phones as Jon had ever heard: brash, shrill, aggravating. He'd once spent forty minutes teaching the older man how to set the clock on his microwave, but the teacher had now risen above his master in knowledge of all things technological. Jon's ringtone was still the factory default.

"Hello, Max." Jim Fitzgerald's voice sounded somehow deeper over the Volvo's stereo than it did in person.

"Shalom," Rabbi Max replied. "You answer the phone for yourself? What happened to that fancy young secretary of yours?"

Fitz laughed. "It's her day with the grandkids."

As the two old friends continued to banter, Jon concentrated on his driving. In another ten minutes, they would pull into the Church of the Resurrected Faith Center. There, they would meet Phillip and the rest of the family. It had been Phillip who had called Jon to arrange the meeting. The circumstances made close contact with Chelle's family inevitable, and the thought of seeing Lisa, Phillip, and P. J. made Jon uncomfortable. He smiled across at the rabbi, who had insisted on coming along. Jon appreciated the support but wished he would wrap up his chat with Fitz so the lawyer could bring him up to date.

"Jon?" Fitz said at last. "How are you doing?"

"I'm fine," Jon lied. "Anything new?"

Fitz sniffed. "Maybe. Castro checked in. I thought you'd like to hear what he's come up with so far."

Jon did, of course. "At this point, any progress is good progress."

"We're going to find them, Jon," Fitz reassured. The words sounded hollow to Jon.

"I know." It hit Jon that Fitz hadn't specified they would find Chelle and the boys *alive*. "Let's hear what you've got."

The sound of paper rustling came through the stereo, then Fitz said, "I don't want to oversell this. There's nothing here that takes us to Rochelle and the children, but it may tell us something about the path they took to get there. The tattoo parlor, Devil May Care. Castro spoke with the artist who did work for Rochelle."

He went on to summarize the PI's conversation with Sketch. Jon had never met him, or any other tattoo artist from Devil May Care, but he knew Sketch's work intimately. If he had to pick a favorite tattoo of Chelle's, the phoenix bird on her thigh was it. He knew its every line and angle, every tone and hue—or *thought* he did. He knew how it stretched when Chelle frolicked in the surf and creased when she sat in the sand. He had seen it glisten after a hot shower and prickle when she entered the cold bedroom. He could so very easily recall its fine detail whenever they made love. And yet, Jon knew nothing about the hidden fiery outline, the horns and the halo, and the snake clutched in the talons, until Fitz told him. He knew tattoos could be prepared for viewing under UV light because of his medical training, but had no idea his wife had such artwork on the body he knew so well.

"Turns out the design is easy to find online," Fitz continued. "If you know where to look."

"You mean aside from Google?"

"Google is an okay start. The interesting part is where Google gets the picture. *NeverEnd-dot-game*. It's in the section about in-game collectibles. It's called *Infinitus*, 'the ultimate reward for the ultimate test,' on the site."

Jon could see the image in his mind's eye, a figure so like Chelle's tattoo, he should have made the connection. He didn't know it was from *NeverEnd*, having never played the game, but it had been on a pin Chelle had used to decorate her work bag while the game was but a twinkle in her eye.

Jon groaned. "Of course it's from the damn game."

Fitz said, "A rare prize, apparently. It lets the holder retrieve all the equipment they lost in a previous life. The symbolism is interesting."

"Life from death," Rabbi Max offered.

"I was going to say *immortality*," said Fitz, "but I guess that's also true. The phoenix dies and is reborn. As for the halo, it dates back to ancient Egypt as a mark of God's favor. The gods' favor, *plural*, I should say. I was stumped by the horns at first, but I did some digging—"

"*Wehinneh karan owr panaw*," interrupted the rabbi. "'And see, there shone the skin of his face.' You Latin types—doctors and lawyers and translators—get 'karan' wrong. It comes out 'corona' in medieval translations. That could be shiny or horned."

Fitz laughed.

"What's so funny, Fitz?" said the rabbi.

"I've been called many things before, but never a Latin lover. Anyway, you're right, Max. Or close enough. The word is *cornutum*. Its ambiguous translation is why medieval sculptors gave Moses goat horns. As a symbol, I'd say the meaning is the same as the halo, only lacking the pedigree. Any thoughts on the snake, Max? Jon?"

Jon had no idea what the snake could mean, unless— "Was it eating its own tail?"

"It was. That mean something to you?"

"So it's Ouroboros: *another infinity*."

"*Another* life from death," Rabbi Max chipped in.

"And another symbol from ancient Egypt." Fitz's voice boomed from the Volvo's speakers.

Jon paused and imagined the complete image flashing by on a highway billboard. When he had shaken off the chill, he threw in, "Phoenix and Ouroboros. Infinity squared."

"I'm law, not math," said Fitz, "but that sounds about right."

Jon tensed. His exit was coming up, and after that, his meeting with his wife's family. Fear and frustration colored his voice. "So what does it get us?"

If Fitz noticed his tone, he kept it to himself. "I'm not sure. The tattoo artist, Sketch, told Castro that Rochelle asked specifically for that tattoo to be touched up that Friday. In fact, she asked him to touch up the *UV* ink, specifically. I know most people think lawyers are all about book smarts, but we spend a fair amount of time thinking about *mindset*. I want to know why Rochelle drove herself and the boys out of town in the dead of night. Aside from where they are now, that's the biggest mystery to me in this whole disappearance. If we can solve that, I'm convinced we'll know most of what happened, and we'll stand a good chance of finding your wife and sons, Jon."

Jon felt a wave of sadness tinged with anger. Not at Fitz, but at Chelle, whose mindset was often illogical and rarely predictable. Sadness was pointless, of course, the anger unfair, considering her mental illness. He tried desperately to push both emotions to the back of his mind as he turned off Highway 12.

He said, "Mindset. I've thought about that a lot. Chelle's bipolar complicates things, but one thing we can be sure of is Chelle needed plenty of energy to make the lake house trip. I'm not a psychiatrist, but based on experience, I'd say she was having a manic episode. Her thoughts would be quick as lightning and just as dangerous; she'd make decisions in a snap and forget them just as quickly. Did I tell you about the night dress?"

Fitz said, "No."

"It was laid out on the bed, as if Chelle had started to pack and forgot halfway through. A set of Luke's and Paul's pj's were missing from the drawers, plus an overnight bag for each of the boys, but it doesn't seem like Chelle packed anything for herself."

"But she *meant* to," said Rabbi Max. "That's important."

Fitz added, "I couldn't agree more. I'll level with you, Jon. Until we find your family safe and well, there will be two possible narratives for the police. Narrative one is the mentally ill mother who comes off her meds and does something unspeakable to her children. I know you've never believed that narrative, and neither do I. Just look at Castro's discovery. Rochelle was making plans on the day she disappeared. She went to Sketch so he could highlight a symbol of a long life, and of blessing by God—if we've got the horns and the halo right."

Jon remembered Rabbi Max's interpretation: "Life from death" could easily have been the mantra of a disturbed person entering a suicide pact. So did highlighting its symbols. He tucked that thought away as he made a turn onto the winding forest road that would take him to the main gate of the Faith Center.

"What's narrative two?" he asked.

"Sorry?" said Fitz.

Jon didn't really need to ask. The second narrative was the one that placed him as the villain of his family's murder. If the police clung to that one, he wouldn't have an established psychological diagnosis to fall back on.

The car reached the main gate. Jon told Fitz, "Another time. We're here."

"You don't have to do this, Jon," the lawyer said.

Rabbi Max reinforced the advice. "He's right. You don't."

Jon pulled to the side of the road. He was close enough to the gate for the guard there to see him, but not so close they would feel compelled to come over.

"I *do*, actually. For Chelle. And for me."

"Peace be with you, my friend," Fitz said, a strangely affectionate gesture.

The men said their goodbyes and hung up. Jon opened his contacts.

"Who are you calling?" the rabbi asked.

"Phillip," said Jon. "We're his guests. I expect him to meet us in person."

Jon didn't expect speed, and didn't get it. A full twenty minutes passed before Phillip pulled out of the main gate in a black limousine. Jon was surprised; he'd thought Phillip would be driving one of the church's Chryslers. Instead, he had chosen to ride in style.

A man in a black suit stepped out of the limo's front passenger seat and approached the Volvo. He made an exaggerated gesture for opening one door and climbing into another, and Jon left the Volvo where it was and made his way over to the limo. Rabbi Max followed him, but halfway between the two vehicles, he stopped.

Jon looked back. "What's wrong, Rabbi?"

"Nothing. I thought— I'll tell you later." The rabbi

stepped up behind Jon and paused for Jon to climb into the limo.

Phillip sat far back in a seat kitty-corner to the door Jon had used to enter. The seat next to him was taken by a woman Jon had shared a church with for years but never actually got to know. She was small, wiry, and muscular, her auburn hair tied back in a stern ponytail that appeared too tight. Then he remembered that Tasmin Beale's face always wore that pinched expression.

"Thanks for coming, Jon." Phillip spoke first.

"Phillip. Tasmin. This is my friend, Rabbi Sophar."

"Please," said the rabbi, "call me Max."

Beale stared blankly out the limo's window, as if formal introductions were a waste of her time.

Phillip was more gracious. "Any friend of Jon's is welcome, Max," he said.

Jon chose not to comment on the irony. "Are we going straight to the house?"

"We should, I think," said Phillip. "Mom is there, with P. J. She was calm when we left her. You know that won't last."

Jon knew all too well. He had witnessed his share of Lisa's tirades, though he'd never been the target. The Berger children—Rochelle, Phillip, and P. J.—bore the brunt nine times out of ten.

"Let's get this over." Beale finally spoke, her voice a low growl.

"One moment, please, Tasmin." Phillip raised a hand to silence her. "Jon, I don't want you to feel compelled. We really do appreciate you coming. Mom has some ideas about what may have happened to Rochelle she thinks you should hear. Of course, I can't promise you *will* hear them, but I hope so. I think there's a good chance—she has several lucid minutes a day, you know, and they tend to cluster around dinnertime."

"It's all fine. Take me to Lisa—if she has something to say that will help us find Chelle and the boys, I'm all ears."

Phillip nodded and signaled the driver, who executed a full about-turn in three points. As the vehicle pulled through the gate, Jon leaned over to whisper to Rabbi Max. "What was your pause back there?"

The rabbi looked hesitant, then leaned in to say, "I'm sure it's nothing. Only, the man who came to invite us to the limousine . . . for a second there, I could have sworn he was James Earl Ray."

The name had a familiar ring, but it took the rest of the drive for Jon to remember what he'd learned in school about Doctor Martin Luther King Jr.'s alleged assassin. He'd been early middle-aged at the trial, if Jon remembered correctly, and had died an old man. The man who now sat in the front passenger seat of the limo was far too young to have even met Ray in person, let alone to be the dead man. Did Ray have children? Jon couldn't recall. Of course, the more likely explanation for the rabbi's mistake was just that, a mistake, and people looked like other people all the time. Jon had enough to think about, so he put the rabbi's comment out of his mind.

A minute or so later, the limo pulled into the driveway of the Bergers' private house. A huge, imposing, red-brick building, it stood on a hillside level with the top of God's Footstool, the central tower that housed the Church of the Resurrected administration offices. Jon recalled that Pastor Korvus had an office there, as did Phillip and Beale. Or at least, they had the last time Jon visited, many years ago. He wondered if Ezra had picked the site of the house for its view of the tower, or vice versa. He was the sort of man who just couldn't leave work at work. He wore his responsibilities like a stack of hats, never taking one off except to put on another. No wonder the poor man died young.

Jon and Rabbi Max were out of the limo, Beale climbing after them, when the wide, dark-oak door of the house opened. P. J. appeared. It was light outside, but the house had enough of an overhang to leave her framed in shadow.

Concern showed on P. J.'s face. "Where's my brother? Where's Phillip?"

"Here, P. J.," Phillip said. "I'm coming."

As Phillip stepped out from the limo, P. J. went back in the house. The way she hurried from the door told Jon all he needed to know; something was wrong. He rushed past the fretting rabbi and mounted the steps. There were footfalls behind him, but whether they belonged to Beale or Phillip, he couldn't tell.

"What's wrong?" Jon asked P. J. the moment he was inside the house.

She stood in front of him, biting nervously on her hand. She pointed. A pair of gold Mary Janes and the fringes of gray, pin-striped trousers were all Jon could see. He stepped past P. J. and ran down the hall, to where Lisa Berger lay in a lifeless heap. Jon dropped to his knees and saw the old lady was breathing rapidly. He touched her neck, found the pulse.

"Lisa?" Jon said as he counted mentally. When Lisa didn't stir, he spoke to P. J. "She's arrhythmic. When did this happen?"

"A minute ago. She forgot you were coming. I told her—"

Lisa's eyes fluttered open and her cold, boney hand closed tight around Jon's wrist. She was strong for a woman having a heart attack.

"Murderer," said Lisa. The word came out as a breathy hiss, but when she repeated, "Murderer," Jon was sure what he heard. "You killed her. You killed—"

Lisa's voice trailed off as she fell unconscious. Jon had

lost count of the pulse, but he was sure she would live, providing she got help quickly. Hate could make the weak strong, for a while at least. Behind him, he heard Phillip on the phone to 9-1-1.

Jon got to his feet. "Is this why I'm here?" He rounded on P. J. She stared at him. He clarified. "I'm here to be accused of killing my family?"

P. J. didn't answer. She didn't have to. Jon returned to his patient and held the hand of the woman who thought he was a murdering monster.

PART THREE

21

It had been a busy week for Charlie Castro. The meeting with the boss, Doc Edom, and the rabbi had been on Tuesday. He'd met Sketch on Wednesday. Sketch and *Nette*—he couldn't forget that curvy little inkblot.

Sketch's picture of the phoenix hadn't conjured Rochelle "Shay-Shay" Berger-Edom out of thin air, but the boss thought the angle interesting. And when the boss was happy, he gave Castro a long leash. For the past few days, he'd allowed Castro to chase leads around town pushing him in any particular direction and only checking in now and then. That was how Castro preferred it, especially as most of his leads, lately, were about the doc.

The boss believed Doc Edom's innocence, of course. He believed in the innocence of *all* of his clients—until something proved them otherwise. More than once, he'd told Castro it was just part of the job. But Castro's job was different: He never started an investigation with an idea of how it would end. The boss knew his policy and didn't mind, so long as Castro delivered the goods. Which he did, most of the time. On the rare few occasions he had to disappoint the boss, it wasn't his fault. Sometimes, the facts just wouldn't play ball.

Today, they'd put him on the trail of a psychopath gun nut named Murphy Gore. It didn't sit right with Castro that the doc's hospital got shot up just over a week ahead of his wife and kids going AWOL. Two major life events happening back-to-back gave Castro an itch. All the instincts he had been born with, all the cynicism his police training had trained into him, told Castro the events were connected.

He parked the El Camino on the side of a dirt road, next to a patch of dingy woodland. It hurt him to take Betty out on rough terrain, but it hurt him more to be parted from her for too long.

"Don't worry, girl." He patted the steering wheel. "I'll give you a wash and wax as soon as we get home."

Castro rolled down the window. Twenty feet to his left, he saw a section of chain-link fence, the rest of which stretched out of sight in both directions. Satellite pictures of the fence showed it surrounded a field; tax records stated the owner of the field was the United States government. Other records said that the Church of the Resurrected had paid big bucks to purchase, survey, and level the field. Beyond the fence and the neglected scrub stood a circle of broken-down buildings that were all that remained of the church's hard work, a complex that had been known in its heyday as the Youngsport Grace Foundation. Something really heavy had gone down there.

The FBI, or somebody wearing FBI jackets, had raided the place looking for guns or drugs or a bunch of dedicated church-goers about to drink the proverbial Kool-Aid. Castro recalled watching the news on the raid and being disappointed by the lack of commitment from the press. For example: What was the government's beef with the church? Nobody seemed to know—or care. Amateur video showed guys in FBI-branded raincoats rushing the property with rifles and handguns, but nobody had an official line on *why*.

Unofficial explanations, on the other hand, were easy to find, especially on social media and among the conspiracy theory lunatics. They ranged from the usual worries about armed nut jobs setting up a death cult to rumors way out on the fringe.

Castro's personal favorite was that the Second Coming had happened at Youngsport. That meant the videos showed the hit squad on its way to take out the Savior. They'd been bankrolled by the wealthy elite, who were worried about an appearance by Christ tanking their mutual funds. As entertaining as Castro found it, he thought the fact none of the attackers were seen melting to goo, *Raiders of the Lost Ark*–style, argued against it. Few other stories he uncovered were more credible, so he'd come to Youngsport himself to find the truth.

Pulling out a pair of binoculars from Betty's dashboard, Castro zoomed in on the decrepit buildings. It was clear nobody had been near the place since the government took over: The walls were alive with kudzu, moss, and mold, the growth so bad on some buildings they looked like overgrown topiaries from a long-neglected hedge maze. Other buildings were only slightly better off, the best of them being the complex's centerpiece—a four-story oblong with an overhanging roof. It was impressive, if architecturally brutal, and reminded Castro of the famous footage of an immense mushroom cloud blooming over the site of an A-bomb test site.

Castro grimaced. None of the spots he could see through the binoculars was any good for a picnic. He was preparing to fetch the snips from Betty's trunk and get started cutting through the fence when his view of the buildings was blocked by a giant hand.

Startled, he pulled the binoculars away from his eyes

and saw a black-haired beauty with tense muscles and short sleeves glaring at him. She clenched the hand into a fist and drew it back like she meant to punch him in the mouth.

"Whoa, chicky!" Castro raised his hand to protect his face. "Be nice, okay? This job don't come with dental."

The woman glowered, and Castro desperately searched his memory for the name for the pretty, lean face and dark, brooding eyes. He got the impression the woman was something professional, which she confirmed as much by pulling out her badge.

"Cavallo," she growled. "Austin PD. You're Castro. I've heard about your car." She wrinkled her nose at his beloved El Camino.

Castro grinned. "My Betty, she's famous. That's so cool."

Cavallo relaxed a tad. "What are you doing in Youngsport, Castro? It's outside your usual hunting grounds. No ambulances to chase here."

"I could ask you the same question, Detective."

Cavallo stood to her full height, several sinches taller than Castro when standing. She crossed her arms over breasts that had a nice, plump shape but weren't in the same league as Nette's deliciously inked bosom. She grimaced at the PI, as though she'd smelled something she didn't like.

At last, she spoke. "We're on the same side, Castro, and I've got the badge. I need to know what you're doing here."

"Detective Danielle Cavallo, Missing Persons, Austin PD. I do my homework too." Castro gave her a sardonic smile.

Cavallo let her shoulders relax some. "Call me Dani. Now spill."

So, Castro spilled, and Cavallo listened quietly as he explained what had brought him to the dusty road outside the former Youngsport Grace Foundation, an abandoned satellite complex of the Church of the Resurrected. The story wasn't long, and it started with Murphy Gore.

"I had this idea about the hospital shooter," Castro told the cop. "He popped up so close to the Berger-Edom disappearance, I thought there had to be a connection. So I asked the doc, and he knew Gore as the father of a patient who died—a little girl. That was it, no bigger picture, at least none the doc could think of. But the internet? Always plenty of imagination there. It took me about fifty minutes to find a connection between Edom and Gore that predated the girl in the hospital."

Cavallo interrupted, arms still crossed. "Let me guess. They were both members of the Church of the Resurrected."

"Maybe," said Castro. He felt annoyed and a little suspicious of the cop. It hadn't been easy digging the dirt on Gore. Halfway up the digital trail, Castro had become sure someone had put in a lot of work to scrub it clean. Who might be responsible for that was a mystery, and a possible solution was now staring him in the face. He watched the wind ruffle Cavallo's coal-black hair as he unbuckled his seat belt and stepped out of Betty.

Cavallo took a step back. "This place." She nodded toward the cluster of old buildings. "Youngsport. Gore was employed here."

"Was he?"

"You know he was. Why else would you come?"

"It seems you know the story already."

"I did my research, like you." There was a tone of one-upmanship to the cop's voice Castro didn't much care for. He would let it slide—for now. "Gore was a member of Edom's church, though they never crossed paths. Did you know he was also a member of the Texas Cross Guard?"

"Never heard of 'em."

"No? Then I've got one over on you. Not that it means much. The Guard was formed by another ex-member of the church, and he poached a lot of members away, most of them men who did time. Gore's record is clean, aside from being on-site for the FBI raid. He joined the Cross Guard years ago, but it looks like he didn't stick around. They've got a commune on a ranch outside Austin. It's adults only, strictly no kids on account of all the pedophiles living there. I think they kicked Gore out after his lady got pregnant."

"Interesting." Castro was impressed. He took a few seconds to crack his back and roll his shoulders, working out kinks from the road, and then pointed at the derelict buildings. "The Youngsport Grace Foundation. What a name, eh? Sounds like a drug outreach program to me. I knew Gore worked security and that he was here for the raid. Do you know about the abandoned civil case?"

It was Cavallo's turn to show surprise.

Castro grinned. "There were papers I found from a case that never made it to trial. Don't ask about my source. The upshot is, six upstanding members of the Church of the Resurrected died in the raid. Gore was an eyewitness to at least one death."

"What happened to the case?"

"It was settled and sealed."

"With six dead. How much did that cost?"

"I'd like to know that too. Anyway, I read enough to boost my interest in Gore's time in security. I came up here to see if I could spot anything illuminating. From a distance, naturally. If I went past that fence, Detective, that would be trespassing, and I would never break the law."

That appeared to break through Cavallo's icy defenses. She smiled with lips that were made for the job, and suddenly, Castro's day seemed several degrees warmer and a good deal brighter. She drew something out of her back pocket. It was a flashlight.

"I had a similar thought." That smile again. "And fortunately, I've got a cousin with the park service up here.

I had him let me in the front gate. That was two hours ago, give or take. So I can save you some time. There's nothing here, Castro. This place is a dump. Some of the doors are off their hinges, and that's pretty much it. I had a good look. There's nothing but cobwebs, snakes, and moldy furniture. No filing cabinets, no books, no computers. No records I can find of any kind—the place was stripped clean after the raid. I've been walking off the disappointment and waiting for my cousin to come back to lock the gate." She punched her leg, swore. "I should have known. My lieutenant said— Never mind. Point is, I'm done chasing shadows. If you take my advice, you will be too."

Castro tucked his hands in the pocket of his hoodie. It was the same one he'd worn to meet Edom. The PI liked the color because it reminded him of a dog he used to have, an old hunting dog. "Thanks for the advice, Detective."

She cocked her head; her smile oozed skepticism. "Like you're going to take it. Well, it's on you if you go snooping around in there."

Castro watched the cop walk back up the dirt road and toward the gate he hadn't thought to check when he arrived—he'd simply assumed it would be locked. When she reached a fork in the road, she turned back briefly to wave before finally disappearing from sight. Castro counted a full a minute to make sure she was well and truly gone before opening up Betty's trunk. A thick, brown tarp was inside. He folded it aside to reveal his duffel.

There were ways onto the Youngsport field that didn't involve bolt cutters, but Castro felt too achy to try any of them, so he'd packed a pair. He had gloves in the duffel, too, leather on the outside and steel mesh within, that would help him bend the fence's links. There was a length of rope in the duffel, a face mask, his favorite flashlight, a lock-pick set, and several technical odds and ends that would allow him to probe the walls for a hidden safe. He reckoned that was something Cavallo wouldn't think to check for; she'd only brought a flashlight, for heaven's sakes. Castro had spent some time on the other side of the law. Not much, true, but enough to think like they did.

It was his brief, dangerous time knocking over houses that had taught Castro the value of the last piece of gear in his duffel: He checked the safety on his sawn-off shotgun— he didn't want the thing going off while he was jogging across the field. Done, Castro rezipped the bag, swung it over his shoulder, and put a hand up to close Betty's trunk.

That was when he heard the snap, like someone had stepped on a twig—deliberately, he guessed.

For an instant, Castro thought Cavallo had come back. After all, she'd snuck up on him before, while he was distracted.

Slowly, the PI eased his free hand to the duffel's zipper. If he could reach the shotgun in time . . .

Something hit him. Hard.

The PI went sprawling and a heavy body fell on top of him, a man. With a huge hand at the back of Castro's skull, he shoved his head down, trying to make him eat dirt.

Castro didn't eat dirt, though. Instead, he aimed an elbow at what he hoped was his assailant's spleen and jabbed the arm upward. The pained grunt told him he'd hit his mark, and Castro rolled onto his back and kicked out at his attacker, who sprang away.

Four men stood in a loose circle around him. The one he'd elbowed was younger than the others and had a lot of doughy fat, which added to his formidable bulk. The others were as big or bigger than him, and every bit as dangerous. Castro knew their leader instantly: He was thick at the shoulders and narrow everywhere else, his head was shaved smooth, and he was missing his left ear. The scars on that side of his face showed the ear had been lost in a fight.

"You're Weaver, right?" Castro gasped for air. "*Bill*

Weaver. You do security at the church. Ain't you out of your territory?"

Weaver pointed at the old buildings on the other side of the fence.

"Got it," said Castro. "You follow me up here?"

"No," Weaver said in a voice that was almost a whisper, "that's the funny part. We followed the cop. You showing up is a bonus. We were nervous about doing a cop."

"She found nothing." Castro eyed the big man warily; this situation was going to take some real smooth talking to get out of.

"I know." Weaver grimaced.

"I could find nothing too."

Weaver shook his head.

The duffel had fallen between Weaver and Castro. The PI man shifted his weight. He would fake a lunge at Doughboy, he decided, and go for the bag. Weaver would catch him, but maybe, just maybe, he could arm himself faster than the killer could twist his neck. It would help if he could knock Weaver off his guard.

"You know," Castro said, "for such big guys, you sure are quiet. I don't guess you'd like it if I shouted for help. I don't guess you'd want the cop to hear."

"She can hear," Weaver said patiently. "Or she can live."

At that point, Charlie Castro saw his future: It was short. It was ugly. But it did pose a certain nobility. "Yeah," he said. "I see how it is."

In an instant, he feinted at the fat boy and dove at the duffel. His fingers wrapped the straps . . .

Weaver laughed softly as he jerked the bag away and out of Castro's grasp.

"Well," he said, listening with some amusement to the rattle of sharp, heavy objects within the bag. "What's in here, I wonder? Darrin, get me a gag. I want to take my time finding out."

21

All the way home from the hospital, the Uber driver regaled Jon with stories of life in Cape Town. Back home, apparently, he was a surgeon's assistant, though some of the tasks he described should have been carried out by the surgeon himself, in Jon's opinion. But, surgeon or assistant, his skills were being wasted in the States.

"I tell the man, I tell him, these hands save lives," the driver went on. "They save men. They save women. They have felt the warmth of a beating heart, and they have done more. Once, there is a woman. She is choking. I cut at the neck for the tube. To open the cut, I use the teaspoon handle." He demonstrated, moving his thumb gently downward in the air while he steered the minivan. "I run the tube. She breathes! I save her life. But here, it means nothing. Here I drive the van, my own van, for wages that would keep a beggar on the street. If not for the tips . . ." He made a dismissive gesture.

Jon nodded, but it was an effort to feel sympathy. Not that the driver's story was unmoving—it reminded him of an article he'd read back in medical school, about Hamilton Naki, a Black South African who was assistant to a White surgeon. Naki's work with animals paved the way for human heart transplants, but because of apartheid, his contribution to medicine went unacknowledged until much later in his life. The driver resembled Naki, and Jon understood the frustration.

Still, the driver had his health and a family back home; Jon would have swapped lives with him in an instant. His right arm burned, as it had since his mother-in-law accused him of killing Chelle and the boys. Based on the feeling alone, Jon would have sworn his extensor digitorum was roasting on the bone, but if that were true, his nerves would long ago have melted away to nothing. Instead, they sizzled as thought over an open flame, which showed no signs of guttering. The pain was too much for him to turn a door handle, let alone a steering wheel, and so Uber was a godsend.

"This is you, yes?" The driver slowed the minivan. "A nice neighborhood."

"Thanks," said Jon. "You can pull up the drive."

The driver did as asked, and Jon got out of the car and reached into his left pocket for his wallet. He fished out a twenty-dollar bill and handed it through the open window; he'd paid in advance on the cell phone app, of course, but wanted to give the guy a little more money that Uber wouldn't skim its percentage from. The effort of holding the bill with his right hand was enough to make Jon's forehead break out in sweat.

"You don't look so good, Doctor." The driver was genuinely concerned. "Probably a virus. Try honey and mint tea. Drink it hot. Good for the lungs." He slapped himself across the chest with vigor to emphasize the point.

Jon smiled to cover his wince.

The car, some breed of Subaru Jon couldn't remember

seeing before, reversed down the driveway and drove off down the street. Jon turned and approached the front door. The double garage was open and Jon saw his ancient Volvo parked in its spot, but his son Simon's sporty blue Honda was missing. In his son's car's place sat a silver Mustang. It wasn't a new model and wasn't old enough to be called vintage. Jon approached the door and pushed the button for the intercom.

"Cass? Cass, if you're there, let me in."

He hoped his daughter was inside. His keys were in his right-hand pocket, and the anticipation of getting them out was almost worse than his pain. Jon gritted his teeth. The stress, the pain, the worry—it was all so frustrating, it made him furious. He hadn't felt that helpless since he was a little kid.

The deadbolt thudded and the door flew open. Jon jolted with surprise and clutched his burning arm in a protective reflex. The woman who opened the door wasn't his daughter. She was tall, with long, jet-black hair and cool, dark eyes. The slacks and button-down shirt she had on looked like a uniform.

She said, "Welcome home, Doctor Edom."

Jon took a moment to connect the voice, which he knew, with the woman he had never met in person. At last, the name came to him.

"Detective Cavallo."

"You have news?"

"I have *questions*, Doctor. Won't you come in?"

The detective stepped aside so Jon could enter his own home. Jon stayed put. His phone conversations with the cop hadn't been friendly, and having her at his house unannounced felt like a bad omen.

She stuck a hand on her hip. "Sorry, it's your house, Dr. Edom. If you want to have our talk in the doorway, we can."

What Jon wanted to do was to leave, or to make Cavallo

leave. Neither course of action seemed likely, though. Sensibly, Jon knew it would be good for him to have the detective on his side, so he gave a compliant shrug that awoke the aches in his arm and his stomach, where he felt the ulcer forming, and stepped inside.

The hallway past Cavallo led to the combined kitchen, dining room, and living area. He started along it, leaving her to shut the door.

"Cass?" he yelled.

"In the kitchen!" John's daughter shouted back.

Jon passed through the hallway in time to see Cass straighten up from pulling a pan out of the oven. The smell of fresh chocolate chip cookies hung sweet, sickly, in the air. Coffee, too. A slim man with a thin, Clark Gable mustache sat at the counter. He held a steaming mug in his hand. His face was leathery in color, texture, and the way it crinkled with every expression. A black leather jacket lay on one of the breakfast bar stools. Jon guessed it belonged to Cavallo, as the older man wore a dark-blue three-piece suit.

"Afternoon." The stranger tipped the coffee mug in greeting.

Jon didn't answer; he figured the older guy was Cavallo's partner—they always traveled in pairs. He crossed the room to stand as close to Cass as the pan allowed.

"Are these people bothering you, baby?"

"No, Dad." Cass's tone was light. "They're detectives. They're going to find Mom, Luke, and Paul."

Jon had to squeeze his eyes shut against his frustration. Chelle and the boys had been gone for ten days, and for all that time, the police had hovered around the fringes of his life, harassing his coworkers, and making vague threats and accusations over the phone. He wanted to tell Cass not to be fooled by them. Instead, said, "I know they are, baby."

The stranger set his mug on the counter and stuck out a hand. "Saul Troyer, Dani's partner. It's good to finally meet you, Doctor Edom." His voice had the unmistakable rasp of a lifelong smoker.

Jon shook the hand. "Detective Troyer."

Cavallo stood at the end of the hall, at the junction of the carpet and the hardwood floor, arms folded. "I guess you're wondering why we've taken so long to come see you in person, Doctor."

"You think?" Jon instantly regretted the sarcasm. It made Cass pause halfway through removing her oven mitts to stare at him, no doubt puzzled that her typically polite father was being so rude.

"Dad?" Cass frowned at him.

"It's all right," said Cavallo. "Your father has every right to be angry. We should have visited sooner. But there's a lot of legwork in a situation like this, and Detective Troyer and I have done a lot of running around."

"Is that what you call it?" Jon snapped. "*Running around.*" He knew he ought to watch his mouth, but the pain in his arm and gut was too urgent for niceties. "My colleague, Rohan Majumdar, told me the questions you've been asking. No wonder the nurses give me odd looks now. Aren't you people supposed to presume a man innocent until proven guilty? Especially one who's just lost his wife and sons."

Jon saw the hurt his words caused on Cass's face and felt a new stab from deep in his gut. He didn't want to burden her with it all; he wanted his daughter to believe her mother and brothers were coming home. He wanted to believe it too.

"The questions we've asked were routine in a case such as this, Doctor," insisted Cavallo. She left the hall and crossed the floor to join her partner. "They're certainly nothing an innocent man should take personally."

Jon glanced over at Cass, who shot a warning with her eyes. He sighed. "I know you're just doing your jobs. It's just, after Chelle disappeared, work become a haven for me. Lately, it's not."

Cass set the loaded plate of cookies in front of Troyer. The clatter made Jon and Cavallo jump. Cavallo slid into the empty stool at the counter. She took a cookie between thumb and forefinger but didn't bite.

"That's unfortunate," the detective said. "Please understand. In a case like this, you have to watch for patterns. And patterns are found in day-to-day life. So . . . we've being asking questions of your workmates and friends. We've been meticulous, and some people don't like that. They misunderstand it as accusations. They feel that if police are asking questions about somebody, that person must have a secret. That's wrong, of course, but I assure you, Doctor Edom, it is necessary. It's how our job is done."

Jon didn't much appreciate the job they were doing but held back from saying so.

Cavallo watched for his reaction. When he didn't give one, she raised an eyebrow. "If you don't believe me, you can ask Mister Castro."

The name caught Jon off guard. What did the little PI with the bulldog lip have to do with the police? Then he remembered what Jim Fitzgerald had told him: Castro was ex–Austin PD. Cavallo would know him, or know *of* him, at least.

He said, "I'll make sure to do that, the next time he checks in."

"Please do," said Cavallo.

Cass shot her father another warning. She lifted the plate to offer him a cookie. He declined. With a shrug, she set the plate back down in front of Detective Troyer, who scooped up a cookie and began nibbling around its edge.

"Detective Cavallo and I have a couple of new questions for you, Doctor," Troyer said between nibbles. "Do you want to talk here or in private?"

Cass tipped her spatula upright, as if staking her claim on her father. "There's no need for secrecy. Dad doesn't keep anything from me."

It was the sort of thing a trusting child would say, but still mostly true. But Jon saw the detectives wanted to speak to him alone. He touched Cass on the shoulder and said quietly, "Don't take it personally, baby. Some things are better said in private."

Jon saw his daughter frown, and for a moment, he saw the little girl she had once been. Always older than her years and too eager to grow up, she was always annoyed whenever adults cut her out of conversation. At last, she said, "I'll be in my room if you need me, okay?"

"Okay." Jon squeezed her shoulder.

Cass set aside the spatula and untied her apron strings. She left through the front hallway, her footfalls sounding on the stairs.

"Nice kid." Troyer took another bite of cookie.

Cavallo seemed to have forgotten the cookie she was holding. She gave it a sniff before returning it to the plate.

"Watching your figure, Detective?" said Jon.

"I had a long drive this morning," she said. "I'm still sick from the road."

Jon turned away for a moment, looking at the mugs Cass had laid out. "I guess you don't want coffee?"

"No, thanks," said Cavallo. "Not one of the tribe."

"Excuse me?" said Jon, turning back. In his mind, "tribe" meant one of the twelve tribes of Israel—or could she be referring to her Native American heritage? Then again, a dose of anti-Semitism would explain Cavallo's hostility toward him.

Troyer waved a hand. "Coffee drinkers, Doctor. She

means coffee drinkers. It's a thing we do. She says, 'Not one of the tribe.' I say, 'Eight-billion strong' and take a sip. Sometimes we fight about how many people drink smoothies or tea. I say they're in denial, she says Folgers owes me a kickback. It's silly, I know, but it gives us something to fight about besides my love life."

"God knows we need the break from that." Cavallo rolled her eyes.

Jon frowned. "The *coffee* tribe. Right. I'd have to get the blender down for smoothies, so maybe it's better if we just get on with your questions."

Cavallo's smile was tight. "Sounds good to me."

She produced a folded piece of paper from her pocket, along with a pen and a small notepad. Jon rubbed his arm as she unfolded the paper.

Cavallo pushed the paper across the counter. "First question, Doctor Edom. Can you explain this?"

The paper showed a table of numbers. There were six rows, four columns. The first column in each row showed a set of four numbers. Each number in the set was separated from the others by a period. The second column showed a time and a date in a computer-friendly format. The third column showed different times, but the same date as the second column of the same row. The fourth column showed a second set of four numbers delineated by periods. Most of the sets in this last column were identical, unlike the sets in the first column, which were all unique. Jon thought the number in the flanking columns had something to do with the internet, but beyond that, he was mystified.

He said, "I have no idea what that is."

Cavallo pointed at the paper. "This first column, here. This is a list of IP addresses. Do you know what an IP address is, Doctor?"

"I think so. It's what a computer looks up when you type something dot-com."

"It's a computer's unique address, but that's a good enough definition for our purposes," said Cavallo.

Troyer made a swooshing gesture over his head, as if that was where the technical talk went for him.

"As it happens," Cavallo continued, "this is a list of IP addresses, with times of first and last access, that you visited, Doctor." She pointed at the fourth column. "This is the IP of the device that made the request. See? This one is your phone. The third down is the desktop computer in your office at the Violet Crown Medical Center."

"My *shared* office, you mean," Jon corrected.

"Right, sorry. We can ignore that one for now. But leaving it out, we're left with five devices we're pretty sure are used only by you."

"Fine. So, this is my internet history?"

"Part of it. The part where we found searches for a particular term. Do you know what term that is?"

Jon didn't dignify the question with an answer.

"Domestic homicide. These are searches you made for *domestic homicide*, Doctor Edom."

The pain in Jon's arm fell away; he was sure it would have surged if the situation had been less susceptible to a ready explanation. But under the circumstances, the detectives' confusion came as a relief to him.

"It's for a paper I was working on," he explained. "I've been researching domestic homicides carried out by players of *NeverEnd*. Do you know the game?"

Cavallo shared a glance with her partner. Troyer crunched loudly into a cookie. "I do."

Jon pointed to the first date on the printout. "This is the day after the shooting at the Crown. On that same day, I saw two teenage cosplayers who'd tried to kill each other. I operated on one, I saw the other in recovery." He then pointed at a date in the fourth row. "This is the day I saw a pair of grown-assed adults get into a fistfight while playing characters from *NeverEnd*. Can you understand what that meant to me?"

When Cavallo kept silent, Troyer said, "Why don't you tell us, Dr. Edom?"

Jon was bending over the counter, like a chess player over a board. "I'm a doctor, Detectives. I save lives. And my wife was a programmer on the game that's caused more domestic violence in this country than all the unrest of the past hundred years. It hurts me. It *haunts* me. But it's put me in a unique position to study the surge, to try to understand it, to hopefully end it before more people get hurt. *That's* what those searches were about. *Ending* domestic homicides, or at least reducing their numbers to what they were before the *NeverEnd* Effect."

Cavallo's stony face flexed, and the smile she turned on Jon was tight, the clench of her jaw muscles adding animation. She pressed her palm flat to the counter.

"*NeverEnd* Effect? That's amazing, Doctor. You're already a hero, and now we find you're on a quest to cure the plague that's killing children. And of course, in the twenty-first century, that plague happens to be a video game."

"You don't believe me?"

"About the surge in violence? Of course I do—I'm a cop. We hear about it every day from our colleagues on the beat. I don't know if it's down to *NeverEnd*, but I've heard theories that were crazier. It's interesting what you said about your wife, that she was the programmer. I'd say that makes her responsible, doesn't it? I wonder if someone thought justice would be served if she disappeared."

"Unbelievable." The pain blazed hot in Jon's arm; he cradled the aching limb. "I didn't kill my wife because of a job she did, Detective Cavallo. I can't begin to tell you everything wrong with that idea."

Troyer started to speak, but Cavallo stopped him with a

firm hand. "You're jumping to conclusions, Doctor. I didn't say *you* killed your wife. And if you did have something to do with the disappearance, I think her old job is an unlikely motive. It's just funny you mentioned that job at all. It just so happens there's another piece of search history I found interesting. I don't have a printout of this part, but . . ."

Cavallo set the notepad aside and unclipped a phone from her belt. After unlocking the cell she tapped at the screen then held it up for Jon to see.

"Do you recognize these dates, Doctor?"

Jon squinted at the tiny numbers on the screen. There were four rows of internet addresses and dates, arranged in a table like the one on the printout. Only, on this table, the number sets in the first column were identical. Those in the last column were also a match to each other. So far as Jon remembered, he had seen neither number in the previous table.

Some of the dates, however, *were* familiar.

"Well, Doctor?" said Cavallo.

"That oldest date, it's the day after the hospital shooting. The most recent is the Friday of the conference."

"The Friday you last your saw your wife and sons, right?"

The fire in Jon's arm could have smelted iron. His ulcer gave a sympathetic flare.

"Yes."

"Are you okay, Doc?" asked Troyer. He set the remains of his cookie on the counter and walked around it to offer Jon an arm.

Jon pulled away.

Cavallo said, "He's fine. Do you recognize the sender's address in the last column, Jon?"

"Sender?" Jon paused to fight a wave of nausea. "What sender?"

"These are emails, Doctor. The number in the last

column is an IP assigned to your wife's laptop. The IP in the first column belongs to an encrypted email server. We don't know the contents of the emails, but thanks to a lot of legwork and a court order, we know the recipient. What do you know about a colleague of your wife's, Vivek Singh?"

"Vivek? We're friends. I . . . ah!"

The ground seemed to shift, and the next thing Jon knew, he was sitting on the floor of the kitchen, back pressed to the dishwasher, a shooting pain in his ass. The pain that had knocked him off his feet had gone. He couldn't even remember it as pain, only as an overpowering wave of sensation that had dragged him under.

Troyer knelt at his side. "Doctor Edom?"

"I'm fine. Touch of vertigo. Give me a moment."

Detective Cavallo didn't move to check on Jon. Instead, she sat stone-still on the stool watching him like a hawk.

"You said you're friends with Mister Singh," she said. "How would you categorize your wife's relationship with him?"

"Dani," said Troyer. "We've got a sick man here."

"It's all right," said Jon. "I'll answer. They worked together. That's all I know."

"Are you sure about that, Dr. Edom?" said Cavallo.

Cass reappeared in the hallway and ran across the room. "God, what happened, Dad?"

"I'm fine, Cass." Jon struggled to pick himself up. Cass and Troyer each took an arm to help, but Jon found he didn't need it. His mind had drawn a curtain on the arm pain, the ulcer, and the vertigo, and he somehow felt stronger than he had before Cavello's interrogation. It was like his body had decided it was time for a break from pain—the time had arrived to act. He told the detectives, "I'm afraid the rest of your questions will have to wait. I just remembered an appointment."

Cavallo looked doubtful. "Is that so?"

"It is." Jon looked defiant.

Dani gave her partner a curt nod, collected her jacket, and left the room. Troyer tugged at Jon's arm, as though testing that he could stand, before he followed on. He grabbed a second cookie from the tray as he went out.

Once the cops were gone, Cass said, "Let's get you to a seat, Dad."

"Let's not." Jon offered a reassuring smile. "I'm fine. Really. I'm actually going out in a minute."

"But you just got home."

"I won't be gone long. We can have a late lunch when I get back, okay?"

Cass started to protest, but the strength her father displayed appeared to change her mind. "What's gotten into you?"

"I don't know." Jon was honest. "An idea, I guess. Where's your brother gone, by the way?"

"Simon? He ditched me an hour ago." Cass's eyes widened. "Do you remember Ximena Ibarra?"

An image of too-tight jeans and low-cut, frilly blouses flashed through Jon's mind. "*Bonita* Ximena? Don't tell me she picked up the phone."

"Simon called, she answered. God only knows why."

Jon turned to face Cass an instant before the significance of her words hit. It didn't take God to guess why Simon's ex-girlfriend had taken pity on him. He'd just lost his mother and his two baby brothers. Cass's eyes overflowed with tears, Jon's likewise, and the two held each other, crying, in the kitchen that held so many memories.

22

"Ow!" Ximena yelped as Simon smacked the bridge of his nose into hers.

He pulled back a little; Ximena breathed in.

"Sorry, babe." Simon tried to kiss her again. She shoved him away with strength that surprised him.

"Babe? Who the hell is *babe*?"

Stumbling backward, Simon tripped over a chair. He fell flat on his back, softening the impact by slapping the thin rug that covered most of the laminate floor in Ximena's bedroom with his left arm. The jarring pain was no big deal; it didn't bother him as much as the ache in his groin.

"Queen!" He got to his knees. "Empress!"

Ximena twirled. She wore jeans so tight they could bounce a flung quarter, and a white satin top that would have hung like a sack on most girls. On Ximena, however, it clung to her voluptuous figure and swelled and curled like waves on the ocean.

"Better," she said. "*Much* better. But isn't there something more magnificent than empress?"

Simon tucked in his chin. "Goddess? Venus. Bonita

Ximena, the Venus of Austin."

She bent over to pat his head. The shimmery top clung like a second skin to her generous, round bust and washboard belly.

"It'll do," she told him.

Simon prayed silently: *Say something dirty. Say something dirty.* He wasn't asking God, though. Mom and Dad did the God thing, and Cass sometimes too. Simon was more practical: He cut out the middleman and prayed directly to the person he wanted something from. There were times it worked and times it didn't. So far as he could tell, all the prayers to God had the same track record.

This time, sadly, the prayer didn't work.

Ximena flopped her perfect, denim-clad backside onto the bed and patted the quilt. Her demeanor remained quite prim, which was fine by Simon. The offer was awesome enough. He crawled to the bed and sprang up beside her. He closed his eyes and leaned in for a kiss. But none came.

Simon opened his eyes to see Ximena staring intently into his face. Her lips trembled, there were tears in her eyes.

"Not this again," Simon groaned.

Ximena turned her face away. "Sorry."

"What is it this time?"

"It's just, I couldn't help think . . ."

"What?"

"You look like your mom, okay? You know you look like your mom. Just now, when I saw your face, I thought of her."

Great, thought Simon. *The missing mom. Mood-killer number one.* Of course, Mom and his brothers were the reasons he was with Ximena now, so he tried not to be too resentful. He couldn't remember every detail of his breakup with Ximena— it had happened five months before he started at UT Arlington. What he did recall, though, was the screaming, fingernails, and the names of at least two, maybe three other girls getting tossed around. Ximena had sworn never to speak to Simon again, but just the mention he was back in town and she'd invited him straight over. If only he could get her to forget why he was back for five minutes straight, he'd get what he came for.

"Babe," he whispered against the soft, fragrant skin of her neck. "*Venus*. I missed you so much."

Ximena held him, and he caressed the back of the satiny top, counting the seconds he figured he had to let pass before going in for a kiss again. Was ten enough? Mentally, Simon counted: *ten, nine, eight* . . .

Ximena shoved him away, gentler this time.

"What do you think happened to them, Simon? I mean, do you think they'll come back? Your mother and your brothers . . . I can't imagine. If I lost my family, I don't know what I'd do."

Simon stood up, conscious of the insistent bulge in his jeans. Ximena was crying hard; tears threaded their way through the cracks in her makeup. This wasn't going the way he wanted at all.

"I missed you," he repeated. He couldn't think of what else to say.

A knock sounded on the door. The handle rattled.

"Ximena! Do you have a boy in there?"

It was Julio Ibarras, Ximena's hot-headed father.

"*Dios mío*," Ximena mumbled to Simon. She then marched angrily to the door, threw it open, and shoved Julio. At least Simon wasn't the only guy she got rough with.

Simon lay back on the bed and listened to the Ibarrases debate in Spanish. He knew exactly two words of their language, *te amo*, so he could only imagine what they were saying. Probably Ximena was telling Papa she was a grown woman and it was *her* business who she entertained in her bedroom; the argument was as old as Simon and Ximena's relationship, probably older.

Parents expected their kids to stay kids. That much was universal. Mom had always done her best to make Simon feel like a child. The rest of the Edom family was no better—even Cass treated him like her little brother, which was stupid, since he was twenty minutes older. Mind you, their little brothers had come along at the perfect time: Mom and Dad had been so busy with babies instead of harassing Simon about his partying, drinking, and countless flings with countless girls. Everything had been so much easier with Mom and Dad distracted. It was only within the past year they'd started paying attention to him again. UTA should have fixed that, but it hadn't. Poor Simon barely got to have any fun at all.

The past week had been better, though. Ximena wasn't his first pity lay; the missing family routine had worked on a sweet, dumb blonde thing from his chemistry class, for one. There were other girls he wanted to try his tale of woe on too, once he figured out which of them were the least likely to talk to the others. Still, none of those girls was Ximena. If he couldn't make her move on from their past and give him what he wanted, he would feel *incomplete*, no matter what happened with the other girls.

Julio burst past his daughter and into the room, breaking Simon's train of thought. Ximena followed. The argument was over, and she had won—Simon could tell as much by Julio's flushed face. The little man looked disappointedly at him, shook his head, and rushed back out.

"God," Ximena groaned as she shut her door and locked it. "He gets me *so* mad. You are *so* getting lucky tonight, Simon Edom." She turned to him. "What were you going to do, *fight* my father?"

Simon wondered why she would think that. He was about to ask when an ache in his fingers told him he was making fists. He shook them out and stared at his palms.

"I've got your back, Venus," he said. "Always."

Ximena came to him, clasping his hands in hers.

"Kiss me. Before Papa comes back with an ax."

Finally, thought Simon, and pulled her warm, supple body to his in a lover's embrace.

23

Castro's phone when straight to voicemail. Jon prodded at the hang-up button on his steering wheel and told his phone to call Rabbi Max.

After three rings, the rabbi answered. "No dice, Jon?"

"Good guess."

"Fitz couldn't get an answer either, and he signs the man's checks."

"Where does that leave us?"

"You tell me, Jon."

Jon checked his GPS; he was a minute away from his destination.

"I honestly don't know, Rabbi."

"Try not to worry. There'll be a perfectly plausible reason for Castro's radio silence. I'm at temple. Can you pick me up? We'll talk, have lunch."

Jon was tempted by the offer to let his troubles rest but knew he couldn't afford the time. Detective Cavallo was on the hunt and had him firmly in her crosshairs. He had to do everything in his power to make sure she chased the right prey.

"You're a good friend. A true friend. But I can't see you right now."

"Jon?"

"I can't explain. Let's just say, there are some things a man has to do for himself."

Jon hung up before the rabbi's inevitable objection—something wise, carefully considered, and probably in Hebrew. He knew it likely would have him change course. The surge of adrenaline had made him feel invincible, which was good, as testing his strength was exactly what Jon Edom had in mind.

The building in downtown Austin that housed Endless Loop Games was comprised of ultramodern curves and angular projections that mostly went nowhere but looked like they gave amazing views. A sort of ribbon in bronze had been wrapped around the building, touching two corners on the ground story and two corners on the fifth floor. Seen from the street, the sinuous line showed a twist in the middle to suggest a Möbius strip—hardly subtle at all. As if that weren't enough to make the company name stick in everyone's mind, Endless Loop used up the rest of the full city block it occupied as a parking lot in the shape of an hourglass, minus the flat top and bottom. Brass-colored bricks outlined the lot's edge, while the interior was tarred black and marked with clean, white lines. From above, the design made the mathematical symbol for infinity, another take on the Möbius strip.

As Jon turned off the road and skirted the lot, he saw a group of protesters blocking the main building's front door. There were somewhere between thirty and fifty people as far as he could discern, about half of whom held aloft signs Jon couldn't make out. At first, he thought it was the distance that made the letters appear strange, but the closer he got, the more convinced he was they weren't any letters he knew: They looked more like Nordic runes.

A few of the protesters turned to watch the Volvo pull up. Jon had planned to let the car idle at the curb, but with so many people around, he switched off the ignition and locked the door behind him.

A protester approached him at once. "Excuse me," he said brusquely, "can you park somewhere else? We're expecting the media."

The speaker was tall and appeared somewhat emaciated. He had a bald head and gray, speckled beard, but from the smoothness of his skin, Jon guessed his signs of aging were premature. Peering closer, Jon realized the man was actually wearing a fake beard. The baldness was genuine enough, but what few lines there were on his face had been put there with makeup.

The sign the man held showed a single runic letter, painted to look like a green glow emanating from carved stone. It was clear the sign had been professionally printed; it definitely did not resemble the handmade signs Jon expected to see at a protest.

Jon gestured at the other protesters. "What's this about?"

The protester frowned. "What's what about?"

"Your protest," said Jon. "What are you protesting about?"

The man, and several others within earshot, broke out in derisive laughter.

"This isn't a protest, dude," fake-beard man told Jon with a smirk. "It's a product launch."

So saying, he spun his sign around and held it out for Jon to scrutinize. A smaller version of the glowing rune-thing was in the middle, and above it was a date almost a month ahead. Under the rune was the phrase, "The Backlash Begins!" Jon read "*NeverEnd* and all associated properties © Endless Loop Games, Ltd." in small print at the bottom of the sign. He shook his head in disgust.

"It's a media stunt? Anything for a buck, right?"

The fake protester shrugged. "Forty bucks, lunch, and the chance to be on TV—can't say no to that. Are you going to move your car or what?"

Rage welled up inside Jon's chest like lightning crackling up from his stomach to electrify his muscles. "Tell you what," he growled, fighting the urge to shove his fist down the man's throat. He thrust his key fob at the fake protester's chest instead. "How about you move the damn thing for me?"

Ducking his head, Jon pushed past the man, who juggled the fob as if he'd never seen a car key before. The mob of forty-dollar-a-day extras parted like the Red Sea to allow Jon through, and it was only when Jon reached the door that he had to stop.

A burly security guard in a dark-blue uniform and important-looking hat stepped up to meet him. "You part of this thing?"

Jon took a deep breath and spoke calmly. "No. I'm here to see Vivek Singh." His voice sounded shaky in his own ears, but the guard didn't appear to notice. He gestured toward reception.

"Check in at the desk."

With a nod, Jon entered the reception area with his back straight and heart pounding. As the oversized glass doors swished shut at his back, he had an overwhelming sensation of déjà vu.

Very little had changed since the last time he'd visited Chelle at work. The wall-to-wall carpet, with its giant picture of a knight on horseback waving a silver sword and holding a shield with the infinity symbol, was as ostentatious as ever. The reception desk curving around one end of the circular frame that surrounded the figure was equally familiar. Even the pair of pretty young receptionists seemed to be the same. Both had the high-collar blouse and pink-painted, pursed lips he recalled so fondly. Amused, Jon wondered how much it cost Endless Loop to train them to hold their mouths that way. Why they'd bother was more of a mystery.

In the whole familiar room, only one change caught Jon's attention. A large, plastic banner stretched from one end of the curved back wall to the other, suspended on wire cords from the ceiling. Shining green against a black background, a crowd of runic letters like those on the signs outside framed a motto spelled out entirely in a font resembling charred sticks of wood:

BACKLASH IS COMING

"Sooner than you think," Jon muttered beneath his breath, his lips barely moving.

Of course, he didn't know what *Backlash* actually was, and he didn't want to know. He hated Endless Loop, its business, and its unbearable pretension. He'd never made many friends among Chelle's coworkers, and now it looked like one of the few employees he liked was a snake in his garden. Hanging his head so the receptionists wouldn't see him scowl, Jon passed the knight on his way to the desk.

"May I help you?" asked one of the women with pursed lips, a brunette with a cute, button nose and startlingly blue eyes.

"Jon Edom to see Vivek Singh."

"Do you have an appointment?"

The woman was new; Jon didn't recognize her. Her near-identical counterpart was a veteran and Jon recognized her immediately. She gave Jon a nod.

"It's all right, Janine," she said. "We know Doctor Edom. I'll buzz Mister Singh, Jon. I'm sure he'll want to come straight down."

Jon's cheeks flushed hot. He couldn't judge everyone in the building as a jerk simply because they worked here, and he wished he knew the receptionist better. He flashed a tight smile and started for the elevators.

They dinged nearly at once.

The doors whooshed open, and Vivek Singh appeared. He was dressed, as always, like a fashion model. His suit of the day was ochre in color, set off by a striking peacock blue waistcoat. Vivek stared down at his phone as he exited the elevator and was so focused on it that he didn't see Jon until he spoke.

"Vivek."

Vivek lifted his head and spread his arms wide in greeting.

"Jon!" He strolled over with a hand raised to shake, but dropped it upon catching Jon's sour expression. Flatly, he said, "What's this about?"

"I think you know," said Jon.

Vivek shook his head.

"Were you sleeping with Chelle?"

Vivek jerked his head toward the reception desk, his smile fixed, fake.

"Let's talk in my office." He ushered Jon toward the elevator without waiting for a response.

Staying put, Jon raised his voice. "Did you sleep with my wife?"

Vivek turned back to face Jon but looked past his shoulder at the receptionist instead of meeting his eye. "What would you like to hear, Jon?"

"Don't patronize me."

Vivek shook his head. "You want the truth?"

"Yes."

"Yes, Jon. Chelle and I did have a relationship. But you know that already. Why else would you kill her?"

Blood roared in Jon's ears and all reason left him in an instant. He rushed Vivek with hands open, struck by an impulse to catch the friend who'd betrayed him by the collar and hurl him to the ground.

Vivek tried to step aside. Too slow. Jon caught him by the lapels and tried to trip him. Vivek resisted. Too angry for a clean fight, Jon released his grip and swung a fist at Vivek's prominent cheekbone. The punch connected, and Vivek's feet went out from under him. He fell hard and with a loud grunt. He quickly rolled to an elbow. The cheek was bleeding. Vivek touched it with a finger and stared in disbelief at the blood.

"You . . . hit me!"

Then Jon fell on him, raining blow after blow as Vivek tried to shield his face.

Moments later, Jon felt himself being pulled away from Vivek by two strong pairs of hands. He twisted away, freeing one arm, which he used to aim a blow at the security guard's eye. Swearing loudly, the guard released Jon to dodge the blow, while his colleague jammed a bony knee hard into Jon's gut.

Jon doubled over, the will to fight forced out of him along with his breath. What had he been thinking? The guards weren't his enemy.

Leaping free of the guards, Jon held up both hands to signal surrender; he had no beef with either of them.

Vivek was back on his feet. The security guard Jon may well have blinded had his back to Jon, facing Vivek with arms extended to block Vivek's attempts to run at Jon to gain retribution. Not that Vivek was trying *too* hard; the performance was actually quite pathetic, nothing more than a show of macho bravado for the benefit of everyone in the reception area who'd just watched him get his ass handed to him on a plate.

"Enough," Jon said, panting from the exertion. "I'm done."

"You are, yes." Vivek faced the reception desk. "Janine, call the police."

"They're on the way, Mister Singh," she told him.

"I didn't kill Chelle, Vivek," Jon growled, his ulcer flaring once more. The pain was so severe, it made his knees wobble, but he managed to keep his feet. "I didn't do *anything* to Chelle or the boys. The police are going to prove that, and when they do, they'll look elsewhere. If you had anything to do with any of this . . ."

"Save your threats, Jon," said Vivek. "I love Rochelle. I wouldn't hurt her."

"And my boys?"

"What about them, Jon? What about *your boys*?"

There was something in Vivek's tone that sounded mocking, but Jon blocked out its potential connotations; he had to keep his mind clear. "If you know anything, anything at all, that could help me find my family, you *have* to tell the police."

Vivek glared at Jon; he clearly thought Jon was guilty.

A blare of sirens sounded from outside. Jon looked toward the office block's exit but made no attempt to flee. How could he escape, with his belly on fire and a media stunt blocking the way, not to mention having left his car keys with a stranger?

One more appeal: "Please, Vivek."

Vivek crossed his arms and hung his head, like a man holding back both despair and anger. Watching him as the sirens drew ever closer, Jon actually felt a stab of pity; the man was experiencing the profound pain of loss just the same as he was.

The police arrived.

There came a moment of confusion as the fake protesters outside got back into formation and started shaking their signs and chanting. Once they realized there were no cameras, that the cops who'd arrived were the real deal, they stood aside to allow the quartet of uniformed officers to rush into the building.

As the cops formed a ring around Jon, he raised his

hands. An officer approached with handcuffs and, in seconds, they secured Jon and marched him out.

Vivek followed. "She was leaving, Jon. Leaving you, leaving Austin, leaving that toxic church of hers. If you wanted her gone, all you had to do was wait. You didn't have to kill her."

Although the last thing Jon had ever wanted was freedom from Chelle, Vivek's rant struck him dumb: That Chelle had talked to her lover about leaving her husband came as little surprise and Jon didn't doubt she was serious, but leaving the church was entirely different. So far as Jon knew, Vivek had no strong feelings about Chelle's religion—it was Jon who felt uncomfortable in that church. As CEO of Endless Loop, Jon expected Vivek to be more or less favorable toward the Church of the Resurrected, considering the founder of the company, Chelle's mother, was a major contributor to it. That Vivek had chosen to mention the church gave his words the ring of truth.

If Chelle had plans to leave the Church of the Resurrected, that was news to Jon. Was Vivek confused? Was he lying? If so, Jon couldn't see his motive, no matter how pissed the guy was.

Jon had struggled to imagine what anyone, apart from himself, stood to gain from the loss of Chelle and the boys. Chelle had no enemies, and if she were declared dead, the millions of her royalty dollars in their joint bank account would become Jon's alone. It was easy to see why the detective suspected he was behind his wife's sudden disappearance.

But Vivek's suggestion that Chelle wasn't happy in the church changed all of that. Her family would definitely object to her severing ties, as would any devout believers who found out. A Berger son-in-law leaving was bad enough, but a Berger daughter losing her faith was simply unforgivable. Jon knew there would be a great many who'd be moved to interfere.

The officer at Jon's side had him duck his head as he slid into the back seat of the police cruiser. His ulcer burned like hell and he felt itching all over his body that he could do nothing about, thanks to the handcuffs.

He felt Vivek's eyes on him, their bare, simmering hatred. But all that was nothing compared to the exhilaration of hope he felt at his wife's unexpected motive.

24

The drive from Youngsport to Austin took a solid two hours, the visit with the Edoms an hour more. But Dani's day was far from over: Fifteen minutes after she left the Edom driveway, she got the call she had been waiting for.

"We're a go on the lake house," Lieutenant Randall told her. "The van is ready, plus two black-and-whites. Waiting on your lead."

"Don't wait on me," Dani told him. "Tell them to go."

Saul insisted on a swing through a Whataburger. After Dani obliged, the rest of the afternoon was spent on I-290 all the way to Lake Conroe. They stopped only the once, to check in on the Wagon Hut, where Rochelle Edom had stopped for gas the night she vanished into thin air.

The roadside store looked like it had stood on that spot for a hundred years, and with minimal changes to its decor. No one was manning the counter or out stocking the shelves, so the detectives took a stroll into the greasy spoon diner that took up half the Wagon Hut's interior. The waitresses wore too-short skirts and tight, checked tops, no doubt for the delectation of their mainly trucker clientele. None on them looked to be a day under fifty. The diner wasn't busy, but none of the waitresses took notice of Dani.

Saul stepped past her. "Hey, Mama," he said. His voice was low, but three waitresses spun around immediately. All strolled his way.

"Need a hand, darlin'?" the first waitress to Saul asked with a broad smile.

"At the very least." Saul returned the smile with a salacious grin.

The waitress stuck a hand on her hip. Her coworkers shot sour glances and got back to weaving around the tables.

"What can I do you for?" the waitress said.

Dani flashed her badge. "You can answer our questions."

The waitress sighed. "Sure. Not like a gal's got a job to do." She gestured at an empty booth.

Dani nodded. When she, Saul, and the waitress were all seated, she asked the woman's name. The waitress pointed at her name tag.

"Val," said Dani, "we're investigating a disappearance. Did you see the news about the mom and two children who went missing at the lake weeks ago?"

"Sure I did. It's been all everybody's talked about since."

Dani pressed on. "Were you working the night the family stopped in?"

"I've got two teenage boys and an eight-year-old at home. I work every damn night God sends me. All I can tell ya is one of the young-uns came in for a pee. I saw her walk him to the door. That was as far as she went."

Saul added, "Must have been a slow night, to notice a kid and a mom who didn't come in."

The waitress shrugged. "It was lively enough. We don't

get many kids young as that one after nine. I noticed the little fella and saw the mom through the glass. Pays to make sure the little ones are accompanied—we've had a few runaways in the years I've worked here."

Dani scribbled a note in her pad. "Do you know if anyone else saw Mrs. Edom?"

"No."

"*Nobody* spoke to her?" said Saul.

"Sorry, sugar. You ain't the first to ask. The other cops asked all us girls, plus Pete in the back and Coop over there." She pointed at the store's counter, where a bored young man with a dark, scruffy beard had appeared. "Nobody talked to the woman. It was a fill-up, plain and simple. She paid the machine, walked the kid to the door for his pee. That was it."

Dani nodded. The report from Montgomery County's police force backed up Val's statement of events, but she'd been hoping they might have missed something. It would certainly have made her life a hell of a lot easier. Unfortunately for her, it seemed the local boys had done a good job.

Twenty minutes after they said goodbye to Val, the detectives parked Dani's car at the end of the Bergers' lake house driveway, behind a forensic van and the pair of marked police cars.

The driveway itself was cordoned off with yellow tape, more of which defined a narrow walkway for Dani, Saul, the uniformed officers, and forensics techs to walk along. The three techs Dani passed seemed to be in a hurry; she tried to waylay a couple of them—a tall, bulky woman and a skinny man with a lazy eye—to ask what they knew so far, but both ignored her.

Finally, Dani stopped a man of average height, athletic build, with a shock of bleached-blond hair. He wore a powder blue face mask and held a black plastic bag. Dani cringed inwardly as she realized the bag was just the right size to hold an adult's foot . . . or a small child's forearm.

"Ken, right?" Dani remembered their meeting at a previous crime scene barely a couple months before.

"Afternoon, Detectives." Ken fiddled with the black bag.

"Your colleagues all seem to be in a rush—what's going on?"

Ken held up the bag like a schoolkid at show-and-tell. "Pay dirt," he said. "We're bringing up a cooler from the van, but the boss wants me to type this sample right away. You two will want to head around back. Just watch where you walk."

When Dani reached the back yard of the gray, split-level house, Saul trailing behind, the lead CSI, a woman named Brockard, lifted a hand in greeting. She and her fellow CSIs, all masked and clad in white paper overalls, were crowded around a pit. Next to it sat a small backhoe and the mound of earth it had dug. The foul, cloying stink of waste and decay hit Dani as she neared the pit. She covered her nose with her jacket.

"Hold it right there, Detective," said Brockard. "We've got another one coming up."

Dani did as instructed and looked on as another zipped bag appeared from the pit, at the end of a metal pole. A CSI retrieved the sample and walked it over to Brockard. Carefully, Brockard unzipped the bag partway, looked inside, and zipped it back up again. Dismissing the CSI with a nod, Brockard walked up to Dani, bag in hand.

Saul finally appeared, pinching his nose against the stench. "Cesspit?"

"Cesspit," Brockard confirmed. "Even the rich folks can't get city sewage out here."

Dani, breathing into her jacket lining, nodded at Brockard's sample. "What's with the party treats?"

"I'd get your opinion," said Brockard, "but they're pretty far gone. Body parts, Detectives. Human, in case you have to ask."

"How many?" said Dani.

"*Parts*? Hard to say. If you mean how many individuals, there's easily enough for a nuclear family, minus the dad."

Saul said, "You can tell that much already? I mean, if our perp cut them up small enough to flush, they must be pretty small pieces."

Brockard gave the bag a shake. "These didn't go down a pipe. Somebody opened the pit and dumped them inside. They did a neat job, too. Rolled out fresh sod to make it look untouched."

"Rolled?" said Dani.

"That's how it comes." Saul talked through a handkerchief, but Dani caught the subtle shift in his voice; he was not quite believing Brockard's hypothesis. "Sod, I mean. You buy it in rolls. You're saying somebody opened the pit, stuffed in the body parts, and covered it over? Then they rolled out new sod to hide their work?"

Brockard nodded. "Looks that way."

Saul gave a whistle. "Big job. Were there machine tracks, or did they do it all by hand with shovels?"

Dani shot her partner a look, which he duly ignored. What was Saul's problem? She didn't like the man's skeptical tone.

Neither did Brockard, it appeared. She squared up to Saul. "One man—or woman—could do the whole job with a shovel overnight. They'd have to be motivated, sure, but most killers are."

Dani threw in, "You're right about that." Another warning glance at Saul, who frowned fixedly at Brockard, hands in his pockets. He seemed to have gotten used to the stench already. Dani changed the subject. "What's our status on the house?"

Brockard blinked at her but didn't miss a beat. "We found the same traces as county. Blood, a bit of tissue. Nothing a kitchen accident couldn't explain."

Dani nodded; she decided to quit breathing into her jacket; if Saul could take the fetid air, so could she. She took a few steps upslope, in the direction of the house, but stopped when something caught her eye. She reversed direction and moved slightly downslope, crossing the yard to the fringe of yellow tape.

Saul called over. "Dani?"

Dani didn't answer. The patch of yard beside the excavated pit formed the narrowest part of a triangle of grass, which was framed by spindly trees and ornamental bushes all the way down to a dock, some hundred feet of which extended into the lake. The patch of lawn Dani was on formed a square. The house was behind her, the neck of the triangle in front of her; a privacy fence stood on a hill to her left. She suspected the hill had been built to order, as it looked oddly out of place in the otherwise flat landscape. Its top was high enough that the top of the fence stood level with the middle of the house's second story, effectively cutting off any view a neighbor might have of the yard on that side. The fence ran on down the hill, curving slightly around the end of the triangle's neck and blocking the view from the lake on Dani's side of the dock.

Turning to face Brockard, Dani extended a hand. "It happened here. This is where he— This is where the victims were killed."

"Hold on," said Saul. "We don't even know—"

"Check the terrain," Dani interrupted. "Look at the position of the fence. There were no neighbors up the road, to the right. The deputies said so, based on their house-to-house. But anyone on the lake, or over the water, would have a clear view of the dock. Anyone at a high angle could see into the second-story windows. But this spot, between the house and curve of the fence, is totally invisible. If I can see that, you can bet our killer did. This is where your people should check for traces, Brock."

Brockard said, "Makes sense to me." She started back to the cesspit. "I'll get somebody on that right away." Stopping, she turned to Dani. "By the way, I said the body parts weren't flushed. They weren't cut, either."

"What?" Dani was puzzled.

Saul said, "Then how—?"

"From the condition of the bones," said Brockard, "I'd say they were *bludgeoned* apart."

Dani shot past Brockard and Saul and headed for the front of the lake house.

"Where are you going?" Saul called after her.

"I need some air." Dani reached in her jacket for her phone. "I'm calling in a warrant to search Edom's car."

"Hold on! Wait!" Saul ran to catch up and caught Dani's arm. She tried to shake him off, but his delicate fingers were surprisingly strong.

"Don't you think you're jumping the gun?" he asked. "We've got body parts. Okay. *Somebody* died here. But we don't know who, not for sure. And that thing with the sod? I don't buy it. You're telling me Dr. Edom murdered his wife and kids, bludgeoned their bodies to bits, dug a deep hole to the cesspit, and rolled out half a new lawn in the same night? I understand what you said about *where* the deaths happened, and it shows our killer knew the lay of the land. But look at the angles again. The pit can be seen from the lake. If our perp put so much thought into keeping the killing out of sight, why would he risk doing hours of yard work out in the open?"

Dani wrenched her arm from her partner's vise-like grasp. "You have a different theory?"

"I don't," Saul admitted. "Not yet. But the evidence, it

just doesn't add up."

Dani glared at Saul, suddenly furious. "If you want something to add up, I'll give you numbers. One mom. Two kids. Seven and five years old. What's that add up to, Saul?"

She tried to storm away, but Saul seemed determined to follow. "Is this really about Edom," he said, "or is it about *your* old man?"

Dani stopped dead in her tracks. Her breath hissed out like it had been sucked from her lungs. She had to draw another before she could spin around and point an accusing finger in Saul's face.

"For your information, Detective Troyer, I'm not acting out some vendetta against doctors—murderous or otherwise. So far as I'm concerned, Jon Edom has nothing in common with my old man other than he's a damn doctor. And I will go on believing that until a court says he's guilty. I know Jon Edom isn't my father, Saul. What he *is*, though, is a person of interest in the disappearance of his wife and two children. And, in case you missed what Brockard just told us, it looks like some person of interest, as yet unidentified, bludgeoned multiple people apart and buried their remains in shit over there. Now, let me ask you a professional question. When a perp goes out of the way to mutilate someone and hide the remains somewhere humiliating like that, are they more or less likely to have a deep personal connection with the victims?"

Saul put on the blandest expression Dani could imagine on his face. She'd seen him look at other women that way when he was trying to end confrontation.

"But it's a thin thread to hang a man on," he said.

Dani pointed past him, to the spot she'd asked Brockard to search. A pair of investigators were already there, crouching down to examine the grass.

"DNA's thinner," she said. "Now, hold down the fort

here, will you? I've got a call to make."

25

Cop shows on TV made interview rooms look cold and uninviting, but Jon found Interview Room 4 at the Austin Police Department Main Headquarters quite comfortable, although not quite cozy. The air was pleasantly cool, the seats padded, and the color palate was brighter than any Jon had seen in any police procedural. The walls were a pale lemon that reminded him of the preschool Cass and Simon used to attend. Every room in that building, even the school supervisor's office, had been painted that color. It had always put a smile on Jon's face.

"What's funny?" Fitz asked; he sat across the table from Jon. He'd been alternating between talking to Jon about Vivek and scrolling through something on his tablet for the past five minutes. The table he tapped with his free hand was stainless steel, and most of the wall behind his head was a one-way mirror, so at least there were some details the cop shows got right.

Jon said, "Nothing. A memory. I was thinking of the kids."

"Luke and Paul?"

"The twins. Have you heard anything from Simon?"

"Cassidy got hold of him. She said something about a girlfriend."

Jon smirked. "An ex. Or maybe ex-ex by now. You wouldn't think it, to look at me, but women find us Edom men irresistible."

Fitz set his tablet flat on the table and leaned in to bring his face close to Jon's. After a moment, he sat back. "You look okay to me."

Jon winced, cradling his bruised ribs with a protective arm. His reflection in the mirror showed disheveled, greasy hair and dark, weary rings under each eye. "As a medical professional, I have to disagree with you on that one."

Fitz lifted the tablet, did a bit more scrolling, and set it back down. At the touch of a button, the screen went black.

"I'm concerned about your mental state," the lawyer said. "Not just this situation downtown with Vivek. Have you considered that some of the symptoms you've been experiencing may be psychosomatic?"

Jon pointed at the mirror. "Before we get too personal, are you sure we can trust the discretion of the Austin PD?"

Fitz half turned in his chair. "Will they listen in or record us, you mean? For their sakes, I hope not. Attorney-client privilege goes back four hundred years."

"In that case, I'll speak freely," said Jon. "Is the pain in my gut and arm all in my head? Maybe. Then again, psychology's not my field." He quit cradling the ribs and patted his heart instead. "A clogged aorta? I'm your man. The mysteries of the brain? Ask someone else."

A knock at the door caught both men's attention. They turned in sync to see a police officer open the door and step aside to show in Rabbi Max.

"Shalom," the rabbi said to the lawyer. To Jon he said, "That goes double for you."

The officer pulled out the chair beside Fitz for the rabbi

and nodded when he was thanked. The rabbi sat, but the moment the door shut behind the officer, he leapt to his feet again.

"Starting fights, Jon? As your rabbi and your sensei, I'm very surprised at you—and disappointed, I might add."

The rebuke stung more than Jon could comfortably admit. He tried deflection. "I wasn't after a fight. I wanted *answers*."

"Next time," said Fitz, "come to me for those. It's what you pay me for, all part of the service. Castro going AWOL is unfortunate, but I have other ways to get answers when I want them."

Jon felt the all-too-familiar tightness in his chest. "They had an affair. Chelle and Vivek." He didn't want to speak the words but felt compelled to spit them out.

Rabbi Max said, "This is news to you?"

"Yes," said Jon, "and no. I know Chelle cheated in the past. The manic state, in bipolar, can be hypersexual. But Vivek? He acted like a friend to me."

"There are friends who are brothers, and brothers who will stab you in the back." The rabbi seemed always to have an appropriate quote to hand.

"Scripture?" asked Fitz.

"A paraphrase. Jon, you were betrayed. I understand that. But violence won't help. Fitz and I are here for you. Don't keep cutting us out."

"I'm sorry." Jon's ribs throbbed, his ulcer burned, and suddenly the interrogation room didn't feel so comfortable anymore.

"Listen. I think it's time we compared notes," Fitz weighed in. "An hour ago, I got word that Detectives Cavallo and Troyer were en route to the Berger lake house. You know the county forensic team found traces of blood?"

"You told me," said Jon. "Wasn't there something wrong with the samples?"

"There was," said Fitz. "I'm told they're unusable as DNA evidence. It's how Cavallo got a new team on-site. My contact called them Austin's best and brightest—I think we can safely say there will be no bad samples this time; at least none so bad they taint the whole evidence batch. I hate to ask, Jon, but if there's anything you haven't told me about your time at the lake house, now's the time to come clean."

The pain in his arm and gut ebbed long enough for Jon to look Fitz straight in the eye. "You've heard everything just as it happened."

"Good," said Fitz. "Good. I'd like to go back, Jon. Back to the beginning. In my last report from Castro, he mentioned an idea he had about Murphy Gore. Did you know Gore was associated with the Church of the Resurrected?"

"No." Jon was surprised. "How?"

"Castro wasn't too clear on that point, but it's interesting, don't you think? A man who targeted the hospital you've worked at for six years has a connection that goes back even further."

Jon shook his head. "I didn't know Gore before the hospital. Did he attend services in person? The congregation is vast, and a lot of the attendees meet only online."

Fitz rubbed at his chin. "I got the impression Gore's ties to the church were strong. They date back to before your conversion, but Castro said the membership is contemporary. It's a vast congregation, as you said, and the online presence is considerable. I've done some digging, and, aside from the usual website and socials, there are layers upon layers of discussion forums connected to the Church of the Resurrected."

"I'm well aware of that." Jon recalled Chelle had served on a committee whose sole purpose was to rein in some of the wilder online discussion groups. The members voted to give up the effort as a lost cause after barely three months.

"My favorite find," said Fitz, "was an independent, ecumenical forum set up to debate the merits of Clive Denning's contributions to life and culture. Did you ever meet Denning?"

"No. Before my time."

"At any rate, my point is the church has layers most members have no reason to know about. I suspect that's true even of you, Jon, despite your close ties. The Denning followers are practically a sect unto themselves. I wouldn't be surprised if Gore's connections with the church at large were somewhat obtuse."

"That could be," Jon conceded. "I never had much to do with the digital outreach side." He paused, struck by a shift in Rabbi Max's expression. "Something catch your attention, Rabbi?"

"A stray thought," said his friend. "Nothing that matters, really. The mention of layers brought me back to my studies of Enoch. There are *elevations* in his so-called vision that hint at layers in the spirit realm. Greater and lesser glories, you might call them—like the third heaven of Saint Paul."

"Saint?" said Fitz. "Isn't that heresy?"

The rabbi shrugged. "So much of it is. Why split hairs?"

Jon found the sideline a pleasant distraction. "How many heavens do you believe in, Rabbi?"

"Oh, at least as many as Paul. Remember the temple, Jon, the division of Kodesh Kodashim, the Holy of Holies. The ark rested there, signifying the Presence. God's in his heaven, as the poet said. The rest of us hope for something else."

"I don't follow," said Fitz.

"You're probably not *listening*." The rabbi was clearly trying to not sound too condescending. "I'll go slow. If

Kodesh Kodashim is the heaven of God alone, his sons have to live elsewhere. In the Temple, that's signified by Kodesh, the holy chamber, where the priests serve. If Kodesh is the second heaven, then the courtyard outside is the first. So, first heaven is for the Jews, second for the angels. And third heaven is . . ."

The rabbi paused there, for someone else to complete the thought. Jon saw Fitz's eyes had glazed over, and said, "For God alone."

Rabbi Max nodded sagely. "Some of my brothers would leave it at that. Personally, I think there must be more heavens than just the three. After all, if there's one each for God, his sons, and the Jews, where would the righteous among the nations go? To say nothing of the rest of the goyim?"

"So, there are at least five heavens?" Jon suggested.

"Five, seven, or maybe even *ten*," said the rabbi. "It's not the business of man to count God's creation." He folded his hands over his belly to signify he'd finished with his piece.

Jon leaned back in his chair. Numbness had replaced his aches and pains, as it often did when he spoke of spiritual matters; the brief respite felt good. Still, he could see Fitz was growing increasingly impatient. Jon sat upright with an apologetic gesture. "I'm sorry. We're a bit off track," he said. "Okay, we know Gore had connections to Chelle's church. You called that the beginning, Fitz. What's after that?"

The lawyer relaxed, in his element once more. "Your troubles at home. Gore's attack on the hospital brought tensions between you and your wife to a head, correct?"

"That's putting it mildly." Jon cringed inwardly at the thought of how he and Chelle had fought, of her infidelity with Vivek. "Yeah, Chelle and I fought—mostly over old ground. How it's dangerous working at the Crown, how the neighborhood has gone to hell in a handbasket, how I'm wasting my talents. She admitted to coming off her meds. I got her to go back on the lithium, but it probably wasn't long enough to make a difference."

"Meaning?" said Fitz.

"Lithium becomes effective after one to three weeks of regular administration. In my experience with Chelle, three weeks was when she'd start to notice the effect. The greatest gains, in terms of leveling her mood, took *months* to kick in."

"So, you'd say your wife was in a compromised mental state at the time of her disappearance?"

"She was an undermedicated bipolar patient. *Compromised* is barely scratching the surface."

Fitz let a moment pass before he spoke again. He lowered his chin like a judge passing sentence. "We've been here before, Jon. Let's say Cavallo's team finds nothing new at the lake house. Occam's razor favors someone who knew she was making the trip as the cause of her disappearance. So far as we know, she told no one. Unless it's someone she met at that service station, the most likely suspect is Rochelle herself."

Jon's jaw tightened; he drummed his fingers on the table, trying to burn off nervous energy as he spoke. "You told me last week you didn't believe Chelle was responsible."

"I didn't," said Fitz. "I still don't. But it's not my job to *believe*, Jon. My job is to persuade the police, a judge, and maybe a jury of your innocence. To do that, I need a compelling alternative to you as the villain. Right now, your wife's mental problems are the best I've got."

Jon's anger surged, the pain in his arm flared to white hot, his throbbing stomach threatened to discharge its contents. Shoving back from the table, he jumped to his feet.

"*Villain*?" he gasped. "My family is missing, and you're talking like—"

Jon balled a fist, and it was only Fitz's wide, startled eyes that stopped him from thumping the table. The lawyer had his own hand raised to bring calm; oddly, Fitz glanced over his shoulder at the mirror.

"Sit down," Fitz turn back around to face Jon.

"I thought you trusted the police."

"I trust them to do their jobs. They'll respect our privacy until you get violent, and not one second more."

"I won't . . . I'm not . . ."

Jon eyed Rabbi Max. He was clearly disturbed, as if he couldn't quite believe Jon was the man he thought he knew so well. Finally, the last of Jon's anger ebbed away and he lowered himself into his seat, suddenly feeling small.

Fitz spoke up. "I'm on your side, Jon. Always remember that. Was *this* outburst what happened with Vivek?"

"Maybe." Jon knew damn well it was. "I don't know. The things he said, his attitude— It's all been a nightmare. Not just Vivek, I mean. Everything that's happened since I got to the lake house and found Chelle and the boys weren't there. It's a nightmare."

Jon rubbed his hands together, folded left over right, then right over left, for what felt like far too long. At last, he felt able to go on. "You need a villain, huh?"

"A poor choice of words on my part." Fitz sounded genuinely apologetic. "I need an *alternative*, some story that doesn't put you at the center of your family's disappearance."

Jon felt true despair; his theory about why someone might want Chelle to disappear had seemed so compelling an hour ago, and now he doubted it was even worth explaining to his lawyer.

Thin hope or not, it was all he had.

"There was something Vivek said, after the fight. He said Chelle was planning to leave me. That's no surprise, really; she threatened as much in our last few fights. What struck me, though, was Vivek said Chelle was leaving *that church of hers*. His exact choice of words, I think. Chelle had never said anything like that to me. So far as I know, she was happy as both a member and a trustee. Any other time, I'd dismiss what Vivek said, but I can't figure out why he'd make that up. He knew me well enough to know I'd be delighted about Chelle leaving her church."

Fitz rocked back in his chair. He hummed but said nothing.

"I was thinking," Jon continued, "if Vivek is right and Chelle *was* making plans to leave the Church of the Resurrected, maybe someone there didn't want to let her go. Could be they were afraid of the adverse publicity such a high-profile member would bring them. The daughter of the sainted Ezra cutting ties would be bound to stir the media into a frenzy. Perhaps they thought Chelle was about to commit a sin and decided to do something about it before she did. Either way, they thought it was a good reason to . . . kidnap her and take the kids as leverage."

Fitz leveled his chair. "It's very weak, Jon. But might be a possibility."

Jon's skin prickled, like a million ants were crawling over the entirety of his body.

"You don't look too good, Jon. Maybe we should take a break," said Fitz.

"I'm fine."

"Okay," Fitz conceded with a snort. "We're making progress of sorts, I guess. You've said you have nothing to add to your account of your visit to the lake house. Is there anything more you'd like to say about your actions *prior* to that?"

"If you mean, did I sleep alone in Houston on Friday

night, the answer is yes. The hotel bed was too hard, so I turned down the AC and slept on the comforter. There was no one to object."

"And there'll be no one to contradict your account at trial—should it go to trial, that is."

"If you're referring to Doctor Susan Grunberg specifically, I don't know if she slept alone, but she sure didn't sleep with me."

Fitz cracked a smile.

"I'll take your word for that. And how about the morning you called the police? Your wife didn't return your messages—you got worried—the police made a wellness check, and there was no one at home. An hour out of Houston, you stopped for gas. Your card was declined because the bank placed a hold on it due to unusual activity. That would have been Rochelle's stop at a gas station near Conroe. You followed her trail, found an empty lake house—the same one Cavallo is now going over with a fine-toothed comb."

"She wants my blood." Jon feared the woman like no other. "If she finds anything on me at the lake house, it'll be because her people put it there. And I really wouldn't put that past her—"

Fitz lifted both hands to silence Jon. A cautionary gesture.

"Let's not sling accusations around, Jon. I've seen the detective's record, and it's beyond clean. Now, back to the lake house. After your search, you spent some time with the Montgomery County police."

"I was numb. Sleepwalking."

"No doubt. And when you got back to Austin, you threw yourself into your work. I'd wager a third of all possible jurors will understand that completely. The rest, we can win over because you are the hero doctor. Cavallo called you at work, correct?"

Jon nodded.

"And you and I met the next day. Aside from Castro going radio silent and this trouble with your health, that brings us right up to earlier today."

As Fitz scrolled for something on his tablet, Jon took advantage of the break. "Actually, there's one twist in the tale you didn't mention."

"What's that?" Once more, Fitz was surprised.

"Lisa's accusation and heart attack."

Rabbi Max paled. "It *was* a heart attack, then?"

Jon nodded. "Classic. You know she spent a night in the ICU? Well, I have a couple of friends in Wimberley who still speak to me, and they said Phillip checked his mother out of the hospital twelve hours after she was admitted. The doctors objected, as they should have, but Phillip has power of attorney over Lisa. There was nothing anyone could legally do."

"Poor woman." The rabbi spoke with reverence, as if Jon's mother-in-law had already passed. "I'll make sure to remember her in *mi sheberach*."

Fitz said, "Right. Thank you, Jon. I hadn't forgotten what happened, but I didn't see a reason to bring it up. I don't see a prosecuting attorney getting traction from a baseless accusation from a senile old woman. Is that all I left out?"

Jon took a moment to think. "Yes. I think it is."

"Good," said Fitz. "So, let's talk about today. A couple hours ago, you had a visit from the two detectives. Cavallo showed you some IP addresses and helped you interpret them. It's all in the report she called in to the police transcription service." The lawyer angled his tablet to allow Jon a glimpse of the report. "I know far less about computers than I do about people, so I have to take Cavallo's word that the numbers mean Rochelle and Vivek Singh were keeping in touch."

"That's one way of putting it." Jon's anger threatened to flare once again.

"My point," Fitz said, "is that, affair or otherwise, the smart thing to do after Cavallo dropped her bombshell would have been to lay low. Instead, you chose to confront Vivek Singh at his place of work. I don't need to tell you the optics are terrible on that one, Jon. But again, I expect one in three jurors will sympathize with you, the cuckolded husband. There are millions of husbands, wives, and lovers who would have reacted in exactly the same way. I'm not *excusing* your behavior, you understand."

"Of course."

"All I'm saying is it's understandable. The most significant part of the whole fiasco, in my mind, is you felt so strongly about Cavallo's revelation that you took action at once. I don't think you would have done that if his affair with your wife was old news."

"I wouldn't." Jon stared hard at his lawyer. "Look, the affair was upsetting, but it's not actually why I went after Vivek. When I heard he was keeping close touch with Chelle, as you put it, I thought he could be involved with her disappearance. I thought he might have orchestrated the whole thing. He's got the resources, after all, and I thought that if Chelle was coming on too strong, trying to force his hand, he'd have a motive too."

Fitz pursed his lips. "And now what do you think?"

"That I was wrong about the motive part. It kills me to say it, but I was looking into Vivek's eyes when he talked about Chelle. His passion is genuine; if he has anything to do with her going missing, it's not because he wants her out of his life—and I don't think he's got her hidden away in some secret love nest somewhere, either. Despite what I think of Vivek now, I know he's decent enough not to put me through not knowing where my kids are. That's why what he said about Chelle leaving the church stuck out. I went searching for a motive and I think I found one, only it's not Vivek's."

The lawyer and Rabbi Max exchanged glances. The rabbi shrugged.

Fitz said, "I have to admit, I've struggled from the beginning of all this with the question of a feasible *motive*. Maybe you're on to something."

Jon was pleased he was finally being taken seriously, rather than some hot-headed, wronged husband. "Remember what I said about Lisa's early checkout from the Crown? If someone at the church found out Chelle was leaving and decided to do something about it, Lisa may have caught wind of it—she still has many friends there. Maybe Phillip was afraid she'd slip up and would talk if he left her in the hospital too long."

"Are you accusing your brother-in-law of being the kidnapper?"

"No. All I'm saying is Phillip *always* knows more than he lets on. I'll bet you anything Korvus does too. They're definitely hiding something."

"About your wife and the boys?"

"Maybe. I don't know. You and the rabbi talked about layers. This story has more layers than a wedding cake."

A knock at the interview room door. Fitz stood up as a bulky, broad-shouldered young man in a crisp uniformed entered. A younger officer held the door for him.

"Good afternoon. I'm Lieutenant Randall of the Austin Missing Persons Unit. Please stand up, Doctor Edom."

Jon did as he was asked. The young officer left his place at the door to stand behind him. Jon looked at Fitz, who gave a swift and subtle shake of the head.

"Doctor Jon Edom, I am arresting you for the murder of Rochelle Berger-Edom, as well as that of her sons, Paul and Luke."

"*Murder*?" Rabbi Max pushed back his chair and got to

his feet.

Fitz said, "You found the bodies?"

"We have partial remains, blood typing, and a scene of crime. Doctor Edom, you have the right to remain silent. Anything you say can be used against you in court. You have a right to speak to a lawyer and have a lawyer present when the police question you—"

"I'm his lawyer," Fitz spoke up.

Randall ignored him. "Doctor Edom, do you understand your rights I have explained to you?"

Jon didn't answer.

Couldn't.

His tongue was sealed to the roof of his mouth, his throat felt like a pinched straw, the imagined ants crawled all over him, again, only this time, they were on fire. As he bent his fingers to scratch, the stainless steel table swelled to meet him.

"Catch him!" cried Randall.

Hands seized Jon's elbows; they felt like barbs jabbing through his skin to the flesh and bone beneath.

"Edom?"

"*Jon!*"

The world became a haze of vague shapes. All Jon could see clearly was his own face, red and sweating, staring back at him from the mirror as the rabbi's voice swelled in the cadence of prayer.

Darkness closed in.

26

Since the tower's underground pool was salt water, it didn't reek of chlorine. That meant Tasmin Beale wasn't inclined to cover her nose, which was good, since it spared her the mental energy she needed to keep from covering her eyes. The pool was monstrous: With the overhead lights switched off and the pool lights flickering with the filter pump's tide, the massive pit could have been confused for a flooded canyon on a cloudy night. It could have housed myriad sea serpents and monsters.

It did house at least one.

Jake Korvus bobbed around in the salty water, watching Tasmin approach the edge. When she stopped three feet shy, he called over, "Scoot on up, Pastor. I won't splash."

"No, thanks."

Tasmin kept her eyes trained on the senior pastor. It wasn't that she liked looking at him; keeping an eye on the cunning old hypocrite was part of her job. Besides, watching him beat watching the foreboding dark water.

The wispy fringe of hair Korvus usually kept under his wig was plastered to his cheeks, and the pool lights gave his bare skin a jaundiced hue. If Tasmin tilted her head, she could see every inch of the man's yellowed, pudgy flesh. There was a passage in *The Grand Cycle* about the importance of a spiritual man keeping touch with his inner animal; Tasmin had heard Korvus quote the passage many times at parties to explain why he loved to swim naked.

He swam toward her.

"What's the word, boss?" Tasmin stood her ground.

Korvus quit swimming and went back to his contented bob. Tasmin knew she could count on his ego working in her favor: Anyone else would have known immediately the "boss" was insincere. She'd only used it to distract Korvus, to prevent him bringing his pale, soggy flesh any closer. She wouldn't have minded examining that flesh cold on a slab, or even warm in the moments following death, but the thought of its hot blood circulating beneath that chilled, shriveled skin made her stomach churn.

The so-called boss gave her a smile. "You've read the briefing, of course."

"I have." News that the bodies of Rochelle and her sons had been discovered came as no great surprise. To Tasmin's mind, it had been a long time coming. "Speaking as your chief of security, I'd prefer you to tell me your source."

"Speaking *to* my chief of security, you can trust me to tell you what you need to know. Rochelle's loss is a great blow to our parishioners, Tasmin. And those poor children, too. We will have to make ready to offer comfort, especially to those who were close to them. At the same time, however, we must remain cautious. It wouldn't do to tip our hand too soon, as it were. We can't be seen making preparations until the police see fit to inform the relevant media outlets of their findings."

Tasmin fought the urge to tap her foot. "I got all that from the email. Why'd you want to see me in person?"

The senior pastor's face reddened. He was angry,

although not at her, it would seem. "I've received a warning. Anonymous, so I don't know how credible."

Tasmin leaned in closer, in spite of her revulsion at the old man. "What kind of warning?"

Korvus swam across to the side of the pool. Tasmin stood up straight and tried not to let him see her recoil.

The reddened face lifted until Korvus's eyes met hers. "The direst kind. Someone has promised, and I quote, 'The seed of Ezra Berger shall rest uneasy. When night falls by day shall God's wrath come upon His bitterest enemies.' *Bitterest*. Can you believe it?"

When night falls by day. The meaning was plain enough to Tasmin. The naked old man floating in front of her had wasted no time planning the funeral for his missing lambs. Even while the church remained officially hopeful for their safe return, they were *un*officially prepared for the worst. Korvus had set aside multiple tentative dates for the funeral service and accompanying burial on the grounds they didn't want to schedule a wedding only to have to reschedule should the inevitable happen. Now the discovery of Rochelle and her sons' bodies *had* happened, and the next date was this coming Saturday. Which also happened to be when Texas was expecting a partial solar eclipse.

"Somebody else has sources too, eh?" Tasmin said.

Korvus's face got even redder—quite crimson, in fact. "The warning came by email. Untraceable—something to do with a VPN and encryption; you know I have little to do with such matters. But it came to my personal account, one I don't usually give out. That's why I noticed it so quickly. And it's why I'm concerned, Ms. Beale."

"They must have sources and inside information."

"This is someone *close*, someone who is working against us. I'm afraid to say, there's a serpent in our garden."

"Of course there is."

"Huh?"

Tasmin squatted low to the cool cement floor; all she saw was Korvus's disembodied face, and the pool became a line on the horizon. The vast expanse of water still troubled her, but for the moment she put that aside.

"We've always had enemies, Senior Pastor, and some have come from inside the church. Do I need to remind you how we've dealt with them before? So, somebody who knew about your funeral plans and your personal email address is out to get us. Big whoop. If it's just one person, I don't see 'em doing any harm. If it's not, what worries me is this 'wrath of God' in the warning. Code for a terror attack, if I ever heard one."

Korvus grimaced. "It had crossed my mind."

"Good to hear it." The pool and Korvus's unwelcome nakedness all but forgotten, Tasmin rose and planted her hands on her hips. "I'll get Billy to draw up a roster. We'll want all of E9 on deck, plus reserves, and all the draftees he can muster."

"Is it wise to use Ezekiel Nine out in the open?" asked Korvus.

"If we put enough bodies on the spot, nobody'll notice. We'll make the total number, reserves plus draftees, triple the active force. Will that do?"

Korvus gave her a nod. "I leave everything in your capable hands."

And with that, he kicked away from the wall, floating into a backstroke that made his shriveled old manhood crest the surface.

Stomach lurching at the sight, still watching the old man out of the corner of her eye, Tasmin quickly left the pool, eager to start on her security plan.

27

Cass had never ridden in a police car before. This one wasn't a black-and-white; she didn't think it was what they called an "unmarked car" either. Cass didn't know much about cars, but this one seemed too small to be those ones she'd seen on cop shows. Nonetheless, it *was* a cop car. A police officer was driving the thing, after all.

The uniformed woman appeared to be in her forties: White, slim build, she had crow's feet beside her large eyes, a kindly smile, and large, calloused hands. Cass had known the officer was coming to collect her, thanks to a call from Detective Cavallo.

Cass found the detective intimidating, especially in the way she looked at Dad; her dark brown eyes burned into him with such accusation, Cass imagined the cop wished he would burst into flames. Cass knew Dad's opinion of the detective, that she was out to get him. Cass had argued with him, told him this was the woman who was going to put their family back together! But after witnessing the two in the kitchen together, she had a bad feeling Dad was right.

"We've got about a minute to go," the policewoman announced. They drove to an impound lot, a place the officer knew well enough that she didn't need the GPS.

Cass lifted the shoulder bag on her lap an inch and let it fall again. She heard her keychain clink and felt the hard plastic edge of the key fobs against her jeans. None of the cards in her wallet was a driver's license. She was nervous about driving, unlike Simon, who got his license the day of their sixteenth birthday. But she did have a key fob for Mom's SUV, the one that was missing, and one for Dad's Volvo. They were gifts meant to inspire her to drive. So far, they hadn't worked.

"Will the detectives be there already?" Cass asked.

"Don't worry—I'm sure you won't have to wait long."

In fact, the moment their car passed through the gate of the shrouded chain fence surrounding the dirt lot, Cass saw Cavallo and her partner standing shoulder to shoulder behind the familiar silver Mustang. It was parked perpendicular to a line of other vehicles, in the direct path of two cars and a minivan. Cass guessed none of the vehicles in the lot were going to be leaving anytime soon.

Dad's Volvo sat across from the minivan, its trunk pointed in roughly the same direction as the Mustang, but at an angle. As though someone had driven it in and run off. Except, of course, no one could have driven the Volvo. That was why she was there.

The policewoman came to a smooth stop in front of the detectives. Dani waved, and Cass tried to get out of the car.

The door didn't budge.

"Sorry." The policewoman pressed a button on her door and Cass's unlocked.

Saul met Cass, holding out a hand.

"Thanks for coming, Cassidy." Dani held out a hand too.

"It's Cass."

Dani's perfectly symmetrical eyes looked tired, expression straight-lipped and neutral. As Cass spoke, she made a clear and only partially successful effort to smile.

Cass's heart sank. "Something's wrong, isn't it?"

Saul stared at his shoes. "I'm sorry, Cass. We—"

Dani cut him off by stepping into the gap between Cass and her partner. "We'll tell you everything, Cass. I promise. Did you bring what I asked?"

"The key fob, yes." Cass opened her bag to fish out the fob, then thought better of it. She returned the bag to her shoulder. "Why do you want it?"

Dani's smile faltered. "You know your father was arrested."

Cass nodded. The rabbi had called her before the detective did. He didn't give any details but told her there'd been a fight. He made it sound like Dad attacked somebody, which Cass would have called impossible if not for the strange way she'd seen her father act after the detectives had left his house.

"He was caught on video assaulting another man," Dani told her. "It's clear Doctor Edom instigated the violence."

Cass took a steadying breath. "What's that have to do with his car?"

"His car was at the scene." Dani pointed with her chin at Saul, who stuck a hand in his pocket before he took up the story. He still wore his suit but had ditched the jacket, unlike Dani, who had her leather jacket on.

Saul said, "We asked Dr. Edom for the key, but he said he gave it to somebody outside the office building. We had to have the car towed here."

"We need to do a search of your father's vehicle."

Suspicion grew within Cass; what did this have to do with a fight? "I guess you have a warrant."

Dani pulled out an envelope from her jacket pocket.

Cass took it but didn't bother to read the contents; she

knew damn well what it was. "If you find something, what will that prove?"

Saul said, "We don't know exactly."

"We're keeping an open mind," said Dani.

Cass shifted her feet. "I don't know if I should help you with this."

There came the sound of another car. Cass turned to see her brother's Honda pass through the gate onto the lot. Simon wasn't driving, which was unusual: Simon didn't even let his favorite girlfriends drive that car.

As the Honda pulled up to the Volvo, Cass saw the driver was a uniformed officer, a middle-aged man with buzz-cut black hair. Cass watched Simon climb out of the passenger seat and take in his surroundings, attention lingering on the Mustang.

"Nice ride." Simon turned his full attention—and charm—onto Dani. "Yours?"

"Good guess." The detective offered a thin smile.

"Jacket gave it away. You're the lady detective. Cass told me I was missing out."

Cass felt herself blush.

"And you're Simon," Dani said.

Simon smirked. "You can frisk me and find out."

Saul glanced from Simon to Cass, a look of disbelief they'd come from the same womb.

"Thank you for coming," Dani went on. "I asked you here so I could get her copy of your Dad's key fob. I understand you have the hideaway key?"

"The what?" said Simon. "Oh yeah. The backup. It's at the dorm. Doesn't fit my key ring."

"That's unfortunate."

"What do you need a key for? You're cops." Simon frowned at the pair.

Saul said, "We can get access through a dealer, but it'll take time. Or we could just go ahead and bust it open——but that's going to cause a lot of unnecessary damage."

"Good point," said Simon. "They got a warrant—give them the key, Cass."

"What? Simon, Dad's in jail. They could—"

Saul chipped in, "Actually, he's in the hospital. Had some kind of fit after the arrest."

Heart in her throat, Cass groaned, "Why the hell didn't you tell me that before all this BS? Simon, you'll drive me?"

"Wait." Dani held up a hand. "The truth is, Cass, Simon, we have reason to believe something terrible has happened to your mother and brothers. I'm sorry to have to break it to you like this, as there's a lot we don't know . . . but we don't think they're coming back."

Everything Cass could see became an indistinct blur; feeling dizzy, she put her hands out to steady herself.

In a heartbeat, Dani was by Cass's side, holding her elbow. "All you all right?"

Cass snatched the elbow away. "Fine."

Saul continued, speaking quietly. "I have to ask you, *both* of you, if you think your father could ever be responsible for hurting your mom, Luke, and Paul."

"*No!*" Cass all but screamed.

Simon hesitated but finally replied with a feeble, "No."

"Then we're *all* fine," said Dani. "We don't have a problem. I let you think the vehicle search had something to do with the fight your dad got into. The real reason Saul and I need to search the car is so we can eliminate Doctor Edom from our investigation, and the real reason for bringing you both here was to gauge your reactions. If you believe your father couldn't possibly do anything to hurt your family, there's no reason not to help us."

"Of course he wouldn't hurt us." Cass's voice began to quiver.

"You want to go to Dad?" Simon said. "I'll take you.

Just give her the damn key."

Cass's shoulder bag felt suddenly too heavy. Simon was right, of course. The detectives would get what they wanted in the end. But if Dad was right about Dani being out to get him—

No. Dani was on *their* side.

"All right," she said, digging into the bag. She held the key fob out to Dani, who took it with a thank-you nod.

"You did the right thing." The detective turned toward the Volvo's trunk.

Cass didn't answer. She couldn't. Her sight had gone blurry again. This time, though, she didn't feel dizzy. She walked stiffly to Simon's car, not caring who saw her tears.

28

The first thing Jon saw when he opened his eyes was a huge black-and-white checkerboard. It stretched as far as he could see, and seemed to be swaying like a boat in choppy waters. As it settled, he saw it was not a board at all, but a ceiling of tiles; he was in a small, quiet room with a distinctly familiar odor of disinfectant.

A face swam into view.

"Chelle?" Jon's voice was a whisper.

"Can you hear me, Dr. Edom?" said a softly feminine voice. Then, "His eyes are open."

"Excuse me." A different voice, also a woman.

Nurse Aegypt appeared in Jon's line of vision.

"Doctor Edom?" Nurse Aegypt flashed his eye with an ophthalmoscope. "Pupil reflex is good."

As the light swung away, Jon's vision cleared in time to see the nurse step back and Susan Grunberg take her place.

"Jon?"

"Susan."

"He's coming around."

Jon tried to sit up, but Susan pushed him gently back

down. He sank into the bed with a loud sigh; his whole body felt so incredibly *tired*.

"You'll have to stay put until we get the tests back. Nobody here has seen symptoms like yours before."

There was no point in fighting; Jon's strength was entirely drained. If he'd thought it possible, Jon would have sworn he'd aged forty years since his arrest. He looked out the room's only window, where salmon-pink rays of a September sunset played along the glass. That meant a couple of hours had passed, at most, unless he'd been asleep for more than a day.

Jon took a moment to study the visitors assembled in the small room. The woman who had spoken first was P. J. Apart from her height, she didn't *really* resemble Chelle, although her voice was similar—hence Jon mistaking her for his wife. P. J. watched Jon intently from a few feet away from his bed. In a corner by the window, Susan and Nurse Aegypt whispered together, while Rabbi Max stood at the foot of the bed. Beyond his troubled friend, Jon espied a uniformed police officer standing in the doorway. He had his back to the room, watching the corridor beyond.

Jon cleared his throat. "What happened, Rabbi?"

P. J. took a step forward, as if to claim Jon for her own. Susan and the nurse tensed, poised to pounce if necessary; they had plenty of experience warning family members not to crowd a sick man.

"You fell, Jon. Collapsed," Rabbi Max told him.

"Did I hit my head?"

"No."

"It feels fuzzy, full of cobwebs."

Susan said, "Probably fatigue. Although we're working to rule out a stroke."

Jon pushed hard and, with a loud grunt, managed to raise himself to a sitting position. "It's not a stroke. Unless you mean I was struck by God."

Susan frowned, clearly unhappy her patient was exerting himself. "We'll wait on the tests before making any diagnosis."

"I know the signs of a stroke," Jon reminded his colleague. "This is something else."

Dr. Grunberg narrowed her eyes at him.

Jon then turned his attention to P. J., his wife's sister. Even through his fuzzy head, he could tell she was distressed. Her eyes were fixed on him like a hawk to its prey, to the exclusion of everything else in the room; the two of them might well have been all alone.

"Thanks for coming," was all he could think to say.

P. J. stepped to Jon's side, grabbing his arm. "I know you didn't do it, Jon. You *couldn't*."

He stared, struck by her expression of faith. Not that he should have been: On the list of things the Bergers were good at, faith was at the top. Only, in the past, it had usually put him on the other side of their arguments. Jon was stunned to find himself the object of P. J.'s devotion.

"Thank you."

P. J.'s eyes brimmed with tears. It seemed wrong to sit there and accept comfort in silence while the poor woman was on a verge of a breakdown; Jon glanced over at her and the rabbi before adding, "It's nice to know who my friends are."

P. J. released his arm. "I'm so sorry, Jon."

"For what?"

"For— For Mom and Phil. The things they said to you. I'm *sorry*." The apology seemed to finish P. J., and she rushed from the room. Jon watched her go.

"I need to check those tests, Jon." Susan broke the awkward moment. "Will you be a good patient for me? No pulling out tubes. No deciding you know best and checking yourself out." A glance toward the surly-looking cop at the door let Jon know he'd be able to do no such thing and he was lucky they'd not handcuffed him to the hospital bed.

"I'll do my best," he promised.

Susan gave him a look of genuine concern before she exited the room.

Nurse Aegypt took her place. She gave Jon's monitors the once-over before she followed the doctor out. "I'll check back in twenty," she said over her shoulder as she almost collided with Fitz.

The lawyer excused himself and let the busy nurse pass, and then paused to inform the police officer he'd be speaking with his client and expected confidentiality.

He shut the door.

"How is he doing?" Fitz asked Rabbi Max.

"Well enough to speak for himself," said Jon.

"Glad to hear it," said Fitz. "Are you up for some bad news?"

A stabbing pain in his shoulder made Jon grimace; what could possibly constitute *bad* news after what he'd been through, he hated to imagine. He massaged the muscle there and said, "Half my family is gone. Killed by some maniac with a grudge. Nothing you can say could ever be worse than that."

Fitz broke eye contact. "Of course. I'm sorry." There was a pause as he fidgeted with the beige folder in his hands.

Jon said, "What's that?"

Fitz nodded, as if someone inside his head just told him to pull himself together. Out the window, Fitz noticed the sun had just finished setting.

"It's the latest on your case," Fitz began.

Leaving the foot of the bed for a turn at the bedside, Rabbi Max said, "I was about to tell him. She's searching your Volvo, Jon. Cassidy phoned to let us know."

"Is she here?"

"In the waiting room. Simon was here with her, but he

left. Said there was something he had to get back to."

"That would be the girlfriend."

Fitz said, "You don't seem too concerned about the car."

"Why should I be?" said Jon. "They just arrested me for murder—of course they're going to go through my car. What's in the folder?"

Fitz tapped the file's cardboard edge on the windowsill a couple times, as if in some personal mantra. When he turned back to Jon, his jaw was set. "Forensic report. Still preliminary, but it comes with photos. I had to twist arms to get this copy."

"Show me."

"No. As your lawyer and as your friend, I can't. You don't need the visuals, or the details, for that matter. I'll summarize. There are three distinct bodies. One woman, two boys. They're the right ages for Chelle, Luke, and Paul. The blood types match. There are also scraps of distinctive clothing. DNA will take time, given the circumstances in which they were found, but that's just a formality at this point. I'm sorry, Jon. I truly am."

Jon expected the blow to bring his symptoms crashing back, braced himself for the nauseating grip on his stomach, the fire in his arm that made his fingers tingle. But no, all he felt was tired, so overwhelmingly exhausted, as if he could sleep for a thousand years. It was possible Susan had added something to his saline drip to keep him mellowed out, or maybe he was simply resigned to the fact that Chelle and the boys were gone and he was the number one suspect in their deaths. There was nothing he could do to change either of those facts. He had to put his trust in Fitz to clear his name and keep him out of prison—although, at that point in time, he really couldn't have cared less about a lifetime of incarceration; nothing seemed to matter to Jon Edom anymore.

A ringtone sounded. Some classical piece, nothing Jon knew. Fitz walked back over to the window to answer.

"Yes? I'm with him now. That won't be necessary. No. What? Fine. I'll tell him." He hung up. In a calm, level voice he told Jon, "Cavallo and Troyer are in the building. They'll be at your door any minute. Cavallo wants to show you a piece of evidence. If you're up to it, my advice is to let her. But, for God's sakes, *don't* answer her questions. If you have to say anything, it's *speak to my lawyer.*

"What if my lawyer doesn't know?"

"Then he'll say so. You've been arrested, Jon. You have rights."

Jon opened his mouth to ask how Cavallo would take his silence but was interrupted by a loud knock at the door. Fitz shot him a silent warning and walked over to hold the door open a crack.

"A moment, Detectives," he said. "Are you ready, Jon?"

"As I'll ever be."

Rabbi Max squeezed Jon's shoulder.

Fitz touched a finger to his lips as a final reminder, then opened the door wide.

Cavallo stood in the doorway, slouched, Troyer's thin face over her shoulder. Jon's attention was immediately drawn to the case Cavallo had with her. Long, metallic, and, from the shape, it may have held a shotgun or a fancy pool cue. The detective had one hand on the handle, the other was wrapped around its bottom.

Cavallo straightened her back and entered the hospital room triumphantly, her sedate partner behind her. Lieutenant Randall, the detective who'd arrested Jon, stood behind Saul, conversing with the officer on guard. He nodded to his underling before he, too, walked in. When Fitz pulled the door closed, Jon felt crowded, claustrophobic, *cornered.*

Troyer and Randall occupied the space in front of the window; Fitz folded his hands at the end of the bed; Cavallo faced the rabbi, puzzled as to why he was present; she said nothing.

Fitz broke the loaded silence. "You have something to show my client, Detective?"

Cavallo didn't flinch. She turned to Troyer, who stepped to her side and took the case from her hands.

"Well, I got my exercise in today." She spoke to the room but made it clear she was talking to Jon. "In any state but Texas and Alaska, the miles I put on my car would have put me across state lines by now. I supervised two searches—one hours away, one local—and wouldn't you know it? The find I wanted, the prize in the cereal box, so to speak, turned up here in Austin. You've seen the warrant for the search of your client's car, Counselor?"

Fitz patted his jacket. "I have a copy."

Cavallo worked the clasps of the metal case. "My team was nice enough to wrap this." She reached into the case and lifted something out.

Even with the clear, plastic bag sparkling in the dim light, Jon knew what it was at once. Nine inches in its collapsed state, the signature red-and-black casing with the hint of metal within, hooks projecting from top and middle—it was the *Club 1000* wheel lock. Cavallo turned the security device around to show him a nick in the top hook of the casing: Jon had damaged it breaking into the lake house.

"You recognize this?" Cavallo's question was, of course, rhetorical.

Fitz cleared his throat, and Jon nodded. "It's mine. A gift from my wife."

Cavallo raised her eyebrows at Randall, then turned back to Jon. "Can you tell me where you last saw this object?"

"Under the front seat of my car. There's a plastic lip I wedge it against so it doesn't slip. I guess that's where you found it."

"And did you have your Club 1000 with you when you visited the Berger family lake house in Conroe, Texas, three Saturdays ago?"

"Of course. It's in my statement. I took The Club in case . . ." A thought occurred to Jon that made him stop short.

"Doctor Edom?" Cavallo prompted.

"I took it in case I needed protection. I didn't use it on my family, if that's what you're implying."

Cavallo retained her poker face. "Your fingerprints are all over the handle, and the hook. Some fingerprints are expected, but so many makes me wonder. Perhaps you were changing your grip, trying to find leverage?"

"I didn't *need* leverage, Detective."

"There are traces of glass, too," Cavallo continued. "Small, powdery." She pointed to the split in the hook casing. Per your various statements, you broke the glass door."

"That's right, but that was the only—"

"And *here*." The detective rotated The Club to show Jon—and the room—the rubber handgrip, "is where we found traces of blood, and hair, and tissue. Are they only from your wife, Doctor? Or did you kill your boys the same way? We know what you did to the bodies; I'd sleep better if I knew they were already dead before you began to dismember them."

"I didn't kill my family!" Jon's voice cracked, tears welling in his eyes. He clutched at his head; he was in agony again. The symptoms were back.

As Jon slumped back into the bed, Rabbi Max urged, "Get the doctor."

Fitz ran to the door; Jon couldn't see what was happening, but the sudden, patchy blindness sharpened his hearing. He listened as the footsteps in the hallway reversed, a second ahead of Nurse Aegypt shouting, "Make way!"

There came yet more footsteps, more voices, and Jon heard Cavallo's breath catch as she was herded from the room.

Nurse Aegypt barked something about a spiking heart rate.

Fitz shouted from the hall, "Hold on, Jon. We'll fight this. We'll *fight*!"

Vision returned slowly, but all Jon could see was that imaginary checkerboard. The sounds around him faded; first to go were the voices, then the movement, then the last sound to leave Jon was the cacophony of electronic beeps.

The checkerboard stretched to infinity. In the distance, a mountain loomed. It looked normal at first: a firm, rocky mountain. But as Jon looked on, its color shifted, darkening from stony gray to an earthy, fecal brown. A breeze stirred up a whirlwind of particles to reveal a mountain of dirt.

The dirt mountain faded, the checkerboard vanished, and the last thing Jon saw, before darkness closed over him, was a mass of bright shadows; they reminded him of blurred photo negatives as they clustered above him, tilting heads down to scrutinize him like observers to an execution.

One figure stooped low and extended a hand. Jon didn't take it. There was something familiar about the figure, something viscerally terrifying.

It wore a hood.

29

Silas Bram Bundy pulled on his headset. The video feed he used for the news hung on the augmented reality wall of his office, where he'd pinned it last night. The office was cleaner with the headset on than with it off, but it held all the same furniture. The desk was there, the mini-fridge, the old yellow couch from Grandpappy's house. The virtual screen hid a water stain on the unpainted Sheetrock. A second screen pinned to the top of the desk showed nature scenes. Silas kept a third screen pinned to the virtual surface of a secret drawer in the desk. Like the screen itself, the drawer didn't actually exist in real life; it would remain hidden to anyone else who might happen to put on the headset. By tilting his head at just the right angle, Silas could see *through* the desk to where that secret screen flickered. In idle mode, it displayed the same nature scenes showing on the desktop. Silas had to key in a passcode to change the screen's function. The scenes it showed him after that could be natural or unnatural, depending upon his mood.

Either way, they were private.

"Over air six," Coppersmith told Silas from behind his left shoulder. "No idea what that is on the world wide web." He made the old-fashioned term sound like a disgusting slur.

Silas had noticed Coppersmith *always* spoke about technology that way, as if he found the whole thing entirely distasteful. He didn't watch screens, didn't own a car. Hell, the guy didn't even possess a cell phone! In all the years of their partnership, Silas had never seen the tall man so much as *hold* a phone. It was like he came from another century, like nothing made by modern man was interesting enough to garner his attention.

Silas said, "I got it," and dragged a virtual bookmark in the shape of a flag down from the AR ceiling. The flag had the number six on it. Silas had dozens upon dozens of bookmarks, some on the ceiling, others in the virtual drawer. Those in the drawer were private—he did his very best not to think about them. Coppersmith couldn't see into the virtual office without a headset, naturally, so *couldn't* have peeked. However, Silas had been told for most of his life he had an overly expressive face. Folks who knew him could read him like a book. With Coppersmith, it was more like reading a billboard.

"Is it up?" Coppersmith asked, as if on cue. "And I mean the feed, not that monstrosity I see stirring in your pants."

Silas cursed to himself. Like a billboard.

The Channel 6 feed was, in fact, up. A studio anchor faced the camera in freeze frame. On the studio wall behind her, a screen showed Kate Boldwin, the channel's star reporter. Kate held a microphone beneath her chin. Behind her was grass, a few trees, and amorphous gray blobs. That was all Silas made out.

"It's ready," he said quietly.

Coppersmith smiled that awful smile of his. "Then play

on, Abraham."

Ever obedient, Silas clicked *play*.

The anchor, whatever her name was, gestured at the screen.

"We go now to a special report by senior investigator Kate Boldwin. I have a warning for our viewers. Some of the subject matter, as well as the images, may not be appropriate for the young or viewers inclined to be sensitive. Anyone who doesn't wish to see violence, cruelty to animals, or the desecration of religious objects is advised to switch off now, or skip forward six minutes and thirty-four seconds on the recorded feed."

The anchor paused to allow viewers time to heed her warning. Mentally, Silas pictured a million snowflakes fumbling with their cell phones to save themselves from *offense*. He smiled; even the snowflakes were curious.

On the feed, the anchor gave a patient smile. Silas snuck a peek at Coppersmith—the pass-through image on his headset was true to life: His partner was awkwardly tall, and way too skinny to suit his smooth, confident voice. He was wrapped in his duster, as usual, and sat with his backside perched on the mini-fridge that held Silas's lunch, among other vittles. The man's height meant his boot heels were farther from the fridge than the appliance was tall. Somehow, his eyes had picked the exact spot on the wall where the news anchor waited in the virtual office.

Coppersmith was fooling around, of course. He couldn't see the AR room, and he couldn't read minds. Faces, maybe, but that was his limit. Nonetheless, even as Silas had that thought, Coppersmith turned to grin at him as if he *knew*. The grin was nothing like the anchor's smile; it showed far too many teeth.

Eventually, the anchor spoke. "Kate, can you tell us where you are right now, and what we're seeing?"

The scene shifted.

In place of the studio, Kate and her hill appeared in full size, no longer miniature. At that size, Silas saw the trees swaying in the breeze, but those gray blobs dotting the grassy hillside were still too infuriatingly small to make out.

Kate Boldwin spoke with confidence into her mic. "Ann, I'm on location at Hidden Heart Cemetery in northwest Austin. Hidden Heart sits on twenty acres of what is now public land. It used to be the burial ground for the Hidden Heart Fellowship, an Anabaptist community that's been gone for well over a century. As such, this is one of the oldest cemeteries in Austin. The last funeral was held here in 1975, and since then, the property has been cared for by a public trust. It's our taxes that keep the lawns mowed, the trees pruned, and the monuments maintained."

Kate began walking midway through her monologue. She said "monument" just as she came to a halt next to a tall, marble obelisk mottled with moss. It reminded Silas of the one his Uncle Tommy was buried beneath. Kate's obelisk was missing its top. The upper third of the pyramid shape had been smashed and left in a heap on the ground. Around the patch of the cemetery upon which the obelisk stood was a foot-high stone wall, which was ringed by flapping yellow police tape.

Kate shook her head forlornly at the mess before she continued. "As you can see, some of those monuments are beyond saving. More than fifteen headstones and larger grave markers like this one have been vandalized over the past three weeks. The damage you see here happened last night. According to cemetery records, it marked the final resting place of the Disztl family. Marie Disztl was the last of the line. She died and was interred in 1909."

As Kate lifted a hand, the camera panned left to show more of the Disztl grave plot. There were slanted headstones, standing in pairs and triplets, to mark where family members were buried. The last stone in line was missing. Based on the size of the hole behind where it should have been, Silas reckoned he knew where to find it.

An icon flashed at the top of the news feed. Silas reached for it almost without thinking. He'd invested in the headset for exactly this feature: AI-assisted immersion. All he had to do was pinch the icon and he would be on location with Kate. He hesitated, though. Switching on immersion would switch off the pass-through feature. And that meant he wouldn't be able to keep an eye on Coppersmith. Sharing the private office with his partner was bad enough; just the thought of Coppersmith watching him made his skin crawl.

"Pay attention." Coppersmith left the mini-fridge and stepped in front of the news feed. *Deliberately* in front, Silas felt sure.

Grumbling to himself, Silas pinched the icon for immersive mode.

The room slipped away and, all at once, Silas was standing in front of the hole that had replaced the last Disztl gravestone.

The feed was paused, which it did automatically, to give him a moment to orient himself. Silas looked around. He was on the hill where Kate had been standing. In fact, she was there with him, off to the right. Her image wasn't entirely perfect: the reporter's face and shoulders looked exactly as they had when the camera was pointing Kate's way; the perky bust that kept the male fans tuning in was nice, too. But the rest of Kate—her waist, hips, and thighs in tight, light brown slacks—was far skinnier than they would have been in person. Even so, the AI-generated Kate was realistic enough to make Silas feel he was actually *there* with the reporter.

Grunting in satisfaction, Silas took a moment to glance around at the green lawn, the dull gravestones, and the blinking red dots that represented cameras in the immersive image. There was one camera behind, one overhead. Silas had been in enough feeds to spot where the cone of each camera's POV ended and the AI guesswork began, but he ignored the jagged edges and concentrated on what he'd switched modes to see. With a subtle hand gesture, he nudged his own POV forward until he was peering down into the dug-up grave.

Sure enough, the slant headstone was inside. It rested upside down at the bottom of a pit nearly three feet wide, six feet long, and slightly over six feet deep. Around the pit, scattered earth and splintered wood showed that a casket had been ripped out, torn open, and demolished. There were no bones Silas could see, nor any shrunken head with its tufts of hair and shriveled face, though that would have made for more dramatic TV.

Where had the corpse gone?

Silas unpaused the feed in the hope Kate would tell him. She stirred to life, speaking directly to him, not the camera—another neat trick of the AI.

"The destruction of the grave is eclipsed in horror by the theft of Marie Disztl's body," Kate told Silas. "Police and cemetery officials are working to piece together exactly how vandals were able to dig up her coffin and empty it, before wrecking the coffin and the family marker. The footage you are about to see was taken by a neighbor's security camera."

The sky went dark, and Silas found himself watching the Disztl grave from a distance. A bunch of shadowy figures moved against a backdrop of gray mist, too far away to see what they were doing, how many there were, or what they looked like. After ten seconds of frenzied motion, the figures moved away, dividing into smaller groups, and were gone.

Back to the gravesite; Kate appeared again. Silas took a step back from the open grave, fighting vertigo that threatened to tip him into the gaping hole, albeit virtually.

"As you saw," Kate said, "the camera was some distance away. I spoke to the owner, who swears he heard and saw nothing unusual that night, except for a couple catfights."

The reporter then paused to kneel beside a piece of mold-blackened lumber just beyond the police tape. Silas, with a good working knowledge of carpentry, quickly rebuilt the coffin in his mind and deduced the piece had from a corner, probably bottom left. Someone had likely smashed the coffin with a sledgehammer, since there was no other way he could imagine the nailed timbers snapping all in a piece like that. Unless, of course, the coffin had been literally blown apart from the inside.

"Catfights," Coppersmith's voice broke into the virtual world. "How horribly *vulgar*."

Silas pulled off the headset. "How did you—"

Coppersmith remained in the place Silas had left him, staring at the blank wall with his arms crossed across his chest. Silas said, "Put those goggles on. The best is yet to come."

Silas scowled at his partner and replaced his headset.

". . . far from the only victim of these vandals," Kate continued, "the same, or perhaps a copycat group struck the St. Thomas cemetery four miles east of here. But the worst offenses happened at a location few Austinites even know is a cemetery."

In an instant, Kate and the Disztl graves disappeared., and Silas found himself standing alone in an empty field. It was an overcast, wintery afternoon, the sky an ominous gray. There were scattered buildings nearby, ramshackle, unloved; a bunch of sour-faced women in tattered clothing stood watching the camera dot that hovered over Silas's shoulder like a sniper's mark. One woman covered her face, while another stooped, grabbed a clod of earth, and threw it

Silas's way. He ducked and found himself floating in a void; the dirt had hit the camera.

Kate began speaking in voiceover: "The grass of that field grows over the bodies of smallpox victims along with victims of other epidemics past. It's now the setting for the Austin Shelter for Women and Children. Channel 6's Bill Mason visited there four years ago and recorded the footage you saw for an exposé he was forced to abandon. It would have told the history of Austin's pest camps, the quarantine sites that ringed Austin until the last, Fort Camp Prairie Two, closed in 1938. Nobody is sure how many bodies are buried there. Or, I should say, how many bodies *were* buried."

The scene shifted again. Silas was at the same location, but the sky was now cloudless, bright, and sunny. The buildings had a fresh coat of green paint, and there was no one in sight—not even the mud-flinging old crones. But it was the field that had changed the most: Something had torn the soil and pitted the earth with grave-wide trenches. They appeared blurry, as if the AI hadn't reconstructed them completely, but the general shape was clear. It made Silas think of a great, clawed hand, and he wouldn't have been surprised if Kate told him God himself had reached down from heaven to scrape the corpses out.

"This is the field today," Kate said. "My crew filmed this earlier today, while I was speaking with cemetery officials. If you don't want to see scenes of violence, especially violence toward animals, please look away now."

Silas registered a subliminal change in picture quality as the edge around a nearby trench grew much sharper than the rest. A camera dot hovered over the trench; he moved to check out what it pulled into focus.

There, scraps of tattered, colorless fabric stood out against the dark soil—the remains of a sleeve wrapped around a skeletal arm. Mummified tendons made the hand at its end into a twisted claw, and trapped in its fingers was a raven's head. The bird had twisted its neck completely around; its glazed eyes and gaping black beak looked down the rest of its lifeless body to the tousled tail feathers.

Silas pulled back from the disturbing sight and saw the camera dot rising to bring more of the trenches into sharp relief. There was a second raven near the first, belly-down with its wings stretched out, like someone had knocked it to the ground and stomped hard upon its back. The sharpening effect of the AI continued to spread to show more birds, a dozen at least, lying dead among scattered, skeletal human parts. Not every bird was a raven: There were crows, a few large vultures, and a caracara falcon, the carrion trifecta. In total, at least fifty dead birds were scattered around that desecrated field.

For a moment, Silas forgot he was watching an immersive news feed. Stumbling sideways, he instinctively tried to catch himself from falling into a trench. All he got for his trouble was a sharp pain in his foot and a chuckle from Coppersmith; his real-world office chair had swung around and banged Silas's boot into the desk leg.

"This scene is unique, for now," Kate Boldwin continued. "We can only pray the vandals are stopped before anything like this happens again."

Suddenly, the field vanished. Silas found himself in the studio with Ann the anchor. She had her head down, hand solemnly over her heart. Kate was on screen at the Hidden Heart Cemetery.

Ann swallowed hard, as if genuinely upset by the happenings at the old, forgotten cemetery. "Kate—do the police have any suspects?"

"Too many, Ann."

The studio was replaced by the view of a home's front porch. There were black bars to Silas's right and left, cutting off his view of areas the AI had decided, or had been *directed*, not to create. Directly ahead, a concrete path led to the porch from the sidewalk. The combined effect of walls and path made Silas feel like he was looking at a stage with curtains at either side, so when a black-clothed something ran out behind the left bar and up the path, the effect was really quite theatrical.

The something appeared human until it got close. Getting a good view of the goblin's ugly little face, Silas lurched back instinctively, making the office chair rattle. Sickly green skin; red, glowering eyes; and a sharp, pointed nose flashed before him a split second before the porch vanished.

Head spinning, Silas now stood in the middle of a city street late at night. He was dressed like a cop, a camera dot trained at the middle of his chest. Straight ahead of him lay a railroad crossing; the orange-yellow streetlights shone down on rust-colored rails, desiccated wooden ties, and loose gravel sidings. The crossing itself was concrete and asphalt. The street it joined ran past tenement housing on the right, a parking lot on the left. Graffiti adorned everything, everywhere: Green flames burst from the nostrils of a huge red nose scrawled on the side of a trailer in the lot, and the fence around the tenement was tagged with elaborate tags, crossed-out genitals, and profanity most foul.

None of the details made the crossing special; Silas had seen had a dozen or more spots just like it in Austin. What set this one apart, though, was the body hanging by its neck from a rough old rope attached to the end of the raised crossing barrier.

Small, it was like that of a child.

Silas unpaused and found himself running. A man's voice said something Channel 6 had bleeped out followed by, "*Call for backup!*"

The child's body loomed as Silas drew closer. Suddenly, the camera sweeping him along stopped. A shadow on the grass shifted, and, in an instant, Silas saw it wasn't a shadow at all but a tarp being thrown off a knot of figures clad all in black. As one, they ran at Silas, who threw up his fists as the first two figures began raining blows upon him. A woman police officer flew into the picture, knocking one attacker away with a solid shoulder block. The connection to the porch footage became painfully clear to Silas: the attacker wore a mask, although not that of a goblin this time, but the white-faced slasher from the horror flick.

The cop drew her gun. "Back off! Trey, are you g—"

"Look out!" It was the same voice that had requested backup.

The police woman pitched forward and, behind her, another masked assailant stumbled into view, holding a baseball bat. The scene before Silas's eyes shimmered as the body behind the camera dot tried to get up. The bat drew back, flew forward. The scene disappeared.

With great relief, heart thumping wildly, Silas was back in his office.

The immersive feed had ended, the headset back in pass-through mode. Coppersmith stepped to one side in time for Kate to appear on the virtual screen, surrounded once more by the hills and stones of Hidden Heart Cemetery.

"What you've just seen is but a sample of the disturbing footage police and media have collected. The first was taken by a doorbell camera, the second from a police bodycam."

Ann then appeared briefly, asking for an update on the officers before the scene returned to the cemetery.

"Minor injuries, thankfully," Kate informer her anchor. "The beating was a week ago. I understand both officers are fully recovered and back on the job."

"That's good to know," said Ann. "And the hanging victim?"

"A mannequin," Kate said with a roll of her eyes. "Supposedly put there to lure the police officers."

"So cruel," Ann replied. "Kate, are you suggesting the police believe the same individuals we saw in those clips are responsible for the cemetery vandalism?"

"Either those or associated individuals, yes. Police say they have more security footage of similarly masked people smashing up headstones, but they are withholding details to stop the perpetrators learning from their mistakes."

"Do we have any names or a lead on a motive?"

"No names. Not yet. But the motive question is something the police are considering closely. There is one feature that appears consistent throughout the videos . . ."

Kate disappeared so the feed could show a still image, a sort of collage that repeated a symbol again and again. Each of the repeated symbols was a triangle formed of thick red lines.

"We've been authorized to release this collection of freeze frames. It shows the red triangle symbol that appears on a patch worn by the vandals. The placement of the patch varies, but they all seem to have at least one. The 'goblin' in the doorbell footage wore a triangle on a glove. The assailant with the baseball bat wore it on a backpack. Expert analysis suggests the triangle is identical to one on the cover of a seminal book by the founder of a church in our area. Channel 6 approached Mister Phillip Berger, spokesperson of the Church of the Resurrected, based near Wimberley, for comment."

Berger's unmistakable face appeared on the screen. He stood in front of the tower his old man had paid for in cash. Everything about the man screamed *expensive*, from his bespoke suit to his silk tie to his haircut.

"I don't know what to tell you, Miss Boldwin, other than that the church is not affiliated with any criminal group. And it is just a triangle, after all. Maybe you should speak to the Salvation Army—I believe their buckets use the same color red."

Back at the cemetery, Kate shook her head. "Other than a possible religious motivation, there seem to be far more questions in this case than there are answers. The police are continuing their investigations. If any viewers out there have footage of any of the crimes being committed by this gang, we ask that they contact police directly. Ann."

The segment ended there.

The anchorwoman thanked the reporter and sent cameras back to the news desk. Her partner there began a story about the doctor accused of offing his wife, who just so happened to be the aforementioned Phillip Berger's sister. Silas recognized the two detectives who'd paid him a visit lurking around in the background of a press conference. Apparently the doctor had posted two million dollars in bail out of his own savings. The anchor said something about him falling sick, but Silas couldn't hear clearly, thanks to an interruption by Coppersmith.

"Well," the tall man said, "are we pleased?"

Silas removed the headset and placed it on the desk. He stared Coppersmith in the eye. "Are you out of your mind? We never talked about beating cops. And what was the deal with the dead birds?"

"The *signs*, you mean, Abraham?" That smile again. "I especially liked the ravens. The death eaters, dead. You know I have a weakness for poetry."

"I know you're a sick sonuva —" Silas clamped his lips shut. Like so many of his conversations with Coppersmith, he'd gotten to a point where he didn't want to know more, even though the not knowing ate him up. "These signs . . . the birds, the dug-up graves. Are you telling me you did all that?"

Coppersmith clapped a hand to his heart. "I'm *wounded*, Abraham. You think I would arrange such a spectacle? No. I didn't strangle the beasts—not for this enterprise. As for the smashed graves . . . you know, signs are far more effective with a bit of mystery. Suffice it to say, a higher power is at play here. Rejoice, Abraham! Someone is rewarding our efforts, our planting is bearing fruit, and the soil is restless. Its captives are breaking free."

Silas rose from his chair and stomped away. "You're so full of—"

"Temper," Coppersmith admonished. There was an edge to his voice that spun Silas around on his heels. Coppersmith crossed over to the desk and lifted up the augmented reality headset. "Do you ever look back, Abraham? Do you ever ask this magic eyeglass to remind you what your life was like when you were at your lowest? The place where we met had fewer screens to place in front of you. And it had far more bars."

He tossed the headset to Silas.

Startled, Silas flung out his hands to make the catch. In the split second that cost him, Coppersmith closed the space between them and seized Silas's collar.

"Don't ever forget what you owe me," the tall man growled.

Silas resisted the urge to scream, lash out, or run.

"Don't forget who you are." Coppersmith's voice dripped menace.

Silas's heart fluttered in a way that he hated: a weak, butterfly rhythm. Coppersmith grinned that toothy grin of his and released the collar, patted Silas on the cheek, and returned to the mini-fridge. He held the tail of his duster out of the way as he examined the contents.

Silas swallowed past a dry throat. "I . . . well, at least that triangle idea of yours worked."

"Of course it worked, friend. Where's your faith?" Coppersmith clucked his tongue as he peered inside the fridge. "Too much refined sugar in here, Abraham. Far too many sweets."

Silas didn't listen. He returned to the desk and set the headset down. "No more beating up cops."

Coppersmith shut the fridge sharply and straightened his back. "Excuse me?"

"You heard."

Coppersmith's glare was cold as the grave, and for an instant, Silas felt like he'd slipped the headset back on and was peering once more at the dead birds and ancient body parts. He was sure his partner was blurring at the edges.

At last, Coppersmith released his gaze. "Oh, but Coachman is so good with a baseball bat."

Silas swallowed again, this time with a little moisture. "And no more of that animal stuff, either—I'm assuming you're lying about that part."

Coppersmith placed his hand over his heart again. "*Lying*? Don't you know me at all?"

Silas blinked. It had been Coppersmith who had sold him on the idea of sending ranch hands in Halloween masks to stir up trouble for COTR. Of course, Coppersmith was the one who had arranged the fake *signs*! The animal cruelty didn't bother Silas too much, him being a country boy, but what got him fretting was the thought of his men setting up the scenes on Coppersmith's orders. That was foolish. He knew Coachman and the rest were good, loyal men. They must have figured Coppersmith spoke in Silas's name—unless he was fooling himself. Maybe Coppersmith was an Absalom who intended to tempt the Cross Guard from Silas the way that evil prince tempted Israel from King David. Well, that was fine by Silas—Absalom had lost his head in the end.

"I *do* know you," Silas defended. "Lying ain't your

style, 'cept when you don't like the truth. You said the birds were signs, a higher power? I reckon you're right. You'd need a higher power to bust open those graves. Diesel power, at least, for the backhoe. Oh, you go on and keep your secrets, Coppersmith. God himself will make the truth shine like lightning."

The tall man quit grinning. He didn't care much for when Silas showed backbone. It was ironic, really: Silas was so worried about Coppersmith reading him, when all along, he could read Coppersmith just as easily, if not more so. If Silas was a billboard, Coppersmith was a thin sheet of glass, his thoughts and intentions exposed for the world to see. That comforted Silas somewhat, and would have comforted him more, if not for the fact that when he did try staring through his partner, all he saw on the other side was complete and utter darkness.

30

Despite days of accumulated dust, the Mustang was still too flashy for a burial, so Dani and Saul had caught a lift in a black-and-white. The crowd at Austin Memorial Park Cemetery numbered easily into the high hundreds. Cars of all shapes and sizes lined the street, directed in their slow, steady progress by uniformed officers. In the last fifty feet before the cemetery gate, Dani's driver had flashed his blue and red lights four separate occasions to get people to clear a path and allow them through. Each time, Dani considered telling him not to hurry. Nights had been rough lately.

She'd barely slept a wink since confronting Edom with the alleged murder weapon. That had been Tuesday, and now it was Sunday—hence her fatigue. With Saul riding shotgun, Dani had managed to catch a few winks in the back of the squad car. The noise of the crowds revived her, but she'd have been glad of more time to get herself ready before the hike to the graveside.

It was nice weather for a funeral—only a little cloudy, not too warm. As the police car moved through the cemetery gatehouse, Dani stared out at the hundred-year-old architecture; the sandstone walls and matching tile roofs reminded her of a Hitchcock film she'd seen a thousand years ago. She couldn't recall which one and considered asking Saul, but he was occupied watching the stream from the Faith Center on his cell phone.

Dani tapped the glass partition and spoke through the vent. "Did I miss anything?"

Saul turned his head. "When did you drop out?"

"Let's call it ten minutes into the ride."

Saul chuckled. "You missed nothing, unless you're into church hats."

He held up his phone so Dani could see the Faith Center audience. About 80 percent of everyone who had been present was on the road, but there were a few women left behind with impressive hats.

One was Lisa Berger.

The matriarch sat onstage in her wheelchair, a headful of peacock feathers balanced precariously upon her wispy white hair. The rest of her family was at the cemetery, so she had to watch the burial on the auditorium jumbotron with only the reduced crowd and her private nurse for company. The nurse had an impressive hat on too, a deep red fascinator with elaborate netting. The color went well with her skin tone.

Saul pointed at the woman. "I'll say this for COTR. They don't mind mixing light and dark in the pews."

"Awfully pale in that tower of theirs, though," said Dani.

Saul grunted. "Is it just me or are there more folks here than back at church HQ?"

Dani eyed the milling pedestrians and the cars trying to negotiate the cemetery entrance. Saul was right. There was definitely an increase, mostly in families wearing casual, nonfunereal, clothes.

"Probably went out to see the eclipse and thought they'd join in with the funeral," she said.

The partial solar eclipse, already in progress, was due to reach its peak in forty minutes. At the funeral, Pastor Korvus had used the coincidental scheduling to full effect. *Death is a passing shadow*, he'd told the rapt congregation. *It darkens our life but briefly. The source of our light stays bright.*

Finally, the driver put the black-and-white in park. They were on the single-lane road that wound its way through the middle of the cemetery. Five vehicles ahead sat the hearse with the caskets that held the remains of John and Paul Edom. The hearse with their mother's remains was in front of that. The limo transporting the family, minus Doctor Edom, had taken a different cemetery road and was parked parallel to the hearse. Dani saw an attendant hold the car's door for P. J. Berger as P. J.'s brother, Phillip, looked on. The next person out of the limo was Cassidy Edom. Her brother followed. He held hands with his girlfriend.

Simon's arm candy was dressed in black, like practically everyone else, but her dress was so tight, it might well have been painted on—it showed off every curve and line of what was a formidable body. Dani had studied Simon at the funeral and noted the time he didn't spend checking his phone or copping a feel on the girlfriend was punctuated with yawns and eye rolls. Phillip, too, seemed less crushed by his grief than he was worried about playing the good host. If Dani had been on the lookout for more murder suspects, Rochelle's son and her brother would certainly have made the list.

Next, after Phillip, would have been the scar-faced man standing next to the church's resident hard case, Tasmin Beale. Both were next to Beale's pickup, parked next in line after the limo. Like Beale, the man appeared angry at life and ready to take it out on someone—bruising for any opportunity to use those big, meaty fists of his. Unlike Tasmin, he had a military record, and the scar as a souvenir from an improvised explosive device from back in the desert. His name was William Weaver; Dani was willing to bet Beale called him *Billy*. The guy dressed like a secret service agent, complete with ear piece, while she wore jeans, cowboy boots, and a satiny shirt. At least her outfit was black, if you didn't count the white bolo, silver buttons, and turquoise belt buckle.

Four vehicles ahead of Dani, a mob of pallbearers stood around waiting for a signal to get started with their grim task. Pastor Korvus stepped out of the hearse's passenger side to raise his hand and, at once, his team started the process of unloading the caskets and carrying them on their shoulders to the large, double-sized tent that covered three open graves.

Dani stretched her neck. Showtime. Her purpose at the cemetery was the same as it had been at the Faith Center: She wanted to assure the family of her support, and to keep them all friendly for the trial. At the same time, she wanted to read the faces of Rochelle's family, friends, and the other attendees. Doctor Edom was the killer, of that she was sure. Still, it was always possible he had worked with an accomplice, given the scale of the crime. If Rochelle's affair served as Edom's motive, he might well have drafted in his brother-in-law by threatening a scandal. Drafting Simon was less likely. Dani couldn't see Edom asking his own son to conspire in the brutal murder.

The sister-in-law was another story. P. J.'s grief seemed authentic enough, but Saul had a saying that Dani was sure applied: if a man leaves, there's always another woman. Edom had insisted he wasn't bedding Dr. Grunberg. If that was true, maybe P. J. was his lover? The idea seemed a stretch, even to Dani, but it was less so than if Edom turned out to be shacking up with Beale.

Dani nearly laughed at that thought and had a struggle to put on her game face before she climbed out of the squad car. Saul held the door for her, and together, they joined the line of mourners trailing the pallbearers across to the tents.

Saul leaned in close. "You heard about the weirdos busting headstones and digging up graves?"

Dani had seen the news. "I'm more worried about cops getting beaten up."

"Me too. But it looks like the family's got other priorities." He nodded toward one of several armed guards forming a perimeter around the Berger family plot. They were dressed like mourners, but ear pieces and bulging jackets gave them away.

"The vandals strike at night," said Dani. "Why are they going so heavy in the middle of the day?"

Nodding, Saul veered to one side, on a course that would take him face-to-face with one of the guards. Dani followed him a few steps before something caught her eye.

Most of the mourners were on the march, but a few were standing apart from the rest. One man was half hidden behind a monument, but what Dani could see of him appeared familiar; short, he had dark features that looked vaguely Hispanic. With the clouds limiting the light and the monument in the way, she couldn't make a positive ID. Still, that rust-colored hoodie was familiar.

"Keep going," Dani called to Saul as she left his side. She was sure the hooded man had seen her, had been watching her, in fact, but she circled around the far side of the monument to make sure. He didn't wait for her but started walking away a moment before her approach angle blocked him from her sight.

Dani ran around the back of the monument, only to find the man no longer there. She cursed to herself and scanned the crowd. The sun was still lodged firmly behind the clouds, making it harder to see, but after a few panicked moments, she spotted the rust-colored hoodie disappear behind a sepulcher about thirty feet away. Again, by the time she reached the structure, both the man and his hoodie had vanished. She was perplexed: there was nowhere he could hide, unless he was a better tree climber than Tarzan. Annoyed, Dani shoved her hands in her jacket pockets and started back toward the crowd.

She was halfway there when the scuffle started. The scarred security guy, Weaver, had hold of a man with gray hair and a salt-and-pepper beard by the wrist. A phone was in the hand connected to the wrist. Weaver was growling something about a "family event."

"Big family," said the old man, an instant before Dani recognized him. He was Edom's friend, the one she'd last seen at the hospital. After splitting with the Church of the Resurrected, Edom had gone back to the faith of his adoptive parents and was now a practicing Jew. The old man in Weaver's grasp was Jon's rabbi.

"What's going on?" Dani hurried over. Beale appeared to have left Weaver on his own, but one of the other guards was already on his way. Dani knew she'd have to work fast to take control of the situation.

Weaver snapped, "Nothing to do with you, sweets."

"That's *Detective* Sweets." Dani flashed her badge. "Want to tell me why you're restraining this gentleman?"

"Unauthorized streaming." Weaver pointed at a drone camera hovering overhead. "The church has *exclusive* rights to the service and burial."

The rabbi locked eyes with Dani. "You know me, Detective. He asked me to come, and to show him what I see here."

"*Exclusive*," said the scarred man. "Look it up."

At that moment, the rabbi's phone rang. Startled, the scarred man tried to seize it, but Rabbi Max held it close to his chest. He moved smoothly for his age; Dani thought it was like watching a skilled martial artist or seasoned dancer. Weaver dodged a shoulder block but lost his grip on the rabbi's wrist. The rabbi shuffled backward out of Weaver's reach, and Dani stepped between the two before either could close the distance.

"That's enough," Dani barked, but the rabbi wasn't listening. He stepped aside, holding the phone to his ear.

"Jon?" There was a pause. "You're sure? All right. Get some rest." He pocketed the phone, eyes on his scarred enemy. "Seems I'll be on my way. Jon doesn't want any trouble, and neither do I." He gave Dani a cursory nod. "Detective."

The second security man arrived, but Weaver waved him away. He glowered hard at the rabbi and pointed a hand in the direction of the cemetery's exit. The rabbi smiled wryly and started off.

Once Rabbi Max was out of earshot, Dani addressed Weaver. "You're in charge of security?"

"That's right."

Dani waved a hand. "Isn't this a lot of manpower for a funeral?"

"If you say so." Shrugging, Weaver gestured for his junior to follow and headed for the graveside.

As Saul approached from the opposite direction, Dani said, "Something's off here," and wove with him through the crowd. At their destination, the two stood for a moment watching as the graveside service began.

The family members sat in chairs in front of the open graves. Pastor Korvus stood stiff, still, Bible clutched in both hands at his waist. There was no *Grand Cycle* today. As for the faces under the tent, they were mostly impassive, devoid of emotion. Only P. J. and Cassidy showed their feelings; they held hands and wept softly as one large and two small caskets were lowered into the ground.

"Come on." Dani drew Saul away from the open graves

to talk. Some of the onlookers wore special glasses to watch the eclipse, though the sun was still mostly obscured by the clouds. Dani pointed out Weaver to Saul.

"Uglier than his picture," Saul whispered. "Surprised that's possible. The goon I talked to got real quiet when I asked about the extra staffing, but I managed to coax out the details. Seems your friend Beale—she runs ops on security, while Weaver bosses the grunts on the ground—got a warning or a threat of some sort. Anonymous email, something about the 'seed of Ezra Berger shall not rest easy.' Said to watch the sky for 'the shadow of sin.'"

Dani raised an eyebrow. "That wasn't from Korvus? Sounds like his material."

"The guy didn't have a clue where it came from. All he knew was they're supposed to stay sharp, especially near the peak of the eclipse. Beale, or maybe Weaver, said to be *ready*."

"For what, exactly?" Dani didn't wait for an answer but checked her phone. "Well, if something's supposed to happen at the peak, we'll find out what in four minutes." A thought struck her. "Wait, did you say *Ezra* Berger?"

"Yeah. The warning, or whatever the hell it was, referenced his *seed*."

"Do you remember our interview with Bundy, at the ranch?" Dani asked Saul.

"Sure. What's that got to do with— oh."

Turning fast on her heels, Dani set off briskly in the direction of the tent. Over her shoulder, she said to Saul, "Get on the horn. Tell our officers to widen the perimeter. And see if we can get eyes on all the church toughs."

"There are too many." Saul looked alarmed. "We don't have the manpower."

"Do your best."

Knowing that too much attention could spark a panic, Dani did her best to disguise her hurry as an emotional swell. She covered her heart with a hand and eyes pointed at Korvus, though she was actually looking beyond him to where Beale stood behind the family. By the time Dani was within fifteen feet, the officers were shifting to new positions. Dani swore under her breath. There were too few law enforcement and too many of Weaver's security force. If Bundy showed up with a mob of cowboy zealots, there was no way the police could prevent violence.

A security guard stepped into Dani's path.

She flashed her badge, but the man stayed put.

"I need to see Beale," Dani urged. "*This* says I need to see her right now." She made the badge sway like a pendulum.

With a derisory snort, the guard let her pass.

How much time did she have? Not enough, that much was certain. No longer caring about drawing attention, Dani broke into a run. Murmurs from the crowd swelled into shouts that drowned out the pastor's speech. Security guards ran to meet Dani, hands reaching inside their jackets

. . .

"*Police!*" she shouted.

Beale turned, saw her.

"I need you to stand down your detail," Dani told her, breathless from running. "Officers are in place. They'll take security from here on out."

Dani knew she had to be careful with her words; they didn't want a stampede. Beale seemed to get the gist but made no move to help. She pointed up at the sky.

The clouds had parted. The sun shone brightly through, despite the disk of darkness that covered half its surface. Dani glimpsed at it through her fingers; she knew better than to stare directly at the sun.

There came the throaty roar of engines, too high-pitched to be cars. Dani searched the horizon. First one, then two, then a half dozen ATVs appeared, all driven by masked riders. Dani recognized the style of masks from a news feed she'd seen: two goblins, a horror film slasher, a wolfman, plus a couple of what could have been zombies or vampires.

The wolfman leading the convoy was big, with broad, square shoulders and a swollen beer gut. Dani couldn't be positive, but she guessed it was Silas Bram Bundy in the flesh. He howled loudly as he steered the ATV one-handed.

The other hand held a silver six-shooter pistol.

"Stand down!" Dani shouted across at Beale, anticipating her inevitable move to defend the mourners. She ran back to the guard who had stopped her earlier; his weapon was already out. Panicking, the crowd ran to and fro to get out of the way, which only added to the chaos.

"*Hold your fire!*" Dani screamed at the security detail; the last thing she needed was a whole bunch of innocent folks getting shot up in the crossfire.

The riders shouted something back, but Dani couldn't tell what. Then, gunfire exploded over her shoulder and she saw one of the goblins slump forward on its handlebars. The ATV went into a spin, a front wheel struck a headstone, and the vehicle flipped. A woman screamed loud, shrill, in horror as it landed squarely on the goblin's chest.

From the corner of her eye, Dani saw the wolfman level his pistol in her direction. She hit the ground as more shots rang out. It was impossible to say what—or who—they struck. Dani rolled behind a grave marker that was barely tall enough to cover her head. She reached for the service weapon in her shoulder holster. Off to her left, another half dozen engines roared.

"Dani!" Saul called over.

She pulled her gun and fired two shots at the remaining goblin's tire. She didn't care if they hit; her goal was to show her partner she was still alive.

Glancing around, Dani saw the cemetery was in

absolute chaos. People ran all over, in every direction, ignoring the shouts of the uniformed officers. Weaver's thugs scrambled for cover, while Weaver himself was busy herding the Bergers away from the tent. The air thrummed with the noise of screaming, crying, gunshots, revving ATV engines. There was thick, white smoke in the air; someone was throwing smoke grenades to add to the mayhem.

And there came more of the riders, at least twenty in total, all weaving this way and that around headstones, coming from every direction. Frankenstein's monster on a black ATV drove full speed over a large, slanted headstone not ten feet in front of Dani. The ATV caught air, but the rider misjudged his landing. One back tire came down ahead of the other. The ATV did a brief pirouette and fell on its side, pinning the rider.

Dani saw her chance.

Leaving the pitiful cover, she zigzagged through the smoke, praying for bullets to miss her as she dodged between graves. She reached the monster man, shoved her gun's barrel hard into his neck, and with her free hand seized the rubber mask by the nose holes to tear it off. The rider was tan, blond, and bearded. He wasn't familiar to her, but he smelled like a ranch hand.

"You're Cross Guard, one of Bundy's. Call him. Tell him you—"

There was a cacophonous roar, a shot, a scream.

Dani turned to see Saul standing with his back to her in a firing pose. Beyond him, a rider slumped, his ATV skewing sideways. The rider's arm was extended, a pistol tilted out of his hand.

Saul dropped to one knee, ready to fire another shot. Only . . . no. Saul wasn't setting up to fire again. He dropped his gun with a groan and fell over.

Dani realized what she'd missed among all the confusion. She had heard the engine's roar, Saul's shot, and the rider's scream. She'd been deaf to the other shot, the one the rider fired as he fell. She ran to her fallen partner.

"Get down." Saul tried to shout, but his words hissed out breathlessly.

Dani knelt and applied pressure to the wound Saul covered with his hand. It was concerningly close to his heart.

"Got to keep you safe, Detective." His eyes met hers, then started to glaze over.

"Oh, God, Saul. Stay with me. *Stay with me!*"

The cop's head fell back, limp, eyes still open, a faint smile on his pale lips.

"*Get down!*" Another voice. A hand fell across Dani's back, shoving her against Saul.

Dani rolled to her side and saw Beale plant her elbows in the dirt. Blood smeared across the woman's cheek like warpaint; she clutched a walkie-talkie. Her lips trembled so much, Dani was amazed she could speak.

"Two-three on north one," Beale said into the walkie. "Take out the wolf. Over."

Shots sounded from away in the distance. A distorted version came over the walkie's speaker. A moment later, a man's voice said, "Winged him, one-one, over."

Beale swore. "Try again, two-three. Over."

"This is two-one," a different voice crackled. Dani recognized Weaver. "Hostiles are retreating. I say again, hostiles are retreating. Defensive fire only. Do not pursue. Over."

Beale glared at the walkie, angry at Weaver's overruling. "You heard the man. Over." Carefully, she scanned the area, but the smoke was so thick, Dani doubted she could see anything. "Still want me to stand down?" Beale snarled at Dani with a glance at Saul's lifeless body.

There were no more gunshots, only the resounding growl of retreating engines and terrified screams of civilians. Dani covered Saul's hand with her own, although she knew it was no use. Blood had poured from a wound Dani knew was fatal, and nothing stirred in Saul's eyes. His thin, elegant hand was already growing stiff and cold.

PART FOUR

31

"That breakfast?" Tasmin didn't know the desk jockey's name. His predecessor, Darrin, had moved up in the world. This guy, so pale and skinny he reminded her of a tapeworm, looked custom-built for the receptionist job. He certainly wouldn't be joining E9 anytime soon.

"Uh, yeah." The kid set aside his coffee and took a better grip on his Danish.

Tasmin shook her head. "I don't know how you SADs do it."

"SADs?"

"Standard American dieters. I'm pure carnivore, myself. Muscle, heart, liver, and all that good ol' healthy protein to give me all the energy I need. If I ate plants like you, or all that processed junk, I'd never get out of bed."

The kid tried a smile. "Would that be so bad?"

Her answering glare made him flinch; he dropped the Danish to his plate and opened his mouth as if to apologize, but evidently couldn't find the words.

"Keep barking, hon." Tasmin gave the kid a withering

stare. "One of these days, it's bound to be up the right tree. Now, buzz the senior pastor. I'm expected."

Five minutes later, Tasmin was seated across a desk from Jake Korvus with Billy Weaver standing to her right. Korvus didn't speak, only sat watching her with his hands folded. After a few tense, silent minutes, he lifted a white envelope from the desk and dropped it in front of her. The typed address named Korvus personally, and according to the stamp, the letter had been mailed from inside the Center's zip code. There was no return address.

"Well?" said Korvus. "Go ahead."

She pulled out a pair of surgical gloves from an inside pocket of her denim jacket. Since the early days of her interest in decaying flesh, she'd never been without a pair. As Tasmin snapped on the gloves, Billy gave her a lopsided grin. Examining the envelope, she saw that someone had used a pen-knife to slit it open—the tattered edges showed the knife was dull. Tasmin suppressed her distaste as she drew out the letter.

A message was printed across the top of the page. Like the address, it was typed:

```
DEAR PASTOR JAKE: I WAS THERE YOU
KNOW WHERE.  WEAVER AND B SLOPPY.
PROS  DON'T  LEAVE  PRINTS.  COPS
SLOPPY TOO OR NO DOC IN COURT. YOU
MAYBE? ICAN SHOW YOU PRINTS OR THE
COPS.  IF YOU BE THERE YOU KNOW 1
OCLOCK. OR SEND WEAVER AND B. LIKE
TO  SEE  THEM.  BRING  100K.  SMALL
BILLS. 100K. HIS WORK IN HIS NAME.
A FRIEND
```

Tasmin set the letter and its envelope back on the desk. "Another warning, and this time a demand along with it."

"Same source?" Billy asked.

"If it is, the writer doesn't want us to think so. No high-flown talk. This does a damn good job of sounding like it was written by a moron."

"Doesn't it?" Korvus slapped the desk in frustration with an open hand. "And what if this *moron* is smart enough to get something on you, or fake it well enough to create a whole lot of trouble?"

Tasmin smirked. "I guess you think I'm *B*. I'll try not to take that as an insult. Tell me this. What could he—or she, I guess—have that's worth $100,000? Prints?" She laughed. "Prints on what?"

"Furniture," said Korvus. "Glass, a windowsill. Papers."

"And what does that prove? That me and Billy, a couple guests, invited friends—"

"Hold on, Tas," Billy said. "What papers you talking about, boss?"

The rage on Korvus's face transformed into fear. He folded his arms across his chest, a defensive gesture, plainly not wanting to answer. Billy stared at the pastor until he broke.

"There were papers I wanted photographed. Financials I had reason to suspect Rochelle had with her," Korvus admitted.

"And these papers stayed in the van," said Tasmin. "Whoever did the job took the pictures and put the papers back. There's no reason to think they're in 'you-know-where' as the moron puts it."

Korvus shrank back in his chair. He wasn't a big man, compared to Billy, but he was plenty tall enough to look down on Tasmin when they were both standing. But now he had become so small, it was almost like seeing him through the wrong end of a telescope.

"I had to be sure. If my agent missed something," The

pastor spoke in a quiet, embarrassed voice. "I had to be able to . . . to try again. There was nothing in the case that would mean anything to a stranger. Rochelle only put it together after months of investigating."

Tasmin put a stop to his babbling with a finger to her own lips. "*Case?*"

Korvus frowned. "A *briefcase*. For holding the papers. My agent removed it from the van, photographed the papers, and—"

"Left it in the house," Tasmin stated the now blindingly obvious for him. "And why not? Perfect place to keep 'em safe. I don't guess he bothered to wear any of these?" She tugged at the glove on her left hand, snapping the taut latex loudly against her wrist.

"I'm sure he did," said Korvus. "*Mostly.*"

Stunned silence.

Tasmin cursed at the pastor, not giving much of a damn who he was or about his lofty position within the church. Billy interrupted, pointing a finger at the letter.

"Is this him, your agent, the mole you've got on my team?"

"Not a mole, exactly," said Korvus.

"Right. Just some sad sack who forgot the chain of command."

Tasmin said, "Answer the question, Jake."

Korvus shook his head. "Why would it be? The letter is addressed to me, and it doesn't mention our private arrangement. It's from someone else."

"Who?" Billy demanded, his presence menacing.

"How should I know? Some sort of investigator. Or another one of *your* people."

"It ain't an E-niner. They can spell." Billy's face was red, his lips thin, eyes wide.

"Right," said Tasmin. "Brains have always been a priority in your recruitment efforts, Billy."

Her mind ran riot with a thousand scenarios as she reran every possibly significant second of the past couple months through her mind. She had gotten plenty of leers from Billy's teammates—nothing unusual there—but no one had made it obvious they wanted anything more from her than the usual.

Tasmin clenched a fist, her own frustration showing. Moron or not, the mystery writer had crafted a letter that stung. *Sloppy?!* That angered her—she was anything but! The mission had gone perfectly. The break-in, the retrieval . . .

"So what's the play?" Billy broke the silence.

Tasmin was surprised that he was asking *her*. She wasn't a part of his precious *chain of command*—Korvus was. Although that hadn't exactly gone smoothly.

She told him, "We meet, like he wants. One p.m. You know where."

"I can't," Korvus told them. "I have to be in court. You go, both of you, like the letter says."

"And the money?" Billy furrowed his brow.

"Lose some zeroes in your security budget," said Korvus. "I'll make it up."

"Fine." Billy sounded as cool as if the pastor had just told him to buy him lunch from a vending machine, instead of embezzle one hundred thousand dollars.

Tasmin got to her feet and removed the surgical gloves. "You're really some piece of work, Jake Korvus." Without waiting for a reply, she left Korvus's office with Billy hot on her heels.

Halfway down the corridor, he leaned in close. "I'll pull the same crew; get set to go in heavy."

She was fond of Billy, but he could be dense at times. "You want to go heavy on an empty house?"

"Huh?"

"One of that same crew as before is your traitor. Try to

pull him and he'll do a fade."

Billy thought hard for a moment; his face showed it took a great deal of effort. Finally, he nodded. "I can do it with reserves. It's just one guy."

"Is it?" Tasmin stopped and faced him. "Billy, if this is just one guy we're dealing with, why is he so confident in calling both of us out?"

He didn't have an answer, only a shrug.

Tasmin considered going back to Korvus, telling him to find someone else to back Billy up. Instead, on impulse, she reached out and touched Billy's scar.

"Bless you, my child," Billy said.

Tasmin balled a fist, trying to fight her attraction to everything ugly, decayed, and deformed. She lost, as usual.

"Call me when the troops are loaded," she ordered.

"On it, boss lady."

32

Jon wondered if he looked as bad as he felt. Judging from the faces of his friends, one foot in the grave about covered it. His itch had turned into a rash he could feel from his scalp to the soles of his feet. In places, it formed blisters that festered and burst—as if the insurmountable inner grief at the loss of Chelle and his sons was bubbling to the surface to manifest itself physically. The last round of steroid injections seemed to be holding the festering at bay, but far more important was the strength they gave him. Or *loaned* to him, rather. Jon had no doubt he would have to pay back that particular loan with interest. For now, it was enough that the steroids kept him upright. He wanted to stand for his first day on trial.

Somehow, the crowd outside the Blackwell-Thurman Criminal Justice Center contained at least 75 percent reporters. Every last one knew his name, and they all wanted an interview. They took their invasive pictures without his permission, using cameras, phones, and drones. He'd recognized Kate Boldwin from Channel 6, who had stood quietly watching with her cameraman. Now she was in the spectator gallery, away toward the back.

In the front seats, behind Fitz and his legal secretary, at the defense table were Rabbi Max, Cass, Simon, and Bonita Ximena. Phillip sat across the aisle with Pastor Korvus. P. J. sat a couple rows back, flanked by other Church of the Resurrected members. One was the man who had opened the door of Phillip's limo, the man who reminded Rabbi Max of James Earl Ray. In a straight line behind P. J., in the back row, Detective Cavallo sat all by herself, and Jon wondered where her dour-faced partner was.

Jon felt he had seen about half of the faces scrutinizing him before. Of course, not everyone stared; most of the reporters were hunched over their devices, making live notes.

And there were a bunch of people who didn't appear to be reporters of any kind—most likely nosey members of the Austin public who got off on attending murder trials. They filled their time before commencement of proceedings with their own onscreen activities; Jon mused they were micromanaging the stats of their *NeverEnd* characters. He'd seen plenty actually playing the game or watching others play through a livestream, but Her Honor Judge Evelyn Morrow had put an end to that. She stopped short of taking the phones away but ordered the bailiffs to expel anyone found playing games in her courtroom.

As Jon raised his right hand, he thought how nice it was that some in attendance, at least, would pay attention to his earnest vow to tell the truth.

"You may sit, Doctor Edom," Judge Morrow instructed once he finished his oath.

Jon glanced warily at the padded stool behind him; if he sat down, he feared he'd not be able to get up again. "If you don't mind, Your Honor, I'd like to stand while I can."

Morrow nodded assent.

District Attorney Esilda Perez, a petite woman with a

brunette bob, round-rimmed glasses, and somber dark-blue pantsuit, asked to approach the witness stand. Morrow granted her permission, and Jon watched as she stepped out from behind the prosecution table.

"Doctor Edom, I want to take this opportunity to assure you I am sympathetic to your health concerns," the DA said. "I want to make the next few days as painless for you as possible." She paused midstep to look over to the jury. "And yes, I'm saying this for you jurors as well. I'll be asking Doctor Edom some very pointed questions." She continued her cross to Jon. "I promise you, Doctor, it's all in aid of settling the matter before this court without needless delay."

Perez didn't seem to require a response, so Jon didn't give one. Instead, he listened to the click of her black kitten heels on the courtroom floor as she lifted the tablet she carried. She stopped a few feet from the witness stand and read out the date of Chelle's disappearance.

"According to your statement, Dr. Edom, which was read into evidence, you spent that Friday morning traveling to a conference of health professionals in Houston. Did you see your wife before you left, Doctor Edom?"

Jon's neck felt stiff; his whole body prickled. "Briefly. Chelle had a rough night and slept in. I woke up beside her, got myself up and ready for my road trip. I think we said two sentences to each other before I left."

"*Two sentences?*" Perez repeated. "Was that a typical morning for you and Mrs. Edom, Doctor?"

"Was it typical for me to be in a hurry in the morning? When I had somewhere to be, yes."

Perez gave him a tight smile. "Doctors are busy people. I'm sure the jury are all busy people too. Do you want to leave it to them to decide if two sentences are enough of a goodbye for a loving couple who don't expect to see each other all weekend?"

The stiffness spread to Jon's shoulders, his rash threatening to torment him. Fitz watched him with narrowed eyes, clearly annoyed at the line of questioning. Jon blamed himself. If only he had stopped at *briefly* instead of letting the DA lead him on . . . but it was too late for that now.

"Chelle needed sleep," he explained. "I didn't want to bother her. We'd said our goodbyes the night before."

"Did you have sex the night before?"

Perez's casual tone at such an intimate question caught Jon off guard. He didn't stumble, but definitely felt the full force of the verbal jab.

"Is that relevant?" he snapped back. Perez began her answer, but Jon caught a quick headshake from Fitz and cut her off. "No. We didn't. The last time I had sex with my wife was . . . I'm not sure. Maybe Tuesday of that week."

"And if not Tuesday, Doctor?"

"The weekend. The previous weekend."

"Do you mean the weekend prior to the disappearance, or the weekend prior to that?"

Between the rash, the stiff muscles, and stress about the trial, Jon was in no mood to spar with the wily DA. So, he went for a body blow. "I didn't cheat on my wife, if that's what you're hinting at." He hoped Perez would stumble at his offense.

She didn't.

"You had sex with your wife."

"Yes."

"On a Tuesday, or the weekend prior, or the weekend prior to that."

"Tuesday, I said."

"But you're not sure. *Maybe* on Tuesday. There's no need to answer, Doctor. I think we understand. You're a busy man. You had sex with your wife when you could find the time, but not regularly enough to say for sure. And you definitely *didn't* cheat."

"I did not."

Perez squared up to him, hands on the witness stand. "It's wrong to cheat on your partner, wouldn't you agree? You feel strongly about cheating?"

"It—"

Perez spun away. "You feel *strongly*."

Jon caught Fitz's glare but couldn't help himself; the DA had triggered the anguish he'd experienced upon discovering Chelle's infidelity with Vivek. "*Yes*. Yes, I do."

"So how did you feel when you found out your wife was having an affair, Doctor?"

An electric jolt of pain to his ribs stopped Jon from thinking about answering. Fitz had warned him what to expect from Perez—the personal questions, the attempts to bait him—and told him to restrict his testimony to the known facts with no embellishments. At the time, Jon had thought a lawyer should have more trust in his client, but was starting to regret his attitude.

Perez pointed at the video monitor positioned opposite the jury box. "Exhibit 2, Your Honor. Security footage obtained from Endless Loop Games, Limited." The monitor switched from black to a still image of Jon and Vivek in the Endless Loop lobby. "Will you please identify these people for the jury, Doctor?"

Jon knew he was in her corner, now, defenseless to the blows she was raining down upon him. "That's me, on the left. The other man is Vivek Singh, Endless Loop's CEO."

"Run the footage, please, Julia," said Perez.

The image came to life: Vivek cringed as Jon rushed him, grabbed him, and opened his cheek with a heavy, well-aimed punch. There was no sound, of course, so nobody heard Vivek's taunt that fired Jon up. Instead, everyone in the courtroom saw Jon straddle Vivek, swinging his fists, in what appeared to be an unprovoked assault.

The scene paused with Jon's elbow cocked, all ready to deliver the next blow.

"Exhibit 3." Perez click-clacked back to the prosecution table, where a fat sheaf of papers awaited her. "These are printouts of an email exchange between Rochelle Berger-Edom and Vivek Singh." Perez crossed to Judge Morrow, who accepted the papers and sifted through them. "Members of the jury, my assistant will hand you each a copy. There's a lot to go through, but the main takeaway is that Rochelle Berger-Edom was cheating on her husband. Isn't that true, Doctor?"

Unfortunately, the steroids were failing; his body was wracked with pain. Jon braced a hip on the stool and turned his attention to the defense table in the hope of a sympathetic look from Fitz, or even from the legal secretary, Dee, who just so happened to be Fitz's wife.

Nothing.

Jon stabbed a finger toward the screen. "That video is from the day I found out about the affair. Weeks *after* my wife and sons disappeared."

Perez made her way over to him, leaning in close in a not-so-subtle attempt to intimidate him. She wore a floral perfume, its scent subtle; it smelled *expensive*. "It was the day you found out about these emails, Doctor." She shook the papers at him. "The emails suggest the affair goes back over years. Are you telling this court you really didn't know what was going on between your own wife and the CEO of her company all that time?"

"Not until that day, no."

"The day of the video, you mean. The day you found out your wife and Vivek Singh exchanged a series of incriminating emails. But Doctor, you must have observed her interest in other men."

Jon sat himself down on the stool—he needed it. "I

knew Chelle was human. I understood about her illness." A flood of memories flashed him scenes of weeping Chelle, raging Chelle, and most painful of all, Chelle flirting openly with other men in her desperate attempts at garnering attention. To keep himself from losing control at the DA, he switched to clinical speak. "As a bipolar patient, my wife showed signs of hypersexuality, which is prevalent with the condition—even when medicated."

The prosecutor recoiled, as if in disgust, an obvious theatrical for the benefit of the jury. "A *bipolar patient*. Do you often discuss people close to you in such clinical terms? I'm a professional too, you understand, and I don't recall ever calling my partner *claimant* or *defendant*—even when we were fighting about money."

Someone in the jury laughed. Heads turned in their direction.

Jon started to explain but stopped as Fitz stood up.

"Objection, Your Honor." The lawyer eyed the DA angrily. "DA Perez is voicing an *opinion* about the use of technical terms based on degrees on intimacy. She is not, to the best of my knowledge, an expert in the field."

There were more noises from the jury and some from the onlookers, enough that Judge Morrow banged her gavel.

"Quiet down," she said. "Objection sustained. Let's stick to the facts, Miss Perez."

"My apologies, Your Honor." The DA's smile made it obvious she didn't mind the objection. Why should she? She'd put her point out there, and the effect on the jury was the same. Perez waved her hand dismissively. "Those are all the questions I have for Doctor Edom at this time."

Fitz declined to cross-examine his own client, so Jon was dismissed. As the state called a staff member witness to the fight at Endless Loop, he made his way to the defense table. Between the aggravating pain and the stiffness, every step was a huge, agonizing effort. Still, he had energy—the steroids were at least doing *that* job. For now.

"You did well, Jon," Fitz whispered. "Perez can be a ball-breaker—she went easy on you."

"That was *easy*?"

Dee brushed delicate gray curls from her face and leaned over to show Fitz her phone. The map on the screen showed a swirling vortex moving jerkily landward from the Gulf of Mexico. Fitz gave a grateful nod.

"Rain delay?" said Jon.

Fitz told, "It's might be bigger than Harvey, but don't worry. It won't get this far inland."

Too bad, thought Jon; some respite would be most welcome—Day One, and he was already going through the emotional wringer. As if losing his family in the most brutal fashion imaginable weren't enough, he was now being forced to prove his own innocence. He sat back in his chair and pretended to watch the witness being sworn in, but his mind kept on throwing up pictures of lightning bolts splitting the courtroom and hurricane winds sweeping him away into sweet oblivion.

33

Dani left the Justice Center with her hands in her pockets and chin tucked low to her chest. Lunch was an hour and a half, and she didn't waste time. Months ago, she'd have looked down on anyone who suggested a drink in the middle of a working day, but now she headed straight for a bar two blocks south that was known to be friendly to cops. The sign over its door reads: The Five-Oh Clock Pub.

Subtle.

"Rum and Pepsi," she told the bartender, a woman with a tattoo of a blue fish twisting itself into a triangle.

"It's Coke in the fountain," the bartender said, "but I keep bottles in back for gals who like it sweet. Gimme a sec."

Dani nodded and watched the tattooed woman go. When she was out of sight, Dani spun round on her stool to check out the crowd. It was early in the day, so there wasn't much of one. She saw a lean, buzz-cut man she recognized as an off-duty beat cop, a bearded guy in a trench coat who looked like he'd stepped straight out of a Dick Tracy cartoon, and a young, freckle-faced couple huddled together in a booth watching news of the impending hurricane on a hanging flatscreen. As Dani spun back, weariness caught up with her. She planted her elbows on the bar, sighed, and buried her face in her hands.

"That bad?" A man's voice.

Dani glanced up, startled. The stool on her left had been empty a second go, but now it supported a squat figure in jeans and a rusty-looking hoodie. He had the hood up, and for an instant, she imagined its shadows hid a monster mask, like those Bundy's people had worn in the cemetery attack. By the time her brain saw through the shadows to the man's face, Dani remembered where she'd seen that rust-colored hoodie before. She opened her mouth to say the name of the PI she had met in Youngsport. Before she could speak, he lowered the hood. Dani saw her mistake. This man resembled the investigator, Castro, but had to be ten years younger at least.

"I got something in my teeth?" he said.

"What?"

"My teeth. There something in 'em? You gave me a funny look."

"No. Sorry. You reminded me of someone else, that's all."

"I get that a lot. Mostly from chi— Mostly from *ladies*. I remind them of their exes, usually. After a while, they start missing the old days, and that's why I can't keep a steady girlfriend."

Dani saw where the conversation was going and considered ditching the bar. She wasn't in the mood to get hit on, not even for a free rum and Pepsi. But that hoodie . . . Could it really be a coincidence?

"Are you following me?" she asked him bluntly.

"Why? Are you hard to find?"

"There was a funeral on the day of the eclipse. Security

personnel exchanged fire with an unknown group, thought to be domestic terrorists. Sound familiar?"

He shook his head. "I don't watch a lot of the news."

Dani studied him. "There was a man in a hoodie just like yours . . . stand up."

"Huh?"

"Stand up. I want to see how tall you are."

"Not very."

"Stand."

"What are you going to do if I refuse? Arrest me?"

She narrowed her eyes. "How do you know I'm a cop?"

"This is a cop bar."

"Are you a cop?"

"No." He flicked the cocktail napkin the bartender had left Dani to make it spin. "Not anymore. But we're wasting time. Let's talk about you."

Dani stopped the napkin's spin with a finger. "Let's not."

"Come on. You want to know something about me. Only fair I learn something about you. Tell you what. I've got a question for you. Give me a straight answer, and I'll do the same back to you."

"One question?"

"Just one."

Dani leaned over the bar, to check if she could see the bartender returning. She couldn't, and she still needed her drink, so decided to indulge the guy.

"Fine."

He waved a hand, pointing vaguely in the direction of the Justice Center. "What do you got against Edom, huh?"

"Edom?"

"Jon Edom. Heart surgeon. Wife and sons went missing months back."

"Yeah. He murdered them."

"That's just a theory."

"It happens to be *my* theory. I'm the investigating detective. I'm the reason Edom's on trial."

"Are you? Sorry. That was two questions, and you ain't answered the first yet. Maybe I ought to rephrase. Why did you make your mind up he's guilty?"

She looked him over. "Are you a reporter?"

"Maybe. See, no straight answer. You haven't earned it yet. I'm asking about your process, Detective, how you reached your conclusion."

"Maybe you should tell me."

"It's the one thing I don't know."

The bartender appeared, at last. She marched past the man on the stool without acknowledging him and planted a glass Pepsi bottle in front of Dani.

"Wow," said Dani. "I didn't know they still made these."

"I know a guy," the bartender said. She popped the bottle top and made Dani's drink in a highball glass. Dani's company turned his back and kept it turned until the bartender left to check on the off-duty cop, the bum, and the couple.

Turning back, he told Dani, "We're running out of time."

She swirled her ice cubes. "I've got an hour, at least."

"I didn't say *you*, Dani. All of us."

She set her glass down and turned to him. "You know my name? Who the hell are you?"

The guy reached into a pocket and drew out a card, but as she reached out to take it, he fluttered his fingers to make it disappear with a street magician's sleight of hand.

"Nice try. It's still your turn. I'll ask again. What do you have against the good doctor?"

When Dani thought back on the conversation, later, she was sure her questioner had chosen the phrase deliberately. At the time, his words cut too deeply for her to react differently to how she did.

"*Good doctor*," she repeated in a passionate whisper. "This is a guy who killed his wife and young kids, for God's sake! How can you sit there and talk like I'm the one who did something wrong? I worked the case. I chased the leads. I found the evidence. You want details? Watch the trial. Edom is guilty. Guilty as sin."

"Or guilty as your father, Angel Cavallo?"

Dani was far too angry to be triggered by her father's name. "Yeah. As guilty as him."

"The Burbank Doper." The little man whistled. "Seven victims the police know about. He claimed they were mercy killings. Hard sell on the last one, seeing as she was your kid sister."

Suddenly, the room felt unbearably hot, but Dani couldn't lift her glass, let alone drink her refreshing cocktail. Somehow, she managed to keep her voice below a shout.

"What do you know about—? We're done here. Whoever you are, we're *done*."

She got up to leave.

"Hold on. You held up your part of the bargain, all right? I'll hold up mine. You asked who I am. This is what you need to know, Dani: I'm a messenger, and I carry a message. Time is short, and the job's not done. There. Message delivered. This next part is personal. I want justice, same as you. And concentrating on Dr. Jon Edom is blinding you to what's really going on. Think *bigger*, detective. As big as *that*."

Dani followed his finger to the TV that had so absorbed the young couple in the booth. The screen showed Hurricane Laurence making landfall in Galveston. The stretch of beach at the bottom of the picture was barely visible, most of it covered by tall, crashing waves. There was a pier hosting the midway, and beyond it the rides. She saw a roller coaster, some sort of tower with suspended swings, and a Ferris wheel. None was lit up, but all were in motion, buffeted by the hurricane's brutal winds; the wheel was toppling over, the tower tilting, the roller coaster collapsing in on itself as wind twisted the metal struts and popped rivets out of the structure. The video clip lasted only a few seconds, ending in a chaotic jumble as the camera spun through the air. An anchorwoman appeared, but there was no volume, and Dani was too far away to read the captions on the screen.

Dani turned back to her *messenger*, but he was gone, the seat beside her empty once more. On the bar was her cocktail napkin—the guy had unfolded it, evidently, and written something in swirling, blue cursive: "Get right," it read. "I'll be in touch."

Get right with who? Dani wondered. Had mother said it, she'd have meant God. The *messenger* hadn't struck her as a religious type, but what did she know? Puzzled, she downed half the rum and Pepsi, left a tip for the bartender, and took the scenic route back to the courthouse.

34

" *Ha'kol le'tova*," Rabbi Max said.

Jon and Fitz stared at him blankly.

"Everything is for the best." The rabbi smiled. "Whatever challenge we face, it's a small part of a larger plan."

"I wish I had your faith," Jon groaned.

"What do you need mine for? You've got your own."

Fitz balled up his takeaway bag and made a high, arcing shot into the wastebasket in the corner. They were in the defense's antechamber, a dim room with no windows, exceptionally plush carpet, and a faux-mahogany desk the lawyer was currently using to prop his feet on.

"You can keep the faith talk," Fitz grumbled. "But I do like this plan talk. Here's what I want to know, Jon. Are you ready to join the defense team?"

Jon was genuinely surprised by the odd question. "How can you say that? I'm with you a hundred percent."

"Really? Because when you were on the stand, you seemed more like a pinch hitter for the other side. I won't revisit your attack on Mister Singh—the prosecution will do that again this afternoon. But let's go back to the hospital. You were under no obligation to answer Cavallo. And this morning, with Perez. Is it only women you let bait you, Jon, or can anyone join in?"

The impulse to defend himself was momentary. Jon let it pass.

"I'm sorry. I should be a better client. I've had plenty patients who ignore my advice. The ones who live come back to ignore it again."

"Pleading the fifth is constitutional law for a reason, Jon."

"I'll do what you say from here on out." Jon lowered his eyes, suitably chastised.

Fitz held out a hand for him to shake. "Good. That and a beer will make you teammate of the month. Now let's plan what we're doing after the break. If the DA keeps her questions short, I'll have Singh on cross today. He's sure to talk about the affair, the emails, and the attack you made on him. Is there anything else we can bring out, anything that would suggest to the jury Singh is untrustworthy?"

Jon allowed himself a mirthless laugh. "You mean apart from adultery and stabbing a good friend in the back?"

Fitz sat back in his chair. "Apart from that, yes. Perez is sure to downplay the usual peccadillos. The vices we want to bring up are anything outside the usual."

The rabbi threw in, "You think Vivek Singh is a suspect?"

Shrugging, Fitz refused to commit. "Alternate suspects are a sideline to me at the best of times. What I'm interested in here is *reasonable doubt*. Think of it from the jury's perspective, Max. Miss Perez is about to present a damning character witness. Singh is a victim of violence at Jon's hands and, if he makes the right impression, all twelve of those upright citizens weighing the case will make the logical leap from punching the wife's lover to killing the wife."

"Quite a leap." Rabbi Max snorted.

"Made less with every smile from Singh." Fitz turned in his chair to address Jon. "Listen. Perez has already laid the groundwork with her video show. Next, she's going to portray Singh as the victim of a violent, out-of-control brute. The more the jury likes Singh, the more they'll be inclined to believe you capable of anything. We need to be ready to counter that. So tell me about Singh—convince me he's far from a saint."

"Without the peccadillos? Nothing leaps out. How long can you give me to think?"

Fitz checked his wristwatch and said he could have five minutes.

Jon conceded in one. "There's nothing. I'm sorry."

"Don't give up so easily, Jon," Fitz told him. "Maybe it will help if I ask you questions about your association with Singh. It's good practice, anyway, for what Perez is going to do. A bit of role-play, if you will. Do you mind?"

"My life is in your hands, Fitz."

Fitz shook his head. "Let's not get ahead of ourselves. We're a long way from sentencing. For now, role-play." Changing his tone, the lawyer allowed his pitch to slide up half an octave, stopping shy of doing an outright impression of the prosecutor. "Doctor Edom, how long have you known Vivek Singh?"

Jon sat up straight; it was surprising how quickly his subconscious took to the exercise and reacted to Fitz as a woman. "Eight years, give or take."

"Can you be more precise?"

If he had been asked as much in court, Jon would have said no at once. But in the low-pressure atmosphere of the defense chamber, he took his time to think. Slowly, a memory began to form.

"My mother-in-law introduced us at a party. Some sort of product launch, or an anniversary. That's it. Endless Loop's fifth anniversary bash, eight years ago. Lisa was playing the CEO and ran up and down the ballroom, introducing everybody to everybody else. Vivek wasn't anything special back then—I think his title was second senior accountant. But Lisa insisted we shake hands anyway."

Fitz gazed off into the distance.

"What is it?"

"Nothing," said the lawyer, in his Fitz voice. "Only . . . second senior accountant. That was the title held by Hannah Bernstein, the friend of Rochelle's who was killed, wasn't it?"

"I think it was."

"I'm damned *sure* it was," said Fitz. He leaned forward in his seat, as though inviting the other two men into a conspiracy. "It's funny it should come up now, but my last conversation with Charlie Castro was about the Bernstein case. I remember her title distinctly: second senior accountant, the same as our Mister Singh."

Jon nodded. "Makes sense. She was in his department. Must have taken the job when he became VP of finance."

Fitz was silent for a moment or two. Then, putting on his best Perez emulation again, he said, "Please tell the court, was your wife's relationship with Miss Bernstein more personal, or professional?"

Had someone asked him the same question about Vivek while Chelle was alive, Jon would have said "professional" without a second thought. That seemed an unhelpful comment, though, so he kept it to himself.

"A bit of both, I suppose. They got to know each other when Chelle was pregnant with Luke. She had to wind down her involvement with Endless Loop in general, and *NeverEnd* in particular, pretty quickly. Hannah helped with all that."

"How so?"

"I don't know all the details. There was a royalty deal in the works for some of the game assets. Chelle couldn't step away until it was locked down. In practical terms, that meant Hannah had a regular spot at our dinner table. She would come over after a day's work, we would chat and eat, and the ladies would work a couple hours into the night. I wasn't always around—night shifts at the hospital—but when I was there I could tell they were getting along well."

"And the work got done, I trust?"

"Yes. The royalty deal came through, Chelle severed ties with Endless Loop, and we kept Hannah on as accountant. Looking back, I'm not sure I appreciated what an asset she truly was. Leaving the company was hard on Chelle, and her pregnancy with Luke was no picnic. Without Hannah, I'm not sure she could have coped."

Rabbi Max leaned in. *"Kha'verim mar'im et a'ha'vatam be'et tzara, lo be'et sim'kha."*

"I got part of that," said Jon. "Something about friends."

"They show love in troubled times," the rabbi said with a nod, "not happy ones."

Fitz added, "So very true."

There came a knock at the door.

Dee poked her head in without waiting to be asked. "Three minutes, Jim," she told the room.

"His master's voice," said Fitz with a dry half smile.

As Dee stepped out, Jon stood up to follow, but Fitz gestured for him to wait—a hand held up, palm toward Jon.

"I'm glad you're eager, Jon, but there are two more questions I need to ask."

"As DA Perez?"

"As *myself.* First, was Hannah good at her job?"

Jon considered his answer briefly, but there was never

any doubt. "She was excellent. As good as Vivek, I'm sure, only not as ruthlessly ambitious."

"Ambition is no crime, but it does bring us neatly to my second question. Do you have reason to believe Singh was ever involved in unethical business practices? Is that, perhaps, how he was able to advance so quickly from second senior accountant to vice president of finance to CEO?"

It was a new idea to Jon. He was so used to thinking only the best of Vivek, he was instinctively inclined to defend his former best friend. He decided, in the end, there was nothing that needed defending.

"I'm sorry. I never heard of any malfeasance on his part. Why do you ask?"

Fitz rose from his chair. "Call it curiosity. I find it interesting that two people in the same position had unusual things happen to them. Granted, rapid promotion and death by drive-by shooting are very *different* unusual things, but they're unusual all the same. Now, hurry. We're needed in court."

35

The sleek black Chrysler 300 pulled off the driveway, where two identical cars already stood. Tasmin fidgeted. Riding in such a small vehicle always made her uncomfortable; her seat was too low, too close to the road—she felt like she was riding in a go-kart. Add to that the darkening, brooding sky and the rippling waters of Lake Conroe that seemed *too* close no matter which window she looked out of, and it was no wonder her nerves were so on edge.

Billy Weaver exited the passenger door of the lead Chrysler and jogged back to meet her. He had to stoop low to keep metal between the driveway and his head. They were a couple hundred feet from the gray, three-story lake house, snugged up to a line of trees that had clearly been planted to shield the patch of front lawn from nosy neighbors. Billy pointed past the weeping willow that occupied most of the lawn to the darkened windows of the house.

"There's no pot shots at the glass," said Billy. "That's something. Still think we should have firebombed the place."

Tasmin grimaced. "There are some costs even your budget won't cover. Let's get this op in motion. We're burning daylight."

Billy slouched back to the lead car, rapping lightly on the windows of Tasmin's car as he passed. In mere seconds, a small force of dark figures emerged, checked their semiautomatic rifles, and split into two lines that wound their way in opposite directions around the house. Billy came back to Tasmin's side, holding a walkie. He counted under his breath.

"One . . . two . . ."

He got as high as ninety-four before a series of calls came over the walkie.

"Clear three!"

"Clear one!"

"Clear two!"

"All clear, Commander."

"'Bout time," Billy growled. He then nodded to Tasmin and led the way across the lawn.

She passed him before they reached the yellowing willow, and was still ahead when they rounded the corner to the backyard. A few strands of yellow police tape still fenced in patches of grass. Tasmin steered clear of the tatters and made sure to step lightly, so as not to leave marks. She ran quickly and carefully to the foot of the stairs, where she paused to slip off her cowboy boots. It took only a moment, as she had deliberately chosen a pair a half size too big.

Several other pairs of boots stood in a line next to the stairs. They belonged to the E-niners who had also come this way. The nine men and one other woman were professionals who knew how to leave no trace, which was exactly why Tasmin was nervous about this mission. The letter from the FRIEND of Pastor Jake Korvus hadn't fooled her for a minute. The summons was a setup, she knew, but she also knew it was pointless arguing with Jake. Besides, whoever had accused Billy and herself of being SLOPPY knew too much to be completely ignored.

She left her boots at the end of the line and mounted the stairs to the deck. Nobody was in sight out of doors, but two men were already in the living room. One stood just inside the sliding glass door that led off of the deck, while the other was on the far side of the room, at the head of the spiral staircase that led up to the next floor.

Tasmin approached the guy at the door. Like the rest of the team, which excluded herself but included Billy, he was dressed all in black, from the rubberized pads of his stockings to the top of his full-face helmeted head. She was only able to recognize the ex-lobby attendant, Darrin, because of his bulky size.

"You know the job," she told him and the other E-niner. "Look around. Snipers will let us know if we have guests."

She glanced back at Billy, who stood at the far end of the deck, gazing up at something on another floor. A spotter with a rifle and scope would be at the window, watching the perimeter at lakeside. Seo-yeon Pak would be keeping an eye on the driveway from a different window. Aside from being the only woman ever inducted into E9, she could shoot a tick off a rat's carcass from nine hundred feet. That alone should have made Tasmin feel safe.

It didn't.

The E-niners said, "Yes ma'am," and got started on the search. Tasmin allowed herself a smug smile; she liked getting her way, even if the effort was futile.

"Waste of time." Billy startled her. He stood an inch behind her elbow and had crossed the distance between them without a sound.

"Don't do that," she snapped. "And don't you think I know it's a waste? This thing with the letter stinks to high heaven. And trust me, I know stink when I smell it."

The burner phone clipped to Tasmin's belt vibrated with urgency. She moved away from Billy to check it, and caught the emergency alert flashing across her screen: Hurricane Laurence, still at Category 5, was continuing its route north from the wreckage of Galveston and Houston. Montgomery County residents who had not already evacuated were being advised to stay in their shelters. Tasmin smirked at the *residents* part. Just like a public service not to care about the visitors.

Darrin and his partner set the desk they were done examining against the wall. Tasmin cursed to herself—she should have told the pair not to bother. The last time she'd been in this room, she had searched the desk personally. Of course, it yielded nothing then, and would yield nothing now. The papers Korvus wanted found were unique, and they were all in the briefcase his so-called agent took from Rochelle's van. But pointless as it was, Tasmin was sure no sign of her earlier search had been left behind. When Darrin and the other man stepped down from the split-level section surrounding the living room fireplace and took hold of the white leather sofa, she waved them to stop.

"Leave that. We never touched it. God! I could kill Jake. Check the windowsills, you two. And the baseboards. I'm going upstairs."

Billy puckered his lips, clearly pissed off. He said nothing, though, just turned around and went back onto the deck, lost in his own bitter thoughts.

As Tasmin made her way up the staircase, she slid her glove along the underside of the banister to see if any dried blood flaked off. None did. She emerged on a balcony halfway to the living room's vaulted ceiling and passed through a door to the second floor. There were three bedrooms on that floor, plus a full bath and a common area that gave a glimpse of bruised, gray-purple sky through the waving willow branches. To the right of the windows was a doorway that gave access to another set of stairs. An op was searching the first bedroom on Tasmin's right. No one was in common area, but Tasmin saw the sniper, Seo-yeon, standing in front of an open window at the top of the stairs. She had her hip against a banister. Even as Tasmin saw her, the other woman spun, covering her with the high-velocity rifle.

"Whoa!" Tasmin held her hands out, waist height. "Jumpy much?"

At that moment, the window Seo-yeon had been looking out of shattered. Tasmin registered the gunshot as Seo-yeon tipped over the banister and crashed in a limp, twisted heap on the stairs. Tasmin peered down at Seo-yeon and saw the sole female member of Ezekiel Nine had a hole in her chest big enough to pass a softball through.

Acting on instinct, Tasmin dropped, pressing her belly to the hardwood floor. The window closest to her exploded, the glass turning to sparkling powder as bright, spinning shards fell around her like jagged hailstones.

"Billy!" Tasmin screamed as she reached behind her for the .357 wedged in her belt. She cocked the hammer, rose up on a knee, and fought hard to get her breathing under control.

36

Rohan Majumdar wore his best suit. At least Dani guessed it was his best. As she watched the surgical assistant being sworn in as a witness, she wondered about the guy's salary: How did it compare with Doctor Edom's? They were supposed to be best friends, but Dani didn't buy it. Edom was so very deliberate in his actions—surely he wouldn't waste time socializing with people who couldn't help him advance in some way.

Unless she'd read him wrong, of course.

The meeting with the self-proclaimed *messenger* at Five-Oh had shaken her confidence in her abilities a tad. One result was that she was now second-guessing herself, another was the urge to scan the courtroom every thirty seconds or so. She looked from back to front, watching for familiar faces, monster masks, or a hoodie that might have belonged to a vanished private detective before it was inherited by his kid brother. Except Charlie Castro didn't have a kid brother—Dani had taken the time to look that one up.

She hated being trapped in the courtroom. What was the

point in her being there? The Edom case was over; she'd done her part in bringing him to justice. Now was the time to be outside, active; she should be out hunting the monsters who'd murdered Saul.

After the cemetery shootings, an army of police had descended on the Cross Guard Ranch. They found nothing to link the group with the masked ATV riders, but when the ranch's owner, Silas Bundy, returned from a trip out of state, Dani had been sure to shake him by the hand. His grip was weak, and when she shifted her weight, forcing Bundy to brace his shoulder, he winced. The shot wolfman would have winced the same way, since it was his shoulder that took the bullet.

Dani was pissed. If Castro Jr., or whoever the hell he was, wanted to talk crime theories, he should have come to her with one about her partner's killer. Exactly why he had sought her out was a mystery; his message made no sense.

Time is short and the job's not done.

Wrong.

It *was* done.

The bodies were buried, the suspect on trial. Dani had yet to give testimony, but everything she was going to say was already on record. If hoodie guy wanted to help the *good doctor*, he ought to have talked to his lawyer, not a detective.

She half listened as the district attorney questioned Majumdar about his work at the hospital. It was all background, every question routine, boring. Dani checked the courtroom several more times before Perez moved on to Majumdar's and Edom's relationship. This was more interesting, but not by much. Dani completed a couple more sweeps before Perez got to the topic that finally grabbed her attention: a confrontation between Jon and Rochelle.

The date of the occurrence was almost exactly a year to the day before the disappearance. The court had heard statements from two nurses about the confrontation earlier in the day, statements Dani had gathered herself. Majumdar's testimony was critical, because he had been in the room at the time.

"You were an eyewitness to the fight," Perez told Majumdar.

"Fight is a strong word." Rohan fidgeted uncomfortably on the stand. "But yeah, I was there."

The DA paced away from the witness, her back to him. "Are you saying that what happened between Dr. Edom and his wife was *not* a fight?"

"I'd call it a misunderstanding."

Perez smiled knowingly, but of course Majumdar didn't see. The smile was for her audience, the jurors especially.

"Thank you for clearing that matter up, Rohan." Putting on a penitent face, Perez spun back around. "Forgive me— may I call you Rohan?"

"Sure."

"Thank you. So, Rohan. Set the scene for us. What was this *misunderstanding*, as you call it, and why were you and the defendant, Doctor Jon Edom, present?"

Majumdar appeared more relaxed than he had been talking about the Edoms' fight, but he was still wary of the DA. Before answering, he cleared his throat, a sure sign his answer was well-rehearsed.

"It happened in the family waiting room, second floor of the hospital. Uh, that's the Violet Crown Charity Hospital. I don't think I said that."

"We understand, Rohan. Please go on."

"Right. We were fresh out of surgery. Doctor Edom did great, like always—he saved a girl's life. We went to give the family the good news, and they were thrilled, of course; we did the usual hugs and handshakes. The doc—Doctor Edom—told them how to get to recovery to see the patient. They left the waiting room empty, so Dr. Edom and I kind of camped out. He was exhausted—it was his fourteenth hour on what was supposed to be an eight-hour shift. When Chelle walked in, she . . . well, she took it the wrong way."

"*Chelle*? That would be the victim, Rochelle Berger-Edom, correct?"

"Yeah. Dr. Edom always called her that, so I did too."

A thought struck Dani: It was odd that none of Rochelle's birth family called her by that nickname, or any other, for that matter. Dani could think of six nicknames allocated to her by her family and the friends she made as a teenager on the res. And only a couple of those monikers had to do with her culture.

"Thank you for clearing that up," the DA said. "Now, what exactly do you mean by *she took it the wrong way*?"

Majumdar gave a sigh. "It's like this. The doc was six hours late for going home. I think he'd called, but Chelle was worried about him, you know?"

"Rochelle was *worried*?"

"Yeah. She came to the hospital, found us in the waiting room. The doc was sprawled in a chair. I guess it must have looked like he'd slept there all night."

"I see." Perez paused, and Dani felt the tension mounting around the courtroom as the DA led her witness along her predetermined path. "And Rochelle Edom took exception to that."

"Yeah. Sort of."

The DA's voice rose in pitch. "*Sort of?* She either did or she didn't, Rohan. Which is it?"

Majumdar gave another loud sigh and looked like an animal caught in headlights. "All right. She *did*. But I think what really got to her was that Doctor Grunberg was there."

The face Perez presented to the jury was that of a parent catching a child in a serious lie. "*Doctor Grunberg?* Do you mean Doctor Susan Grunberg, who works at the same hospital as the defendant?"

"Yes." The downcast look on Rohan's face told Dani he knew damn well he'd said too much.

"This court has already heard testimony that Doctor Grunberg was present that night, Rohan. But you didn't mention that until now. Why is that?"

Majumdar took his time answering. Dani's urge to scan the courtroom for the thousandth time evaporated; the only person she wanted to see was Jon Edom. She scrutinized his posture; it had been stiff that morning and somewhat relaxed after lunch; it was now painfully stiff.

Guilty, said a part of her. *He knows what's coming and feels the guilt.*

Another part said, *Maybe. But is it the guilt of a killer or a husband who cares what his wife thinks?* The part that sounded like Saul.

"People get the wrong idea," Majumdar said quietly. "Chelle did, for sure. Doctor Grunberg's a good-looking woman. She knows it. She has fun with it. But the doc—I mean Dr. Edom—he's *devoted* to Chelle. He never even looks at another woman in that way, and never like he's after something. He didn't play Doctor Grunberg's games, didn't take her bait. He was always polite but pushed back whenever she stepped over the line. He's a far better man than I am. It's a shame Chelle couldn't see that."

Perez left the statements unchallenged. And why not? They were favorable to the accused, sure, but they also painted him as a man at odds with his wife. Dani had seen the DA in action before; her pet strategy was to allow the defendant's friends to praise him to the heights and humanize him to the jury. It was when they started to believe his innocence that she would introduce an unexpected twist to the tale. The defendant had endured one too many insult. He had gone off the deep end. Surely they could understand? The hard part of such a strategy was convincing the jury that the doctor's plunge had been into pure evil, not madness. In the case of the State of Texas versus Jon Edom, the murder of the children was definitely going to help with that.

"Perhaps," Perez after a too-long pause, "you could explain to the court why Doctor Grunberg was there."

Majumdar straightened up, and Dani was reminded of a basketball player stepping up to the free throw line. He was still tense but glad to take a break from a hard job to do one that was relatively easy.

"She was part of the team on the patient's case." Majumdar clearly felt comfortable with his answer. "Not in the surgery itself, but as a consultant. The patient had a congenital defect, and Doctor Grunberg is a geneticist. She helped on the treatment plan, and when the surgery was successful, she came by to congratulate the doc."

"And she was in the waiting room when Rochelle Edom arrived?"

"She was sitting in a chair next to Doc Edom. Chelle came in at the worst moment possible."

"What made it the worst?"

Majumdar hesitated, seemed caught in an inner debate whether or not to elaborate further. But, at this point, nothing was going to stop the DA from getting the details she wanted out of him. Dani knew as much from watching her previous trials; she guessed Majumdar sensed it too.

He said, "Dr. Grunberg had her hand on the doc's chest."

Perez paused to give the jury plenty of time to focus their interest. "Her *hand*? Where, *exactly* did Susan Grunberg have her hand? Maybe we can demonstrate. Was Doctor Grunberg to the right or left of Doctor Edom?"

"To his left."

"Like this?" Perez stood to the left of the witness stand. "Was it the right hand she placed on his chest?"

"Yes."

The DA turned her side to the audience and held out her right hand. Majumdar hesitated briefly before positioning it lightly on his chest, palm flat. Perez kept the hand steady for a moment before removing it and backing away.

"Would you call that an intimate gesture, Rohan? Strike that. Don't answer. Let's agree, instead, that most people would. And that is how Doctor Grunberg was touching Doctor Edom when his wife, the mother of his children, entered the waiting room?"

"It was totally innocent. Dr. Grunberg was demonstrating something, asking Jon a question about the surgery. How the doc made the incision, something like that. The touch wasn't for its own sake—she was only pointing out parts of the heart."

"On Doctor Edom's chest." Perez actually snorted. "Instead of, for instance, on her own chest, or by use of a diagram. You don't need to answer that, Rohan. The point here is not what Doctor Grunberg meant by the contact, it's what Rochelle Berger-Edom thought when she arrived and saw what she saw. There was her husband, six hours late for going home, sitting next to good-looking woman—in your own words—who had her hand on his chest. Do I have it all correct? *Do I?*"

"Objection." The defense attorney stood up. "Badgering the witness."

"Sustained." Judge Morrow eyed Perez. "Maybe your witness would answer the question if you gave him a chance, Miss Perez."

"Sorry, Your Honor. Mister Majumdar, am I correct about Dr. Grunberg's hand?"

Majumdar took a long, deep breath. "Yes."

"And, as a result," Perez continued, "there was a *misunderstanding* between Doctor Edom and his wife. I would appreciate if you could now characterize this misunderstanding. Did it involve an accusation?"

Majumdar's pause was brief but significant. "Yes."

"Were there raised voices, shouting?"

"Yes."

"And was it Mrs. Rochelle Berger-Edom who did all of the shouting?"

"The doc tried to make her calm down."

"Did he raise his voice to do that?"

"Yes."

"This is important, Rohan. Did the conflict get physical in any way?"

Majumdar looked desperate, fully aware of the noose he was tying for his friend and colleague. "Chelle put her hands on him, grabbed him. I think she would have hit him, but the doc caught her by the wrist. There was some shoving, and they ended up in the hallway outside the waiting room."

"That was where the nurses witnessed the commotion."

"Right. Chelle was screaming, furious. She acted like she wanted to kill him."

"And he defended himself, physically."

"He had to."

"He caught her wrist. Shoved her. They fell into the hall. Did he hit her, Mister Majumdar? Did Doctor Edom hit Rochelle Edom?"

"He—"

"*Did he hit her?*"

No objection from the defense this time.

Majumdar was on his own; Dani saw the sheer desperation written across his face, and she almost felt sorry for him.

"Yes, okay? He hit her. He slapped her. Open palm. I don't think he meant to. He was trying to cover her mouth to stop her screaming at him. She stepped into it. It definitely wasn't deliberate. The doc wouldn't—"

Perez held up a hand to silence him. "Thank you. No

more questions."

"But he *wouldn't—*"

"*Thank you,*" the DA repeated, voice raised, firm, as she walked back to the prosecution table.

The judge then invited Edom's attorney, Fitzgerald, to cross-examine Majumdar. He took the opportunity to buff the rough edges off the fight story but didn't linger too much on the details. Every experienced attorney understood the futility of trying to erase a bad impression from a jury's collective mind. All Fitzgerald could do was color the impressions, blending them from red to pink. White was unachievable.

As the cross-examination wore on, Dani found that, once more, she couldn't concentrate. The urge to be up and active had calmed somewhat while Perez questioned Majumdar, but now it had returned with a vengeance. She distracted herself by checking news of the hurricane on her cell: It was well north of Houston and working its way along a track that would take it close to Lake Conroe, provided the wind didn't change. When Dani returned her attention to Fitzgerald, he was looking soulfully at Majumdar.

"How long, total, would you say you've known the defendant?"

"Almost five years."

"And in that time, how many arguments, total, would you say you witnessed between Jon and his wife?"

"Maybe three or four on the phone, and that one in person."

"In all those arguments, how often did Jon raise his voice, make threats, or get physical?"

"Just the once, at the hospital, and he didn't mean to, like I said."

"Thank you, Mister Majumdar."

The lawyer sat down and whispered something to his

client. The cross-examination had gone well, but based on the stiffness of both men's backs, it was evident they knew as well as Dani what little good it would do.

37

The DA's assistant, a stumpy, balding man in a dark-gray tailored suit, got to his feet. In a clear, firm voice, he said, "The state calls Mister Vivek Singh to the stand."

A thrilled murmur ran though the court; this was the part they'd all been eagerly awaiting. Jon didn't move but watched Vivek rise from his seat in the front row out of the corner of his eye. Vivek's outfit consisted of cranberry trousers and a matching waistcoat under a blue-and-white checkered blazer. As bold as his dress sense, Vivek marched across the courtroom like he owned the place.

In place of swearing on the Bible, Vivek affirmed to tell the whole truth. Then Judge Morrow struck her gavel and called for silence in court. The crowd quit their excited muttering; nobody wanted to get kicked out and miss what promised to be one juicy testimony. Rohan's evidence had been a disaster for the defense, but even Jon couldn't have made the story of Chelle's tirade sound any better than his friend had.

"Mister Singh," said District Attorney Perez, "could

you please state your occupation for the record?"

"I'm chief executive officer of Endless Loop Games, Limited."

"Your company makes some very popular video games, correct?"

"Our legacy title, *Infinite Quest*, is a two hundred million seller across physical and digital media. We've done triple that with the sequel, *NeverEnd*, on digital alone. That puts us above *Tetris* in all-time sales."

"I watched blocks falling in my sleep all through law school, so I appreciate the comparison. What about the victim, Rochelle Berger-Edom? What was her connection with the company?"

"Rochelle was . . ." He paused there, hanging his head. "She *was* the company, up until some years ago. She was the genius who created *NeverEnd*. After that, she could have had any job she wanted, but the banalities would have bored her to tears. Rochelle was a star to outshine all others. And of course, Endless Loop was the family business."

Jon turned to catch a glimpse of Phillip. He and P. J., who sat a few rows back, were the sole representatives of the Berger family in court. It was a mystery to Jon why they weren't sitting together; sure, like all siblings, they sometimes fought, but if there was ever a time for family solidarity, a murder trial involving three members of the family would be one.

Jon turned farther around in his seat, trying to catch P. J.'s eye. Instead, he caught Detective Cavallo's. She was in the back row and also staring at P. J. when their eyes met. Cavallo broke the contact at once, and, if he didn't know better, Jon might have thought the detective was uncertain about something—maybe she doubted his guilt?

On a better day, Jon would have laughed at that thought.

Having finished her questions about business and the family, Perez asked Vivek, "How would you characterize your own relationship with the victim?"

"We were lovers," he said without hesitation.

Perez was more cautious. "Lovers?"

"We had an affair. Is that how you would like me to put it? Rochelle and I had a years-long sexual affair. We loved each other in ways most people will never experience. We were perfect together."

As the news reverberated through the audience, the DA signaled to the judge she wanted to approach the bench. Her assistant handed her a paper, which Jon immediately recognized: It was the printout of computer IP addresses Cavallo had showed him what seemed like a lifetime ago.

Perez handed the printout to the judge. "Exhibit 4-A, Your Honor."

The judge nodded, and the contents of the paper appeared on the court display screen.

"This is a record of contacts between computers belonging or accessible to Rochelle Berger-Edom and Vivek Singh. The dates suggest they were in contact for a period of weeks before her disappearance. Do you dispute that, Mister Singh?"

"Why would I?" Vivek straightened his jacket. "We were back together then."

Jon balled his fists under the table and fought hard to contain his anger; it was better he not let his feelings show.

"*Back* together, you say?" Perez acted surprised.

"Because she cut me off." The poised and confident Singh seemed disgusted, as though the thought of someone not wanting him made him physically sick. "This was a year ago. After the death of her friend, Hannah."

"That would be Hannah Bernstein, another Endless Loop employee."

"Yes. Rochelle said we were through, that she wanted to fix things with her husband. I put it down to a phase of her grief over Hannah. We'd been broken up before, but this time it stuck: Rochelle stayed away, blocked my emails, wouldn't answer my texts. I heard nothing from her for nearly ten months. And then, a few weeks before she disappeared, she got back in touch. She said we had much to discuss and asked to meet in person."

"And did you meet with her, Mister Singh?"

"We tried. Our schedules—mine mostly, I admit—conflicted. I'm sure we would have worked it out eventually, but we never had the time. Saturday morning, the day after she went missing, I got an email. A private email, through an account I use only for private communications. It had been written the night before and said Rochelle wanted to meet at her family's lake house. She'd be staying there with her sons and wanted me to come over. Jon knew nothing—she didn't want him, only me."

The surprise Perez showed was definitely faked, but the emotion on Detective Cavallo's face was the real thing. Jon's attention was drawn back to her when Rabbi Max, who sat behind him, a waist-high wall between them, whispered, "*Jon.*"

Twisting around, Jon saw Cavallo standing in the aisle next to her seat, face frozen, cheeks flushed. Surprise didn't do the detective's emotion justice—Cavallo was in turmoil.

Rabbi Max nodded at Cavallo a second after Jon had seen her and mouthed, *What is this?*

Jon couldn't waste time on speculation as Perez was continuing her questioning.

"Let me get this straight," the DA said to Vivek as she rested a casual arm on the witness stand. "Rochelle emailed you Friday night to say she wanted to meet at the lake house. But you didn't see the email until *Saturday morning*."

"That's correct," said Vivek. "I text much more than I email, and I kinda got out of the habit of checking my private inbox during our break. I never bothered to set an alert, like the one Rochelle had on her phone. I look at the emails in that account only when I remember, and this time . . ."

"You got the email late."

Vivek's natural arrogance retreated, if only for a second. He showed a brief look of regret that Jon couldn't help but think genuine. Either he blamed himself for not reading the email sooner and missing a chance to save Rochelle, or he was swapping some other anguish into this one's place.

His, "I did," sounded so heartfelt, Jon was reminded of the Vivek he once thought he knew.

The DA paused to stand up straight and cross her arms. "Why didn't she call you, Mister Singh?"

"Rochelle was a deeply emotional person. It was easier for her to say some things in writing."

"I understand." Perez addressed the jury. "I think we can *all* understand. It can be easier to express feelings in print, especially on a sensitive topic."

"Rochelle censored herself so much in real life," said Vivek. "In text, she could be herself."

Jon rocked back in his chair and put a hand to his forehead in an attempt to press away a stab of pain. It was one thing listening to Vivek talk about his romantic relationship with Rochelle, and another to hear him reveal insights about her Jon himself had never gained. Between fresh sympathy for Vivek and a temptation to self-pity, Jon found it hard to focus on the DA's next question.

"Mister Singh, was that all Rochelle said in her email—that she wanted to meet?"

"No," Vivek admitted. "She was afraid I wouldn't come. The children were there. We sometimes fought about them. They were the reason, the *only* reason Rochelle refused to leave her husband and be with me."

Vivek looked directly across at Jon. The challenge sharpened Jon's focus once more, and he made sure to return the gaze for as long as it was offered, which was more than Cavallo had done.

Perez said, "I can understand your reluctance to take care of another man's children."

Vivek shook his head. "Actually, I adore children. What I can't stomach is the thought of separating sons from their father. My own father died when I was young." He paused, his face clouded. Jon sensed a storm was about to break through. "And then she told me, and everything changed."

"*Told you?*" Perez jumped straight on that phrase. "Do you mean she wrote something to you, something important, maybe even life-changing, in that last email?"

"Yes."

A faint smile crossed the DA's lips. Jon knew she knew what was coming and couldn't wait for the jury to hear it. He couldn't even begin to guess.

"And what did Rochelle tell you, Mister Singh?"

Vivek's anguish dissolved and his confidence returned. "She told me the truth, that I'm the boys' father."

The words set off an earthquake in the audience. Murmurs and indistinct chattering rumbled from every mouth. Someone gasped and, from the direction of the sound, Jon guessed it was Detective Cavallo. Those not murmuring began to whisper between themselves. There came a noise like a tiny stampede: fingers tapping wildly on screens.

Jon felt unnaturally calm. He knew Vivek was lying. So, why should a lie upset him? *It was only a damned lie.*

"Sit down, Jon," said Fitz.

Jon hadn't realized he'd gotten to his feet.

"Lying," he said. Loudly he said, "*It's a lie!*"

"Order!" Judge Morrow raised her gavel.

Jon's shoulders slumped; he pressed his fists onto the

table for support. None of the weakness he felt reflected in his voice.

"He's lying, Your Honor."

Morrow banged the gavel. The crowd settled somewhat. Jon remained standing.

Perez raised her voice. "Can you clarify, Mister Singh? To which boy are you father?"

"Both of them," Vivek told her. "Rochelle was positive about Luke, and promised to have the same tests run on Paul—but she *knew*."

Jon fell backward into his seat. At the same moment, he heard a loud cry of "No!" It sounded like P. J. He didn't have the strength to find out. Someone rushed from the courtroom and, a moment later, Simon dragged Ximena to her feet and exited Jon's peripheral vision. Cassidy and Phillip kept their seats in the front row, though Phillip turned to stare at Jon. Jon didn't return the stare.

Jon squeezed his temples as Fitz raised a hand and was saying something to the judge Jon couldn't make out over the crowd's redoubled tumult. He felt a touch on his upper arm and found Rabbi Max was leaning over the partition. Jon couldn't hear him speak, either, but even the sight of his friend's lips moving was a comfort.

Again and again, Judge Morrow banged her gavel. Her calls for order went unheeded until, with a baritone shout that shook the heavens, the bailiff announced, "Court will come to order or the onlookers will be cleared!"

Shushing replaced the murmurs, followed by a series of awkward coughs. Order was finally restored, though it was plain to see it wouldn't last. The judge banged her gavel once more and waited while everyone standing sat back down.

Perez opened her mouth, but Morrow silenced her with a jab of the gavel.

"Mister Singh," said Morrow, "let me get this straight.

You are telling the court Mrs. Berger-Edom informed you by email that you're the father of her children."

"Of the two youngest boys, yes. She had DNA tests run on Luke, the seven-year-old. She became pregnant with him shortly after we met."

"But, Mister Singh, how could you be unaware of this test before the email? Didn't you give a sample?"

Vivek shook his head no. "The test ruled out Jon as the father. It detailed Luke's heritage—the boy was Rajput, like me." He brought a fist down on the witness stand and used the same hand to point at Jon. "*He* knew that. At the end, he *knew*. It's how he was able to kill those boys. They were *my* sons, not his."

Clamor broke out once again. Clearly, Judge Morrow knew then that nothing more would get done in her court that day. She struck the gavel and said, "Counselors, my chamber. Court is adjourned."

In the confusion that followed, Morrow exited through a side door, only pausing to give orders to the bailiff, who went to the witness stand and gestured for Vivek to follow him out. The bailiff kept a sharp eye on Jon, no doubt expecting trouble, but he needn't have bothered. Fitz and Dee were on their feet and Jon couldn't move; his back ached, his arm was throbbing, his stomach burned—the very thought of attacking Vivek was ludicrous.

All Jon could do was stare straight ahead, past the judge's seat and at the court's back wall. His head felt light, his attention miles away, his thoughts on Detective Cavallo. Why had she been so thrown by Vivek's testimony about Chelle's final email? Was the problem, perhaps, that it suggested he didn't know about Vivek and Chelle's affair until she'd told him? Jon remembered saying as much to the court, and Cavallo hadn't been surprised then. That was the trouble with cops: They didn't trust anyone.

The thought cheered Jon enough that he was able to

smile at Fitz when the lawyer asked if he needed a hand. He held up two fingers in answer and extended both arms.

38

"Gimme five rounds, two o'clock!" Silas pointed at a window on the second floor of the lake house. Shots rang out. Glass shattered. There were no screams this time, but the sheer destructive mayhem was enough to bring a fuzzy feeling to Silas's innards. He turned to Coppersmith, who watched from beneath the low-hanging branches of the willow tree. "What do you think? I'd say they're soft enough."

For the past fifteen minutes, the tall man had been huddled there in his duster, barely even lifting his head to watch the effect of the volleys. Each time Silas asked if the enemy was soft enough for the boys to bust through a door, Coppersmith gave him a glare that was exactly like the one Silas saved for federal tax inspectors. The only thing more obvious than Coppersmith's hostility was his disdain.

This time, the response was the same.

Silas glowered; he'd taken about all the bad attitude from his partner as he could take. There was no special reason Coppersmith had to be in charge of the mission today. He hadn't planned the attack on the COTR security team, only told Silas where to find them. Sure, he'd dropped plenty hints about luring ol' Bill Weaver into a trap, but that was just talk. The tall man had connections—that much Silas knew all too well—but he wasn't about to kowtow to Coppersmith simply for passing along a tip.

"We ain't getting any younger, boys," Silas said into the headset that connected him to his men. "Squad Two, move out!"

The plan he made with Coachman called for one squad to break in the front and one in the back of the lake house. Between the two, Coachman was the better at sneaking. Even now, Silas could barely see the long, lean cow boss lying belly-down in the brush beside the driveway. It would have hidden Coachman perfectly, if not for his chalky white vampire mask. Silas didn't bother with masks anymore because the figure he cut was too distinctive. Hiding his face behind a wolfman mask, or a mask of any description, was of no use anymore. It only made him sweaty and uncomfortable.

Coachman gave him a "ten-four" through the headset and, a moment later, the brush started to sway: Coachman's squad was on the move.

Silas watched their subtle ripple approach the back of the house. Okay, a few more seconds and it would be his turn. He slapped the shoulder of the man lying in the grass beside him, one of the goblins. There had been four cowboys in goblin masks at the cemetery. Now there were three, one here and two at the ranch, near where the fourth man was buried on their version of Boot Hill. Silas hissed at the surviving goblin to get ready to move.

Using his left hand, Silas pressed himself to a half crouch. His right hand, in fact the whole of his right arm, was useless; it sat on his belly like dead meat on a cold plate. The shoulder strap that held it was the latest in a line of nuisances that had kept Silas uncomfortable since the cemetery shooting. He had no idea who'd gotten lucky enough to peg him one in the shoulder, but good money said the shooter was on the other side of those lake house walls, already bleeding or waiting to be bled. Despite the arm's inconvenience, and the pain of its frayed nerves, Silas was glad to be where he was. Enough time had passed since the cemetery for his revenge to be served cold.

And that was going to make it so very sweet.

The big man braced his haunches and started a count. Three more seconds, he told himself, and he would signal the charge. Across the yard, up the front stoop, shotgun to the door and then? Revenge. In three . . . two . . . one.

"You're late, Abraham," said Coppersmith. He wasn't wearing a headset, of course, and raised his voice as he added, "*Too* late."

Furious, Silas stared hard at the tall man. He was fifteen feet away, or Silas would have throttled him left-handed first for exposing their position and second for calling him *Abraham* in public.

Coppersmith made a gesture, a long, thin finger pointed vaguely at the window Silas's men had shot out just a few minutes before. A shadow could be seen there, aiming a rifle.

"*Two by!*" bellowed Silas. The man closest to him was up on a knee in the blink of an eye. He aimed quickly, squeezed the trigger.

There came a flash far too bright for muzzle fire, a cacophonous boom of thunder. *Literal* thunder.

Silas let out a surprised yelp as the willow tree shattered like ice struck by a hammer, its branches ablaze despite the drizzling rain. Silas lurched away from the splintering tree as limbs crashed down and chunks of smoldering wood spun high through the air. Silas looked back where Coppersmith had been standing. It was empty. Only the burning leaves and the split trunk of the once-magnificent tree, insides scorched black by the lightning, remained.

Overhead, the sky was an ugly dark, every storm cloud blending into its neighbor. Another lightning bolt flashed up high, followed immediately by a thunder clap so violent it almost knocked Silas off his feet. The wind had been whistling menacingly all day, but now it hollered and howled, and the rain hissed as it fell, changing from drizzle to fat, bloated drops in less time than it took Silas to cuss.

A shot rang out from the house.

Silas felt a blast of heat roar past him, just a hair's breadth from his damaged shoulder.

"*Run!*" he shouted, already following his own order. "It's the Judgment!"

The COTR cars were parked beyond the sloping lawn and across to the driveway. Silas lurched that way, seeking cover; his own vehicle was a quarter mile down the road. He wasn't a fast runner, but Silas reckoned he could make it in ninety seconds if his heart held out. He ran full tilt for the first thirty, to get himself out of range of the enemy rifles. Then, once the first of the black Chryslers was between him and the lake house, he paused to watch his fellow guardsmen race past him. When Coachman caught up, he slapped Silas on the back, and Silas got moving again.

The rain was a veritable torrent, driven sideways by the vicious wind so mighty it bent the tall trees sideways. It made the grass dangerously slick, the ground beneath it mud, so Silas lurched onto the gravel shoulder to finish his run.

"Make it four to a cab," ordered Coachman as the men reached the vehicles. "It don't matter who you ride with."

The men ran to their respective jeeps, pickups, and sedans. Hurriedly, they bundled into every door to escape the hurricane's onslaught.

Not Silas, though.

He stood in the street and stared back the way they'd run. What little of the lake house could be seen through the storm was a tiny gray blob under the roiling storm clouds.

"Eyes on Coppersmith?" Silas said to the headset. The tall man hadn't passed him, he was sure of that, and he wasn't anywhere to be seen.

Coachman's voice came back over the headset. "This storm will kill us all, boss. We going, or what?"

Silas narrowed his eyes, trying his best to see through the almost impenetrable rain. The house was entirely invisible now, and he could only barely make out the dark shapes of the Chryslers. Shadows moved through the dimness, edges frayed by the driving rain. Plenty of the shadows Silas could see were tall, plenty were the right shape to be human, or something that could pass for human if Silas didn't look too close. He'd never looked close at Coppersmith. It was his strictest policy.

"Going," Silas said, and clambered into the nearest pickup.

39

The wait in the defense's antechamber wasn't nearly so long as Jon had expected. Fitz walked in after barely ten minutes with Judge Morrow. The first thing he did was ask where Dee had gone.

"That bailiff, the angry one," said Rabbi Max. "He came for her."

Fitz looked alarmed.

Jon said, "He wasn't angry. That's just his face. Narrow forehead, tight orbicularis oculi. Squinty eyes, in layman's terms—just makes him look angry. Dee's fine, I'm sure. The bailiff said something about a delivery. She went with him to check."

Visibly relieved, the lawyer took his seat at the desk. He didn't prop his feet on top, as he had at lunch. He wasn't that relaxed, but he did seem generally pleased with his meeting with the judge.

"What did she say?" Rabbi Max asked.

Fitz smiled, showing clean teeth. "Her Honor kindly let me watch her chew the district attorney's ass. She didn't care too much for the prosecution's style when questioning

Mister Singh. *Grandstanding* was the word she used."

"The shoe fits," Rabbi agreed.

Fitz grew somber. "Is Vivek's claim true, Jon?"

The steroids had washed out of Jon's system an hour ago, leaving him physically and mentally weak. The pain remained manageable, but he knew much worse was in the offing. Those two facts combined made Fitz's question seem more intrusive than it was surely meant to be. Jon had to work hard to keep his emotions in check.

"I never asked Chelle." Jon's voice trembled. "I never suspected someone else could be Luke's father. I didn't know *she* had any doubts. She never said anything, anything at all, to even suggest it. The other affairs were long ago, years before Endless Loop existed."

Fitz leaned in closer. "You mentioned before, you knew she cheated. You never had suspicions about Luke. What about the other children?"

"I'm sure Paul is mine. *Was* mine. He had his mother's eyes, the Berger eyes, but he had my nose. All our friends said so."

Fitz nodded, appearing to accept that as conclusive evidence. Jon knew better than to believe appearances.

"What about the twins?" Fitz prompted.

Jon drew in a sharp breath. The looming aches and pains hopped up on their toes, ready to pounce on his throat. He couldn't meet Fitz's eyes; the scars the lawyer was asking him to uncover ran too deep.

He said, "Bipolar is a monster, Fitz. Most people know about depression, the havoc it can cause, but the mania can be just as harmful, or even worse. Nineteen years ago, when Chelle got pregnant with Cass and Simon, she told me she thought somebody else could be the father. We'd been trying for a long time, and the things she said made me question my masculinity. I got over that soon enough, but it hurt deeply. It wasn't her fault, though, you understand.

Chelle was in one of her manic episodes. If I'd understood her condition better back then, I would have dismissed her ranting and accusations out of hand. She told me later she made up the whole thing and had no idea why. There was no one else, never had been. I didn't believe that, I'm not that naive, but I'm confident the twins were mine. If Vivek or anyone else has any claim on my children, it's on Luke. I'm definitely the father of my other children."

From his wooden-backed chair next to Jon's, the rabbi asked, "About Luke. You believe what Vivek said about a DNA test?"

Jon's muscles along his right side tightened as his body prepared for a symptom attack.

"Rochelle told me about the test. A nutrition screening, she said. It was meant to optimize Luke's diet, and give us insight into diseases to which he might be prone. We were supposed to discuss the results, but there was the shooting at the hospital, and we never got back to it."

"How do you know the test came out the way Vivek said?" asked the rabbi. "Maybe Rochelle lied to him in the email like she lied to you all those years ago. If the children were the issue, she might have pretended he was the father so he'd go to her."

"It's possible," Jon was forced to admit.

"And Singh may be lying about the email's contents," Fitz put in. "That was Judge Morrow's chief point, that Perez allowed Singh to make statements based on facts not in evidence. She wants the email, *all* the emails presented. The DA should have done that already—she was lucky the judge stopped at a dressing down for such a serious omission. In fairness, the DA should have given an official censure."

Following a knock at the door, which had been left partially open, Dee entered from the hall with a cardboard box under her arm. It was about the same height as a shoebox but twice as wide. Fitz raised his eyebrows.

"Dropped off by courier," Dee said as she lay the box on the desk. Someone, presumably a security official, had cut the tape that had once sealed it. Jon saw papers inside—some loose, others in plain, light-blue folders. Dee drew out one of the folders and handed it to Fitz.

The lawyer took a few seconds to peruse the contents. As he did so, his eyes widened. He set the folder down in front of Jon and flipped to the first page.

"It's a cold case file from Austin PD. See the name of the victim?"

Jon followed Fitz's finger. "Hannah Bernstein."

Rabbi Max let out a grunt of surprise as Fitz spun the folder back around for better reading.

"The whole investigation is here. Forensics, witness testimony." Fitz flicked through the pages, stopping three-quarters of the way through the file. "Now, *this* is interesting."

"What is?" Jon tried his best to read upside down, as did Rabbi Max and Dee.

Fitz held up a finger, asking the others for patience. He skimmed the page, then the next, and one more. Finally, he flipped back to the page that had first caught his attention. He held it up for Jon to read. It was a report. Fitz tapped the header at the top of the page.

"Financial Crimes Unit," Jon read.

"It seems Miss Bernstein found irregularities in Endless Loop's accounting," Fitz explained for the benefit of his wife and the rabbi. "She contacted the police shortly before she was killed. The last pages in this file summarize an investigation by the Financial Crimes Unit. An investigation, I'm sad to say, that went cold shortly after her death."

A thousand questions ran though Jon's head. He asked the most pressing. "Who sent the box? Is there any way to tell?"

Dee said, "None that I noticed. There's no return name or address. Not even handwriting we could analyze." The three men stared at her. "What? Like I wasn't going to check."

Fitz smiled and pulled the box closer. A quick search through the rest of the papers proved fruitless.

"Everything here is germane to the Bernstein killing," he told them all. "There's no cover letter, and there's nothing on the box besides my name and the courthouse address. And that's typed." He gave Dee an indulgent look. "All together, based on the contents, I'm inclined to credit Castro as our benefactor. Bernstein's death having something to do with Rochelle's disappearance was his hypothesis."

"I'm still not sure of the connection," Jon threw in.

Fitz admitted, "Neither am I."

"If this is Castro," said Dee, "where's he been all this time?"

Fitz shrugged.

Rabbi Max said, "The cunning man hides from harm."

"You think he's gone undercover?" Jon's mind was in overdrive, despite its weariness.

"Maybe he figured something out, and whoever did this horrible thing to your family came after him." The rabbi scratched at his face, deep in thought.

The logic made sense to Jon. He turned to Fitz, expecting an opinion on the rabbi's suggestion, but the lawyer didn't appear to be listening. For the next few seconds, he sat quiet, reading intently from a portion of the financial case. What he saw in there conjured surprise on his usually stoic face.

"Listen to this," he said. "'Interviewee'—that's Miss Bernstein—'reports a series of credits to corporate accounts. Identical amounts are recorded from different creditors over a period of four years.' The last was roughly three years before the report date. 'All credits are cited as loans, but no record of payment or demand exists. Interviewee suggests creditor names may be aliases or dummy corporations obscuring the true source of funds.'"

Jon took a moment to digest the information. "She found someone sneaking money *into* Endless Loop?"

"Something like that." Fitz frowned; it evidently made little sense to him either. "Reading on, it seems there's a paper trail of amounts similar to the credits *leaving* the company. Bernstein never worked out where they were going, but she had a short list of suspects for the creditor. The FCU traced a few possibilities before they hit a dead end. Are any of these names familiar?"

The list he presented included several names that struck a chord in Jon's memory. One in particular resonated.

"Korvette Holdings, Limited," Jon said. "*Korvette* with a *K*, as in Korvus."

"The pastor?" Rabbi Max voiced what Jon was thinking.

"*Chief* pastor of the Church of the Resurrected." Fitz cracked a thin smile. "An interesting notion, indeed." Flipping to the last page of the report, the lawyer spun it around on the desk for the others to see. "It seems Financial Crimes thought of it too. They questioned Korvus about being a creditor and he declined comment. A warrant was sought to search church records, but the judge flatly refused. Inside of two months, Bernstein was dead. There were modest efforts to pursue the other creditors, but without her as a source, the investigation folded."

"You think it was mothballed on purpose?" Jon interlaced his fingers, resting them on the smooth desk.

"I wouldn't be surprised."

A moment of silence fell as everyone processed what they'd just heard. Jon spoke first: "How far back did you say those loans went?"

Fitz flipped back through pages to refresh his memory. "They were over a four-year period, starting roughly three years prior to the report. Considering when it was filed, that's around eight years ago."

"The same time Vivek Singh was hired," said Jon.

Fitz made a noise something akin to a gasp *and* a laugh. "*And* he was hired into the same position later taken by Miss Bernstein."

Another thoughtful silence.

Dee broke it this time. "He cooked the books."

"Who?" said Rabbi Max.

"Vivek," Jon stated the obvious. "Based on the timing, I think he might have been hired for exactly that purpose. He buried that series of credits and whatever Endless Loop did with the funds."

Fitz said, "And Hannah Bernstein found out about what looks to be classic money laundering."

"So they killed her." Dee sat down in one of the empty chairs.

"But who are *they*?" Rabbi Max asked.

"Most likely someone at the company," said Jon. "Or the church. Whoever they are, they also had a motive to kill Chelle."

The others stared at him, waiting for him to spell out the connection he'd made.

"She was obsessed, near the end," Jon went on. "Obsessed with Hannah's death. She investigated it on her own after the cops gave up, talked to mutual friends, even hassled the police. At the time I thought it was a quirk of her mania—she was prone to fixate on a subject to the extent it dominated her every thought. She usually let it drop once the manic phase passed, but this time, she persisted."

"You think she rediscovered the credits," said Fitz.

"And maybe the creditor."

"How?" Fitz and Dee said in perfect sync.

"Chelle had unlimited access to Endless Loop's files. She basically built their security system from the ground up, back when Lisa was CEO. Their cyberwalls were solid, firewalls impermeable, but Chelle knew a back door—because she'd programmed one in without anyone knowing. She showed me once, when we lost some old pics during a phone upgrade. Chelle logged into the company servers and downloaded the backup without anyone in the system knowing she was there—no trace whatsoever."

"So far as you knew," Fitz added. "Around eight years ago, the newly hired second senior accountant of Endless Loop Games, Vivek Singh, processed a series of credits *into* the company. We don't know if he processed the transactions *out* as well, but it would certainly have helped to keep them secret. All this went on over the course of four years, after which time Singh left his position to become vice president of finance. Later, he became CEO. In the meantime, his successor, Hannah Bernstein, studied the company records and suspected malfeasance. She reported her suspicions to Austin police, and was murdered for her trouble. Rochelle investigated her death and had the means to access the same financial records as Miss Bernstein, and more."

Jon's heart raced; he couldn't help but take the theory a step further. "And during the time she was looking into Hannah's murder, she was in direct with Vivek. Think about it. He admits to reading *one* of her emails, but we know there were several. Detective Cavallo showed me that list they put out in court."

"You think Rochelle wrote something to Vivek that tipped him off?" Fitz pondered.

"Maybe. They were *lovers*, after all." The word stuck in Jon's throat, made his stomach churn. "There's plenty

Vivek may have lied about, but that definitely fits. You heard what he said up there—Chelle didn't censor herself in her emails. Psychology is not my field, but I've got a feeling Singh was laughing at us when he mentioned that. His words had a double meaning, and what he meant was Chelle was careless and trusted the wrong man. We all know the result."

Fitz shut the folder and dropped it into the box. "Do we, though? There are several important details missing. The first and most vital is who actually committed the murder. Did Singh act alone, or was he part of a conspiracy? If it was the latter, was Singh the mastermind, or simply a flunky? I'd like to know how—and where—Korvus fits in. You mentioned a theory about motive, Jon: Singh told you Rochelle was leaving the church. You thought someone might have kidnapped her, and now we know *killed* her, to prevent her from going. I'm beginning to think you may not be far wrong."

The lawyer got to his feet and lifted up the box as if to weigh the contents. Dee and Jon watched him with furrowed brows.

"Where are you going?" Dee asked her husband.

"Back to chambers. If I hurry, I can catch the judge and maybe, just maybe, we can have these papers submitted as evidence. I'm not sure where it'll lead us, but I think it's worth a shot. Chin up, Jon. We'll beat them yet."

Fitz's confidence was both infectious and invigorating. Jon felt his weakness recede, and the aches and pains threatening him slunk back on their haunches. He considered standing up to usher Fitz out, but his muscles were still too tight and he chose not to push his luck. Fitz swept from the room with the box with a wink at his wife. She gave a wave before taking his seat; she propped her feet up on the desk as she pulled out her cell phone.

"It's been a long day, Jon." Rabbi Max stated the

obvious for all of them. "Your medicines, the injections. They've worked?"

"I couldn't have made it on my own," Jon told him. "I'll be back at the Crown tomorrow morning for another round of injections."

Dee clucked her tongue. "Awful."

Surprised, Jon and the rabbi turned to face her. It was clear at a glance, though, her comment had nothing to do with Jon's medical routine.

"The latest pictures of the hurricane are just awful." Dee used her finger to scroll, eyes glued to the tiny screen. "Its path of destruction looks like the wrath of God."

"The world turns," said Rabbi Max, "but the Judge of All shows mercy."

"Maimonides?" guessed Jon.

"No," said the rabbi with a sardonic smile. "That one's mine."

40

Tasmin clung onto Billy as the scarred mass of sin and grit kicked open the front door and half dragged, half carried her into the driving rain. She was hurt, bleeding profusely, her left leg numb. Every bullet had somehow missed her, but the final barrage had made a mess of the window frame she was standing behind, not to mention the wall housing the frame and the pictures of the Berger family on the wall beyond that. Tasmin reckoned she had a cord of wood worth of splinters in the leg, plus enough glass in her face, chest, and arms to glaze a greenhouse. Her rifle was somewhere in the rubble upstairs, keeping company with Seo-yeon's corpse.

Of all Tasmin's injuries, the chunk of flesh taken out of the foot was the most troubling. Not because it hurt her—adrenaline was doing a good job of masking the pain—but because she wasn't able to pause the retreat to enjoy the rare dive into her own anatomy. There she was, with a perfect opportunity to study her own raw gristle and bone, and all she could do was blink down at the bloodied surface as Billy helped her run.

At least what remained of the foot seemed solid. Tasmin reckoned she was sure to have a few cracked bones, in the damaged foot and elsewhere, and she looked forward to setting them herself. In the meantime, nothing the shooters had done was enough to make her stop; the damage they'd done only slowed her down and made her lean on Billy, who was also bleeding, only not as much as she was.

She tightened her grip on his shoulder. Billy responded by wrapping a hand around her belt and lifting up until her feet left the ground.

"Hang on," he growled.

The front door of the lake house let out onto a porch with three steps. The steps had a railing and a perfect view of the smoldering timber of the willow tree. Billy squeezed off a round from his M4 as he leapt, setting his hip on the railing and starting a slide that took him and Tasmin to the ground. There were no answering echoes of gunfire; all Tasmin heard was the relentless thud of the torrential rain that stung her torn cheeks and soaked her clothes through. Cursing, she checked over Billy's shoulder.

She saw Darrin race out of the door—the new recruit slipped on the wet wood and nearly fell, saving himself at the last second by grabbing the railing. An E-niner Tasmin didn't know followed Darrin out, his footing much steadier. So far as she knew, they were the only survivors of the firefight. Twelve people, including Tasmin, had entered the lake house. Only Billy, Tasmin, Darrin, and the other E-niner had come out. An impressive body count. Whoever had set up the ambush had done their job well.

The unfamiliar E-niner shouted something across at Tasmin and Billy, but the wind and the rain snatched his words away. It didn't matter, though, because Billy got the message and shoved Tasmin away. She rolled hard on a shoulder and skidded in the sodden grass. Looking back, she saw Billy crouching, covering his helmeted head with his hands. Behind him, where he'd been standing, lay a thick limb from the destroyed willow. As she watched in disbelief, it tipped upright, shook violently, and was swept away by the wind.

". . . *late! Won't make it!*" the E-niner shouted again.

Billy blinked at Tasmin through his goggles. He then turned and gave a *help me!* gesture to his remaining team. The E-niner called out something inaudible and pushed past Darrin to sprint, as best he could, through the rain and toward the cars.

Billy drew his sidearm from its holster.

Tasmin covered her ears.

A shot rang out, splitting through the howling wind and pounding rain.

Immediately, the E-niner crumpled, shot in the back of the knee. He rolled on the wet ground yowling in pain, clutching his bloodied leg.

Without comment, Billy hooked an arm under Tasmin and lifted her up. Her leg ached terribly, the adrenaline wearing off, and she was grateful when Darrin took a place under her other arm.

None of the three spoke as they passed the willow tree. The wind was howling still louder as they reached the E-niner, thoroughly drowning out his sobs. Billy kept his gun trained on the man, and left Darrin to help Tasmin as he approached the fallen grunt for a word.

They reached the lead Chrysler. Darrin fumbled for keys while Tasmin watched Billy wrench the E-niner's weapon out of his hand. The man shouted something that sounded like a plea, and then a powerful gust of wind blew the rain sideways to erase both men from her view.

A sharp report of a gun rose above the buffeting wind.

The next instant, Darrin opened the door. Tasmin clamored into the back seat while Darrin slid behind the steering wheel and turned the key.

A sudden flash of lightning lit up the sky, and Tasmin saw Billy's black clothes set off by the glaring light. He jerked open Darrin's door; without question, Billy climbed over to the passenger seat.

As Billy settled in, Tasmin said, "Friend didn't want a ride?"

Billy snorted. "Said he'd thumb a lift."

He tossed something in Tasmin's direction. She caught it. Gunpowder and gore painted the stump of a severed thumb.

She said, "Good luck."

The fallen man writhed in pain as Billy wheeled the Chrysler in a tight semicircle. A second later, he was hidden by the rain, along with the wreck of the willow tree. The house vanished next, seconds before the car left the gravel driveway and drove on to the pavement. That was when Billy put the pedal down. Thanks to the spiral of the hurricane, the wind was coming in from the south. It buffeted the Chrysler hard, threatening to blow it off the road.

"We're not going to make it," Darrin groaned.

"*Shut it!*" Billy snarled and drove around a bend. The windshield wipers, whooshing at full speed, were worthless in the storm; they just couldn't keep up with the deluge of rain. Billy switched them off, telling Darrin, "Watch for mailboxes on your side."

"Yessir." Darrin scooched forward and pressed his face to the glass.

As they rounded another bend, Tasmin was amazed that Billy could make anything out at all; it felt like they were riding a roller coaster through a car wash.

Tasmin didn't see what they hit, but she sure as hell felt the effect: The driver's side of the car lifted and the vehicle flew through the air. Momentarily weightless, Tasmin's shattered foot struck the ceiling, the window, and the seat as she was flung around. Mercifully, her back hit the door and stuck there as the rest of the world turned over and over. With a sickening *crunch*, the windows cracked into spiderwebs.

For a splinter of a second, Tasmin Beale's world went dark.

Then it brightened again. A light shone from somewhere. Tasmin blinked, and the light was gone.

"Billy?" she called out. "*Billy?*"

No answer.

Lightning flashed brightly outside. It was sharper than the brief, shining light and far less inviting. It also showed Darrin lying in a heap below the upside-down passenger seat. His neck was broken—she knew instantly by the unnatural angle of his helmeted head. For the first time in many years, the thrill Tasmin felt when faced with death failed to spark. She suppressed a scream and called out again for Billy.

"Naw." A voice came from the front seat. It sounded like Billy, but also *not quite* like Billy. Stripped of his usual control, Billy Weaver's voice was reedy, panicked. "It ain't gonna be this way," he said and bashed at his window with what could have been an elbow or his pistol.

"Billy! Help me. Billy!"

He didn't seem to hear her.

Outside, the rain beat and the hurricane howled. The car gave a lurch, and Tasmin realized it wasn't sitting flush on its roof—it tilted sideways. Tilting and sliding.

Swallowing down her panic, Tasmin peered out of the cracked window to see where they were sliding toward. The broken window at her back buckled inward with an audible *bloop*.

"Damn it," Tasmin grumbled.

Billy had somehow flipped the vehicle all the way into

Lake Conroe. Likely he'd steered down a driveway or along a service road, and the bump she'd felt was a sign reading Bridge Out.

Billy struck the glass with another cry of, "Naw!"

It broke and water gushed in.

Tasmin's stomach lurched at the thought of drowning trapped in the car. The water's weight made the car tilt faster and, in less than a second, the extreme angle sent Darrin's body tumbling over the center console and back into the driver seat.

Tasmin cursed against the pain shooting up her leg and pushed herself upright. She scrambled into the front seat in time to see Billy's feet disappear through the hole he'd made in the window.

She couldn't follow him because Darrin's lifeless corpse blocked her way.

"I'm a good swimmer," Tasmin reminded herself. "A *strong* swimmer."

That much was true, so far as it went. Daddy had taught her to swim the old-fashioned way when she was just six or seven: picking her up by a belt loop and tossing her into the water one pitch-black night. He'd been drunk at the time, naturally, and kept his balance in the boat by what must have been a miracle. It had the desired result, though—Tasmin could swim like a damn fish. She just didn't care for it much.

The light vanished, and it was as dark in the car as on that night in her father's boat. Only the muffled *thump* told Tasmin the car had struck the lake bottom—the momentum had her bumping hard into Darrin's body. The car no longer tilted; it lay on its side, mercifully blocking Billy's broken window.

Seizing Darrin's shirt, Tasmin heaved with all her strength. The body shifted slowly away from the exploded driver's side window, but all that exposed was sucking mud and clinging weeds. She got to her knees. The water was at her waist now, rising quickly, and so very dark and cold.

Tasmin was actually glad she couldn't see the icy lake water snaking its way up her belly on its way to steal the breath from her lungs; it brought her a strange sensation of comfort. The windshield, along with the passenger window above her, seemed to be holding. They had been weakened, though she pictured in her mind's eye the cracked glass. Why didn't they break, though? Tasmin's only hope was she could smash one of them as Billy had his and she could swim out—oh, God—to safety.

The water reached her breasts.

Tasmin pulled a knife from her pocket and tried chipping at the windshield. She struck once, twice, and at her third strike, the blade pierced through. There was a moment when the knife hung suspended, held in place by pressurized glass.

Then the glass split.

Too late, Tasmin saw her mistake: The incoming water was a torrent, far too heavy to swim against. Instead, it drove Tasmin down, bowled her over, held her under its icy grasp. She bounced once more against Darrin's limp body and clawed at the water in a blind panic as she fought to gasp in the last of the frigid air.

By the time she got hold of herself, Tasmin had lost all sense of direction. She wasn't even sure if she was still in the car. The water no longer rose or gushed toward her; it pressed her under like daddy's hand.

She tried to swim, but her hand struck something hard. So, she swam in a different direction and was caught up in a strong current. The storm above was churning the lake to create whirlpools. It occurred to Tasmin that all the snakes and gators the area was famous for would be busy swimming against the currents, away from her. That was her only positive thought.

Something battered Tasmin's shoulder, and she saw lights swirling before her eyes. She guessed they may well be inside her oxygen-deprived brain but swam after them anyway, fighting hard against the water despite the terror that gripped her and the agony in her damaged foot.

Her chest ached for air like nothing she'd ever experienced before, a white-hot pain that clawed at her lungs like some malevolent beast, and her throat itched like she'd swallowed thorns. It didn't matter. She still fought that current until its grip weakened.

She was free! Somehow, Tasmin Beale had found a still place in the hurricane-churned water.

But it was still so dark in the depths of the lake, so bitterly cold. She swam toward that pinprick of light in the distance, fighting the urge to take a gulp of lake water and let herself sink—to give in.

No! Not like that. *Never!*

Tasmin had pictured herself dying a thousand times, in a thousand different ways. None of those involved water. Not one! She hated the thought of being found floating face down, of someone hauling her bloated, fish-eaten corpse into a boat and carrying her to a morgue where doctors would poke and prod her and carve out her secrets. She wouldn't die this way. *She just wouldn't!*

A hand closed around Tasmin's ankle. Not her Daddy's, but still a hand of flesh and blood. Yet, it felt too cold to have hot blood inside it. Still, it was strong and most welcome. The long, bony fingers dug hard into her skin, making the ankle bone throb with dull, aching pain.

Tasmin fought to look and, with only that pinprick of light to see by, the thing holding onto her was all but invisible. All she saw was the faintest smudge of a hand, the hint of a long, slender arm, and the nebulous impression of a long, billowing jacket. Making out any other features in the darkness was impossible.

So why was she positive its face was grinning at her?

Tasmin tried to swim free. It held her tight. She stretched to her limit, reaching out for the light. The water pressed her ever downward, but Tasmin defied it. The hand chilled her even more than the icy waters of Lake Conroe, but Tasmin fought against it with a fierce inner fire, a hellish warmth.

The light blossomed, yet somehow, it didn't reach her. Tasmin drifted away from it, tugged by the current and that cold, evil hand. As darkness closed around her, Tasmin quit swimming. Not permanently, she promised herself, just for a moment, just for a short rest to catch her . . .

Tasmin was surprised to find she could hear the storm raging above.

The chaos was quite musical. It reminded her of a song. There were voices in the storm; they sang words she couldn't quite recall. Tasmin was sure she'd heard them before.

She was sure she would never hear them again.

41

Thunder woke Dani for the fourth time that night. Or morning, she corrected herself. Fresh, early-morning light shone through her bedroom window. She checked the time: seven thirty. Later than she normally got up, but still plenty of time to get ready for court at ten. If yesterday's testimony had convinced her of anything, it was that she didn't want to miss a minute of the trial. Not when everything she thought she knew about the crime could shift so easily.

Vivek Singh's testimony had called into question everything Dani intuited about Rochelle. She'd read the murdered woman as a psychological captive: The overachievement at work, the religious fervor, and the doubling down on a second batch of kids told her Rochelle Edom *wanted* to change her life but lacked the agency to make it happen on her own. The affair with Singh was her attempt at a way out, and the fact she'd involved Singh in the attempt just screamed that her confidence was shot. No doubt the poor woman suffered decades of gaslighting, repression, coercion, and psychological torture at the hands of her husband. It *had* to have happened that way; nice guys like Dr. Edom pretended to be didn't just change into brutal killers overnight. If the doctor *was* a monster, he'd been one for years.

The notion that the children, or at least Luke, might have had a father who was not Edom had thrown Dani's entire understanding of the crime into disarray. Rochelle's way to a new life had been in place for at least seven years. She could have gone to Vivek at any time following her penultimate pregnancy. That she hadn't done so suggested she wasn't a virtual captive at home, as Dani had originally thought.

It was evident Rochelle Edom had more agency than Dani had thought, so she must have had reasons for staying in the marriage. Was it for the twins? No. Dani had seen too many couples break up when the kids reached their teenage years to think Cassidy and Simon were the answer.

The detective pondered the conundrum as she crawled out of bed and went to look herself over in the mirror. The other side of her bed was empty, of course, had been for a while, so it wasn't like anybody cared how tangled her hair was in the morning. Neither did Dani. What she wanted to see was the stern, confident face she used to present to Saul Troyer. Today, it was missing. In its place sat a pinched brow and deep, dark shadows beneath the eyes.

"Worried, Detective?" she asked her reflection before tucking her long, black hair behind her ears and attempting to splash the troubled face away with cold tap water.

Her phone rang, loud, insistent. Dani snagged a hand towel off the sink counter and rushed back to the bedroom. The phone was on a table over by the wall—Dani had the habit of keeping it out of reach overnight to prevent herself from doomscrolling instead of sleeping.

"Cavallo." She prodded the speaker button.

"You're the detective?" a woman's voice asked.

"Yes. *Detective* Cavallo. Austin PD."

"I have information." The caller paused so long Dani turned up the volume, listening for background noise. At last, the caller spoke: "Dr. Jon Edom is innocent. He loved his wife. He did not know about the affair. And he couldn't have killed his children because they're not . . . They're not—"

She hung up midsentence.

Dani glared in frustration at the phone, willing the unknown woman to call back. When it seemed clear she wouldn't, Dani pulled up her recent calls. NUMBER UNKNOWN showed on the first line. Obviously, the caller wished to remain anonymous.

The voice was familiar, though, but Dani couldn't quite place it. If she'd heard it someplace before, the conversation must have been very brief. She made a mental note to call the phone company the moment she got to the station—sometimes they could help trace even a masked number. She also reckoned that if she skipped a shower and threw on yesterday's clothes, she could be on the road in five minutes.

Pausing halfway through shaking the wrinkles from the pair of slacks she'd discarded in a heap on her bedroom floor the night before, Dani asked herself what Saul would do in her situation. If she showered and put on a fresh suit, she might still have time to look into her mystery caller. She wouldn't get an immediate answer from the phone company, anyway—until after her day in court. Tossing the slacks aside, Dani raised her eyes to the ceiling.

"All right, partner. This time we do it your way."

42

Pamela let the phone fall from her hand to the smooth, white surface of the comforter. What had she done? The detective wasn't stupid; she'd soon learn who'd called her. And when she did, she would come asking questions. What would Pamela do then?

She considered telling Phillip about the call. He would be angry with her, of course, but she thought a good fight might be what she needed to forget her fears. It turned out she didn't need to bother. A sudden, loud shout from Phillip reverberated down from the hallway, and Pamela's fear for herself was replaced with that for another.

She rushed from the bedroom, buttoning her blouse. Phillip's voice had come from Mother's bedroom, two doors down from her own. Pamela caught the end of a word she thought was *yesterday* and an incoherent murmur from Mother. When Pamela peeked in the door, Phillip stood over Mother, who sat on the bed fussing with the belt of her dressing gown.

"You don't have a choice," Phillip was telling her as if she were a naughty five-year-old. He wasn't shouting anymore, but Pamela could tell his temper was as fierce as ever. Angry outbursts had a long history in the family, though Phillip was quite unique in keeping his private. That tended to make them worse. "The prosecutor expects you. You're her prize exhibit. She's going to call you to testify after that red detective."

Mother slouched. She lost interest in the belt and let her arms hang limply by her sides. The dressing gown was a mass of wrinkles, a detail that would have made a fully aware Lisa Berger cringe. She hated untidiness, and considered sloth the most deadly of the sins. Pamela felt a moment of satisfaction at seeing the once-stern woman like this. Her pleasure was just as quickly swallowed by guilt: Mother was in a pitiful state, and she certainly had no defense against Phillip.

"Leave her alone." Pamela entered the bedroom. She stepped past Phillip to touch Mother gently on the shoulder. Mother brushed her away like some troublesome insect. Undeterred, Pamela rounded on Phillip. "Don't you see how she is? You should be ashamed!"

Phillip squeezed his temples. "Ashamed? I think you've forgotten your priorities, P. J. Number one is the trial. You remember the trial? It's the one that will make sure Jon Edom gets locked up for killing your sister and nephews. It's very important. I can't get Mother to realize that."

He faced Pamela now and held one arm to the side, the other by his head. She interrupted by stepping closer, as though about to either hug him or punch him on the chin. Phillip didn't flinch but kept on looking down at her. She was two inches shorter and absolutely hated to be reminded of that fact.

"It's not about *realizing* anything." Pamela met his icy stare. "Mother can't remember, Phillip. Can't you get that through your stupid head?"

They each took a breath, eyes locked in a grim sibling

stare. Finally, Phillip said, "You've got no family spirit, Peej. You make a fuss when you ought to be helping." He relaxed his arms, softened his tone. "Don't fuss. We're family. Look, Perez wants us at the courthouse at nine. Talk to Mother. Get her up and dressed. God knows she listens to you better than me."

Pamela considered that a moment. Her brother was right, of course: The trial *was* important, and Mother did listen to her better—probably because she didn't shout. If only Phillip hadn't called her "Peej," she might have agreed to work on Mother's wardrobe. But the nickname triggered too many troubling memories. Pamela remembered the last time she'd heard it, the night of the dinner party, the same night some maniac shot up Jon's hospital. It all seemed a lifetime ago.

"I smoked that night," she said out loud.

"Huh?"

"The last night you called me Peej. You know what, Phil? I think I need another smoke." She turned to Mother, saw she'd straightened herself up somewhat, and put on a smile. "Lisa, get your clothes on, hon. We're going someplace special."

Confused, rheumy eyes blinked at her, but the smile Mother gave was the clear, trusting smile of a child. As the old woman stirred into movement, Pamela turned away.

"Was *that* so hard?" She gave Phillip a condescending grin. "I'll be outside, smoking."

So saying, Pamela scooted around her brother and left the room. She paused briefly to acknowledge Phillip's snarky "Go, then" with a middle finger. As soon as she was around the corner, Pamela broke into a brisk walk. Who was she fleeing? Phillip or Mother?

She honestly didn't know.

The hallway took Pamela past the staircase to the door of the patio. She considered going out there, remembering the night of the party, another time she'd felt helpless and lost. To his credit, Phillip had tried to comfort her. Tried and failed. Then Rochelle had called, and their talk about the kids had made Pamela's night. It was amazing Rochelle could do that with nothing but her voice at the end of a phone line. Rochelle was a wonder; Pamela knew that better than most.

She wiped her eyes to clear away the tears and returned to the staircase. Phillip was talking calmly to Mother, leading her patiently through a selection of clothes. The patience was an act, Pamela knew, and keeping it up would keep Phillip distracted. She had to take a chance. She had to do it now.

Pamela descended the stairs quietly. To her left on the first floor was a large open room Phillip insisted on calling the lounge. He entertained guests there most often. To her right was the main hallway. Glancing along it, Pamela could see the door to one of the downstairs bathrooms and a narrow passage that led off to the kitchen. Beyond the hallway lay the expansive dining room where Phillip's friends sipped wine from gilt-edged glasses and debated whether or not the next update to their eco-friendly hybrid cars would finally be smart enough to let them fire their drivers.

Pamela held her breath and listened for a moment to check that Phillip was still intent on his task. The whispers from above had ceased: Phillip might be coaxing Mother along, or he might have finished and be coming her way. She had to hurry.

Jogging to the passage, Pamela no longer minded her footfalls; she practically *ran* into the kitchen.

Would Phillip actually stop her from checking the basement? He never had before, but he always insisted on going with her whenever she visited their guests. With Phillip by her side, she couldn't speak for herself, or listen for herself, or decide for herself what ought to be done. This time, things would be different. This time, she would be going in alone.

She crossed the kitchen to the basement door. It was tall, broad, and solidly constructed of old, hard oak—it was actually an exterior door. Phillip had it installed specially, not long before the guests arrived. There was a deadbolt on the door, in addition to a keyed lock and chain. Phillip, always practical, kept the keys safely in a drawer. The locks were for keeping the guests *in*, after all—her brother harbored no particular fear of someone letting them out. She smiled to herself at that thought; Phillip could be stupidly blind, especially when it came to the people he thought were under his control.

Pamela was on her way to unlock the basement door when she realized something was wrong. The chain was off. She touched the door handle. It felt warm. The lock had been turned. The deadlock was open. Nervously, she stepped away from the door; sounds came from the other side, dull thumping sounds, like footsteps coming up the stairs. For a moment, Pamela could only stare at the door. Her heart leapt. Behind her came the sound of yet more feet.

Phillip.

"What are you doing?" he demanded, his face angry.

Before Pamela could answer, the footsteps from the basement stopped. Pamela sensed a presence behind the door; someone was there on the other side, waiting, radiating heat. Pamela had a choice. Rush to Phillip or—

She seized the handle and swung it wide. Light flooded out, and she screamed. A powerful, unseen force blew her over.

Phillip screamed too.

"*You!*"

43

"Get up."

Silas groaned.

"Get up, Mister Bundy."

Silas groaned again.

"We don't have long."

Silas tried to ask who was talking but found he couldn't. He just didn't have the breath.

"Get up!"

Discomfort moved Silas like a stranger's voice never could. He forced open his eyes—they felt pasted shut—and wrestled with the seat belt that squeezed his gut too tightly. The latch clicked and he was able to breathe properly at last.

Where was he?

Then he remembered. The pickup—Coachman had been driving, and now he was dead. The head of the Cross Guard Secret Militia lay pinned against the steering wheel, his vampire mask bloody and cracked. A telephone pole, propelled by the hurricane, had done the man and the mask in. The militia member directly behind Coachman was dead too.

The pickup lay in a ditch, cocked at a crazy angle. The man who'd been behind Silas was missing. Silas guessed he had left through the window, and decided it would be a good idea to follow suit. He lowered his own window—thankfully, the pickup was a hybrid and the electric motor still had juice, so of course it was running. Taken unawares by the flying telephone pole, Coachman never got a chance to turn off the car.

Silas climbed out the window, his movements awkward, thanks to the dead arm and his ungainly bulk. It took him a full minute of grunting and sweating to haul himself out, but in the end, he made it. He lay in the road breathing heavily, eyes on the pickup.

It was a sorry sight to behold: The telephone pole had split the cab nearly in two. More poles were down farther up the road. Silas figured the power was down, because no transformers were sparking. Past the poles, he saw uprooted trees strewn all over the place. Most of the other trees he could see—those still rooted—were stripped of their leaves, even the evergreens, and their trunks slanted from the ground at odd angles. It looked like a tornado had hit the place. As Silas studied the wrecked pickup among all the scattered debris, he asked himself what the dead men had possibly done to make God *that* angry.

"You with me, Silas Bram?" The strange voice interrupted his woolgathering.

Silas started. He'd made up his mind the voice was in his head. Instead, its owner turned out to be a small man standing six feet or so away. He appeared to be Mexican, or near enough, and had on blue jeans and a hoodie the color of red clay, maybe rust. At least he wore cowboy boots, which Silas always took as a good sign. Of character. The stranger leaned forward, bracing his hands above his knees.

Silas glowered at the searching eyes and jutting lower lip and asked the obvious question, "How do you know me?"

The stranger straightened up again. "Don't know you from Adam, pardner. But I was sent to find you, and now I have."

Silas eyed the small man suspiciously, guessed he couldn't have been much taller than five feet one or two, and hundred ten pounds soaking wet.

The stranger waited, not helping Silas, but not doing anything threatening, either. Silas eyeballed the sky. The pouring rain was gone, the pole-tossing, tree-destroying wind was no more than a light breeze.

"Storm's over." Silas struggled to get the words out, his breath still short.

"Yeah. You slept through a day." The stranger pointed to Silas's forehead.

Silas felt there with his good hand and found a gash there that was sore but scabbed over. "Are you *really* here?"

The stranger laughed. "You think you're dreaming me? Come on, Silas. You can dream much better than that." He walked across and stuck out a hand. "Let me help you up."

Silas scoffed at the offer, but the man took his hand anyway. He was stronger than he looked and pulled Silas to his feet like he weighed nothing.

"I'm sorry for your loss." The stranger sounded genuine.

"Who are you?"

"I'm a messenger. I came to bring you a message."

"Yeah? And you reckoned on finding me here, at the side of the road, in a pickup with two dead men?"

The stranger shrugged. "It worked, right? Listen to me carefully—we don't have much time. That friend of yours, the tall guy with all the teeth, the one who is always staring? He's distracted right now, but he won't be for long. I need to give you the message before he starts paying attention again.”

Silas was used to such obtuse talk from Coppersmith, but hearing it from somebody else set his nerves on edge. He considered what he would do if the stranger turned hostile: Even with one good arm, given the stranger's diminutive stature, Silas reckoned he could throw him down and give him a good stomping without too much trouble. Then again, there was the unexpected strength to consider. If the guy was some sort of miniature athlete, the last thing Silas wanted from him was a fight. He decided it would be best to ignore the mystical talk and play along.

“Okay, shoot,” Silas said.

“Are you ready?” The stranger eyed Silas with suspicion. “You have to be *ready*.”

Silas really wasn't ready for much of anything; he was groggy, his body hurt like hell, and the stranger was making him angry with his dumb riddles. He studied the stranger's face; the man was young, in his twenties, maybe thirty at most. But his eyes were much, much older, deeper, frightening. Silas sighed. “Yes. I'm ready.”

The stranger cleared his throat. “*It'll matter.* That's the message.”

Silas blinked. “That's it?”

“I know it doesn't sound like much. Not worth tracking you down or making you climb out a window. But trust me, Silas Bram. You'll be glad you listened, in the end.”

Something in the stranger's tone gave Silas an eerie feeling of peace. It was like the stiff breeze that was once a hurricane was carrying away all that ailed him.

“Thanks.” Expressing gratitude always made Silas feel awkward, so to fill the dead air between them, he added, “Why do you keep using my middle name?”

“Bram?” The stranger grinned. “It's cool. Like Bram Stoker. Quite the writer.”

"I ain't named after him."

"Oh, I know. *Abram* is who Grandmama had in mind. She hoped you'd go on a spiritual journey, prove your faith on a mountain, get Bram changed to Braham."

Silas was struck speechless. Only two people in the world knew that story, and the other one, Grandmama Bundy herself, was long dead. There didn't seem a point to asking how the messenger got his information. He'd only tell Silas to guess.

When he found his voice again, Silas told the stranger, "That journey never happened."

"It still *could*." The stranger turned to leave, but halted and returned to Silas. "Almost forgot."

He stepped up to Silas, who instinctively stepped back. In that instant, the stranger seemed to move in a blur; reaching out, he touched Silas's shoulder, where the bullet hit home. The effect was immediate and agonizing. Silas doubled over and clutched his shoulder, which felt as if it was being penetrated by myriad hot needles. He screwed his eyes tight shut and fought the urge to scream.

The white-hot piercing sensation burned through Silas and he dropped to a knee, enveloped by the all-encompassing pain.

But then, even as unconsciousness beckoned, the pain grew less insistent but somehow more . . . *complex*.

Silas let out a whimper and the heat subsided. He bent his other leg until he rested upon both knees on the road. The stabbing, the heat, the pain lessened . . . lessened . . . stopped.

When Silas opened his eyes, the stranger was gone. However, his gift remained: The pain was entirely gone. Silas loosened the strap holding his arm and flexed his elbow, the wrist. He wiggled his fingers and found to his delight everything was working just fine. After the shooting, Ol' Doc Harley had informed him the nerves might need a year at least to reroute themselves. Most of Harley's patients were cattle, sure, but Silas didn't figure he was too far wrong.

He cracked knuckles he hadn't been able to move in what felt like forever, the sound bringing him great joy. A weight was off Silas's shoulders. It felt so incredibly good.

Silas Bram Bundy searched the horizon, breathing in the moist, earthy, post-hurricane air. He reached for the holster on his belt where he kept his phone, but before he could call for a ride, a helicopter appeared over the naked trees, buzzing low. Silas flagged it down with both hands.

44

There was still a voice, Jon was sure, in the thunder. The reason he couldn't hear it was because the storm outside the hospital and the storm inside his head were too alike. They amplified each other's chaos, the waves of sound and panic and pain building on one another to the point where nothing peaceful could break through.

At least this storm wasn't a hurricane. The devastating winds and rain that had torn through Houston, leaving what Dee Fitzgerald had described as a trench, never swung far enough to the west to touch Austin. Where Hurricane Laurence did reach, though, it took hundreds of lives and destroyed thousands of buildings in a meandering south-to-north track from the Gulf of Mexico to Houston to the Davy Crockett National Forest. One of its victims happened to be the Omni Houston Hotel, the place Jon had slept before the worst day of his life.

He felt like he'd been tossed from a train. And, from what he could see of himself, Jon fully expected to look about the same too. His skin was pale, clammy, blotched with bruises. He was exhausted—so much so, it was hard to hold up his head. These symptoms were all too familiar, but the thin dribble of fresh blood oozing from his left arm was new. It wasn't the nurse's fault, because, as the young man had bent over Jon to insert the IV needle, a jolt of nervous energy had made Jon's forearm involuntarily clench. The needle had gone wide, blood oozed, the nurse recoiled.

"I'm *so* sorry, Doctor."

Jon didn't know the nurse personally and couldn't see well enough to make out his name tag. He was young but competent, and took only a few seconds to apply a wad of gauze to the wound. After a second apology, the nurse moved on to strapping the gauze in place with surgical tape and finding another vein to tap for Jon's IV.

Jon studied the divots in the hospital room's ceiling. They weren't the same ones he'd once interpreted as a checkerboard—those were in another room. However, the divots in this room were similar enough to remind him of that checkerboard's vast expanse. He wished he could reach that infinite landscape. He wanted to visit the checkerboard, or stand on the peak in the fantasy mountain range and listen to the voice that dwelled within the thunder. But try as he might, they remained heartbreakingly out of reach.

Jon was trapped.

Weakness confined him to a chair by a window, close to the wheelchair the nurse had used to wheel him in. The thunder inside and outside his head didn't speak clearly enough to lead him along a spiritual passage to freedom, and he wanted freedom badly—not only from the pain and the grief that consumed him, but from the agony of the trial. Granted, the latter couldn't go on for long.

He was dying; of that much Jon was certain. The disease at the root of his physical pain was killing him. His long march to the grave had started the night he lost Chelle and the boys. His analytical side took this as evidence the problem wasn't truly physical, but psychological. He suffered because of a psychosomatic reaction to all the stress. His fearful side said that didn't matter: Whether the disease was of the body or the mind, it would kill him just as dead in the end.

Jon called his pessimistic side "fearful" because he couldn't think of another way to counter its argument. Deep down, he knew the fateful pronouncement didn't come from fear alone. It came from what Rabbi Max would call his *lev*, his heart, his inner person. Whatever it was, the take-home message from all his bitter experience was simple: "The end is near."

What would happen after the end? Based on how the voice and the checkerboard eluded him, Jon guessed his prospects were pretty grim. It could be the agony he felt now was just a preview of so much worse to come, and he was destined to suffer in fire until the stain of sin was burnt from his soul. Was that his Judaism talking or his abandoned Great Cycle Christianity? Jon honestly didn't know. The dogged materialist he kept in the lev's basement said death was oblivion. After the disease killed him, he would be nothing and nowhere.

He tried hard to imagine oblivion, and failed. It was like trying to imagine the universe before the Big Bang. The only way he could picture it was as another universe. The still, sightless, infinite void was far beyond his ability to conjure.

"Are you ready to try again, Doctor Edom?" The nurse had a fresh needle in hand.

Focusing outward helped keep the inner storm contained, so Jon studied the nurse intently before he said, "Go ahead."

The nurse raised the new needle with the IV catheter attached. Jon concentrated on slowing his breathing. If he delayed the insertion again, he might not be ready when

Rohan arrived to drive him to court. Fitz wouldn't allow him to take a ride share; if something went wrong, he said, the drivers and ride share companies were too hard to sue.

The nurse stretched the skin of Jon's arm and was about to pierce the skin when he was interrupted by a knock at the door. The nurse turned to see a man in a white coat nudge the door open with his shoe. He held a clipboard in one hand, a shiny black briefcase in the other, and wore an expression so arrogant, it made Vivek Singh humble by comparison.

"Oh, good," the man said. "I caught you." Shutting the door, he held out the clipboard. "Thank you, Nurse Svenson. We won't be needing you further. Doctor Edom is under my care now."

Obediently, Svenson set aside his needle and accepted the clipboard. He studied the printout clipped to the front as Jon tried hard to place the newcomer. He seemed familiar, but with his blurry vision, he couldn't be sure they'd actually ever met.

"Do I know you?" Jon asked.

"Andrew Grant, MD," came the answer. The name, too, was annoyingly familiar, but Jon couldn't place from where. "We met once at Longevity Therapeutics—briefly. You had the whirlwind tour."

That explained it. Before the old man's death, Longevity Therapeutics had been as close to Ezra's heart as Endless Loop was to Lisa's. The "whirlwind tour" Grant mentioned was actually a recruitment drive. Chelle never quite got over Jon's refusal to be part of her father's business, and she'd revived the argument more than a few times during their tumultuous marriage, but that was all water under the bridge. What Jon needed to know now was what Dr. Grant had to do with his steroid injection.

"I think I remember you," Jon ventured. "I'm under your care?"

"Your family asked me to check on you personally, Doctor Edom."

"Jon, please."

"Call me Andrew." He returned his attention to Svenson. "Everything in order, Nurse Svenson?"

Frowning deeply, the nurse replied, "Yes, Doctor," and handed back the clipboard. "Everything looks to be in order."

"Good. Now, if you don't mind, I would prefer to treat my patient in private."

"Hold on." Jon experienced a twinge of panic.

"It won't take long, I promise," Andrew told him, "and afterward, I promise you'll feel so much better, Jon." He nodded at Svenson, who glanced once more at Jon.

Jon tried to ask the nurse to stay but found his throat was too dry to create sound. Instead, Jon coughed weakly and watched Svenson exit, leaving him alone with Andrew.

The doctor set his briefcase and clipboard down on the windowsill. He studied Jon, seemingly waiting to see if the cough would have a sequel. When no second cough came, he smiled and began removing Jon's IV bag from its hook.

Jon swallowed hard and forced out, "I need that."

Andrew dropped the clear plastic bag on the windowsill. "You need *something*, that's for certain. You look like Death, if you don't mind my saying so. And not one of those cute ones with a black hooded cape and scythe, like in the comics."

A wave of fresh exhaustion washed over Jon. He could only stare as Andrew held his thumb over a glass plate fixed to the top of the briefcase. Something clicked, and the briefcase's latches clunked opened.

Andrew lifted the lid.

"You've had a very difficult time, Jon," he said. "I'm happy to say, though, your luck is about to change. You are about to receive a gift, something truly amazing. I'd be jealous, honestly, if I didn't feel so . . . *fulfilled* to be part of your healing process."

Andrew leaned over Jon, as if to ensure his patient saw his satisfied smile. He then leaned back over the briefcase and withdrew some of the contents. The IV bag in his hand appeared similar to the discarded one on the windowsill. But while that one contained a clear solution, that in Andrew's IV bag was pale yellow. Suspended within the yellow were specks Jon wouldn't have been able to discern at all, except for the soft blue glow they emitted.

Panic gave Jon back his voice. "You're not putting that in me."

Andrew held the bag to his chest protectively. "Be reasonable, Jon. You're a very sick man. The formula in this bag is the culmination of much of what your father-in-law worked for in his life. It's not conventional medicine, but it is perfectly safe. I oversaw development and testing after Doctor Berger's death, and I can assure you, the treatment I'm offering is revolutionary, absolutely cutting edge."

A hundred cautionary questions sprang to Jon's mind, but he couldn't help but be curious. "Safe and revolutionary don't always go together. What's in the bag, exactly?"

Andrew quit hugging the bag and held it over Jon, inviting inspection. "We don't have time for *exactly*, I'm afraid. Even a man with your training would need months, if not years, to absorb the detail. I'll tell you what. I'll explain what I can in the time it takes to prepare you. If you're not convinced when I'm on the point of putting in the needle, I'll swap you back to *that*." He eyeballed the original IV bag, showing clear disdain.

Jon wasn't sure he would be able to resist Andrew's jabbing him with the mystery medicine, anyway, so he nodded his head.

Placing his self-proclaimed cutting-edge formula on the

IV stand and returning to the briefcase for a needle and catheter, Andrew started his pitch.

"You're familiar with the basic tenets of *ex vivo* gene therapy? A subject donates a cell sample, cells are edited using CRISPR-Cas9 or a similar system, and the altered cells are reintroduced to the donor. The detail I'm excluding concerns how the alterations are made to propagate in the donor's body; that's unnecessary if all we wish to do is generate some novel protein or express traits of a cell that are typically suppressed over the short term. But it's *very* necessary if the problem we want to fix is systemic, and we're looking beyond the short term to permanent remission. That's the goal in your case, naturally. We want to put your illness into complete remission. To give you a *cure*, in other words."

With a final flourish of the hands, Andrew finished connecting catheter and needle. He showed the needle to Jon, whose head swam with all the connotations the doctor had conjured there. The possibility of permanent remission from whatever was killing him was so far from where Jon thought his illness was heading, his impulse was to simply dismiss Andrew's words out of hand as quackery. At the same time, what he said was too intriguing to dismiss.

Jon said, "How can you cure me if nobody knows what's wrong?"

"We do know."

"How?"

Andrew set the needle aside and pressed a hand to Jon's forehead. The reflex that should have had Jon blocking the hand made him squirm in his seat, instead.

"You're burning up. Let me help you."

Jon summoned the last of his strength and growled, "How do you know what's wrong with me?"

Andrew may have sighed or he may only have parted his lips to breathe—Jon couldn't make out the difference through his inner storm.

"Ex vivo, Jon. You remember the blood sample you submitted to Longevity Therapeutics? Part of a genetic testing package, I believe, for your son."

The memory of that long-ago day when he'd drawn a sample of his own blood, packed it in ice, and sent it away by courier flashed through Jon's mind. Chelle had said the sample was needed as a sort of control, that the geneticists would compare what they read of Luke's genetic code to that from both parents. It would, apparently, help them identify any genetic-based problems Luke was likely to have later in life. If he had the same genes for clearing LDL as Jon, for instance, he would probably have the same elevated levels. If his blood pressure genes were similar to Chelle's, they would have to keep an eye out for signs of hypertension.

It had all sounded most reasonable to Jon at the time; simple, even. Of course, he didn't know back then that the tests would show he was not the boy's natural father. The process of sending the sample had been routine, and Jon had actually forgotten Longevity Therapeutics was the laboratory that did the testing.

"So the blood sample showed, what, some genetic mutation?"

"Oh, dozens," said Andrew. "That's normal. You know that if babies were just CC'd from their parents, the whole human race would have died of the sniffles during the ice age. What your sample showed us, Jon, was a weakness to certain pathogens all of us encounter in our day-to-day lives. The body can put up with a lot, as I'm sure you know, but the immune system can get overloaded if it becomes compromised. Put enough stress on an organism and it goes into defense mode. And as anybody fighting a serious viral infection can tell you, some of those defenses can be quite nasty. What happened to you, Jon, is simple. You got overstressed and you got sick. And I'm here to help."

"With ex vivo gene therapy."

"It works. Your weakness, as I called it, is just an overreaction to what your body ought to be able to deal with. It's panicking because it's forgotten how to fight, so the edited cells we have prepared will remind it—simple as that, really. The rest of the formula will get you back on your feet, much like the steroids Nurse Svenson was about to administer. The difference being that if you accept my help today, you won't need an injection tomorrow. In fact, before twenty-four hours have gone by, you'll shed the worst of your symptoms. Inside a week, you'll forget you were ever sick."

Lightning flashed outside the window, as if the heavens themselves were endorsing Andrew's grandiose claims.

Jon forced himself to say, "Sounds wonderful. You understand why I find it hard to believe?"

"Certainly. And you understand why I say you would be a fool not to try?"

The doctor was right. Between the weakness and the pain, Jon had so little to lose—even if he was facing life imprisonment for a murder he didn't commit.

"How long will it take to get on my feet?"

"If you stop talking and let me stick you, twenty minutes."

"I'm due at court in thirty. Make it fast."

Andrew got to work and, as the yellow fluid began to squeeze its mysterious blue specks through the catheter, Jon remembered the final question he should have asked.

"You said my family sent you. *Who exactly*?"

Andrew stepped away from Jon's side. "That's confidential, I'm afraid." He locked the clipboard in his briefcase and started for the door.

"Stop," said Jon. "What do you mean?" He already felt stronger, so was surprised when he tried to sit up and found his muscles sluggish. "Why won't you . . ." The words froze in his mouth, Jon's lips felt leaden, his vocal cords frozen.

"Don't try to move, Jon. The formula includes a mild neuromuscular blocker. I'm sorry I didn't mention that, but I was afraid you might worry about the timing. You'll be fine for your appointment, I promise. Just don't try to walk until you're fully recovered."

Jon watched the doctor and his briefcase leave.

Over the next twenty minutes, the storm outside blew itself out and, by the time Rohan appeared, ready to load Jon into the wheelchair, the storm inside was calmer than it had been in months. Despite the trick with the muscle-blocking drug, Dr. Andrew Grant, MD, appeared to have actually delivered on his promise. Jon felt a surge of hope that was quickly crushed by the thought of what lay ahead. The supposed cure had set him up to be bright and attentive on what promised to be yet another contender for the worst day of his life.

45

The judge raised her gavel and the courtroom hushed. A woman in the fourth row was already sitting quietly, and so were her young charges—one on her right and the one on her left. She was proud of how brave they were both being, how calm and well-behaved. She was so proud, she almost forgot where she was and praised them out loud.

But before the words left her mouth, she remembered and bit down on her lip. Not too hard—there was no need to draw blood.

"District Attorney Perez, Mister Fitzgerald, please approach the bench," said the judge. Earlier, the bailiff had announced her as Judge Morrow. The woman in the fourth row thought Morrow was a pretentious name for a judge, at least for one who was human. Morrow, as in *to*morrow, suggested a permanence that belonged only to the divine.

The district attorney and the attorney for the defense rose from their tables. The woman in the fourth row saw the defense attorney nod to his client. Jon looked strong today: He sat with his back straight and his eyes fixed firmly upon the judge. He also turned his head to acknowledge his lawyer, which he couldn't have done had he been close to exhaustion. The woman in the fourth row was happy to see him doing well and took a moment to glance from him to his children, Simon and Cass, who were seated in the first row with Rabbi Max. Simon had a girl, Ximena, next to him. The woman in the fourth row didn't know how to feel about that.

She opened her purse and took out a compact, and, as Perez and Fitzgerald spoke privately with the judge, she checked her reflection. Her hair was hidden by the hood of her raincoat, the shadow it cast concealing most of her face. Still, she could make out enough to tell she had done a decent job with her lipstick. Actually, it wasn't hers, it was borrowed, and not quite her color. It was close, at least. In the family, as it were.

The other thing the woman in the fourth row wanted to see in the mirror had nothing to do with her appearance. Behind and to her right, at the end of the back row on the prosecution's side, sat an attractive woman with dark, straight hair. She was dressed in slacks and a button-down top and gave no sign she knew she was being observed. The man sitting in front of her, however, did notice, and winked. He had long hair, a goatee, and a crooked "X" tattooed low on his forehead. The woman in the fourth row shut the compact with an audible *snap*.

DA Perez and Fitzgerald were finished talking with the judge. As they returned to their tables, the woman in the fourth row put the compact away. There was very little else in the purse—the borrowed lipstick, some ancient receipts that belonged to the owner, and a hairbrush—so she didn't worry about where it fell.

She remembered a habit she used to have of pulling out her wallet before adding anything to her purse because she wanted the wallet to stay on top. Now she had no wallet, and no money or credit cards or ID to put in one. It was strange to think how much of her life used to fit in such a small space. It was stranger still to think how little she missed what was gone.

Judge Morrow cleared her throat. "Members of the jury, I need to update you on a change in the scheduled testimony you were supposed to hear today, and to inform you of some additional evidence recently submitted by the defense. Mister Phillip Berger and Miss Pamela Berger, the brother and sister of Rochelle Berger-Edom, were to testify this afternoon. I am told both witnesses were involved in some sort of household accident early this morning. I don't know the details and I will not hear speculation in my courtroom. Is that clear?"

The stir of voices that had risen at the mention of an accident died quickly away.

The judge continued. "Suffice it to say, we do not expect to hear from Mister and Miss Berger today. We *will* hear from Detective Cavallo as scheduled. I am also told the defendant, Doctor Jon Edom, is prepared to take the stand, should his attorney deem it beneficial to his defense."

This time, Morrow raised her gavel as she surveilled the audience with piercing eyes. That Jon might take the stand was exciting news to the reporters, but they didn't dare stir. The only sound was of caught breath as fingers hovered over phones, all ready to text a scoop.

"I mention this as a reminder to everyone, including Doctor Edom, that we are going to hear all sides of the case at hand. There is no cause for anyone to create or to participate in a disruption. After what we experienced yesterday, I will need very little provocation to permanently remove anyone apart from the defense, the prosecution, the jurors and witnesses and courtroom staff. Today will be peaceful, or the rest of this trial will happen behind locked doors."

She paused to stare across the courtroom as if daring anyone to be the first to be expelled. No one gave her an excuse, so she set the gavel quietly down.

"As to the evidence I mentioned, it has been brought to my attention that a connection may exist between this case and a violent crime that was never brought to trial. Please understand that the connection is yet to be confirmed. The defense asked to present evidence in an effort to explain both crimes. I have allowed this. Depending on the length of Detective Cavallo's testimony and cross-examination, we may or may not hear the new evidence presented today. The jury should be aware that it exists and will be presented at the right time."

The judge appeared about to end her speech when her eyes fell on the woman in the fourth row. She frowned.

"One more thing. In view of certain events of the past year, I think it's important we see everyone's faces in court. Remove all hoods, please."

She continued watching the woman in the fourth row, who looked passively back at her from beneath the shadow of the rain hood.

"Ma'am," Morrow said brusquely, "don't test me. Either remove your hood, and the hoods of your children, or leave my court. If you choose not to leave voluntarily, I will instruct the bailiff to escort you out."

The woman in the fourth row made no move. She was actually pleased the judge had drawn attention to her. It meant she didn't have to wait for the best time to say what had to be said. Extra attention meant the time was close, but not quite yet. The tension in the room was building, she could feel its electricity in the air. The reporters turned her way—the woman in the fourth row wanted *all* heads to turn. More than anyone else, she wanted Jon Edom to turn and look at her. She wanted *him* to hear what she had to say.

"All right. You've left me no choice." Judge Morrow had reached the end of her patience. "Bailiff Trent. Remove that woman and the children who are with her."

A murmur ran around the audience. Jon turned around, curious, not impatient. There was a healthy glow to his cheeks which the woman in the fourth row wanted to believe was his own inner light.

She got to her feet.

The bailiff was in motion.

In the few seconds she'd been watching Jon, the bailiff had advanced and in a few seconds more, he would reach her. She had to act fast.

"I have something to say the jury needs to hear," she said, waking horror in Jon and anger in the judge.

Jon's face changed, and the woman saw his curiosity turn to profound confusion. As she spoke, a tinge of horror crept in. She was so very sorry

Bailiff Trent was almost upon her, but the woman wasn't watching him. Instead, she watched Jon Edom.

The woman in the fourth row wondered who would reach her first—Trent or Detective Cavallo, who also was up on her feet and moving toward the fourth row. The woman offered a hand to each of her charges.

Trent reached the third row; Cavallo, the fifth.

The boys let go of the woman's hands. All three then pinched the fringes of their hoods, following the plan she'd explained in the car on the way to the court that morning.

The woman in the fourth row swept back her hood in unison with the young boys. There were murmurs and gasps from around the courtroom, even though not everyone understood what they were seeing, and those who did know doubted their eyes.

Bailiff Trent reached for one of the boys on his side even as the three unhooded faces turned on him. He stopped dead in his tracks.

Detective Cavallo, on the other hand, stopped moving the moment those hoods came off.

"Impossible," was all she managed to utter. "*Impossible*."

The woman in the fourth row focused her attention on the judge. "Jon Edom is innocent of murder, Your Honor." Beaming with a mother's warm pride, she placed a hand on the shoulder of each boy.

From his place at the defense table, Jon's lips formed a name.

"I am Rochelle Berger-Edom," the woman said quietly. "These are my sons, Luke and Paul. Jon didn't kill us. He's a good man, and he's suffered. He's suffered so much. Be strong, Jon. Know that your suffering is not in vain."

END OF BOOK ONE

About the Author

Blake Rudman enjoyed a former, successful career in executive management, building his own companies from the ground up.

Success or not, Blake's heart has always been in the written word, and the myriad ideas he spent much of his spare time jotting down in notebooks, Post-Its, and scraps of paper whenever the inspiration hit him.

A breakout author of bestselling noir thriller novels, Blake's destiny of becoming a writer of some renown is well under way.

When he's not working diligently on his next novel, Blake spends quality time with his family and tropical fish.

Follow Blake at: blakerudman.com
Facebook: @BRudmanThriller
Instagram: @BRudmanThriller
Twitter: @BRudmanThriller

For all Blake's books, visit him at:
www.hellboundbookspublishing.com/authorpage_rudman.html

Blake Rudman Novels from HellBound Books:

Available in Kindle, paperback, hardcover, and audiobook.

The Gentleman's Choice

"Caught in a whirlwind of adverse publicity following a viewer's death, the streaming show, The Gentleman's Choice becomes the target for a sadistic killer – and it's up to PI Vanessa Young to put a stop to it before more young women are murdered."

A sleazy internet dating show blamed for a viewer's death, a host with a dark, secret past, and a killer with a sadistic grudge…

Someone is kidnapping and murdering previous contestants from the popular streaming show *The Gentleman's Choice* – a strictly-for-adults hybrid of *The Bachelor* and *Love Island*. Private Investigator, Vanessa Young, is hired by a victim's family to infiltrate the show as a contestant to expose and capture the killer.

Vanessa and the show's charismatic star, Cole Gianni, begin to fall romantically for each other, until Vanessa's plan goes terribly awry when they're drugged and taken to a remote location to take part in their captor's own brutal, ultimately fatal, version of *The Gentleman's Choice*.

With the clock ticking toward their fateful final night, Vanessa and Cole are forced into a battle of wills to survive their tormentor and escape with their lives before it's too late…

Dark Beauty

Tessa and Kristin Morgan are identical twins, exquisitely beautiful, and have the world at their perfectly pedicured feet; they are also profoundly different beneath their stunning facades.

Tessa is the laser-focused academic with her eyes firmly fixed upon a career in neurology, while Kristin exploits her striking looks and undeniable power over men to carve out a single-minded path to fame and fortune as a model and actress; an ambition she also holds for her sister.

But, on the night of the pair's debut as top-tier models, and with a high-profile movie role in the bag, tragedy strikes the twins in the form of a cruel acid attack by an unknown assailant. Thus, a gruesome chain of events begins - one that leaves a trail of blood, death, and devastation behind both Tessa and Kristin.

As Tessa fights to rebuild her life and uncover the truth behind the attack, she finds herself getting closer and closer to an uncomfortable truth about her sister and her search for the truth turns into a nightmare struggle to stay alive.

Goodbye Stranger

"As with *American Psycho*, Blake Rudman's *Goodbye Stranger* has a wealthy, successful man whose wonderful family life masks a much darker side. Throw in a once-trusting, increasingly suspicious wife, and the stage is set for twists and turns you'll never see coming!"

Danielle Harrington has the life many women envy: She's beautiful, rich, has two wonderful children, and is married to *the* Preston Harrington - the handsome, charismatic, retired quarterback who won two Super Bowls.

Unfortunately, something is very wrong with Preston. Having suffered more than his fair share of injuries and concussions, he becomes quiet, withdrawn, and distant. As Preston spends more time away from his family, Danielle begins suspect an affair without realizing her husband is involved in something much, much worse...

Following a series of tragic incidents and the return of an old nemesis from the past, things begin to spiral out of control for Danielle as Preston's dark side puts her and their children in terrible danger.

Redline

"If Lee Childs' Jack Reacher or Clive Cussler's Dirk Pitt tackled a terrorist scheme that utilized subliminal messaging to sow social and economic chaos on a global scale, it would look a lot like *Red Line.*" Baltimore Police Detective Mitch Wilson wants a nice day out with his wife and son. Instead, they are all caught up in a catastrophic terrorist attack that has repercussions across the USA and triggers events that could alter the course of civilization.

Having lost everything, Mitch sets out to seek justice – and revenge and stumbles upon a global conspiracy.

On the other side of the world, renowned linguistic professor, Yasaman Karami, flees her native Iran for the freedom of the west; she holds one of the keys to defeating the terrorist organization.

Yasaman and Mitch's worlds collide as, alongside federal agents and allies, they race against the clock to hunt down the terrorist masterminds and prevent worldwide catastrophe.

Kutri

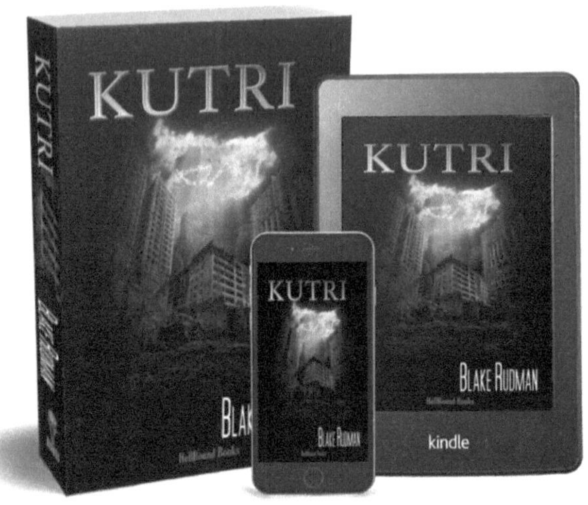

The Slow Plague, a gender-targeting infection with no cure, killed billions of women and girls worldwide and created a dystopian society in which the survivors are treated as highly valuable commodities. Although their market value is high, women's rights decline as they become objects of avarice, awe, and worship – possessions to be owned or won in high-stakes games.

Kutri Chandigarh, a rare beauty, is shipped from her native India to Los Angeles, a shattered metropolis barricaded behind a radiation-proof wall. Within the city stronghold, a bleak, broken, male-led society is mesmerized by stupefying programs pumped out by Little Angel Studios: an endless parade of reality TV shows.

The studio's #1 hit is Good Breeding: a bevy of ethnically "pure" young women compete to marry a chosen suitor and produce a "perfect" family under the scrutiny of the public eye.

Kutri has dreamed of wining the competition since early childhood. But, when she arrives in LA and meets Jakob Freeman, her assigned matchmaker, the fantasy quickly turns sour and twists into a horrific nightmare extending far beyond Kutri and the man she chooses for herself.

As Kutri tries to escape the fate she once coveted, Jakob is swept up in events that threaten him body and soul and spark memories of a past he has so desperately tried to forget.

Follow Blake at: blakerudman.com
Facebook: @BRudmanThriller
Instagram: @BRudmanThriller
Twitter: @BRudmanThriller

For all Blake's books, visit him at:
www.hellboundbookspublishing.com/authorpage_rudman.html
www.hellboundbooks.com